THE HOOKUP SITUATION

LYRA PARISH

CONTENT WARNING

This book is a spicy romantic comedy that contains on-page adult content and language not suitable for minors. It also briefly discusses grief after the loss of a loved one (not shown on page).

OFFICIAL PLAYLIST

Slim Pickins - Sabrina Carpenter

Somebody To Love - Queen

Eternity - Alex Warren

Bad As The Rest - Jessie Murph

The Chain - Fleetwood Mac

Mr. Brightside - The Killers

All Of The Girls You Loved Before - Taylor Swift

Someone New - Hozier

Dive - Olivia Dean

Don't Smile - Sabrina Carpenter

Delicate - Taylor Swift

Coming Home - Leon Bridges

Picture You - Chappell Roan

Movement - Hozier

End Game - Taylor Swift, Ed Sheeran, Future

LISTEN TO THIS PLAYLIST:
https://bit.ly/hookup-playlist

This one is dedicated to those who get just as excited about pumpkin season...

Nick Banks is waiting for you, Fall Queen.

Every dead-end street
Led you straight to me
Now you're all I need

-Taylor Swift, Lover
All the Girls You Loved Before

1

NICK

I press my forehead against the floor-to-ceiling window of my penthouse at Park Towers, which overlooks Central Park. It's cold to the touch. The early morning traffic fills the streets below, and I can see people walking on the sidewalks in a line like tiny ants. The sun is just beginning to rise, but this city never sleeps. Shit, I barely do these days.

It's mid-September, and the leaves are preparing to change from green to orange and yellow—a sign that fall has arrived. Unlike my siblings, I grew up in the suburbs, where harvest festivals, hayrides, and pumpkin patches were a regular part of our weekends. In the heart of the city, there's only steel and glass and a billion-dollar view that might as well be a prison. Some days, I feel like a damn robot, going through the motions of life.

I was convinced that living in this luxury high-rise with this view would make me happy. My brothers, Asher and Dyson, have penthouses here, along with many of my friends and acquaintances. However, this place has only made me feel lonely.

I'm convinced nothing can make me happy anymore. Hockey did at one point, until I tore my ACL for the third time and had a hard recovery. That's when I knew I'd never play again. The game was my everything.

Money sure as fuck doesn't make me happy, and probably never will. Undoubtedly, it might make some parts of my life easier, but the attention it carries isn't always worth it. There should be balance, but like most things, I don't have any, and unfortunately, I don't care anymore.

The thirty-thousand-dollar Italian espresso machine that my older brother, Dyson, insisted I buy hisses behind me. It's the third shot I've brewed this morning, and so far, I haven't touched a single one. They're lined up on the marble counter resembling tiny monuments, showcasing my disinterest in everything.

Every autumn, I'm like this. Ever since my sister, Eden, passed away, I can't avoid it. I was hoping this year would be different. So far, it's not.

I suck in a deep breath, and I catch my reflection in the window.

I'm wearing a designer suit, perfectly tailored for me, while sporting five days of stubble that's transitioned from sexy but trying to not giving a single fuck. I have a neck beard, for crying out loud. The thought makes me groan. The man staring back at me used to be a hockey league defenseman for the New York Angels—one of the most successful teams of this decade. Five years ago, I had fire in my eyes and ice in my veins. Now I'm just another hollow-eyed billionaire who forgot what winning feels like.

Eden would hate this for me.

Memories of my sister flood in; losing her isn't something I will ever just get over. Even though it's been years, somehow, her opinions still affect my life choices. I lost one of my best friends.

I can almost hear Eden's voice. *"Nicky, you're pathetic. Look at you, turning into one of those rich, boring assholes we always made fun of as teenagers."*

I fucking am. *Shit.*

Not long after she was gone, I spiraled. I made bad decisions, was selfish, and nearly destroyed my friendship with my childhood best friend, Zane. I didn't respect myself or like the man I'd become. Even now, we're still repairing our friendship, and one day, I hope it will be a fraction of what it was before I messed up. Worst mistake of my life. I was in a bad place, and what I did was inexcusable; however, I was also taken advantage of when I was at my weakest. Two things can be true at the same time.

My phone buzzes, and the monthly reminder flashes across the screen.

Donate to Eden's favorite literacy program.

I tap through to the notification without thinking, bumping this month's donation from fifty thousand to one hundred thousand. The foundation has put libraries near twelve inner-city schools this year. Eden would've visited each one and read to every kid who listened.

I stare at the confirmation screen until it blurs. This is what I do now. Write checks to fill the crater my sister left behind. I throw money at my problems because facing them would be me admitting too much.

The espresso machine gurgles one last time and falls silent, just like everything else in this place.

I line the shots up like they're tequila and take all three. My phone dings, letting me know that the driver is downstairs, waiting to deliver me to the office. I grab my briefcase and leave.

When I arrive at Banks Advertising and Marketing Firm, it's as quiet as a morgue. I enter the conference room for our first meeting today and sit next to Asher.

"Good morning, all," Mr. McDaniels says.

He's the young CEO of a new start-up for a revolutionary app, and he needs our company to help boost him to the stratosphere, because that's what we do. We can make or break anyone of any size in any industry. This kind of power comes with great responsibility, one neither Asher nor I take lightly.

The overhead lights reflect off the polished black table, and if I hear Mr. Big Mac say this app will disrupt human connection one more time, I might lose my cool. He's twenty-six, wearing sneakers that cost more than most people's rent, and he keeps using the words *synergy* and *vibe* like they're going out of style.

"The beauty of our platform," he says, clicking through slides that hurt my eyes, "is that we're removing the inefficiencies of traditional human interaction."

Something inside me snaps.

Maybe I've had too much espresso, and it's finally hit my bloodstream, or I'm over this shit. Or maybe how he reduced human connection to an algorithm pissed me off.

"Stop." The word comes out harsher than I intend.

The room freezes, and everyone goes quiet.

Asher clears his throat and glares at me. Maybe I've finally lost my mind. The rest of the team exchanges glances, not sure how to react to my outburst.

"Did you have a question about the projections?" Mr. McDaniels asks, unfazed by me. I'm not sure he can't read basic social cues.

"I have a question about your integrity." I stand up, and my chair scoots back and falls backward with a loud thud. "You're twenty-six years old, and you think human connection needs to be more *efficient*? When's the last time you had a conversation that wasn't about market penetration?"

"Nicola—" Asher starts.

"No." I'm already moving toward the door. "We're not marketing this. We're not promoting anything that makes people lonelier than they already are."

The silence behind me is deafening. I know what they're thinking. Nick Banks, the ice-cold closer, has feelings. They're treating me like I'm crashing out. Maybe I am.

I'm halfway to the elevator when Asher catches up to me. He's the only person in this high-rise building who isn't afraid of me.

"That was the most dramatic fucking exit I've ever seen you make." He falls into step beside me. "Reminds me of when you used to play hockey and your testosterone was out of control."

"Not now, Ash."

"Oh, definitely now." He clenches his teeth. "You just torpedoed a ten-billion-dollar deal because you're suddenly concerned about human connections. We need to talk."

The elevator opens. I step in, and Asher follows, hitting the button for the top floor, where our offices are.

When we're alone, he turns to me. "What the hell is wrong with you?"

"I'm not working with that entitled prick," I explain as we ride to the top.

When the doors open, I step out and move to my office. Everything is exactly where I left it yesterday. Papers and file folders are scattered across my desk. I take a seat and then log in to my computer. If I don't acknowledge him, hopefully, he'll disappear.

I glance up at Asher, and based on his expression, I know he's pissed.

"I'm putting you on leave."

My brows furrow. "You can't do that."

Asher may be the CEO of this company, but I helped start it with Eden. When she passed away, she left it to Asher and me to manage. My little brother is levelheaded and not as irrational as I tend to be, which is saying a lot, considering he takes more risks than anyone I know. However, it's always calculated and not built on emotion. Asher quickly figures out the probability of the outcome he desires the most and gives his full self to every project he commits to. Eden chose him to help keep me grounded. Asher is intelligent, a built-in fail-safe.

"It's effective immediately," he continues.

"That's extreme, don't you think?"

"Actually, I don't. You need to figure out what the hell is going on with you. The way you acted back there is unaccept—"

"Asher, I—"

"Look." He holds his hand up. "You've been walking around with a chip on your shoulder for months now. Anytime I try to talk to you about it, you blow it off. Either you need to get laid or go on vacation. Maybe both. You figure it out. Consider this payback for you forcing me to do the same a few months ago."

I roll my eyes at him. "That was different. You were starting shit with the Calloway family. You know they—"

He continues talking over me. "I'll decide when you can return."

"Do not do this to me right now. I have projects that are important."

Asher doesn't seem to give two shits about any of it.

"At this point, I don't want to see your face in here until November first. We have an investors meeting on the second. Don't return before then."

"November? That's six and a half weeks from now."

He nods. "Very good. Thrilled you can count. You haven't taken a true vacation since Eden died. It's been five years, Nick. I know how close the two of you were and how important this marketing firm is to you, but when was the last time you enjoyed yourself and had fun? I'm worried about you."

I don't answer because I can't. I'm a workaholic—I know that. But what else is there to life?

I can't keep a relationship for over a month. I push people away when they get too close. Not to mention, the internet watches my every move.

"When's the last time you felt anything besides angry or numb?" he continues. "And don't try to pull that jokester, happy-as-can-be, fake-self bullshit on me. I see through it."

I can't move.

"I know grief has no time limit. I miss the hell out of Eden too," Asher says. "But you've been slowly losing yourself. She'd hate this,

Nick. She'd hate what you've become. You refuse to have a work-life balance, every relationship you rush into fails, and you're not living your life. You have tied my hands, and now I'm forced to do exactly what Eden would want."

"Don't." My voice cracks on the word.

"You need a reality check, Nick." He shakes his head. "You're taking a break. A real break. Go somewhere and get lost so you can find yourself. When you scan out, your credentials will be deactivated."

Asher moves toward the door.

"This isn't fair," I tell him.

He laughs. "Oh, boo-hoo. Life isn't fair. Build a bridge and get over it."

The door slams shut, and I sit in the silence, allowing it to swallow me whole.

I slump into my chair and glance up at my computer, seeing my schedule immediately grayed out. If anything, Asher is thorough.

Fifteen minutes pass, and I'm still in the same place because when I leave, I will be locked out.

"Nick?" Lauren, our executive assistant, says from the doorway. She's holding two cups. "Saw Asher storm out, mumbling under his breath. Figured you could use this."

She sets the mug in front of me, and I notice the tea tag hanging from the side. She's been bringing me mugs of Earl Grey since she worked for my dad at our family's finance company.

When Asher quit the family business and took over the marketing firm, he took our father's executive assistant with him. Lauren didn't hesitate to leave. She's been watching us since we were kids. Now we're adults, and she's often the only voice of reason we have.

"Tell me what happened." She settles into the chair across from me.

"I walked out of that bullshit meeting." I take a sip, letting the warmth spread through my chest.

"I heard. A few directors are currently having heart palpitations because of that little scene you caused."

"Mr. Big Mac doesn't get it. If I didn't know better, I'd say he was a terminator."

Lauren lets out a small laugh. "You know what your problem is?"

"Please, enlighten me."

"You're thirty-eight years old, and you're already a ghost," she says matter-of-factly. "You float through these halls, meetings, and life, but you're not really here anymore."

"I show up every day—"

"Your body shows up. But Nick? The real Nicolas Banks? The one who used to throw baseballs in the hallways and bring me wildflowers from the park?" She shakes her head. "I haven't seen him in a long time."

The tea suddenly tastes like ash. "That Nick had nothing to lose."

"That Nick had joy, and you need to find it again." She leans forward, plucking a chocolate from the candy jar next to a stack of invoices I was auditing. "Where would you go if you could go anywhere in the world?"

The answer escapes before I can stop it. "Cozy Creek."

Her eyebrows rise. "Where Zane is?"

"It's nothing. Forget I said—"

"When were you last there?"

I do the math, even though I know the answer. "I visited for a few days in January and ended up cutting it short."

"Why?"

"A huge contract came in, so I traveled back to the city. It was abrupt." I spin the teacup on its saucer.

"What really happened?" she asks.

A sigh escapes me. "Shit got too real."

She takes a sip of her tea. "I'll schedule a private plane to take you there. I'll have everything booked for you within the hour."

"Lauren, please."

She lifts her hand. "No. I asked you where you'd go, and that was your answer. So, that's where you're going. Call Zane. Let him know."

"Lauren!"

With that motherly expression on her face, she glares at me. "You've been punishing yourself for far too long. I think you walk out of meetings about human connection because you've convinced yourself you don't deserve any."

I open my mouth, but she doesn't let me speak.

"I'm not done." She returns to my desk and places her palms flat against the cool wood. "This isn't a vacation. It's a lifeline. If you don't go where your heart leads you, you'll become what you're afraid of being—a hollow asshole, just like your dad, who forgot how to be human."

Her words are a slap to the face.

"What if I go to Cozy Creek and come back in November and nothing has changed? Then what?"

"It's a possibility. But also, what if you go and remember who you are?" She straightens up. "You are *Nicolas Banks*. That means something. You're the happy-go-lucky guy who loves ice skating, skiing, baseball, and bonfires. You never miss an opportunity to tell a joke. You're not like your brothers and sister, Nick. You grew up differently from the other Banks kids, and somewhere along the way, you lost your true self. It's time to find you again. And your relationships, honey? Don't get me started on those."

"Thank you for that last little cherry on top," I say sarcastically.

She heads for the door, pausing at the handle. "Go to Cozy Creek, Nick. If not for yourself, then for Eden." She gestures at me, at the office, at everything. "She wouldn't want this to be your life."

"How do you know that?"

Lauren grins wider. "Because she told me that no matter what, she never wanted *you* to become a cunty cliché like the rest of the

Banks family. Asher, on the other hand, there was never any hope for him."

I burst into laughter as the door closes with a soft click.

I sit there, tea growing cold, and realize I'm smiling.

I guess I'm going back to Cozy Creek. And for the first time in years, I'm excited.

JULIE

The Tuesday morning rush hits Cozy Coffee like a caffeinated hurricane. I'm in my element as I move like a bartender behind the counter. Steam hisses from the espresso machine while I pull two shots at once. The smell of cinnamon and freshly ground beans wraps around me like the quilt my grandmother made me when I was a kid.

"One maple latte, extra hot, for Mrs. Henderson." I slide the cup across the reclaimed wood counter, already starting on the next order. "Tom, your usual black coffee's ready. Yes, I put it in a to-go cup even though we both know you're staying until eleven."

He's an older gentleman with bright blue eyes, a perfect smile, and a white handlebar mustache. I shoot him a wink. Tom grins and plops down in his favorite armchair by the window. When he crosses his legs, I see he's wearing his favorite boots that have been through some shit.

"You know," he says in his thick Southern drawl, "I have a few sons your age."

"I know. Tell them to come visit me and say hello themselves. No one wants a matchmaking parent," I remind him for the hundredth time.

Tom Valley owns Devil's River Ranch in Texas. He also owns a vacation escape thirty minutes away, up in the mountains. When his sexy-as-sin sons visit Colorado, they party at Silver Sky, the next town over. Everyone knows about the Valley boys—cocky, homeschooled Texas cowboys who mostly keep to themselves but always show up for pumpkin season.

I glance around the shop, and everyone seems happy, thrilled to be here. It's one of the hottest hangouts in Cozy Creek, where most come to get their piping hot gossip after the sun rises.

Cozy Coffee is my second home, where I'm sure of myself, where everything works out for me. This is my family's eighty-one-year-old business that runs like clockwork when I'm managing. Here, I know exactly who I am and what's expected of me. Here, I'm the boss. I don't ever question the future, and there's no confusion about my career path. Now, my relationships? That's a whole cluster of a conversation.

"Jules, honey, you won't believe who I saw at the Maple Inn this morning when I stopped in to grab a newspaper." Mrs. Patrick leans across the counter, eyes bright with gossip.

She's part of the women's group that I nicknamed the Fairy Godmothers over a decade ago. They play matchmaker and are always meddling in relationships around Cozy Creek under the guise of a romance book club.

"Oh?" While I don't have time for this right now, I lean toward her with a smile to appease her.

I pour more roasted beans into the machine, knowing we're getting low as orders print nonstop.

"Let me guess. A sexy pumpkin peeper who's staying for the season that I should totally hook up with?"

Pumpkin peepers are what we call the tourists who have zero self-awareness, who show up just for the festivities.

"Craig Downing." She drops my ex's name like an atomic bomb. It's been nearly a year since anyone has mentioned him to me.

"*What?*" It comes out louder than I meant.

Blaire clears her throat from the register, and I quickly turn back to the espresso machine, grateful for the grinding that's drowning out the silence.

"He's still in love with you," Mrs. Patrick continues like it's nothing. "I overheard him telling Jeanette at the front desk he had regrets. Said he missed home. Apparently, he moved back and broke it off with your replacement."

I keep my voice flat. "That's impossible. They were engaged."

"People change their minds," she offers. "But remember, a tiger never changes its stripes."

The two of us have this toxic cycle. He returns to Cozy Creek, says sweet things, makes promises, and then we have sex.

But not this time. I promised myself never again.

Mrs. Patrick watches me with the intensity of a teacher who's taught hormonal seventh-grade students for forty years—because she has. "Figured I'd give you a warning. Don't be shocked if he strolls in here."

"Mrs. P, it won't matter. Trust me when I say, Craig and I are ancient history." I flash my million-dollar smile, the one that says, *I'm fine*, while I force my hands to stay steady. "I want a real man."

A college kid at the register counts out crumpled bills and loose change for a large latte. As Blaire waits for him, I wave him off, sliding an extra chocolate croissant into his bag.

"Student discount," I lie.

We only have a senior discount, but he looks like he's living on ramen and anxiety. I try to spread good vibes when I can.

"Thank you," he says graciously. No way he's a day older than nineteen.

"You're too nice for your own good," Mrs. Patrick says as the guy walks away, but she's smiling. "You remind me so much of your grandmother."

"Thank you. But don't forget, Gran kept a metal baseball bat under the counter and wasn't afraid to use it." I wipe down the already-clean machine, needing something to do with my hands as

Blaire rings in the following order. "I kill with kindness, caffeine, and croissants."

The bell above the door chimes, and Mike Ashford stumbles in, nearly walking into a table and chair because he's staring. At me. Again.

"Hi, Jules." His face goes red as he fumbles with his debit card.

"Hi, Michael," I say.

He's adorable, but I'm eleven years older. At thirty-five years old, I do not want to date someone who could only recently order a drink at a bar.

"Still denying me?" He looks up at me with googly eyes.

"Yes, I am," I say with a laugh.

I blame his reaction on my genetics. Sometimes, being a ginger goddess is a blessing, and other times, it's a curse.

At the thought, I glance at my reflection in the espresso machine. My red hair refuses to be tamed, and my eyes—the ones my mother insists on calling "emerald" instead of just green—stare back at me, almost hollow. Freckles multiply across my nose anytime I even think about sunshine. Most guys say I'm intimidating just because I have a sassy mouth and an attitude that matches my hair. Sometimes, I'm exhausted by the attention I receive from men.

"Did you do something different with your hair?" Mike manages, still hovering by the register like he's afraid to come any closer. "You're glowing."

"It's called downing double espresso shots before nine. Caffeine makes the world go round. But thank you. I appreciate the compliment."

He orders a simple coffee with two sugars and a splash of cream before he practically runs out of the building.

Mrs. Patrick chuckles. "That boy's been crushing on you since high school."

"I know, but I just can't. Last week, I gave him dating advice and explained how having confidence is attractive." I shake my head. "We just need to work on the execution."

"Mm-hmm," she says with a nod, but she's kind enough not to push. "Well, I'd better get going. Garden club is judging autumn arrangements today to decide which ones will be displayed in big potted plants around the town when fall officially kicks off next week. I want to win that title. I'm sick and tired of Patty winning each year. It's rigged, I tell you! Rigged!"

"Good luck," I say with a laugh as she leaves, and I'm grateful that the conversation is being dropped.

Five minutes later, when I look over my shoulder, Blaire is smirking at me. And that's when it's confirmed she heard every damn word.

"So, Craig is back?" she whispers close to me.

I meet her eyes. "I can't bang him while he's here. Seriously. I'm done with him. I'm going on almost a year of no contact."

"We have to find you a distraction."

A chuckle releases from me. "Put me next on your love spell list."

"I'll make you one tonight," she says with a wink, and we go our separate ways as the second rush comes in.

When we're nonstop busy, I lose track of everything.

Four hours later, the shop is practically empty, and there is too much quiet and not enough distraction. Blaire and I clean so we can leave right at three when the afternoon shift comes in.

As I'm emptying and replacing trash bags by the condiment station by the door, I catch sight of a blacked-out Range Rover sliding past the wall of windows. My traitorous heart does a stupid little skip. Lots of people have fancy cars, and hundreds of thousands of people drive through Cozy Creek in September to catch sight of the large pumpkin patch that's constructed in the middle of the town square.

I work on making the shop sparkle as Blaire stocks everything. Cozy Coffee is my sanctuary, my legacy, my perfectly controlled universe, where no one leaves without saying goodbye and everyone gets exactly what they ordered.

"Jules!" Finn Morrison pops his head in, still in his fire chief gear. "Just wanted to warn you, Autumn's on her way, and she's got that look."

"What look?"

"You know the one."

Autumn is my best friend, my ride or die, who used to work the morning shift with Blaire and me. That is, until she met the love of her life, Zane Alexander, and married him. Now, she lives in a haunted house on top of the hill that overlooks Cozy Creek—Hollow Manor. Sometimes, when I think about it, I can't help but laugh. That house was the feature of our childhood ghost stories, and now it's where Autumn calls home.

"Thank you," I tell him, preparing myself, wondering if Mrs. Patrick ran into her and snitched about Craig being back.

"Uh-oh," Blaire says, her crystal earrings dangling as I move behind the counter.

"Yeah. Thanks for the support," I mutter. "If Autumn knows Craig is here, she's going to track him down and drag him through the town square by the balls."

Blaire bursts into laughter. "He deserves everything he has coming to him."

I straighten my apron, tighten my ponytail, and prepare for Hurricane Autumn. At least I know how to handle her.

When the bell chimes, I know it's her before I even look up. There's something about the way Autumn enters a room, like sunshine and storm clouds, all at once. I miss my best friend so much, but I'm happy she's enjoying being in love. She deserves it.

"Julie Loveland." She uses my full name, which means I'm in trouble. "We need to talk."

"Good morning to you too, Autumn Alexander. Coffee? Chocolate croissant? Did you bring me pumpkin bread, or do you have an explanation for why you're using my government name?"

She stalks to the counter, dark hair pulled back in a messy bun, wearing one of Zane's flannels over her yoga clothes. "I just ran into Craig at the grocery store. *Craig. Downing.* I nearly panicked, watching him buy organic brussels sprouts. He asked about you."

"Brussels sprouts?" I focus on the important part. "He *hates* vegetables. Must be an impostor."

"Jules."

"What? He used to count a serving of ketchup as vegetables. It's hard for me to believe."

Autumn shakes her head. "He moved back. You cannot see him again."

"I know." My stomach drops, but I keep my voice steady. "You and everyone else in Cozy Creek know that. I'm not falling for it again. I refuse."

"Good, because I might have told him that you're thriving, glowing, and dating someone that you're madly in love with." She pauses. "I'm sorry. I couldn't help myself."

"Autumn!"

"He was so jealous. No way I was giving him any hope. I'm sick of him! He needs to go away—forever!"

Blaire nods. "I agree with her."

I hand Autumn a lavender latte without her asking. She's addicted to them.

"Everyone knows I'm not with anyone. He won't believe it."

"I don't care. You're unavailable." She grimaces.

"This sucks," I whisper. "Craig being back wasn't on my autumn bingo card."

"I know. I'm really sorry. But that's not actually why I came to see you." She takes a sip of her latte, suddenly looking uncomfortable. "I needed to warn you about something else. Someone else actually—"

The bell chimes, cutting her off.

"Shit," she mutters, and I turn to see why.

"Oh. My. Goddess." Blaire freezes when she sees him.

Nick Banks stands in the doorway like he's stepping out of one of my dreams. Dark slacks; button-up shirt, rolled to his elbows; and messy, dark hair. His honey-brown eyes are tired, but when our gazes meet, I feel that familiar gravitational pull that makes my stomach do somersaults.

"Nick!" Autumn practically squeals, which is weird because Autumn never responds this way to anyone. She rushes over and gives him a side hug. "Zane said you might be coming to town."

He hugs her back, but his eyes stay planted on mine. "Hey, Autumn. How's married life?"

"Amazing. Exhausting. But oh so worth it." She pulls back, glancing between us with barely concealed panic. "I was just here to get a coffee from Jules and was, uh ..."

"Gossiping about my ex," I offer, trying to stay calm, but I am completely unwell. He's the last man on the planet I expected to see today. "It's just the usual Tuesday morning entertainment."

"Right. That." Autumn backs toward the door, shooting me an apologetic look. "I should go. I'm making pumpkin bread today."

"Autumn," I say as she floats across the dining room.

She mouths, *I'm sorry*, behind Nick's back as she escapes. "Bye! Good talk, Jules! Back to the grocery store I go! I literally left my basket in the produce section."

The bell chimes as she flees, leaving me alone with the man who's been haunting my thoughts since last year.

Blaire can't stop laughing and moves to the back so she doesn't interrupt us.

And then Nick and I are alone.

The electricity that always seems to stream steadily when we're in the same room is alive and well.

"Hi," he says, plump lips lifting in that dangerous half smile. "Come here often?"

My mouth twitches. I pour his coffee with hands that remember exactly how he takes it. Black. Simple. No room for anything extra. "Occasionally. I hear the manager is a real hard-ass though."

"Really? I heard she's gorgeous. Sassy as fuck."

"Sassy?" I raise an eyebrow, falling into our same old rhythm as I hand him his cup. Our fingers brush, and it nearly undoes me. "That's a big word for a hockey player."

"Former hockey player, babe. Currently a suit-wearing corporate asshole who knows words like *quarterly projections* and *synergy*." He takes a sip and closes his eyes. "This is perfect."

"I know. I made it."

"Confident, per usual."

"Nah, you just don't intimidate me like you do most women." I lean against the counter, trying to ignore how good he looks.

"How've you been?" he asks, trying to make small talk—something he's great at.

"Fantastic. Living my best life. Thriving with your read receipts and no responses."

I met Nick Banks last year when his mom was getting married. We sat at a local bar called Bookers and chatted for hours. I shared things with him I'd never said out loud, and he told me his secrets too. I thought I'd never see him again until he showed up in January to stay with Zane and Autumn. We exchanged numbers, but after three days, he left. I haven't seen him since.

I texted him a few months ago and got zero response. I gave up the ghost.

"I deserve that," he says.

"Oh, you deserve *much* worse. I was trying to be friendly and wanted to check in on you."

"I know. I suck." He doesn't move.

"What brings you back here? Another family wedding? A three-day drive-by, where you show up and pretend like you're going to stay but leave?" I ask as he tries to pull his credit card from his wallet to pay. I shake my head at him.

"None of the above." He sets down his cup and meets my eyes. "But I am staying."

My heart twirls. "I don't believe you."

"I don't care. I'll be here for six weeks, through the season. I'm scheduled to return to New York at the beginning of November. No sooner." He says it like a promise.

"Scheduled?"

"Long story short, I had a meltdown at a meeting and was forced by my bratty little brother to take a vacation." He runs a hand through his dark brown hair, messing it up more.

I blink at him with my head tilted. "And you chose *here*? Why?"

"Why not?" The way he looks at me makes my stomach flip.

I don't have an answer for him.

"There is no other place to be during fall. I rented a cabin until November. I think it's called Riverside?"

My eyes widen. It's a luxury mansion that's ironically called a cabin. It costs ten thousand dollars a day to stay there. "Riverside? That's fancy for a temporary escape."

"I want to do temporary right this time." He pauses. "You should come see it. Tonight. At seven."

"Nick." I shake my head.

"Have dinner with me. It would be an honor to catch up." His voice is casual, but his eyes say so much more.

I cross my arms over my chest. "You're serious?"

"You're the only person who's tried to check on me this year. And I'll have plenty of wine." He leans forward slightly. "Come on, Little Red. When's the last time you did something just for fun?"

Little Red. He gave me that nickname the first night we met at Bookers. It's a sports bar, and the Cowboys were playing the Eagles. It was a random night full of nothing but conversation that I'll never forget.

"Pfft. I have fun every day," I tell him.

"Outside of work." He licks his lips. "You can love your job, but there's more to life than this."

My heart thuds because it doesn't know better. I try to remember the last time I had a good time, and it was with him, when we talked all night about nothing and everything. I thought

I'd never see him again until he showed up at Autumn's house. That was when I learned he was Zane's stepbrother and ex–best friend.

He grins like trouble as I replay memories of sharing my deepest secrets with him. I thought I'd never see Nick Banks again.

"You can't just show up nine months later, after completely ghosting me, and expect me to be receptive to your invites."

He gives me a look, almost like I struck a nerve. "I knew it was a risk, asking you, but I took it anyway. The truth is, I wasn't ready to have any new friends."

His words catch me off guard.

"And you are now?"

He smiles. "Now I have nothing to lose."

"What makes you think I don't have plans?"

"Do you?" he asks with a brow lifted.

The coffee shop suddenly feels too small, too warm, too full of possibilities I can't afford.

"I might," I say.

"Cancel them."

"Cocky as hell," I whisper, finding him too hot to handle.

"I wanna see you, Jules. Finish our conversation." He heads for the door, pausing to look back. "Wear something you don't mind getting wine spilled on. I'm professionally clumsy when distracted."

"What's going to distract you?"

His eyes do a slow sweep from my face down and back up. "Mmm."

Nick pushes the door open and strolls toward the Range Rover. My head and heart swim.

Moments later, Blaire walks back to the front and glares at me. "Holy shit."

"What?" I ask.

"If you don't date him, I will."

I burst into laughter. "Shut it. He's not dateable."

"Is he fuckable? Because I'd be his blowup doll."

I'm wheezing. "Stop."

I wipe tears from my cheeks, and she pauses, staring at me.

"Oh my goddess."

"Tell me. If I have something in my teeth, I'll be mortified."

She shakes her head. "You're going to fall in love with that man."

"No, I'm not," I huff out. "I know too much about him."

Blaire doesn't look convinced. "Did I eavesdrop correctly? Did he say he's staying until November?"

"Yes," I whisper and realize I'm smiling. "But we'll see. That means nothing. Last time, he was supposed to stay two weeks, but within seventy-two hours, he was gone without a goodbye."

"I think he'll be the perfect distraction for you. Poor Craig." She rolls her eyes and then bumps me with her hip. "This season is going to be different for you. I can feel it in the air."

"Don't jinx me," I say as the afternoon crew enters.

"It's a good thing," she confirms.

For the final hour of my shift, I'm in my head, thinking about Nick and what it means now that he's here. I secretly hoped I'd get the opportunity just to chat with him again. His conversations are good, and it helps that he's not bad to look at. The invitation is a new beginning, a way for us to start over.

I glance at the clock, counting down to seven. I have four hours to decide whether to go or not.

"Is a planet in retrograde or something?" I ask Blaire over my shoulder. "Why is it raining men on me right now?"

She shrugs. "Mercury's in retrograde, but Venus is ascending. You know what they say—third time's a—"

"If you say charm, I'm burning all your sage."

She mimes zipping her lips, but her eyes are dancing with hope.

Somehow, I'm the only one who remembers that some patterns are meant to be broken, not repeated. If Nick leaves again without saying goodbye, I'll forget that he exists.

Meeting him the first time was by chance. The second was a coincidence. But the third? It would be a choice. Right now, I have a big decision to make.

3

NICK

I sit in the Range Rover outside Hollow Manor—the black mansion that overlooks Cozy Creek—for a full minute with the engine off. I'm still trying to convince myself that being here is a good idea, even if I have nowhere else I'd rather be.

The house looks exactly how I remember it from when we were teenagers, before Zane's mother passed away. There are new additions though. Dark wood flower boxes are now under the windows, full of orange and deep purple flowers. A sparkling wreath made of golden autumn leaves hangs on the oversize door, and pumpkins are lined up on the steps. It's the little details that show signs of the life Zane has built while I was hiding in my Manhattan office. He's made this place a home, and I'm happy that he's found true love. He deserves it.

I suck in a deep breath, trying to get my shit together before I get out. We're on the mend, but it's still hard because I carry so much guilt.

In January, I flew here so Zane and I could reconcile. We've gotten together a few times when he's visited the city, and we text occasionally. We're trying, now that his dad married my mother. It's impossible to avoid one another during the holidays.

The last time I was here, I ran into Julie again and learned she was Autumn's best friend.

My phone dings with a text. I unlock it.

ASHER

Did you make it there okay?

NICK

Sitting outside of Zane's as we speak.

ASHER

Good. Quit being a chickenshit and go inside.

I shake my head, wondering how my brother knew. Before I go inside, I text another one of my old hockey friends, Patterson Cross, knowing I have to make an effort with the people who care about me.

NICK

Have to take a rain check for our drinks next Friday. I'm in Cozy Creek until November.

PATTERSON

What the hell? Why?

NICK

Asher said I needed a vacation. If you get bored, you should come check out the harvest festival. Got a place for you to stay.

PATTERSON

Might take you up on that. Tell Zane I said sup.

NICK

Will do.

I force myself out of the Range Rover and up the steps to the door. I give three knocks. Seconds later, Zane opens the door, and we look at each other for a moment. He's in jeans and a flannel, and the gold of his wedding ring catches the light. Happy suits him in a way that makes me proud. He found what he'd always been searching for—love and happiness.

"Nick." His voice is neutral.

He's not surprised. I texted him and let him know I was heading to Colorado for the season.

"Zane." I try for casual. "You always *this* excited to see me?"

Something in his face shifts. It's a smile. "Honestly? I halfway expected you to bail on the way to the airport. You weren't always a flake."

"Yeah, you're right." The admission comes out easier than I thought.

"My manners. Welcome in." He steps to the side, letting me enter. "Want a beer?"

"Yeah. I'll have one. Thanks."

The dark wall is lined with wedding photos of Zane and Autumn laughing, dancing, looking at each other like the rest of the world doesn't exist. There's one of my mom and Zane's dad—our parents—and they're beaming at the camera. I missed one of the happiest moments of his life, and that hurts.

My eyes slide to the fridge.

Zane pops open two beers and hands me one.

"You look happy," I say.

"I am," he tells me. "Life is great."

I glance down at the label wrapped around the dark bottle and see it's a local craft beer that probably has an interesting story behind it. We drink in silence for a moment, the kitchen feeling too normal.

"Marriage suits you," I say, watching him subconsciously twist his wedding ring. "Never pictured you so domesticated."

"Never pictured you apologizing." He leans against the counter, smirking. "Guess we've both changed."

"You do have a point ..." I trail off. "I have a lot of regrets in life. I'll never be able to apologize enough."

He smirks. "Save it. I've forgiven you. I'm ready to get back to how things used to be. Doesn't mean it's not still weird though."

"Which part?"

"All of it. You fucking my ex. Our parents getting married. You being here. Us talking like adults. Me not wanting to punch you in the face."

I raise my beer. "Progress. I'll toast to that."

"I have missed you," he admits. "I sometimes think about the old days, when we didn't have to worry about anything but where we'd be skiing for the upcoming season. The slopes here were great last season."

I grin. "Remember when you thought a black diamond meant to go as fast as possible?"

He smirks. "Remember your backflip attempt off the lift?"

"Hey, I landed that shit with flying colors."

"Yeah. You landed on your face in front of all those college girls." He grins.

"Didn't stop them from coming to my room," I say, waggling my brows. "We were fearless idiots. Sometimes, I wonder how we survived half of that."

"You were an idiot. I was following your lead every single time."

It feels good to chat and laugh, like old times. It makes me believe that we can salvage something from the wreckage.

"So," Zane says too casually, "how long are you staying?"

"Until November first. I'm on permanent vacation until Asher lets me return."

"Uh-oh. Do I even want to know what you did?" His eyebrows rise.

"I crashed out in a meeting about the human experience," I admit, not regretting it. "CEO was a punk. Asher said I needed a break. So, here I am."

I'm not ready to admit my brother thinks I'm a ghost.

Zane smirks. "Good choice. When I showed up last season, I wore the same expression you did. Now look at me."

I pick at the beer label. "Yeah, this time, I'm hoping to deal with shit instead of running from it."

"Plan to see Jules?"

My hand stills. "I invited her to have dinner with me."

He considers me for a long moment, then grabs two more beers. "You know that's Autumn's bestie ..."

"I'm not here to use her. It's not like that with us. We just ... *talk*."

"Good." He slides the beer across the counter. "Because Autumn will make you regret your life choices, and I won't be able to stop her."

As if summoned by her name, the front door swings open.

Bags rustle, and Autumn immediately speaks. "Zane, my love! I was just at the coffee shop, and you'll never believe who—" Autumn rounds the corner and stops dead in her tracks. "Oh. You're here."

"Long time no see," I offer.

Autumn stalks into the kitchen with determination, setting everything down on the counter. She kisses Zane hello, but her eyes assess me.

"You're back," she says.

"Here I am."

She grabs a beer from the fridge, pops it open, and takes a sip. "For how long this time? Please say longer than three days because that was very annoying."

"Six weeks. I can't return to the city until after November first. Per my asshole little brother."

"Hmm." She hops up on the counter. "You look tired."

I wasn't expecting that. "I'm exhausted by everything."

Autumn studies me, then seems to make a decision. "Look, I'm going to be straight with you."

My brows lift, and I glance at Zane, who chugs his beer. "Okay ..."

"Jules is my person. My bestie since we were kids. My chosen sister in every way that matters." She swallows hard. "And you, Nick Banks, have a very bad reputation. I googled you."

"Happy to know you've done your research," I offer, smirking.

She sets down her beer and meets my eyes. "The universe is invested in the two of you because you keep popping up at the right time."

Zane groans. "Autumn, don't start with the universe stuff."

"I'm just saying." She turns to me. "Maybe you and Julie can help each other."

"Really? How?" I take two gulps of my beer.

"Well, for starters, she needs a fake boyfriend to slide in when her shitty ex tries to win her back."

Zane glares at her. "Craig is back?"

"I assume Craig is the ex?" I ask.

"Yes," they both say, annoyingly, at the same time.

"Tell me about him," I say.

Autumn groans. "He's Julie's really shitty, sorry excuse of an ex. She has a hard time resisting him, and he just uses her. Promises her the world, gets what he wants, then leaves again. It's a toxic cycle that has to stop. I do not want her in his arms this fall."

I take several gulps of my beer. "How can I help?"

"Be aware." She hops off the counter. "Craig will try to win her back. Julie needs someone who will keep her away from that son of a bitch." Autumn looks annoyed. "He always treated her like she was too much and not enough. That's Craig Downer. He's his namesake." Her jaw tightens. "I want her to forget he exists."

"Autumn, I can't commit to anything," I say.

"My bestie doesn't need a commitment." She sighs. "She needs a distraction."

Zane stands and pulls some chopped watermelon from the fridge. "He asked her to dinner tonight."

Autumn's eyes widen. "Yes!"

"It's a friendly dinner. That's it. I owe her an apology for being a dickhead and not responding to her texts."

"That's a start." She grabs some fruit. "Want a piece of advice?"

"I bet you're going to give it to me anyway."

She grins and heads toward the stairs. "You're right. You have six weeks, Nick. Make them count. The universe doesn't give fourth chances."

Seconds later, she disappears, leaving me with Zane.

"Is she trying to hook me up with her best friend?" I ask, surprised.

"I have no idea," he offers. "But you two would be good together."

I check the time. "Shit. I should probably get going. I'm cooking penne alla vodka."

"Really?" He's smirking.

"What?"

He shakes his head. "Nothing."

Zane walks me to the door.

"Let's not be strangers while I'm here, okay?"

"You're the one who left early in January," he says. "But I'm glad you're back. The mountain air has a way of healing someone. I came here last year and found myself."

I chuckle. "I hope I'm as lucky."

He claps me on the shoulder. "You will be. Just go with the flow. Learn to be spontaneous. Follow your heart. That's the magic of Cozy Creek. Also, if dinner turns into a disaster, don't panic. Call Cozy Pizza; they'll deliver. Julie's order is thick crust with pepperoni, mushrooms, and extra black olives."

"Thanks," I say.

He grins. "Six weeks, man. Hope you have the autumn of your life."

"I hope I do too."

Zane leans forward and pulls me into a brotherly hug. He holds me tight, and it's only then that I realize how much I've missed him.

"I'll see you."

"See you," he says.

I get in the Range Rover and take the switchbacks down the mountain to the road where the Riverside cabin is. I follow the gravel to the end until I approach the home. Calling this place a cabin is ridiculous. I think it has ten bedrooms and eight baths, and it's pure luxury with marble floors and countertops.

When I walk in, I admire the vaulted ceilings, exposed beams, oversized fireplace, and a kitchen that puts my state-of-the-art penthouse to shame. I unpack groceries because, tonight, I'm making one of my sister's favorite recipes, one I haven't made in years. I set the bags on the counter, then wash my hands before I get to work.

Prep goes smoothly until I reach for the bottle of booze, realizing it's missing. I walk out to the Range Rover to make sure it didn't fall out, but it's not there. Before I panic, I check the cabinets to see if anyone happened to leave vodka behind, but there's nothing other than a bottle of unopened tequila.

"Shit," I hiss, checking the time.

It's already six o'clock, and the store is twenty minutes away. It's not enough time.

I stare at the sautéed garlic, onions, and tomato paste, knowing I need the vodka now.

After I release a long sigh, I grab my phone and call Cozy Pizza to order.

By the time I've changed clothes and hidden all evidence of my attempt at making a nice dinner, it's seven o'clock. The pizza arrives on time, and after I tip the delivery guy, I scan the driveway.

At 7:10 p.m., I pour a glass of wine and check my phone. Maybe she's running late.

After I read the last text she sent me, it only confirms that I deserve to be ghosted.

UNKNOWN

Thinking about you. ☺

I remember I was at a swanky party with Asher and his fiancée, Billie Calloway. I could've responded, but what would I have said?

You've been on my mind since we met?

We'd both made it very clear that neither of us was in the right space for a relationship. Friends only. But then she sends me texts like that.

Another ten minutes pass, and I'm convinced she's not coming.

After I gave her months of silence, I expected us to pick up as friends? How truly fucking delusional and presumptuous am I?

By seven thirty, I swallow down the rest of my glass of wine and refill it. When I open the lid of the pizza box, I notice headlights sweep across the windows.

I freeze and move toward the kitchen window watching Jules park. She sits in her car for a while. She's officially thirty-five minutes late.

Get out of the car and join me. Please.

Eventually, she does. She's wearing a brown sweater and tight jeans and carrying a bottle of wine in her hand. She takes her time strolling to the door, almost as if she's still deciding if she should turn around.

I open the door before she can knock.

"You're late," I say.

"You noticed." She studies me, then smiles. "I was trying to decide if this was a terrible idea."

"What's the verdict?"

"Jury's still out." She steps past me into the house. "But I brought more wine for us, so I'm committed to at least an hour of fun."

"Fair enough." I let her in, closing the door behind her. She smells like wildflowers and a dash of vanilla. "I ordered pizza. My cooking plans fell through."

Her emerald eyes sparkle, and her red hair glows in this light as she turns to me. "What happened?"

I hear the concern in her voice.

"Turns out vodka sauce needs vodka. Who knew?"

She laughs, and the sound echoes off the vaulted ceiling. "You forgot the main ingredient?"

"It was a travel day, and I've had a lot of shit on my mind," I admit.

"Clearly." She sets her wine on the counter and notices the packaging in the trash. "You bought fresh penne from Marcello's?"

"You know it?"

"Who doesn't? Fancy." She touches the package. "You were actually going to cook for me."

"Of course. But also, don't sound so surprised. I know how to cook," I explain. "I can be domestic when needed."

"Really? I learn something new about you every time we're together."

"I've missed your fire," I tell her.

She laughs. "I could say the same about you."

I slide a plate from the cabinet and hand it to her with a napkin. "I'm glad you came. I thought you weren't."

"Truthfully, I wasn't, but I flipped a coin." She opens the pizza box and grins. "My favorite. Lucky guess?"

"Zane told me," I say. "Wait, wait. You flipped a coin?"

She nods. "I even did the best two out of three. Then I did three of five. The answer was clear, so here I am."

I snatch a piece of pizza from the box and take a bite. Julie does the same.

"Sorry it's cold," I offer.

"My fault," she says, covering her mouth with her hand as she speaks. "You know, the night we met, I thought I'd never see you again."

The words hang between us as I grab her a wineglass and fill it.

"I thought you were just some guy passing through town. If I'd known you'd keep showing up, I might have kept some things to myself," she says.

"I'm glad you didn't."

She plucks a black olive off the top of her slice. "Can I ask you something?"

"Anything."

Her voice softens. "Why didn't you text me back?"

A breath releases from me. "I didn't know what to say."

"I can accept that," she says. "But I can't be ghosted by people who try to call themselves friends."

I nod. "You're absolutely right. I should've done better, and I apologize. You'll never have to worry about not getting a response from me again. Apparently, I've been needing to work on my human connections, and since I left the city, that has become my new priority."

"Wow. Thank you," she says.

We stand in the kitchen, eating pizza and drinking wine, and I feel something shift. The awkwardness slowly melts away.

"God, I've been lonely," she admits as we move to the couch. "Is that weird to say?"

"Not if it's the truth." I grab the remote and flick on the gigantic television that fills the wall. "Lately, I've felt the same. It's almost like I've been living the same day over and over again; it was a nightmare I couldn't wake up from. Then I lost my shit in a meeting, and here we are."

Her eyes are kind as she takes another bite of pizza. "I'm happy you're here."

"I am too."

She raises her glass. "To friendship. And answered texts. And remembering the vodka next time."

"To having the best damn autumn of our lives," I counter, excited for pumpkin patches and apple cider.

"Amen."

We clink glasses, and her smile is worth every minute I spent panicking that she wouldn't show.

"So," she says, settling in, "catch me up on your so-called life. I need entertainment with my pizza."

"Only if you share."

"Deal. But don't you dare skip the embarrassing parts."

I lean against the cushions, careful to keep a distance between us. "Okay, but remember, you asked for this …"

And just like that, we fall into a rhythm, like the eight months that separated us never happened. We're just two people who found each other again at the right moment. We're honest and raw. I tell her about work, and she talks about the coffee shop. This is the friendship I've been missing.

We talk until the pizza box is empty and the second bottle of wine is almost gone. She throws her head back and laughs at my stupid jokes. Throughout the night, I can't stop staring at her lips.

"Your turn," I say after I explain one of my embarrassing relationship moments.

She grows quiet, spinning her wineglass. "My ex-fiancé, *Craig*, showed up at my parents' anniversary party with his new girlfriend three months after our engagement ended." She looks up at me. "Want to know the pathetic part?"

I move closer without meaning to. "Tell me."

"For about thirty seconds, I thought he was there to win me back. After everything, some stupid part of me thought …" She shakes her head. "Anyway, he just wanted to return my grandmother's ring in front of everyone."

"Jules—"

"His new fiancée was wearing a necklace I'd bought him to celebrate our second anniversary." She laughs, but I hear the pain. "So, yeah, that's my most embarrassing. Nothing beats being reminded very publicly that you're replaceable."

"You're not."

"Everyone's replaceable."

"I don't believe that." I set my glass down and turn to her until we're facing each other. Our legs briefly touch, and I can see the gold flecks in her green eyes. "Some people leave marks on you and make it impossible to go back to who you were before you knew them."

She stares up at me. "Do you really believe that?"

"Yeah. You're unforgettable, Little Red."

The air between us shifts. Her lips part slightly.

"We're friends," she whispers.

"We are friends."

"Friends don't look at each other like this."

"How?" I ask.

"Like …" She sets her wine down and shifts toward me.

We're too close now.

Neither of us moves.

She sucks in a breath. "Nick, I—"

The doorbell rings, shattering the moment.

We jump apart like teenagers caught by their parents. Jules smooths her sweater, looking everywhere but at me.

I answer the door to find a woman in her sixties, holding a clear dish.

"Hi! I'm Sheila Galloway. I own the place and rented it to you. Just wanted to come and give you a warm welcome and a fresh pumpkin pie."

She glances around me and spots Julie on the couch like a typical nosy, small-town neighbor.

"Oh! Julie? I didn't know you two knew each other," she says over my shoulder.

"Hi, Mrs. Galloway." Julie appears beside me, cheeks flushed. "I was actually just leaving."

"Don't go on my account, dear. You two continue your date; don't let me interrupt."

"It's not a date," Jules says.

"We're just friends," I add, knowing how rumors start in small towns.

Mrs. Galloway looks between us with knowing eyes. "Well, regardless, enjoy the pie. I plan on winning the pie baking contest with that very recipe. Hope I can count on your vote." She leaves with a wink.

The door closes, and Julie groans, pulling her keys from her pocket. "Great! Mrs. Galloway will tell the entire town I was here."

"And? I can't let you leave," I tell her, gently pulling her to me. "You've had too much to drink."

Her cheeks are flushed, and she breathes out, "I'll call Autumn to pick me up."

"Just stay," I say. "I don't bite."

She narrows her eyes. "Yes, you do."

"No way I'm letting anything happen to you."

Her face softens, and she chews on the inside of her cheek. "You're a bad influence."

"Undeniably," I say with a smirk. "But bad influences have the most fun and make the best of friends."

She playfully rolls her eyes but finally sets her keys down. "Promise to be a gentleman?"

"I always am." My voice is casual, even as my pulse speeds up. "Honestly, this house is huge. Any bed is yours. What's the worst that could happen?"

Her eyes swirl with amusement and skepticism. "That sounds like someone's famous last words."

4

JULIE

Comfortable warmth is the first thing I notice when I wake up. It's not the kind that comes from the fireplace in my condo. It holds me tight. I drift in that hazy space between sleep and reality, feeling safer than I have in months, maybe years. Everything smells like expensive cologne mixed with clean cotton.

My eyes jolt open, and I see the gray shirt and feel solid muscles.

Shit. Shit. Shit.

I'm on Nick's couch, but more specifically, I'm lying on top of him, holding him like he belongs to me.

My head rests on his chest, his strong arm wraps heavy around my waist, and our legs are tangled in a way that suggests we've been like this for hours. Because we have.

Memories from last night rush back, and when I try to lift my head, it pounds. We shared pizza and wine, then talked until our voices became rough. We shared a lot. At one point, I laughed so hard that I nearly cried.

We eventually started streaming *When Harry Met Sally* because neither of us had ever seen it to the end. We spent half the movie arguing about whether men and women could have sex and be just friends while Billy Crystal proved it was impossible.

Truthfully, I dislike that movie. I know it's a romantic comedy classic, but there's something about it I can't stand. Every year, I try to watch it all the way through, but I always give up. Nick thought we'd be able to pull it off. We didn't.

I fell asleep somewhere around one of Harry's speeches. Total snoozefest.

Nick shifts, his arm tightening around me. I freeze, unsure of what to do.

Friends don't wake up wrapped around each other like lovers. My heart shouldn't flutter when we shift closer, and we absolutely shouldn't fit together so effortlessly that when one of us pulls away, it feels wrong. But here we are.

We're just friends because anything else leads to complications that neither of us needs or can deal with at this point in our lives.

I need to leave before he wakes up because I don't want any awkwardness.

I stay perfectly still as I calculate my next move. His arms are my biggest hurdle because they're heavy and warm and make me want to stay instead of pulling away. By some miracle, I slide out from under them, holding my breath when he stirs.

"Mmm," he mumbles, still asleep. Reaching for the space where I was before, he turns onto his side.

My traitorous heart flutters again.

I quickly find my shoes. One is hidden under the couch; the other is by the leather chair, large enough to fit two people. I slip them on, trying not to make a sound.

Before I go, I take one last glance at him with his messy, dark hair and his face relaxed. Somehow, he looks unfairly gorgeous without even trying.

I grab the receipt from last night's pizza and write a note on the back.

THANKS FOR THE PIZZA AND THE COMPANY. NEEDED THAT. WE SHOULD DO IT AGAIN SOMETIME.
   LITTLE RED

THE DOOR CLOSES BEHIND ME WITH A CLICK, AND I NEARLY SPRINT TO my car. The crisp autumn air is sharp in my lungs, and I try to gulp it down, wishing it would clear my head. It doesn't work, not when his cologne still clings to my sweater like a secret. Not when the memory of how perfectly we get along plays on repeat.

"Friends," I mutter as I start my car, then laugh at myself.

I leave the thought in the driveway as I pull away. I'm not searching for a relationship, and neither is Nick. The reason why we so easily gravitate to one another is because we're both broken. It's why we're honest with one another. There are no expectations, and what you see is exactly what you get. I've never met a man like him before.

Each time we're together, I realize how much I enjoy his company and how our conversations flow freely. It's as if I've known him forever when, in reality, it's the third time we've met up.

Last October, when I was at Bookers, crying about Craig at the end of the bar, Nick talked me off the ledge. I shared my weaknesses, and he told me my ex was an idiot. He also explained how I shouldn't take relationship advice from him because he sucked at them.

He was there for me that night and listened to me bleed out, and his kindness is something I'll never forget.

I drive to my condo in the middle of town, watching the thick fog twirl close to the ground. Mornings like this are my favorite—a reminder that fall *officially* begins on Saturday, and that's when the town celebration will kick off. I park and check my surroundings before I unlock the door.

The sun hasn't risen yet, but it will within the next thirty minutes, which means I have to shower and get ready for work.

My place feels too empty and cold in comparison to where I just came from.

I drop my keys on the kitchen island and grab two aspirin for my head. After I swallow them down, I go straight to the bathroom to desperately wash away the lingering feeling of being held by Nick. I turn on the water, undress, then step into the shower.

The hot water pounds against my skin, and it barely removes the cologne that still lingers on me.

"Just friends," I say aloud, as though repetition might help cement the thought into place.

But when I close my eyes, my mind drifts back to the effortless laughter, his flirty gaze, and how dangerously good it felt to be close to him. I twist the dial to cold, hoping shock therapy works. It doesn't.

After my shower, I stand in my bedroom, staring at the sweater I wore last night. It smells like him, and I should wash it immediately.

Instead, I hold it to my face and breathe deep, wanting to remember that scent.

"Get it together, Jules," I mutter, then throw the sweater in the hamper.

Just as I pull on some clothes for work, my phone dings in the kitchen.

AUTUMN

How was dinner with Mr. I'm Back, Baby?

I stare at the text, thumbs hovering over the keyboard.

What am I supposed to say to her? That we talked until three in the morning? That I fell asleep on top of him on his couch and woke up in his arms? That neither of us made it through *When Harry Met Sally*?

Another text appears before I can respond.

AUTUMN

Zane said your car was still at the cabin at four a.m., when he drove to town to get doughnuts for me! ● ● ⫼

Great. Guess there will be no denying that I stayed over.

It's barely after six, but I'd be willing to bet half of Cozy Creek already thinks Nick and I were together doing everything except sleeping. I sigh. By lunch, the Fairy Godmothers of Cozy Creek will be picking out centerpieces for our wedding.

I turn my phone face down and don't respond. I can't deal with this right now, not when I need to be at work in just fifteen minutes.

My phone buzzes again, and when I glance at it, I'm disappointed to see it's a reminder text from my coffee supplier, confirming delivery later today.

"Get it together," I tell my reflection as I pull on a cute black sweater that swoops down in the front and some jeans that make my ass look perfect.

Last year, Blaire made me some super-cute black cat earrings with dangling legs and arms, and I slide them on. After a touch of lipstick and some mascara, I'm ready to leave. I grab a jacket and hurry out the door.

The streetlamps lining the sidewalk are still lit, casting pools of soft golden light against the lingering darkness, but the sun will rise at any moment. Several people jog through the town square's park, others stroll with their dogs, and in the distance, tiny headlamps bob rhythmically as runners scale Lookout Mountain's trail.

Autumn used to be obsessed with jogging, and I'd always be so worried about her. She and Zane now run it together. The two of them are just a reminder of how much can change in a season.

When I arrive at Cozy Coffee, I slip inside quickly and lock up behind me again. Blaire has keys and will arrive in about fifteen minutes, giving me enough time to collect myself and start our opening tasks.

I start in the office, counting the cash drawers, then move to preheat the ovens. As soon as Blaire arrives, she'll dive straight into pastries and brewing coffee. When the doors open, we'll be slammed with the morning rush for hours. Lately, we've been running the day shift with just the two of us, except on the weekends, but I'll eventually have to start scheduling someone else to help us once fall kicks off.

After I quickly finish my opening checklist, I carry the cash drawers to the front and slide them into the registers. When I glance up, I spot Blaire strolling past the large front windows that line the sidewalks, already giving me a curious look. A few early customers gather in line by the door outside, eagerly waiting for their caffeine fix.

Blaire enters, locks the door behind her, and immediately tilts her head, eyes sparkling with suspicion.

"Good morning," she says, her gaze locking on me. "Someone looks super guilty."

"Who? Me?" I ask.

"Who? Me?" she repeats in a high-pitched tone as she walks to the back. I hear baking racks clanking as she quickly makes croissants. "Who else would I be talking to? The Ghost of Christmas Past? Let me guess. You had dinner with Nick after all."

I snicker as Blaire continues running her mouth.

I grind the beans for the coffee makers. When she returns to the front, she adjusts her quartz crystal necklace. It's the exact one she always wears to repel crazy ex-boyfriends with bad vibes.

"So," she says, lingering long enough for me to fill in the silence, but I don't say a single peep.

She groans. "Are you gonna tell me why you're glowing like a human lava lamp, or do I need to read your tea leaves before I unlock the door?"

I busy myself stacking pastries that don't need arranging. "Nothing to tell."

"It's so weird, but for some reason, I don't believe you." She leans against the counter, studying me like I'm one of her tarot spreads. "Your aura is screaming in vivid colors. Bright orange."

"Before you even say it, nobody got laid." The to-go cups suddenly need to be reorganized.

"Maybe not, but *something* happened." She checks the napkin holders and the receipt paper. "And not to mention, you keep chewing on your inner cheek."

I didn't realize I had been doing it.

"Nothing happened. I swear. We watched a movie. I fell asleep on his couch. End of story."

She grins. "Oh. What movie?"

"*When Harry Met Sally,*" I say.

Her jaw falls to the floor. "You gave him your relationship test."

I make a face at her. "What? No."

"Yes, you did. You make every guy you might be into watch that sucky movie. You didn't finish it?"

I shake my head. "Nope."

Blaire moves closer. "You know it's okay to have a crush on him. No one cares."

"He's fun, but he's not long-term-relationship material." I fidget with a loose thread on the corner of my apron.

She elbows me. "Not everything has to be long-term. Live a little. You can have an autumn hookup."

"That's absolutely ridiculous." I shake my head.

"Why?" she questions. "You're literally glowing, like you swallowed the Andromeda Galaxy. Neither of you is in a position to commit. Why not have fun until he leaves in six weeks?"

I exhale. "I don't think he's attracted to me, and it would complicate things. We're trying to be friends."

Blaire refills the brown sugar at the end of the counter. "I vote for friends who fuck. It's just sex. That's the point. Leave your feelings at the foot of the bed, have an orgasm, then continue on with your day. New besties."

"You make it sound easy."

"It is," she says, like there is no other answer.

Before we open the doors for the morning rush, Blaire spends some time making us each a latte with extra shots of espresso.

"Maybe you can help each other with your relationship issues," Blaire says, handing me the first one. "Regardless, I'm happy for you because one of us needs some excitement in their life this season."

My phone buzzes. We both freeze, staring at it like it might explode. It's another delivery confirmation.

"You're disappointed that it wasn't him even though he's never texted you," Blaire says.

After Nick left in January, I told Blaire everything. I needed to vent, and she usually has sound advice, even if it's sometimes sprinkled with a tarot card pull or a crystal being shoved in my pocket.

"Pretty please, get out of my head," I tell her as she moves to unlock the door.

"No can do, babe. I'm reading all your thoughts!" she says, and I toss a rag at her that she easily catches.

The morning rush saves me from my thoughts, but Blaire's words stick to me like honey. An autumn hookup would be fun, and it would have an expiration date. But I know the type of women Nick has had flings with. His list includes models, actresses, tennis players, and pop stars. I don't see coffee barista being added anytime soon, which is welcome. Honestly.

I lose count of how many shots of espresso I make, and I'm surprised Mrs. Galloway hasn't come in and called me out for being with Nick.

We work nonstop, barely able to take bathroom breaks until the afternoon rush has moved to just a few lingering customers. At 2:47, I start counting down the seconds until it's time to leave. The evening crew is here and restocking supplies while Blaire and I clean. The night manager, Tracy, has already switched the cash registers and updated the deposit logs.

I move into the dining room and sweep the croissant crumbs from under the tables, then rearrange the autumn flower basket and sparkly pumpkin decorations on the mantel of the fireplace.

When the bell above the door rings, I glance back to offer a welcome and see Craig. I have to hold back a groan.

He immediately smiles.

I breathe out because he looks good. But that's not new. I've always found him to be attractive with his sandy-brown hair and hazel eyes.

As he moves toward me, I notice he's carrying a bouquet of yellow roses, and it takes all my strength not to shake my head. We were together for three years, and he never cared that my favorite roses were pink or white. This is proof that I can't let him weasel himself between my sheets ever again. It's over.

His hunter-green collared shirt fits tight around him, and I can tell he's been working out and taking care of himself.

"Jules." He says my name like it's sacred as he approaches me with that confidence that used to make me feel special. Now, after realizing he uses it as armor in relationships, it exhausts me.

"Craig," I say, returning to the mantel to rearrange the Halloween town buildings, just to stay busy. "What do you want?"

"To talk." He sets the roses on the mantel. "You look beautiful."

I give him a pointed look, and his grin widens.

This is the charming man I fell in love with, but it's a mask, one he removes when the newness of the relationship wears off.

Over my shoulder, I know there are two tables of ladies trying to listen to every word we're saying. To my right, Mrs. Caldwell sits with a cup of tea while she does a crossword puzzle in the newspaper.

The Fairy Godmothers are everywhere. This conversation isn't safe unless I want rumors started.

"You should go."

"Wow," he says with a sigh. "I've missed you so damn much."

Blaire appears from the back room, takes one look at the situation, and promptly disappears again.

Traitor.

"Why are you here?" I place the spooky graveyard scene back where it was and stare at him.

"I'm back in town. For good this time."

He leans forward, almost removing the space between us, but I take a step away.

"I owe you an apology. I've changed, Jules. Therapy has really opened my eyes. After being without you, I know you're the only woman on this planet for me."

My brows lift, and my mouth falls open. I promptly close it. "Glad you're finally going to therapy, but we're over. There are no more chances. We're too toxic for one another."

I glance at Mrs. Caldwell, who pretends she hears nothing, but I see how she's leaning in.

"Julie, baby." Craig reaches for my hand, but I pull away. "I know I messed up bad, and I'll do whatever I can to make sure that never happens again."

"No," I firmly say, not liking to have to repeat that word.

I'm a people pleaser, and I have the urge to make people happy. Saying no is hard; repeating it is harder. And what sucks is he knows this, but instead, he continues to test me.

"Now, please leave. You're embarrassing me. I'm at work." I glance around and see Harold Jenkins pretending not to eavesdrop on this conversation, but I'd bet every dollar in our overflowing tip jar that his wife will know about it before supper.

Shit.

"I was an idiot." He admits it, which is new. "I get it now. You're meant to shine, and I didn't let you. I didn't support you."

"Let me?" I glare at him.

He'd freak out on me if I smiled at other men, who were

my customers. He'd tell me I was asking to be stared at by dressing certain ways. One thing Craig is wonderful at is gaslighting. His words were chosen wisely, but almost too carefully.

"That's not what I meant."

"It's exactly what you meant. You used to make me feel so small. It's a no, Craig. A very firm no. I don't need your or anyone's permission to be myself. I will never change who I am for you or any man." I move the roses aside, their sickly sweet scent making my stomach turn. "You lost your chance."

His jaw tightens, and he's losing his grip because I won't lie down for him and submit, like he requires from a woman. "Autumn said you're seeing someone."

It's not a question, but it doesn't matter because I ignore him. He doesn't deserve to know anything about me anymore.

"Who is he?" Craig steps closer, and suddenly, the space between us disappears. He grabs my left hand, holding it in his. "Because until there's a ring on this finger, I won't give up. I still love you. I realize now I always will."

I pull my fingers from his grasp, not liking how pushy he's being. Maybe this is why Autumn was protecting me from his weird persistence.

"Do you remember what you told me the day you ended things with me?" I raise my voice a little more so that the rest of the eavesdroppers can hear and spread this fact around town.

"No," he mutters. "I wasn't myself."

"I think you were exactly who you are." I smile, but it's forced. "You said you wanted a more submissive woman, one who wasn't asking for attention from men and who knew how to listen." I cross my arms over my chest. "Let me be clear. I've not changed. I will not be submissive to you or any man."

"I don't want you to change because I have," he tells me. "I want you exactly how you are."

He looks almost hurt, and my self-doubt kicks in. I try to

remember this is part of his manipulation, part of the cycle that keeps bringing us back together.

"Come on. Remember all the good times we had? You were mine, Julie, baby. It was me and you. All those late summer nights, lying in the back of my truck, waiting for fireflies to appear. We were perfect together. Everyone said so."

I think about those summer nights and the vibe of it as the crickets chirped. Then I remember how he humiliated me in front of my friends and family when he brought his new fiancée to town. Sometimes, it's hard to believe the man who promised to love me forever could've been so cruel. It erased the good times for me.

"Everyone is delusional. They have no idea how controlling you were."

Sometimes, when I'm lying in my bed at night, I think about what I'll say to Craig the next time he tries to beg me back. I promised myself I'd never sleep with him again after the last autumn. It happened to be the same night I met Nick.

I'd asked the goddesses, how Blaire had instructed, to give me a sign to never see Craig again. Nick appeared like an angel.

After Craig and I fooled around, he left and met another woman for a date. That was when I realized I was his hometown fuck buddy, his sneaky link, and he'd used me to get what he wanted. Thanks to Blaire stalking him, I learned he had taken that woman to his brother's house. Meanwhile, I went to Bookers and drank the night away.

"Admit that you feel something when you look into my eyes," he whispers. "I need to know."

"Craig—"

The bell chimes so hard that the door rattles, and that's when I see Nick standing in the threshold. His stance shifts when he looks between me and Craig, reading the situation in seconds. He pushes his expensive designer sunglasses on top of his head, and I meet his piercing honey-brown eyes.

His brow lifts as he approaches us, and he's already reached the correct conclusion.

As soon as Nick is close, I reach my arm out, and he wraps his around me.

"I missed you," I say.

"Damn, me too." He smirks, kissing me on the forehead. "Especially after last night."

Nick tucks a loose strand of hair behind my ear and smiles. Those butterflies swoop in, and I wish they'd stop it because it's too confusing.

Craig clears his throat, clearly intimidated. Nick's jaw clenches tight, and it's obvious how he wants to rip Craig to shreds.

"Can I help you?" Nick finally asks, treating Craig as if he's the biggest inconvenience of his life. The confidence, the no-shits-given persona, is sexy as hell.

"I don't think we've met." Craig squares his shoulders, trying to match Nick's presence. It just doesn't work. "Craig Downing. Jules's—"

"Forever ex," I interrupt firmly. "Craig was just leaving with these flowers he bought for his mother." I pick up the bouquet and push it toward him.

There's something in Nick's eyes that makes Craig take a step back.

"I didn't catch your name." Craig's voice carries a challenge.

I panic.

"Because I didn't throw it to you. However, I'm Nicolas Banks. Jules's boyfriend."

"Boyfriend," I repeat as my heart ricochets against my rib cage.

Holy shit, did he just say boyfriend?

Heat rushes up my neck, embarrassment mixing dangerously with excitement. The ladies are watching with eyes as wide as saucers. I'm so screwed, knowing this won't stay within these walls. My cheeks heat more.

Nick's smile doesn't fade when he meets my eyes. "Soon-to-be fiancée, especially if she keeps looking this damn gorgeous. Going to have to make sure to put a ring on that finger so I can keep her all to myself."

Craig freezes, and I see his heart rate tick upward.

"Oh, stop," I say to Nick with a nervous chuckle, wishing he would, because this will push Craig to spiral.

His thumb brushes against my cheek, and I stare into his brown eyes. He carefully reads me like a message in a bottle.

"Come on. We both know you'll eventually be my wifey. Mrs. Julie Banks. Sounds so sexy." Nick chews on his bottom lip as he studies me, noticing how I'm not squirming.

He's having too much fun, but I know this will backfire.

"It has a ring to it," I say.

Nick grabs my left hand and kisses my ring finger. "Can't wait to put one here."

He's really rubbing it in, and what I hate the most about it is how damn believable it is.

"Julie, baby," Craig whispers, using that stupid nickname he gave me, "I'm not giving up."

"On what?" Nick asks, searching between us, dropping my hand, and pulling me into his arms. "What am I missing, darling?"

"Craig thinks he's going to steal me from you," I say.

Nick chuckles as he runs his fingers through my hair. "I'm not letting you go, *Julie, baby*. Especially not for your trash-can forever ex, Craig."

I'm not sure what happens next, but Nick leans in, and I lift on my toes. His mouth gently slides across mine, and everything changes.

The kiss is brief. Just enough to make a point, but it completely resets my brain chemistry. A moan escapes me as heat slides straight through my veins. My pulse pounds so loudly in my ears that I almost miss the quiet, satisfied sound Nick makes as he tastes my pumpkin pie ChapStick.

When I pull back, we're both breathing a little too hard. I don't know what just happened. Nick's thumb gently traces my cheek, and it takes everything in me not to lean into him and capture his lips again. It shouldn't have felt like that.

"Bye, Craig," Nick says, not taking his attention from me. His eyes are soft and unreadable as Craig stays planted.

"We were having a conversation," Craig says.

"It's over. Leave my girlfriend alone," Nick tells him, glaring before returning back to me. "Apologies. I was going to come earlier."

"I'm just so damn glad you're here now," I say, meaning every word. I can't imagine how this would've gone had Nick not shown up.

Craig's jaw clenches hard enough that I see the muscle twitch from my peripheral vision. Craig stares daggers into Nick, then storms out.

I laugh as Nick pulls me into his arms. I'm not sure what just happened, but we stay locked together and giddy. Our eyes meet, and he's wearing his signature smirk.

"You can let me go now," I whisper, half hoping he won't.

"You're right; I *could*," he says, his gaze dropping to my lips before meeting my eyes again. "But maybe I don't want to."

5

___

NICK

My arm is still around her waist, and neither of us moves. The scent of coffee and baked goods mixes with her sweet perfume that's been on my skin since she fell asleep in my arms.

"Thank you for showing up at the right time," she whispers, her voice shaky. "I seriously owe you."

"Nah, he needed to fuck straight off," I say, still not happy with how overbearing he was being. "You were uncomfortable. I saw it on your face."

Before Julie can respond, Blaire screams from behind the counter with excitement, "Oh, it's Nick. For five seconds, I thought you were kissing Craig!"

Her hands clasp together, bracelets jangling.

"Blaire." Julie's cheeks are pink.

She straightens her apron, glancing around the coffee shop, making note of the audience size. All eyes are still on us and have been since the moment I entered. But that's not anything new. I'm used to people staring. That's what happens when you're revealed as the love child of a well-known and highly followed billionaire.

"I saw the sparks," Blaire whispers.

Julie tenses beside me. Without thinking, I slide my arm tighter around her, pulling her closer against my side. She relaxes, melting into me like she was made to fit there.

"Oh, hush." Julie tries to hide her embarrassment, and I chuckle, finding it adorable.

She turns to me. "Wait for me, okay? I'm about to get off."

"Of course." There's no other option because we need to discuss what the hell just happened.

After a long pause, Julie sucks in a deep breath and pulls away. She walks through the dining room, avoiding eye contact with everyone. I immediately miss her closeness, exactly how I did this morning when she thought she was sneaking out. I was awake, but I didn't want to make it awkward for her. The thought makes me laugh.

I move to the register to order a drink, and Blaire grins at me.

"What are you having today? The normal black serial-killer coffee, just like last season?"

"I'm a changed man," I admit. "I'll have an Earl Grey with a dash of milk, a spoonful of honey, and one raw sugar."

When I pull out my wallet, she shakes her head.

"So bougie. This one's on the house."

Blaire punches a few buttons on the computer, and I hear the order print. I catch a glimpse of Julie in the back, chatting with the other manager. My eyes slide over to the evening crew, making my tea, while Blaire stares at me.

"You'll never be able to read me," I tell her.

"Ahh, you're not as obtuse as you believe, Banks." Curiosity radiates off her in rolling waves. "But I'd love to listen if you care to explain."

"I plead the Fifth."

"Typical billionaire response," she says.

"I'll let your bestie tell you what's going on." I move to the end of the counter, and she follows me.

"Oh, you'd better believe she will tell me everything," she

whispers, which does absolutely nothing. "I have at least fifteen follow-up questions after that kiss."

"Honestly?" I laugh. "I do too."

My Earl Grey appears, and as I grab it, Julie approaches me, sliding her hand into mine.

"I want all the deets," Blaire yells as I'm tugged outside, around the building wall, and away from the nosy customers of Cozy Coffee.

Her face is still red. "I don't know what to say."

"Can I walk you home?" I hold my arm out for her, and she loops hers through it with a nod.

Her green eyes and bright red hair practically sparkle under the afternoon sunlight. She's a dream.

On the stroll to her place, we don't say much. The two of us are too lost in our heads—or at least I am. Julie lives close, but I've never been to her place before.

"That was …" She removes her arm from mine as we cross the busy street.

"Intense?" I glance over at her as we file in behind a crowd of tourists.

"I was going to say unexpected, but intense works too." She chuckles. "I don't know what happened back there."

"I don't either," I reply, brushing my fingers against hers as we walk. "You needed an out, and I gave you one. Just didn't expect you to kiss me."

We turn up the sidewalk to her place.

"Ohhh, no, no, no, you were the one who kissed *me*," she says.

"Nope. I'm a gentleman. I *always* ask first. You stood on your tiptoes, and I couldn't deny you in front of that piece of shit."

"You were moving close, so I thought you were … wait, so it was a pity kiss?" She sounds offended.

I don't know how to respond. "Hell no. The opportunity presented itself, and it happened. But you *totally* kissed me."

"That won't be how I tell the story," she says, wearing a soft smile.

"That's fine. The truth always lives somewhere in the middle," I say.

"Well, regardless, thank you for being a good *friend.*"

The word hangs between us.

I've never kissed a friend and felt so right. I'm tempted to ask her if the world stopped spinning for her, like it did for me, but I don't. That kiss will forever be burned on my lips.

The electricity between us crackles stronger as I taste her ChapStick on my lips. Julie's sweet and addictive.

As we arrive at her door, I shove my hands in my pockets so I'm not tempted to reach for her. "If you ever need me to rescue you again, just text me. I'll even answer this time."

Her laughter lights me up inside. "Careful, Banks. I might take you up on that."

"I'm counting on it." I grin, heart pounding harder as she turns to her door. I'm not ready to say goodbye yet.

We stare at each other for an eternity.

"Want to come in?" she asks.

"Abso-fucking-lutely," I say, and I'm relieved.

When I step inside, it's how I imagined it would be. Warm and cozy with color everywhere. The accent walls in her living room and office space are painted deep jewel blue and purple. Several mismatched throw pillows that somehow work lie neatly on her couch. Big plants are in every corner of the room, reaching toward the natural light of the windows. It feels like home, a place where life happens.

"Wine?" she asks.

Before I can answer, she's already pulling two glasses from her turquoise-painted cabinets.

"Sure."

I watch her move around the kitchen, noticing more eccentric decorations, like the chili pepper string lights hanging above the window. A collection of coffee mugs with sarcastic quotes dangle on a rack.

"Your condo is great," I say, settling onto her couch, twisting my body to watch her.

"It's no New York penthouse, but it will do, I suppose."

She pops open the cork and pours us two glasses. I take one as she sits on the opposite end of the couch, legs tucked under her.

"You know, I actually grew up in a small town that's not much different from Cozy Creek."

"Oh? Really?" she asks, intrigued.

"Most assume I had a silver spoon in my mouth because of who my father was, but that wasn't my life. After my stepdad passed away, it was just me, my mom, and my older sister, Miranda. My mother raised me to be humble."

"Wow, I'm sorry."

"He was the man I considered to be my dad. I took it hard, but also I'm grateful he was such a big part of my life. I think about him and smile now."

Her face softens. "How did you and Zane become friends?"

"We took lessons from one of the best coaches in the country, who trained Olympians. Our friendship wasn't formed because of who our fathers were. It was because of our interests. Before I got into hockey, I thought I'd professionally snowboard like Zane."

Julie drinks her wine, watching me. "Wow. You were a normie turned billionaire baddie? How did you adjust?"

This makes me laugh. "Who said I have?"

"Oh. Fair."

"I never played hockey for the money. I played for the game," I tell her.

"And why do you work at the marketing firm?" I ask.

"Hmm. That's interesting." I blink over at her. "No one has ever asked me that question before. No one has cared."

She scoots a little closer. "Is it your dream job?"

"No," I say out loud for the first time.

Her brows furrow.

"I work there because of my sister. Now, it's about continuing her legacy."

She thinks about it. "What is your legacy?"

"You're asking the hard questions today."

This earns me a grin as she runs her fingers through her hair. Our eye contact is intense, and I can't help but study her lips or watch how her tongue darts out when she licks them.

"We should probably talk about earlier," I say before we lose track.

She glances up at the clock above her mantel of photos. "Right. We should probably figure out how to squash this before the rumors start."

"Or not," I say, standing to grab the bottle of wine from the kitchen counter.

Julie finishes her glass, then swipes the bottle from my hand and takes several gulps.

"I'm sorry, what?" she asks.

"Let people believe whatever they want." I meet her eyes. "A love story is great for business. The women sitting in the dining room today were invested."

She groans. "They were. This could get out of hand very quickly."

"Well, if it helps, I can be your fake boyfriend until I leave," I say with a pause.

Her eyes widen.

"Under one condition," I add.

"Yes?"

"You give me relationship advice."

Julie bursts into laughter, but my smile stays planted.

"Wait, you're serious. You don't need relationship advice. You're a playboy."

"I *was*. You're levelheaded enough to be able to give real feedback. I want to be a good partner for whoever comes next."

She holds out her hand. "It's a deal, but you have to help me too. I don't want to die alone, and I'm rusty on my dating game."

"Okay." We shake on it like it's the easiest thing in the world. "My brother is expecting me to return to the city changed. This is a start. Any opinions about me, I want them, good or bad."

"Oh, that's so dangerous, Nick," she says. "Sometimes, my opinions are things that shouldn't be said out loud."

"Then whisper them," I mutter.

She leans forward, her mouth close to my ear, her breasts pressing against my body. "You shouldn't be looking at me like that."

My expression doesn't change, but my heart rate increases. "For this to work, I think we need rules."

"Rules are made to be broken." She drinks more.

"That's usually *my* line," I tell her.

The wine continues to disappear, along with Julie's filter. "This could get out of hand. You're Nick Banks, and I'm …"

"Gorgeous," I say without hesitation. "Everyone will believe it *because* I'm Nick Banks, and I shuffle through women—"

"You don't have to finish that sentence," she interrupts. "Your reputation doesn't bother me." She offers me the bottle as she hiccups.

"Okay, but don't believe what you read on the internet. The character they've created of me is so far from the truth that it's comical."

We finish the bottle of wine. Julie leans her head back on the cushion and watches me.

"If we're doing this, you're right about needing to make rules." She slides a notebook and a pink pen from her coffee table and flips it open to a blank page.

"You're actually writing them down?"

"Documentation is important." She clicks the pen a few times, then taps it against her lips. "Rule number one: Friendship comes first. I don't want to ruin what we have."

I nod. "That's essential and probably the most important rule of all. Um, number two: Total honesty about what's working and what's not. If I do something that gives you the ick, tell me. And vice versa."

"Brutal honesty," she says, writing it down.

"Rule three: We are both aware it's fake," she says.

"Yep, can totally do that," I add.

She writes it down, then pauses. "What about PDA and all that?"

The air shifts as I think about capturing her lips again.

"That should probably happen only when it's necessary," I offer. "Hand-holding, casual touches. Nothing that crosses lines."

"Should we define those lines?" She's not looking at me now, very focused on the notebook. "If we're going to make this believable, there might be moments when we need to …"

"Kiss?"

"Yeah." The word comes out breathy. "But only when it's absolutely necessary. An example is if Craig shows up or if someone questions us. Or if eyes are on us."

"That's fair. Performance kisses only." I clear my throat. "What about a safe word? In case either of us gets uncomfortable and we need to reel it back or walk away?"

"Smart." She thinks for a moment. "What about *pumpkin spice?*"

I stare at her. "Really? *That's* your safe word?"

"It's seasonal and easy to throw into conversation without it being obvious." She writes it down. "Oh, and our end date is November first. That's when you're planning to leave?"

"That's right."

"Okay. And …" She hesitates, pen hovering over the page. "What happens if one of us develops actual feelings?"

The question lands between us like a grenade with the pin pulled. We both know the chemistry is already there, crackling under the surface of this friendship we're trying to build.

"We won't," I say finally. "Rule number one comes into play. I'm bad at love, Jules."

"Right. Of course. Oh, we should do another rule of no jealousy. If either of us wants to talk to someone else—"

I look at her like she's lost her damn mind. "During our fake relationship?"

"After. Or … I don't know. We should be prepared if the situation presents itself, right?"

Something hot flares in my chest at the thought of her with someone else.

"For this to work, we should probably be exclusively fake dating," I tell her. "The last thing we need is a scandal."

She gives me a look that says she heard the edge in my voice. "That's fair. We have to keep it believable so Craig will leave me alone—at least until November."

I lean back, studying her. "What about dates? How often do we need to be seen together?"

"Two or three times a week. Coffee shop appearances, maybe dinner at Bookers, where locals can see us. All the fall activities." She clicks the pen a few more times. "We should probably establish our backstory, too, because we'll be asked a lot when the town catches wind. When we got together, how long have we been hiding it, you know, that sort of thing."

"The truth is always the best answer to that," I suggest. "It's a new development. We've been talking to one another for about a year and just decided, why not?"

"That's actually perfect." She sets down the pen, looking at our list. "I think we've covered everything. Clear rules, clear boundaries, clear end date."

"Very professional."

She's smiling, some of the tension easing. "This is crazy, right? We're actually doing this?"

"Apparently, we are."

The notebook full of rules sits between us, but somehow, it feels more like a challenge than a safety net.

This is the start of something dangerous, disguised as something safe.

I already know I'm in trouble, and I should leave before I do something silly, like kiss her.

"We should figure out our couple style. Today was a bit chaotic."

"Chaotic is generous." She laughs, not a trace of embarrassment now. "Next time, we should aim for less desperation, more casual. But you're right. What's our vibe? Are we touchy-feely? Reserved but intimate? Do we use pet names?"

"No pet names. We want believable, not nauseating," I tell her.

"Agreed. So, about the casual-kissing thing. Maybe we should practice that," she says, blinking up at me.

There's something tempting about the offer, but the anticipation is more gratifying.

"Nah," I say, standing, knowing that's my cue to go. "Where's the fun in that? I say we wing it. Live *dangerously*."

She looks genuinely surprised. "Mr. Corporate Strategy wants to improvise?"

"Hey, I'm trying to be more spontaneous. When we kiss, it will just be a peck. We can handle it." I stretch and move toward the door. "Besides, half the fun is the unpredictability of it all."

"That's a good point." She walks me to the door. "I'm looking forward to this."

"Want to have dinner tomorrow night at Bookers?" I ask.

"I'd love to," she says.

"Night, Little Red."

"Night, boyfriend."

As I walk away, I feel lighter than I have in months.

My phone buzzes before I'm even at the end of her sidewalk.

JULIE

Forgot to ask ... are you a hand-holder or arm-around-the-shoulder type of boyfriend?

I grin, typing back.

NICK

Depends. Are you a snuggle-into-my-side or maintain-your-independence type of girlfriend? I'm following your lead.

JULIE

Hmm. Guess we'll both find out tomorrow.

6

―――――

JULIE

I've reorganized the coffee bean display three times this morning. The Ethiopian blend doesn't need to be alphabetically arranged by roast date, but here I am, labels facing forward.

"Jules, you're spiraling," Blaire announces, not looking up from the espresso machine she's cleaning. "And before you deny it, you've been humming for the past twenty minutes."

"I'm not—" I stop myself. I am spiraling.

"Is this about yesterday? That kiss with Nick?" She sets down her cleaning rag, full attention on me now. "Because I haven't been able to stop thinking about it either, and I was just watching."

"It felt …" I trail off, unable to find the right word.

She doesn't say anything, allowing me to get my thoughts together.

"Incredible," I confirm. "Electricity shot through every nerve."

Blaire moves closer, lowering her voice. "Jules, he looks like a Greek god. Of course you felt something. Any woman with a pulse would feel something, kissing Nick Banks."

"You're right. It's probably just physical attraction."

"Really, really intense physical attraction," she confirms. "That man could make a nun reconsider."

63

I burst into laughter. "You're damn right about that."

"Just a human response. And a horny one. When's the last time you had really good sex?"

"Blaire!"

"What? It's a valid question. Craig was about as exciting as plain oatmeal in bed. Your body is probably just screaming, *Finally, a man who knows what he's doing!*"

The bell chimes, and my stomach drops. Nick walks in, carrying a leather messenger bag, hair slightly messed up from the morning wind. He looks uncertain, almost nervous, which is weird because Nick is usually Mr. Confidence.

"Speak of the devil," Blaire whispers. "The hot-as-hell devil."

"Shut up," I hiss.

"Morning," he says, his voice carrying that rough edge that means he didn't sleep well either.

"Hi."

We stare at each other. The entire coffee shop seems to pause, waiting. I can feel the ghost of yesterday's kiss on my lips.

Mrs. Henderson actually leans forward in her chair.

"Could we talk?" Nick gestures to the corner booth. "I have a … proposal."

"A proposal?" Mrs. Henderson gasps loud enough for everyone to hear.

"A business proposal," Nick clarifies.

I lean against the counter. "Sure. *Pumpkin spice* latte?"

"Make it two," he says with a wink.

We're both uncomfortable right now.

Blaire steps up next to me as I start the espresso. "That man is looking at you like you're his favorite dessert."

"It's just attraction," I remind myself as much as her.

"Are you imagining climbing him like a tree?"

"Blaire!"

"What? I guess it's just me."

She's not wrong, which is the problem. I finish making our lattes.

"Want to meet me in my office?"

He grins. "Good idea."

I lead him through the back, past the ovens and the storage area, to the small office that used to be my grandmother's. It's cozy—just a long table that acts as a desk, a computer for inventory, two chairs, and walls covered in photos of the coffee shop through the decades.

Nick follows me in, and suddenly, the space feels even smaller. He sets his messenger bag on the floor as I close the door, muffling the sounds from the dining room.

"This is better," he says.

I hand him his coffee and pull one of the chairs away from the desk, angling it toward the other. He does the same, and when we sit, our knees touch. Neither of us pulls away.

"So," I say, wrapping my hands around my cup for warmth, "a business proposal?"

"Right." He pulls out his laptop, balancing it on his thighs. "Don't laugh."

"No promises."

He turns the screen toward me, and I nearly spit out my coffee.

The first slide reads *Strategic Relationship Development: A Comprehensive Approach.*

"You made a PowerPoint about us?"

"I know how it looks—"

"Oh my gosh. You're a nerd!" I giggle. "You made a business presentation about us kissing."

He laughs. "Okay, maybe I am, but this is how my brain works!" He clicks to the next slide. It's a graph. "Look, we went from zero to sixty in approximately three seconds. That's not sustainable."

I study the graph, which has *Intimacy Level* on one axis and *Time* on the other. There's a sharp spike labeled *Coffee Shop Incident.*

"You graphed it out?"

His knee presses more firmly against mine. "I process better with visuals." He's fully blushing now, and I find it so damn adorable. "The point is, we need practice. Small interactions. Building comfort gradually."

"So, exposure therapy, but for fake dating?"

"Exactly." He clicks again.

The next slide reads *Phase One: Casual Public Interactions.*

I'm trying not to smile, but I'm failing. This overly structured, analytical approach is so opposite to how he kissed me yesterday. But it's also sweet that he's put this much thought into protecting our friendship.

"So, what does Phase One involve?"

"Coffee together. We're doing that now. Walking through town. Grocery shopping. Normal couple things, but low stakes."

"You want to practice grocery shopping with me?"

"Do I put my hand on your back while we walk? Do you hold the cart, or do I? These are things actual couples know without thinking."

Our knees are still touching, and I can feel the warmth of him through my jeans. "You've thought this through."

"I couldn't sleep." He runs a hand through his hair, messing it up more. "That kiss … Jules, I don't want to screw this up. Our friendship, I mean. This situation. Whatever this is."

My heart pounds hard in my chest. "Me neither."

"So … practice?"

"In front of the whole town?"

"That's kind of the point, right? Being seen together? Making it believable so Craig gives up."

He's right.

"Where do we start?"

"Right here with the steps I've laid out in my very professional presentation."

I laugh, and the tension breaks. "You're such a dork."

"You appreciate it."

"I do," I admit.

He closes the laptop, then reaches over and takes my hand. His thumb strokes across my palm, and my breath catches.

"Too much?"

"It's perfect." The words come out softer than I intend.

We sit here in my tiny office, holding hands, knees touching, and it feels more intimate than yesterday's kiss. Maybe because we're choosing this, deliberately and privately crossing lines we drew.

"This is weird," he says.

"So weird."

"Want to get weirder?"

"Always."

He grins. "Come grocery shopping with me after your shift. Riverside cabin has nothing but wine and cheese."

"Very bachelor of you."

"Hey, they're very good cheeses."

I squeeze his hand. "I get off at three today."

"I'll be waiting," he says.

"Stalker."

"Strategic planner," he says with a laugh.

A knock on the door makes us jump apart like we were doing something we shouldn't.

"Jules?" Blaire's voice calls through. "The afternoon rush is starting, and Tracy can't find the vanilla syrup that was supposed to be delivered."

"Coming!" I stand, and Nick does too.

In the small space, we're suddenly very close.

"This is going to be fun," he says.

"I'm actually looking forward to some excitement this fall," I admit.

He steps back so I can open the door, and Blaire is standing there with a knowing smirk.

"Business proposal go well?" she asks, waggling her brows.

"As expected," Nick says.

Blaire openly swoons. "Please tell me your brothers are available."

He laughs. "Dyson, but trust me when I say, he's not your type."

I lead him through the back exit like he's a celebrity. He kinda is.

"See you at three, Little Red."

"Can't wait," I say, then turn to see Blaire staring at me when I lock the door.

"Phase One," she repeats. "That beautiful man made a whole presentation about fake dating you, didn't he?"

"Maybe. Were you eavesdropping? What the hell?!"

"And you're going grocery shopping together?"

"Yeah, his place needs food. It's an essential part to being a human."

"Uh-huh." She follows me back to the front. "What is this going to solve exactly?"

"Being believable so Craig will get the hint."

"Babe, the sexual tension between you two is believable from outer space."

"That's just—"

"Physical attraction, I know." She grabs the vanilla syrup from exactly where it always is, and I narrow my eyes at her. She was just being my nosy bestie. "Oh, look, here it is."

"You're so evil," I tell her.

"Nah, just supportive. Also, Phase One sounds like foreplay to me."

I gasp. "Did you hear everything?"

"I'll never tell," she says.

I follow her to the front, where a line has formed. As I make the espresso, I can't stop thinking about Nick's knee pressed against mine, the warmth of his hand, the way he said, "Want to get weirder?" like it was an invitation to adventure.

It's just fake dating, I remind myself.

Really elaborate, PowerPointed, multi-phased fake dating.

The next two hours pass in a blur of customers and knowing looks from Blaire. When my shift ends, Nick waits for me by the door, hands in his pockets, looking unfairly good in his casual clothes. The afternoon sun streaming through the windows catches the gold in his eyes, and I have to remind myself that this isn't real. It's a friend offering a favor.

"Ready?" he asks, holding out his hand.

I take it, ignoring how perfectly our fingers fit together. "Lead the way."

The walk to Harvest Market is short, but approximately thirty locals see us holding hands. Each time someone waves or calls out a greeting, Nick's grip tightens slightly—a little reminder that we're in this together.

"You're thinking too hard," I tell him as we enter the store.

"How can you tell?"

"You get this little crease right here." I reach up without thinking, smoothing the spot between his eyebrows.

He catches my hand, holding it against his cheek for a moment. "You're right."

"It's not a bad thing. Welcome to the Overthinkers Club. We meet on Wednesdays. There are cookies."

He laughs, and I realize I'm already looking forward to making that happen again. The physical attraction makes everything feel more intense.

"Okay," he says, grabbing a cart. "Teach me your ways."

"Oh, this is easy. You push the cart. That's what hot boyfriends do."

"Noted," he says. "And then?"

"And then they tell their girlfriends to buy whatever they want."

He smirks, moving close to me. "Buy whatever you want, sweetheart."

The way his voice lowers, along with the pet name, causes a shiver to run up my spine.

"Okay, that was good."

He turns the cart and crashes the corner into an apple display, causing three to roll across the floor.

"So smooth," I say, helping him chase them down. "Relax. No pressure."

"Right. No pressure."

He takes a breath, and I slide in beside him. He wraps his arm around me as we walk side by side, both of us keeping one hand on the cart. We look like an inseparable couple.

"You know, Craig used to criticize all my food choices and insist on organic everything while complaining about the prices."

"What a dick."

We move through the produce section, and I load the cart with different fruits and vegetables I enjoy. Nick listens like I'm sharing secrets, asking questions about why I choose one apple variety over another. It's oddly intimate.

In the cereal aisle, I reach for Cinnamon Toast Crunch, and he gasps.

"That's pure sugar."

"That's pure joy, you mean." I toss it in the cart with a thud. "What do you usually eat for breakfast?"

"Protein shake or eggs."

"That's the saddest thing I've ever heard."

"It's efficient. I was on a super-strict training schedule for years of my life. Some habits die hard."

"Sounds depressing," I say. "We're fixing your breakfast situation immediately."

"We?"

The word hangs between us.

"Yeah," I clarify. "Can't have my boyfriend eating a sad-to-be-alive breakfast every morning. And what if you get hungry late at night? Cereal is always the solution."

He chuckles.

We're standing too close in the aisle, as Mrs. Lutcher—one of the librarians—takes photos of us with her phone.

"We should eventually practice PDA," I say. "Small stuff. It can't look forced."

He steps closer, his hand coming to rest on my lower back. It's barely a touch, but I feel it everywhere. I enjoy the heat of his palm through my shirt and how my body automatically leans into him.

"Like this?"

"Yeah." My voice comes out breathy.

"And this?" His other hand tucks a strand of hair behind my ear, fingers lingering against my cheek, giving me a smile.

"That's … that's really good."

"Julie?"

"Hmm?"

"At least five people are watching us."

"I know," I say with a grin.

We have an audience, pretending to be fascinated by pasta sauce and canned vegetables.

"Should we give them something to talk about?" I ask.

"What do you have in mind?"

Instead of answering, I rise up on my toes and kiss his cheek, letting my lips linger just a second longer than necessary. He smells like expensive cologne and coffee, and I have to resist the urge to capture his lips again.

"Perfect," he mutters, and I'm not sure if he means my performance or something else.

We finish shopping, the cart full of a variety of foods from healthy to horrible. At checkout, Linda, the cashier, gives me a smile.

"You two are adorable together," she says. "About time you found someone who matches you, Julie."

"Thank you." I try not to blush as Nick loads the bags.

"He's a keeper," she whispers. "Any man who lets you pick the cereal is marriage material."

Nick chuckles, slipping his arm around my waist. "She's the keeper."

The drive back to his cabin is comfortable, filled with easy conversation about nothing important. I help him unload the bags and put everything away.

"This place needs some life," I say, arranging the fruit in a bowl.

"It's a rental."

"Still, you're here for over a month. Might as well try to make it feel like home."

His smile slightly fades. "I haven't been anywhere that feels like home since I moved out of my mom's house when I was eighteen."

This hurts my heart. "Why?"

He shrugs. "I'm not sure. Maybe because I haven't been happy in a long time. Nothing has ever felt permanent."

"Are you happy now?"

"I'm working on it," he admits.

"Well, if I were staying here, I'd have already hung string lights and bought a stack of fun throw pillows."

He's smiling at me in a way that makes me forget everything. "Tomorrow, I made reservations to do sunrise yoga in the square."

"You're joking. I *love* yoga."

"Autumn told me." Nick licks his lips. "Fake boyfriends love doing yoga with their girlfriends. It's a very coupley thing to do."

I laugh. "Fine. But it's going to be hard. You have to promise not to complain the entire time."

"Are you kidding me? My stamina … unheard of. I can do planks for *hours*," he says.

"I look forward to it," I tell him as we load into the Range Rover and he drives me home.

After parking on the street, Nick walks me to my condo, and there's a moment where we both pause. In a real relationship, this would be when he kisses me goodbye. The air between us crackles with that knowledge.

"Thanks for today," he says instead.

I unlock the door but hesitate. "See you at dawn."

"It'll be fun."

"That's what you're saying now. The instructor, Jessie, is a beast."

He leans forward and gives me a tight hug. I walk inside and look in the peephole, watching him walk away. He's grinning, and so am I.

I move to my kitchen, needing water because I feel parched.

AUTUMN

Saw the grocery store pics. You two are ADORABLE.

BLAIRE

Linda says he called you a keeper!!!

AUTUMN

WHAT?! Details. Now.

JULIE

Holy shit. I just got home. How did you know any of this happened?

I move to my couch and turn on the TV.

BLAIRE

Fairy Godmothers are camped out all over Cozy Creek, trying to get a peek of you two.

She sends a photo of Nick's hand on my back, and me looking up at him with what can only be described as heart eyes.

JULIE

Please tell me that picture wasn't sent to the entire book club chat.

AUTUMN

I really need to join book club again.

BLAIRE

It was. It's like a live action feed of what's going on with you two.

JULIE

We are JUST friends!

AUTUMN

Friends who look at each other like they're
starving and at a buffet.

JULIE

Okay, but he is hot! What do you expect?

BLAIRE

I want a hot man for autumn. WTF?! I'm so
jealous! I'm going to die alone with my cat!

AUTUMN

No, you're not. It's just a matter of time.

JULIE

IT ISN'T REAL!

My phone vibrates with another text.

CRAIG

Really? Already parading him around town? I
thought you had more respect for yourself.

My heart immediately races when I see it's Craig. It's not a welcoming feeling. I take a screenshot and send it to my bestie chat but refuse to respond to him. I'm not letting him ruin this ... whatever this is.

AUTUMN

Wow, he's jealous!

BLAIRE

He should be.

Another text comes through.

NICK

Thanks for today.

He sends me a picture of an oversized bowl of Cinnamon Toast Crunch.

NICK

Girl dinner.

JULIE

Happy for you.

NICK

Happy for us.

I set my phone down and head to my bedroom, already planning what I'll wear in the morning for our yoga session.

I pull out a sports bra and some sexy leggings with cutouts on the thighs.

For the rest of the night, I'm going to let myself enjoy the flutter in my stomach when I think about his hand on my back, the way he said, "She's the keeper," and how he listened to me talk about apples and cereal like it mattered.

I shouldn't be enjoying myself this much with him, but I am. And I don't give a single damn about it. Neither does he.

7

NICK

I'm awake at five fifteen a.m., staring at the ceiling of the Riverside cabin, wondering what possessed me to suggest sunrise yoga.

The truth is, I haven't felt this alive in years. Yesterday, walking through a grocery store with Julie, letting her teach me about the foods that brought her joy, was the most normal and extraordinary thing I'd done in decades. I felt like a real person instead of the hollow corporate ghost I'd become in Manhattan.

My phone dings on the nightstand.

ASHER

You're up early. Even for you.

NICK

How did you know I was awake?

ASHER

You're active on Instagram. When did you start liking posts about pumpkin recipes?

I check my activity.

Shit. I've been subconsciously liking every post from Cozy Coffee's account for the past twenty minutes.

NICK

Research.

ASHER

Sure. How's the girlfriend?

NICK

Fake girlfriend.

ASHER

The fact that you felt the need to correct me says everything.

I don't respond because he's not wrong. Nothing about yesterday felt fake.

I put on some athletic wear, grab my keys, and head into town. The streets are empty, except for a few early morning runners. The sun hasn't risen yet, but the sky is starting to lighten at the edges, painting the mountains in shades of purple and pink.

The town square is already set up with yoga mats in neat rows. A woman with long gray hair in elaborate braids is arranging blocks and straps at each station. This must be the instructor, Jessie.

"Good morning, Nick," she says without looking up.

"How'd you know?"

"Never seen you here before. Think you can handle it?" Jessie looks up, studying me with kind eyes.

"I hope," I say with a laugh.

"You look like you can," she says.

"I played professional hockey. I think I can manage some stretching."

Jessie's laugh is knowing. "Oh, sweetie. This isn't *stretching*. It's a spiritual journey through physical torment. But don't worry; I have a one hundred percent survival rate. Tomorrow might suck."

Before I can respond, I spot Julie walking across the square. She's wearing purple leggings with strategic cutouts that make her legs look impossibly long and a sports bra that leaves very little to the imagination. Her red hair is pulled up in a messy bun, and she's carrying two coffee cups.

"Close your mouth, dear," Jessie says. "You'll catch flies."

Julie hands me one of the cups. "Figured you'd need a little pre-workout caffeine."

"You're a lifesaver." I take a sip, and she made it exactly how I like it—strong. "Ready to do this?"

"Oh, I'm ready to do a lot of things."

The way she says it, with that little smirk, makes me lose my train of thought.

Other couples start arriving; most are in their thirties and forties.

"Nicolas Banks!" Mrs. Henderson calls out. "Didn't expect to see you two here."

"Didn't expect to see you." Julie narrows her eyes. "You realize this is partner yoga?"

"Well, that's why I asked Mrs. P to join me," she says.

They're both too cheery—and only here to do recon.

Julie chuckles. "Hope you two have fun."

Jessie claps her hands. "All right, everyone! Let's begin with partner poses."

"Partner poses?" I whisper to Julie.

She's trying not to laugh. "Don't worry; I'll be gentle."

"Liar."

The first pose involves sitting back-to-back, arms linked, trying to stand up together. It requires complete trust and coordination. Julie and I fail spectacularly the first time, both of us laughing as we tumble sideways.

"You're supposed to push back," she says.

"You're supposed to communicate," I counter.

"I'm communicating with my back pressure."

"That's not a thing."

Jessie appears above us. "Less talking, more breathing together. Feel one another. Quit fighting it."

We try again. This time, I focus on matching Julie's breathing, feeling the rise and fall of her back against mine. We stand smoothly, perfectly synchronized.

"Better," Jessie says. "Now hold the tree pose while maintaining contact."

The next hour is a special kind of torture. Not because the poses are challenging, but because every move requires me to touch Julie. Her hands are on my waist for balance. My palms press against hers for warrior pose. The warmth of her skin when we move through flowing sequences does something to me.

At one point, she's in downward dog, and I'm supposed to place my hands on her hips to help deepen the stretch. The position is innocent, therapeutic even, but the way she looks back at me with those green eyes makes it feel like foreplay.

"Breathe, Nick," she whispers, and I realize I've been holding my breath.

"Trying," I manage.

Jerry—an older guy who's partnered with his girlfriend, Margaret—chuckles from the next mat. As Julie walks away to grab some water for us, he chats with me.

"Jessie's classes have saved more relationships than counseling in this town."

"Why's that?" I ask.

"Forces you to pay attention to each other," Margaret says. "Can't fake connection when you're trying not to fall over."

By the time class ends, I'm sweating, and Julie's face is flushed pink. We're lying in final savasana, side by side on our mats, pinkies touching. The sunrise has painted the sky in brilliant oranges and golds, and I can't remember the last time I felt at peace.

"That concludes class," Jessie says, then dismisses us with a series of breathing techniques.

"That wasn't so bad," Julie says as we roll up our mats.

"I had a good time," I admit.

As we help pick up the accessories we were using, Mrs. Caldwell approaches us with her phone out. "You two are just adorable. Mind if I get a picture? For the book club newsletter."

"The book club has a newsletter?" I ask.

"Oh, honey, the book club has everything," she says, already snapping photos.

"The Fairy Godmothers need to stop." Julie grabs my hand and leads me away.

"That will never happen," Mrs. Caldwell says with a laugh.

"Breakfast after that intense session?" Julie asks.

"I'd love to," I admit, not wanting our day to end so quickly.

"I think your plan is working," she says, then seems to catch herself. "I mean, people are definitely buying that we're together."

"That's the point."

She steers us across the street so we don't pass the windows of Cozy Coffee. "Come on. We're going to Cozy Diner. Best food in town, and I need real food after that workout."

"Is there a reason why you're avoiding the coffee shop?" I ask.

"Blaire will interrogate me for an hour if we show up sweaty from couples yoga. Plus, the diner has the best pancakes in Colorado."

When we enter Cozy Diner, it's exactly what I expect. It has red vinyl booths, a black-and-white checkered floor, and walls covered in vintage signs. It smells like bacon and strong coffee. Heads turn to watch us.

"Julie!" an older woman with silver hair piled high calls out from behind the counter. "Some booths by the window are open, honey. Any one you want."

"Thanks, Marge!"

We slide into the booth, facing each other, the morning sun streaming through the windows. The menus are laminated and sticky, with pictures of enormous portions that would horrify my nutritionist back in Manhattan.

"Everything here is amazing." Julie doesn't even glance at her menu. "But the blueberry pancakes are life-changing."

"Sold."

Marge appears with a coffeepot, filling two mugs without asking. "Who's this handsome stranger?"

"This is Nick, my *boyfriend*." The word rolls off Julie's tongue so easily now.

"Well, aren't you two adorable together?" Marge winks at us. "First meal's on the house for new couples. It's tradition."

"Marge, no—" Julie starts.

"Don't argue with me, young lady. I've known you since you were stealing candy from the pie counter."

"I never stole anything!"

"Sure, honey." Marge winks at me. "She was a little thief. Luckily, she turned out so well. What'll you have?"

We order blueberry pancakes, extra bacon for me, and fruit salad for Julie.

As Marge walks away, Julie shakes her head.

"She tells everyone I was a childhood criminal."

"Were you?"

She peeks up at me. "Maybe once. It was a Snickers bar, and I was seven."

"Hardened criminal."

"The *hardest*."

Our food arrives so fast that I barely had a chance to drink half of my coffee. The pancakes are the size of dinner plates, and we drown them in syrup and butter. Julie immediately steals a piece of my bacon.

"Boundaries," I say, moving my plate away.

"What's yours is mine. Dating rules."

"I don't remember that in my PowerPoint."

"Slide nine, section two. Look it up."

She takes another piece of bacon, grinning when I don't stop her. Being with her is everything I didn't know I was missing.

"So, what's Phase Two?" Julie asks, adding even more syrup to her pancakes.

"Haven't figured that out yet."

"Really?"

"Still to be determined." I tilt my head, admiring how pretty she is. "Truthfully, you make me want to be more spontaneous."

She pauses, looking at me with those green eyes that see too much. "That might be the nicest thing anyone's ever said to me."

"That's impossible."

"No, I mean it." She sets down her fork. "Most people think I'm too impulsive. You're the first person who makes spontaneity seem like a good thing."

She makes me feel alive. I haven't randomly done anything since I stopped playing hockey and locked myself in my corporate castle.

"What are your plans for the rest of the day?" I ask.

"Not much. I switched shifts so I could do yoga with you. I have to be at work at two."

"That gives us six hours."

She grins wide. "What do you have in mind?"

"No idea."

"Sold."

We demolish our pancakes while the diner fills up around us. Every few minutes, someone stops by our booth to congratulate us or make small talk. Julie handles it all with grace, introducing me, making everyone feel important. She belongs here in a way I've never belonged anywhere.

"You're good at that," I tell her after the fifth interruption.

"At what?"

"Making people feel like they're not a burden."

She shrugs. "Small-town survival skill. Everyone wants to matter."

"You matter," I say without thinking.

Her cheeks turn pink. "So do you."

We stare at each other across the booth, and I want to kiss her again. Not for show, not for the woman who I can see walking past the window, staring at us. Just because.

"We should go," Julie says, breaking the moment. "Before Marge tries to feed us pie."

"Too late!" Marge appears with two slices of apple pie. "Made fresh this morning."

"Marge, we just ate enough for four people," Julie protests.

"That's why I'm boxing it up to go. You kids have fun today." She winks at me again. "Take care of our girl."

"I will," I promise, meaning it more than I should.

When we walk outside, I glance over at Julie.

Then I notice a lady across the street, phone out, obviously watching and texting someone.

"We're being surveilled," I say.

"That's Craig's aunt. Mrs. Mires." She doesn't even look to know who I'm talking about. "She's been his spy network since I moved into my neighborhood. Want to give her something to report?"

Instead of waiting for my answer, Julie turns to me, goes up on her toes, and kisses me. Not on the cheek this time. Full on the mouth, right there on Main Street at eight a.m. on a Friday.

It's playful as she nips at my bottom lip before pulling away, leaving me stunned on the sidewalk.

"There," she says, satisfied. "That should keep her busy."

"That was very spontaneous," I whisper.

"That's why it's fun." She takes my hand. "Come on."

We end up at the local antique shop because Julie insists my rental needs personality. She makes me buy string lights and throw pillows with bears on them. I pretend to protest as she keeps adding things to our basket, but honestly, watching her light up is worth it all.

"This is perfect to spruce up the cabin," she says, holding up some vintage coffee signs.

"I don't plan on being here that long."

"Might as well make it feel like home while you are though."

We carry our purchases to the Range Rover, and I realize I haven't checked my phone in two hours. There are a handful of texts from Asher and three missed calls from Zane. I silence my phone.

"Everything okay?" Julie asks.

"Perfect," I say, meaning it. "Where to next?"

"Trust me?"

"Always."

"We need to go on a drive," she says, and I unlock the door for her to climb in. "Go toward the cabin."

As we take the second switchback, she directs me to a pull-off on the mountain road, then leads me down a trail. We exit the SUV and hike for twenty minutes before emerging at an overlook that takes my breath away. I can see the entire valley spread out below.

Cozy Creek looks like a miniature town. It's easy to see where they're setting up for the festival. Carnival rides, food trucks, the pumpkin patch, and a corn maze. This festival will have it all.

"Is this place secret?" I ask as the breeze brushes against my cheeks.

"It's nicknamed Make-Out Lookout," she says, sitting on a large, flat rock. "A quiet place where we can just be."

I sit beside her, our shoulders touching. "Thank you for sharing this with me."

"You looked like you needed it." She studies my face. "You get this expression sometimes, like you're drowning on dry land."

"That's exactly how it feels."

"When did it start?"

I know I should deflect, make a joke, keep things light. This is supposed to be fake, but sitting here with her, overlooking this valley, I find myself wanting to tell her all my truths.

"When I couldn't play hockey anymore, my life changed. Then my sister died, and everything good about our family went with her. She was the glue that had held us together, the one who remembered birthdays and organized dinners and made sure we all stayed connected. After she was gone, it stopped."

"What did?"

"Feeling. Connecting. Living. I went through the motions of working, dating, and socializing, but none of it meant anything. I'd lost my career and my sister, who was my sounding board for everything. I felt dead inside."

Julie takes my hand, interlacing our fingers. "And now?"

"Now I'm sitting on a mountain with a beautiful woman who makes me want to eat Cinnamon Toast Crunch for dinner and wake up at the butt crack of dawn to do sunrise yoga."

"Lucky you," she says, grinning.

"I agree," I say.

We sit in silence, watching clouds drift across the valley. This feels too intimate for something with an expiration date. But I can't make myself care.

My phone buzzes again. This time, it's one of my best friends from my hockey days, Patterson.

PATTERSON

Yo, how's Cozy Creek?

NICK

Great. I've been busy as hell.

PATTERSON

Busy with that redhead?

I look at Julie, who's now lying back on the rock, soaking up the sun like a cat. Her hair spreads out like fire against the stone.

NICK

How did you know?

PATTERSON

Asher told everyone at a party last night that you're no longer single.

NICK

I'm going to kill him.

PATTERSON

Nah. It's about damn time you found someone worth unplugging for.

PATTERSON

Don't fuck it up.

NICK

Trying not to.

"Work?" Julie asks without opening her eyes.

"My friend was just checking in."

"Good friend?"

"The best. You'd like him. His name is Patterson. He's also commitment-phobic and emotionally constipated. Biggest asshole teddy bear I've ever met."

"More than Zane?" She laughs.

"Oh, yeah. He makes Zane look tame because he's an extrovert."

I lie flat against the rock with her, and we stare up at the clouds. She grabs my hand and holds it tight.

"This is nice," I say.

"Yeah," she agrees. "It really is."

We stay here until we have to head back for her shift. As I drive her to her condo, she reaches over and places her hand on my thigh.

"Thanks for being spontaneous," she says.

"Thanks for making me want to be."

She squeezes my leg. "We should do this again."

"Deal."

I walk her to her door, and she takes a step forward, giving me a tight hug. I hold her until she pulls away.

"Want to have dinner tonight?"

"I get off at eight."

"Great," I say. "It's a date."

Her brows lift. "Oh, a *date*. Sounds official."

I laugh. "See you then."

As I'm driving out of town and back up the mountain toward my cabin, my phone rings. It's Asher.

"Finally," he says when I answer. "I thought a small-town serial killer had murdered you."

"Just living in the moment."

"Who are you, and what have you done with my brother?"

I think about Julie.

"I'm currently trying to figure that out."

"Well, whatever you're doing, keep doing it."

"I think I might."

"Good. Don't overthink it."

After we hang up, I sit in the Range Rover for a moment and smile. Am I happy? Such a simple word for such a complicated feeling. The back seat holds string lights and bear pillows, and I think about what Julie's lips tasted like.

I want to find happiness, and that terrifies me more than anything else. I thought it didn't exist anymore—at least not for me.

But Asher is right. I do run from people at the thirty-day mark. And in forty-four days, I *have* to leave. So, things are complicated.

For now, I'm going to hang string lights in a rental cabin and put pillows on a couch I don't own.

Today, I want to live like this is real and like my deadlines don't exist.

This must be what Eden meant when she told me to live in the moment.

8

———

JULIE

The evening shift at Cozy Coffee is brutal. After being up since dawn, I'm running on fumes and caffeine. Every tourist in Colorado needs a complicated coffee drink fifteen minutes before we close. My body is sore from Jessie's torture session, I smell like espresso and pumpkin spice, and there's definitely whipped cream in my hair somewhere.

"Go," Tracy says, practically shoving me toward the back. "Your man's been sitting outside in that ridiculously expensive car for ten minutes."

"He's early."

"He's *eager* and putting in effort. There's a difference." She waggles her eyebrows. "I'll finish closing. You've been glowing all day, and I want that energy to continue through your date."

I glance through the window and see Nick scrolling on his phone in the driver's seat. Even from here, even after a long day, the sight of him makes my stomach flutter.

"Thanks, Tracy."

I grab my stuff from the back and head outside. Nick looks up from his phone and smiles, getting out to open my door.

"Hey," he says. "Long day?"

"The longest. Plus, I'm sore from yoga, and I smell like I bathed in sugar coffee." I gesture at myself. "Can we stop by my place first? I desperately need a shower before dinner."

"Of course. We have a reservation at eight thirty, so there's plenty of time."

"Bookers doesn't take reserva—"

"Money talks." He grins as I slide into the passenger seat.

"I could get used to this," I say with a wink.

The drive to my condo is two minutes, tops. When we step inside, I immediately kick off my shoes.

"Make yourself comfortable," I say, heading toward the stairs. "Actually, come up with me. You can sit on the toilet and talk to me while I shower."

"I'm sorry, what?"

I pause halfway up the stairs, grinning at his expression. "Blaire does it all the time. We chat while I shower. Otherwise, you're just sitting down here, alone, like a weirdo."

"How is that any different from sitting in your bathroom like a weirdo?"

"Oh, come on. I want to talk!"

His ears turn pink, but he follows me up the stairs. "This is what female friendships are like?"

"Oh, yeah. Prepare to be educated."

He follows me into my bedroom, immediately distracted by the organized chaos.

"Is that a stuffed llama wearing a sombrero?" He points to my bed.

"His name is Fernando. He helped me get through a rough patch, so no judgment."

"I already like him." Nick picks it up, then notices my bedside table. "You read three books at once?"

"Different moods require different books. Romance, thriller, and self-help." I head into the bathroom, scooping up my workout clothes and throwing them in the laundry basket.

"Come on, boyfriend. Bring Fernando if you need emotional support."

He follows me in, still holding the llama. "We're really doing this?"

"Yes! Now, be a good boy and sit." I point at the toilet lid. "And close your eyes while I get in."

"This is definitely not what I expected when you invited me up."

"What did you expect? A striptease?" I say, turning on the water.

"A man can only dream."

"Eyes closed, dreamer."

"They're closed. Scout's honor."

I undress quickly and step into the shower. "Okay, you can open them. Tell me about your afternoon. What did you do after you dropped me off?"

"Spent an hour arranging those bear pillows you made me buy," I say.

"Please tell me you took a picture," I say, as I scrub away the remnants of a day in the life of a barista.

"No, I absolutely didn't document my pillow arrangement."

"Should have. It's always nice to have evidence that you're being a real human. And you could've updated your Phase One slides for your PowerPoint presentation."

"Harsh." I can hear him shifting on the toilet lid. "Oh, I picked up a coffee maker."

"Why? I saw one on the counter at the cabin."

"I bought a normal one that makes normal coffee for normal people."

"Look at you, embracing your inner basic bitch. I love this for you."

"Is that what we're calling it?"

"Of course. You're giving up your rich people's elitist ways and living a humble, regular-coffee-maker life. But I'll be honest with you, an espresso machine is a must. It's one thing I'm a total snob about. But then again, caffeine runs in my veins."

Nick howls with laughter as I finish rinsing my hair and washing my body.

"Can you grab me a towel? In the closet next to you."

I hear him moving around, then laughing.

"Jules?"

"Yeah?"

"Why do you have seven bottles of the same shampoo?"

"It was on sale, and I had coupons! That stuff is expensive. Stop judging me and hand me a towel."

The shower curtain moves, and his hand appears with a fluffy towel, his eyes comically squeezed shut.

"You look ridiculous." I laugh, taking it, patting the water from my face.

"I'm just being respectful."

"I guess." I wrap the towel around myself and step out. "You can open them."

He opens one eye cautiously, then both, and his gaze does a quick sweep before he deliberately focuses on my face. "Hi."

"Hi, yourself. Come keep me company while I figure out what to wear."

"So bossy," he says.

"Does it bother you?" I ask.

"What?"

"My bossiness."

"No," he tells me. "I appreciate it."

That makes me smile.

Nick follows me to my closet, still carrying Fernando.

"Friends help each other pick out outfits," I say, flipping through dresses. "What should I wear?"

"I don't know," he says.

I stop and look at him. "Haven't you ever had a female friend?"

"Not like this," he admits.

"You're missing out. This is where all the best gossip happens." I pull out two dresses. "Which one?"

"Either one," he says.

"What's your favorite color?" I ask, shoving them back onto the rack as my eyes scan across the many colors.

"Green," he says without hesitation. "Like the color of your eyes."

I grin and pull out my emerald silk dress. "Turn around."

"Seriously?"

"Unless you want a show."

"I mean …"

"Nick!"

He turns, covering his eyes with Fernando. "The llama sees nothing."

I drop the towel and slip into the dress quickly. "Okay."

He turns back, and his mouth falls open slightly. "That's … you're …"

"Words are sometimes hard."

"You're going to cause accidents."

"Don't flatter me," I say with a laugh.

"Honest." He sets Fernando down and moves closer. "You look incredible."

"It's just a dress."

"It's never just anything with you." He reaches out, fingers barely grazing the silk at my waist. "Tonight will be torturous."

"Why?" I ask, picking up the towel and doing my best to dry my hair.

"Because I'll have to perform through dinner, pretending you're mine as everyone wishes you were theirs."

I laugh. "So, sell it. Let them know I'm yours. Give no doubts."

"Don't give me permission to be possessive," he says.

"Permission granted." I walk past him and add some product to keep my waves. I hurry and swipe on some lipstick and mascara.

"Wow," he says as we head downstairs. "You clean up nice."

"So do you," I tell him.

I lock up and grab his hand as we make our way to Bookers. It's only a few blocks away, and the evening air is perfect. It's cool enough to be comfortable.

Leaves from the trees hanging over the sidewalk drift down between us. They're bright orange and brown and scatter across the sidewalk. The air carries the faint smells of woodsmoke and cinnamon—a reminder that it's mid-September. Starting tomorrow, the streets will be packed with tourists and will remain that way through the new year, especially after the ski season begins.

We pass the bookstore, where three teenage girls quickly appear in the window, watching us.

"Is this kind of interest normal?"

"Unfortunately, yes," I say, avoiding their gaze. "They'll move on to someone else eventually. It's just been a while since I've dated, after everyone thought I'd marry Craig. I think the whole town is shocked. And many of them have no idea who you are yet."

The wind picks up, sending more leaves swirling around us like confetti. We pause at the street corner to let a car pass before we cross. Nick turns to glance at me, and I notice how the streetlamp catches the auburn in his hair.

"Serious question," I say. "Could you imagine yourself living here?"

He hesitates as we cross the street. "Yeah. Zane is here. When we were teenagers, we always talked about living close so our kids could grow up together."

"You want kids?" I ask.

Nick is utterly breathtaking.

"Maybe one day." His thumb rubs across mine, and his hand squeezes my fingers a little tighter.

We approach Bookers, and there are huddles of people waiting outside. Nick opens the door, allowing me to enter first.

My eyes widen. "I can't believe you had them reserve a table."

"Why not? It's a Friday night, and they're packed. I wanted to be guaranteed dinner with my beautiful girlfriend," he says.

"You're going to make me blush," I tell him, leaning closer.

The hostess greets us, pulling us away from our conversation.

"Two, for Nicolas Banks," he says, and she cheerfully leads us across the room.

As we pass tables and booths, heads turn to watch us.

"People are staring," I whisper.

"Because you're stunning," he says, gently placing his hand on my shoulder to pull me close.

I melt into him as he escorts me like I'm royalty.

My pulse jumps when I slide into the booth and he sits right beside me. His arm settles around me, and I lean into his warmth. Being close to him is too easy. Our legs touch under the table, and neither of us moves away.

Menus are placed in front of us, but I don't need it because I have it memorized. I open it, though, to give myself something to focus on other than him.

"Would you like to start with some drinks and appetizers?" the server asks, and then pauses when Nick turns to her. "I, uh … Nick, uh … huge fan. I literally had a poster of you in my bedroom."

I smile, understanding because Nick has a way of scrambling people's thoughts.

"Thanks."

"I was devastated when you retired," the girl says.

"I was too." He chuckles, like this is a normal reaction. "I'll have a whiskey, neat. And my girlfriend wants …"

"A margarita on the rocks, salt, with an extra shot of tequila on the side," I say, needing to calm down. "And an order of chips and salsa."

She walks away, leaving us alone.

"Does that happen a lot?" I ask him.

His brown eyes meet mine. "Not as much anymore. Most people have forgotten I ever played and know me from other things."

"Does it bother you?" I ask.

"Not really. Being forgotten comes with retiring, which is inevitable for every player. Part of the game is knowing when to quit. That's why I tried hard to break records—to ensure I'm remembered as one of the best in the league," he answers, then pauses, realizing I'm devouring every word. I could listen to him talk for the rest of the night. "You're so pretty."

"You don't have to do that," I whisper.

Soft laughter releases from his lips as he rotates his body more toward me, almost to face me. "Give you a compliment?"

"Yeah," I tell him.

"Just so you know"—he leans in close and speaks only loud enough for me to hear—"I don't give fake compliments. *Ever.*"

Nick pulls his phone from his pocket and turns the camera on. He snaps a picture and shows me.

"Oh no," I mutter, staring at the picture.

"What?" His brows are lifted.

"I have *the look*." I gasp.

"What look?" He stares at the picture, trying to figure it out.

"I cannot fall in love with you."

Laughter rolls out of him. "Then don't."

"This feels too easy," I say, my voice low, staring at the photo.

"We look good together, like we belong," he confirms, and hearing him admit that does something to me.

"I think we might break some people's hearts on November first," I say, hoping mine isn't one of them. I'm already trying to predict the town's reaction when I explain why we're over.

He smirks. "I'll be your long-distance fake boyfriend as long as you need, babe. I have no plans to hop into a relationship anytime soon. Kinda good on that."

"Agreed. It honestly feels good not to have to try to impress you," I tell him. "It might be you and me indefinitely at this rate."

"I'm down for that," he says. "Would make my life so much easier."

"Me too," I admit. "My mom would stop trying to hook me up

with a different guy every week. I think she's scared I'm going to be single until I'm in my prime."

"There is nothing wrong with that, if it's what you want."

Our drinks are set in front of us. I lift the extra shot of tequila, downing it, wanting it to shake my nerves loose. Nick sips his whiskey and continues to read the menu. Every once in a while, he steals a glance at me and grins. It's adorable.

The chips arrive, along with fresh salsa that has just enough kick to keep my mouth on fire. We order our food. With the lights low and how close we're sitting, I'm suddenly aware of how intimate this feels. I can smell his cologne, feel his warmth, and I want to be closer.

"So," I say, taking a sip of my margarita for courage, "I should probably give you some feedback."

Nick turns and twirls a strand of my hair with his finger as he studies me. "I'm listening."

"You're good at this." The tequila makes me braver. "You actually listen. Being with you doesn't feel forced or too much. You make it comfortable."

"Yeah?" He sounds pleased.

"Yeah." I pause, then add quietly, "The closeness is nice and not too overbearing."

His thumb traces circles on my shoulder. "And what about this?"

"Not too much." Goose bumps trail over my arm, and I try to brush them away.

His brows lift, and before he can say anything, a shadow falls across our table.

"Jules"—Craig's voice cuts through the moment—"can we talk?"

"No," I say.

"Come on. Five minutes."

Nick's arm tightens around me. "She said no. We're actually on a date, and you're rudely interrupting it."

Craig's eyes narrow at our closeness. "This is ridiculous. You've known him what, two days?"

"Actually, a year," I say. "Not that it's any of your damn business."

"A *year?*" Craig laughs bitterly, and I can smell beer on his breath. "Funny how you never mentioned him."

The dining room quiets, and my heart rate increases.

Craig's face flushes red as the restaurant watches our drama unfold like it's dinner theater.

"Funny how you never asked about my life when we were together, but care so much now," I counter.

"You're using him to make me jealous."

Nick starts to respond, but I squeeze his hand, stopping him. This is my battle.

"Craig, I need you to understand something." I keep my voice level. "Not everything is about you. Nick and I are together. You and I are over. Those are two separate facts that have nothing to do with one another."

"Jules—"

"Please leave us alone," I snap.

Craig stands there for another moment, giving me his best *go to hell* look, then storms off, nearly knocking into our server.

"Well handled," Nick says quietly.

"I've had practice. It's not often I have to use my manager tone." I take a sip of my margarita and laugh. "He'll probably text me later with either an apology or more accusations."

"Want me to fuck him up?"

"Yes, but also, he's not worth it."

Our food eventually arrives, and we both ordered steak and baked potatoes. When we're halfway through eating, Nick's phone vibrates on the table. He glances at it and frowns.

"Everything okay?" I ask.

"Yeah, it's just my little brother, who has been a total pain in my ass." He lets it ring.

"Answer it," I say. "It might be important."

He playfully groans, but picks it up, putting it on speaker but keeping the volume low. "Asher, I'm busy."

"You're always busy. Or avoiding me. Which is it tonight?" His voice is smooth, teasing.

"I'm on a date."

There's a pause, and it's followed by sarcastic laughter. "Right. You're on a date. In Cozy Creek. Where the nightlife consists of that one bar."

"I'm dead ass serious."

"Are you going to keep her around longer than thirty days?"

I raise an eyebrow at Nick, who looks embarrassed.

"I'm literally sitting next to her right now, and you're on speaker, so thank you," Nick grumbles.

"Prove it."

He looks at me. I shrug and lean in.

"Hi, Asher," I say. "This is Julie, and I have a feeling Nick is going to beat his thirty-day deadline this time. Would you like to place a bet on it?"

Nick softly chuckles, and it eases his tension. I bump into him.

The line is silent, but I see the seconds still counting down.

Asher scoffs. "Holy shit."

"Yeah, and our food is getting cold because we're right in the middle of a date. So, we should probably let you go."

"Mark your calendar," Asher says. "Thirty days from the first date, he will try to run. Don't let him. Nick will always have the sudden urge to reorganize his entire life or go through a mini self-discovery phase that requires him to be alone."

"Why do I care?" I ask him. "His past relationships don't affect us."

"Also, that's not entirely true and—" Nick starts.

"Remember Jessica? You suddenly had to take up rock climbing in Europe. Or Sarah? You realized meditation was the key to your problems. Then there was Emily and Tiffany and Hannah ..."

"Goodbye, Asher."

"Julie! Get my number from him and call me. I'll talk you through every single one of his exit strategies!"

Nick hangs up, jaw clenched tight. "Sorry about him."

"Thirty days, huh?" I tease.

"It's not intentional. I get restless. Most people are more into me than I am them. I try to end things before someone gets hurt."

"Should I expect you to decide to hike the Appalachian Trail in mid-October?"

He laughs.

"We're different," he says, then seems to catch himself. "Because it's fake and we're committed until November first. Already, you're beating my records. It's a clean ending. No need for exit strategies."

"Right." I do the math quickly. "That's two weeks longer than your usual."

"You're right," he admits. "I guess Asher will have to start telling my dates six weeks, going forward."

We finish our food, and he pays, completely ignoring my offer to split the check. I'm slightly tipsy, and Nick holds me close as we stroll down the sidewalk.

Outside, the September air is cool against my skin, causing me to shiver. Nick drapes his jacket over my shoulders without me even asking. We walk back to my condo, our hands linked together. I'm not ready for the night to be over, but I know we're rounding the end.

The streets are full of tourists, and music streams from a karaoke bar that opened up on the corner. Laughter and the sound of plates clattering echo from the diner. Cozy Creek is full of life, and the season hasn't fully started yet.

"Your brother seems like he enjoys giving you shit," I say.

"It's his favorite pastime. He and Dyson both." Nick squeezes my hand. "They think my thirty-day thing is hilarious."

"Is it really that consistent?"

"Unfortunately." He glances at me. "You'll be a personal record."

"Breaking records makes a person unforgettable," I tell him, recalling what he said about his hockey records. The way he glances at me makes my pulse quicken.

We round the corner to my building, and my stomach drops when Mrs. Mires, Craig's aunt, steps outside with her ancient poodle, Mr. Whiskers. She hasn't seen us yet, but she will in about two seconds. Her phone is already in her hand; she's probably texting Craig right now about her nightly surveillance, telling him I'm not home yet.

"Shit," I whisper.

Without thinking, I turn to Nick, grab his sweater, and pull him down to me. Our lips crash together, and for a second, he's surprised. Then his hands come up to frame my face, and he's kissing me back with an intensity that makes my knees weak.

This is nothing like our coffee shop kiss. This is pure instinct, pure want. His tongue traces my bottom lip, and I open for him, a small sound escaping that I'll be embarrassed about later.

One of his hands slides into my hair while the other wraps around my waist, pulling me flush against him. I can feel his heart racing, matching mine. The world narrows to just this, us, his mouth on mine, the solid warmth of his body, the way every nerve ending seems to spark to life at once.

When we finally break apart, we're both breathing hard. I'm vaguely aware that Craig's aunt has hurried inside, Mr. Whiskers yapping from being rushed.

"Jules," Nick breathes, his forehead resting against mine.

"She was going to see us," I whisper, but it sounds like a weak excuse, even to me.

"Right." His thumb traces my cheekbone.

Neither of us moves. We're standing so close that I can feel his breath on my lips, and it would be so easy to lean back in. His eyes drop to my mouth, and I know he's thinking the same thing.

"Kissing you feels too good," he mutters.

"It's just chemistry," I say, trying to sound practical. "Physical attraction."

But his hand is in my hair, and his thumb is still stroking my skin.

"Is that what this is?" he asks. The question lingers for an eternity.

We finally step apart, and the loss of his warmth makes me shiver despite his jacket around my shoulders.

"I should go inside," I say.

"Yeah."

But we're both standing there, staring at each other like we're trying to figure out what just happened because that kiss has made me forget anything else exists.

"Nick—"

"Six weeks," he says, like he's reminding himself as much as me. "We have six weeks."

"Six weeks," I repeat.

One wrong move could ignite a fire that will burn us both down.

"Good night, Jules."

"Night. It was fun. Hope we can do it again, boyfriend."

"Oh, babe, we will."

He waits until I'm inside before leaving. I lean against my door, fingers pressed to my lips, trying to catch my breath.

My phone buzzes.

CRAIG

I can't stand knowing you're with someone else.

Ig-fucking-nored.

It's followed by another one.

NICK

I'm sorry if that was too much.

I stare at the message.

Too much? Kissing him was *everything.* I keep that to myself.

JULIE

Every part of tonight was perfect. We did great. Thank you for being a good sport!

NICK

Helps when I have a great partner.

JULIE

Do you have plans tomorrow night?

NICK

I don't.

JULIE

Want to join me at the harvest festival kickoff celebration? It's tradition. I never miss it. Will probably head over there around five.

NICK

I'd love to join you.

My heart skips.

JULIE

Can't wait!

NICK

Me neither.

I plop down on the couch, wearing his jacket, with my lips tingling from that kiss. Tomorrow is the festival, and something tells me everything is about to change. I have to remind myself it's only temporary, and six weeks is all we have. And that thought terrifies me more than anything else.

9

—————

JULIE

Once again, I wake up at five a.m., even though I could have slept in a bit longer. Festival day makes me feel like a kid on Christmas morning. I unlock my phone, seeing I already have a text from Nick, sent at 4:47 a.m.

NICK

> Why am I awake? This town has broken my city-boy's sleep schedule. Good morning! Hope you have a great day.

JULIE

> Morning! Welcome to small-town life. Your internal clock now runs on coffee-shop time.

NICK

> Speaking of coffee … are you working today?

JULIE

> Until 3. Then it's ME + YOU + FALL FESTIVAL TIME! AHH!!! 🎃

NICK

> Your enthusiasm for pumpkins is borderline concerning.

JULIE

Says the man who literally graphed our relationship.

NICK

We agreed never to speak of the PowerPoint again.

JULIE

I don't remember agreeing to anything.

I grin and roll out of bed. Even though I don't have to be at work until seven, I'm too wired to go back to sleep. Last night keeps replaying in my mind. Nick was a good sport and chatted with me while I showered, and I can't forget the way he looked at me in that green dress.

By the time I get to Cozy Coffee, Blaire is already there, surrounded by pumpkin-shaped cookies.

"You're early," she says, then looks at me closely. "Oh my God, you had sex."

"I did not!"

"You're wearing that *I had good sex* face."

"I have an *excited about the festival* face."

"That's definitely not it." She studies me. "Or maybe it's *almost sex* face. What happened after Bookers?"

"Nothing. We walked home, and he was a perfect gentleman."

"Boring." She groans. "I'm supposed to be living vicariously through you."

"Before we left for dinner, he sat on my toilet and talked to me while I showered."

Blaire almost drops a tray of cookies and sets it down. "What? That's what I do! And I'm not even trying to get in your pants!"

"Neither is he. We're F-R-I-E-N-D-S. Do you know what that spells?"

"Yes, I do. Friends who absolutely want to bang each other." She shows me her phone. There's a photo of us at Bookers that someone snapped when we weren't looking.

"I'm going to murder the Fairy Godmothers. Who took that?" I ask.

"I dunno, but they keep doing updates of your relationship on Insta."

My eyes widen. "No. They need to stop that. Who do I need to talk to?"

Blaire laughs. "It's a runaway train. Just ride it. Or ride Nick."

All I can do is shake my head.

The morning rush hits before I can process this.

We work like busy bees, and I'm thankful I had Sierra, one of our teenage employees, join us this morning because there was no way Blaire and I could've handled it. Next week, I may add another person to the morning shift just because it seems busier than usual.

Every tourist wants special drinks, and locals keep stopping to ask about tonight. The excitement streams through the air, and I'm counting down to when I can leave work.

"You and that handsome boyfriend coming to the festival?" Mrs. P asks for the third time.

"Of course. It's tradition," I tell her. "I wouldn't miss this kickoff for anything."

She smiles wide. "Can't wait to see you two lovebirds."

"Tell the Fairy Godmothers to stop meddling."

"Sorry, sweetie, no can do." She walks away, giggling.

Around ten, my phone buzzes.

NICK

How's the coffee battlefield?

JULIE

Beautiful, pumpkin-scented chaos. Someone just ordered fifteen pumpkin spice lattes.

NICK

The horror!

JULIE

Tons of people have asked about you.

NICK

Is this where I say pumpkin spice?

JULIE

Why are you making me think about safe words while I'm at work? 🔥

NICK

Behave yourself.

JULIE

Never.

"You're sexting at work," Blaire says from behind me as the orders keep coming.

"It's completely platonic, and I'm one hundred percent multitasking. Plus, I'm the boss, and I can do whatever I please."

"You *could* do Nick."

"Blaire!"

"What? Zero lies detected," she says.

The door chimes, and Tom Valley strolls in with his perfect mustache. "Jules! My boys are coming for the festival. Caden's still single."

"Sorry, Tom! I have a boyfriend now."

"I heard. But if that city boy breaks your heart, Caden's just a phone call away."

I chuckle.

Blaire glances at me. "Maybe you should rub some of that off on me. You have men lined up as backup boyfriends. Meanwhile, I'm hoping the festival fortune teller will predict someone tall, dark, and handsome in my future."

"Maybe she will."

"She predicted I'd find love near water last year. I dated that swimmer for two weeks before he ghosted me."

"Public pools don't count as near water."

"Now you tell me!" she says with a laugh.

The afternoon crawls by. Every time the door opens, I hope it's Nick, but he's helping Zane and Autumn volunteer for festival setup. According to the book club's Insta updates, he's been stringing lights and moving hay bales all morning. He's officially their new real-life book-boyfriend material. The comment section aggravates me.

"Your fake boyfriend is getting the full small-town experience." Blaire shows me a photo of Nick helping the fire department set up the stage.

He looks good. Really good. His T-shirt stretches across his chest as he lifts equipment, and his smile is genuine as he talks to other volunteers.

"That man is not faking anything," Blaire says. "He fits in."

"He's leaving on November first," I tell her. "He's returning to New York."

"Why?" she asks.

"I dunno. Because he has a life away from Cozy Creek," I say, returning to the rush, happy for my thoughts to be captured by sugary drinks.

Finally, three o'clock arrives. Tracy practically shoves me and Blaire out the door.

"Are you going to the kickoff?" I ask Blaire.

"Probably. But I think I'm going home to take a quick nap. I'm exhausted," she says.

We exchange a quick hug, then go our separate ways.

I pull my phone from my pocket and text Nick.

JULIE

FREEDOM! Heading home to shower! Still on for tonight?

NICK

Hell yeah! Can't wait to see you.

JULIE

So much same!

I read his message and smile as I practically run home.

When I reach my door, there's a large white box with an orange ribbon waiting on my porch. No delivery label, just my name in handwriting I don't recognize.

Julie

My heart races as I carry it inside. I set it on my kitchen counter and carefully open it, parting orange tissue paper to reveal the most beautiful burnt-orange silk dress I've ever seen. Underneath is a velvet jewelry box.

With shaking hands, I open it. Diamond earrings shaped like tiny pumpkins catch the light, along with a matching pendant. They're from Calloway Diamonds, which is the most exclusive jeweler in the world. These must have cost a fortune.

I find the card and open it.

The way you light up about fall deserves proper appreciation. They sparkle just like you.

Happy autumn, Little Red. Hope this is your best one yet. Can't wait to see you sparkle tonight.

—Nick

I STARE AT THE GIFTS. THIS IS TOO MUCH.

My phone rings. It's Nick.

"Hi," he says.

"Hi. I can't accept this."

"And why not?"

"They're too expensive. This is supposed to be fake and—"

"Jules"—his voice softens—"I think our definitions of *expensive* are much different. And there is nothing about how I feel when I see you happy that's fake. It's a real gift, not one encouraged by fake-dating standards."

"This probably costs more than my mortgage."

"But you're smiling. I can hear it," he says.

He's right. I am.

"In the grand scheme of things, it's just money. It comes and goes. Let me spoil you if I want."

"Okay, but no more expensive gifts."

"Define expensive. A million dollars? Two? Babe, I could spend a billion on you right now and not even notice."

"Nick!"

"See you soon, Little Red."

He ends the call before I can say anything else.

I shower quickly, then slip into the dress. The silk hugs every curve like it was made for me. It might be. The burnt orange makes my hair look like fire, and my skin glows. When I put on the diamonds, I barely recognize myself in the mirror. I look like I'm falling in love.

"Stop it," I tell my reflection. "It's been less than a week."

But my heart isn't listening.

I walk to the town square since it's only a few blocks away. The festival is already in full swing. Families everywhere, the smell of apple cider and kettle corn filling the air, local bands setting up on the small stages scattered around.

I spot Nick by the main stage, talking to Zane and Autumn. He's wearing dark jeans and a black button-up with the sleeves rolled to his elbows. When he sees me, he stops mid-sentence.

"Jules!" Autumn rushes over. "You look amazing! Wow! Someone is taking my Pumpkin Queen crown this year!"

"Hush," I say, catching Nick's eye over her shoulder.

She and Zane were crowned the Pumpkin Queen and King of Cozy Creek last year. Their love story is one people will tell their kids.

Nick excuses himself from Zane and walks over to us.

"You're beautiful," he says, like it's a fact. He takes my hand and twirls me around.

I'm giddy, and Autumn notices.

"Going to take my girlfriend to get some cider before the line gets too long," he says, interlocking his fingers with mine.

"Oh. My. God," Autumn says as we walk away. "This is the real deal."

She squeals.

"Stop it!" I say to her over my shoulder as Nick drags me away.

We spend the next hour doing festival things. We watch teenagers bob for apples after we get our faces painted. Little kids race past us in costume toward the corn maze. Afterward, we eat caramel apples that get stuck in our teeth. Nick even laughs when I get whipped cream from my hot cocoa on my nose, gently wiping it off with his thumb. He places it in his mouth, and I have to look away because it's too damn sexy for me to handle.

"I haven't done anything like this in years," Nick admits, watching a guy fail at the ring toss.

"A festival?"

"Fun without an agenda. Being present instead of thinking about the next meeting, the next deal," he admits.

"And how does it feel?"

He looks at me—really looks at me. "Like I'm waking up."

Before I can respond, Mayor Hutchinson's voice booms over the speakers. "Ladies and gentlemen, before our main entertainment tonight, I'd like to ask Nicolas Banks to come up here for a moment!"

Nick freezes. "What?"

"Did you know about this?" I ask.

"No. I just helped with setup. I didn't—"

"Mr. Banks, don't be shy!" The mayor waves him forward.

The crowd starts chanting his name, and Nick shoots me a panicked look before heading to the stage. "What do I do?"

"Go," I say, encouraging him.

"Folks, before we start the kickoff, I wanted to give my appreciation to this generous young man. Nick here decided earlier that he would make a very large donation to our literacy program to help us rebuild and expand the library."

"How much?" someone yells from the crowd.

The mayor laughs. "He's funding the *entire* project."

Whispers circle around the crowd, and I stare at him. I had no idea any of this was going on.

"That's millions," I hear someone say behind me.

My stomach drops. Nick isn't just wealthy; he's in a different stratosphere.

"We're so appreciative that you're here, sir. Would you like to say a few words?"

Nick looks nervous as hell. The entire town square has gone quiet, and hundreds of faces have turned toward the stage.

"Hi." He finds me in the crowd, and I give him an encouraging nod. "I didn't expect this. I don't really do speeches. I typically leave the talking to my brother, Asher. And I know he'll see this somehow, so I'll give a preemptive, *Shut up, Asher.*"

"You're hot!" someone yells, and I hear all the women in the crowd swoon.

Nick takes a breath. "My sister Eden loved books. She loved fall. She would have loved this festival." His voice gets stronger. "She passed away five years ago, but she believed in the power of literacy to change lives. This donation is in her memory—because every child deserves to discover the magic of reading."

The crowd is silent for a moment, then erupts in applause. I'm crying, and I don't even care.

"And," the mayor adds, taking back the microphone, "let's give a round of applause to his lovely girlfriend, a local. Nick told me earlier that Julie brings out the best in him!"

Every head turns to me. Phones come out. Flashes go off.

Nick escapes the stage and makes his way back to me, looking overwhelmed.

"I'm sorry," he says immediately. "I had no idea they were going to—"

"Are you kidding? That was amazing. You just changed hundreds of kids' lives."

"But people will find out. The attention—"

"I can handle it. I'm so proud of you."

I shut him up by kissing him in front of everyone. Not for show. Not for Craig, who I can see watching from near the beer tent. But because this man just honored his sister's memory in the most beautiful way. His fingers thread through my hair, and everyone and everything around us disappears to nothing. I can taste the cider on his tongue, and my heart is so full that it might burst out of my chest.

When we break apart, the crowd is cheering.

"That was …" Nick seems dazed.

I feel the same; he makes me dizzy.

"Come on. You need a drink after that ambush," I say, pulling him away.

We escape to the beer tent, where Nick downs half a beer in one go.

"I hate public speaking," he admits.

"You were perfect," I offer as we stand at the edge of the tent.

"I saw you crying."

"Happy tears. What you said about Eden … that was beautiful."

He's quiet for a moment. "She would've liked you."

"Yeah?" I ask.

"You remind me of her sometimes. The way you make everyone feel seen. How you find joy in small things. Your obsession with fall."

"Nick ..." I swallow hard.

"Sorry, that's probably weird—"

"It's not. It's ... thank you for everything. I'm sure I would've liked her too."

"You would've both ganged up on me," he says, laughing, but I see the sadness in his eyes.

"Guess I'll have to go harder on you to make up for it," I say with a wink. "Want to dance?"

"Yes," he tells me.

We walk across the grass to the dance floor that's set up in front of the stage. A country band called The Heartbreakers is playing, and the lead singer, London, is so damn talented. Afterward, we share a funnel cake and end the night by watching the fireworks burst over the mountain. As the festival winds down, he walks me to my condo.

"Want to come inside?" I ask as we take the sidewalk that leads to my condo.

"Is that a pickup line?" His mouth quirks upward.

"Maybe. Or maybe I just want to keep pretending this is real for a few more hours."

He grabs my hand; the streetlight casting shadows across his face. "What if we stopped pretending?"

"Nick ..."

"I know. I know we have rules. But, Jules, today didn't—"

"Come inside," I say softly, not wanting anyone to overhear this conversation. "We need to talk about this. About us. About what we're doing."

"Yeah," he says, following me. "We really do."

My hands shake as I unlock the door, knowing that whatever happens next could change everything between us.

10

NICK

I follow Julie inside her condo. The door closes behind us with a soft click that sounds like a slam in the silence.

"Wine?" she asks, already moving toward the kitchen like she needs something to do with her hands.

"Something harder." My voice comes out rougher than intended.

I watch her pull out a bottle of tequila, her movements nervous. The diamonds I gave her catch the light as she reaches for two shot glasses, and something primal in me roars.

"So," she says, pouring them full, "what did you mean? About stopping the pretending?"

I take the glass she offers, our fingers brushing. That simple touch sends electricity shooting up my arm.

"Jules …" I set down the shot without drinking it. "Can we be honest with each other?"

"Aren't we always?"

"No, we're not." I move closer, and she backs up until her back touches the counter. "We've been pretending this thing between us is just friendship. That the kissing is just for show. That I don't think about you constantly. That you don't feel what I feel when we touch."

Her breath catches. "Nick …"

"Tell me I'm wrong." I cage her in, hands on either side of her on the counter, careful not to touch her. "Tell me you don't feel this, and I'll shut it off right now. I'll pretend it's not true."

She meets my eyes.

"Be honest. That's one of our rules."

"I can't deny it," she whispers.

"Why are we fighting it?" I lean in closer, close enough to smell her perfume, mixed with kettle corn from the festival. "We have six weeks. We both know I'm leaving. We're already exclusively fake dating. Why are we torturing ourselves?"

"What are you suggesting?" Her green eyes search mine.

"That we stop holding back." My thumb traces her jaw, and she leans into the touch. "We already have an expiration date. No false promises. No broken hearts. Just … this. Whatever this is."

"More will complicate things," she says, but her hands come up to rest on my chest.

"We're already complicated." I lower my forehead to hers. "I haven't felt this excitement with someone … ever. And I don't want to leave Cozy Creek with regrets of not exploring this. No lies, no manipulation. Just two people who are attracted to each other, going with the flow." I pull back to look at her. "Six weeks of friendship, fun, and incredible sex. Then I go back to New York, as planned, and we part as friends."

"Sex?" She's quiet for so long that I think she's going to say no. She downs the shot. "We'd need new rules."

"Such as?" I toss my tequila back.

"Still friends first and being honest. That doesn't change," she says, pouring us another round of shots.

"Agreed."

"Exclusive for the six weeks. I do not and will not share."

"Neither do I," I tell her.

"No *I love yous*," she says firmly. "That's completely off the table. Leave your feelings at the footboard. *I love you* kinda freaks me out."

Something in my chest tightens, but I nod. "Fair."

"And when November first comes—"

"We part as friends. No drama. No trying to make it more," I say.

She searches my face like she's looking for any sign of deception. "Do you really think we can do this?"

"We'll explode if we don't. This pull between us is unavoidable. It chases me in the night." I move closer. "Jules, I—"

KNOCK. KNOCK. KNOCK.

We move apart, both startled.

"Julie! I know you're in there!" Autumn's voice carries through the door. "Come answer so I can prove a point!"

"Autumn, this is—" Zane says on the other side.

Autumn keeps pounding, and Julie groans, moving to the door and swinging it open.

She glares at them. "What do you want?"

"I win! Pay up, Alexander! Told you they were together," she says, holding out her palm. "Look at them. Tequila on the bar. His hair is messy. I win."

My brows crease, and I cross my arms over my chest. "You bet on us?"

"Fifty bucks," Zane says, playfully rolling his eyes. "She insists on this."

"And I'm spending every penny on fried cheesecake tomorrow," Autumn says, pulling him away. "Thank you! Carry on, lovebirds!"

We hear them bickering as they walk away, their voices fading down the sidewalk.

Julie returns to me and stares as if my eyes hold the answers.

"If I don't say yes to this, I'll regret it," she tells me. She moves forward, tucking her fingers in the pockets of my slacks. "I need to know something."

"Anything."

"What do you get out of this? You can literally hook up with anyone."

"Yeah." I take a breath. This is the hard part. "But I don't want anyone. I want you. And I think you can help me."

"With?"

"My thirty-day expiration date with women, the walls I put up, the way I run the second things get real. I'm broken." I force myself to be honest. "I want to know why I'm so shitty at relationships. And you … you see through my bullshit. You force me to be honest when it's easier not to."

She studies me. "You want me to be your relationship coach? And then you pay me with orgasms?"

"When you put it like that …"

"Great! I'll do it." She laughs, then moves away, going to her bookshelf. "But if I'm going to help you, you're helping me with something too."

She pulls out a small notebook with a rose-gold cover.

"What's that?"

"My naughty wish list." Her cheeks turn pink. "Things I want to try, but my exes were too vanilla."

"You have a naughty wish list?" I smirk. This is music to my ears.

"Yes, and before your mind goes to the gutter, it's not *all* sex," she says, then flips it open. "Some of it's just *experiences*."

I scan over her neat handwriting. My eyebrows climb higher with each item.

THE "LIST"
SKINNY-DIPPING UNDER THE STARS
SEX IN A SEMI-PUBLIC PLACE
BODY SHOTS
MILE-HIGH CLUB

DOMINATION
PHONE SEX
HAVE SOMEONE GO DOWN ON ME UNTIL I BEG THEM
TO STOP
TIED UP AND BLINDFOLDED
FOOLING AROUND IN AN ELEVATOR
O ON BALCONY DURING A PARADE
MAKE A STEAMY SEX TAPE
SEX IN AN OFFICE
WAKE UP TO ORAL
ORGASM IN A CORN MAZE
SHOWER ORGASM (NOT SELF-INDUCED)

"JULES," I BREATHE, "THIS IS ..."

"Too much?"

She reaches for the notebook, but I hold it away.

"Perfect. You're perfect." I keep reading. "Craig wouldn't do these?"

"Craig was a little bitch," she says.

"Clearly," I tell her, setting the notebook down to meet her eyes. "I'll help you."

"Really?" She laughs, but the mood turns serious. "We're doing this? Exclusive friends with benefits?"

"That's up to you," I tell her. "I'm all in."

"I am too," she says, taking another shot of tequila. "Will you stay with me tonight?"

"Yes, I fucking will."

"Great." She grabs the notebook again, scanning her list. "If we're doing this, let's start small."

I look over her shoulder, reading over it again.

"Body shots." She taps on it. "It's the tamest thing on here, and we already have tequila."

My mouth goes dry. "You want to do body shots? Now?"

"Unless you're scared."

She's challenging me, and I love it. That sparkle in her eyes drives me crazy.

"Do you have salt and limes?" I ask.

"Absolutely do."

She grabs the saltshaker and slices a lime into wedges. The way she looks at me, like I'm everything she's ever wanted, makes my pulse race.

"So …" she says, suddenly looking uncertain. "I've never actually done body shots. It's on my list because it seems fun. Also, I made this list when I was twenty-one."

"And you've never done them?" I'm surprised.

"I wasn't a party girl. I was too busy managing a coffee shop, and I have hobbies." She rolls her eyes. "Teach me."

I move closer. "Three steps. First, you lick where you want the salt. It's usually somewhere sensitive, like the neck or wrist. Then you sprinkle salt there, take the shot, and finish with the lime." I pause. "The person can hold the lime in their mouth."

Her pupils dilate as I place the lime between her lips.

"Tilt your head for me, Jules."

She does, exposing the long line of her throat. I lean in slowly, giving her time to change her mind. When she doesn't, I slowly drag my tongue along her pulse, feeling her whole body shiver. I taste the sweetness of her skin.

"Nick," she gasps.

I sprinkle salt where my tongue was, then grab the shot glass.

Her eyes stay locked on mine as I take my time licking salt from her neck as she places her hands on my shoulders. I lean in for the lime, our mouths barely brushing as I take it.

"How was that?" I ask.

"Perfect," she says. "Can we do it again?"

This time, Julie reaches behind her and unzips her dress. The dark orange fabric falls to a puddle around her feet. She's standing in her bra and panties.

"Go ahead," she whispers. "I know you want to look."

My brain short-circuits. She's standing in black lace, confident and gorgeous, taking control of her own desires.

"Jules," I breathe, "you're killing me."

"That's the point." She takes my hand, leading me to the couch. "My turn to learn. Show me."

I pull my shirt over my head, and her eyes go wide.

"Jesus, Nick."

"Hockey body," I say with a shrug.

"Lie down," she commands, pointing at the couch.

I do what she wants and stretch out on the cushions. She straddles my hips, and the weight of her, the heat … it's almost too much.

"Where do you want the salt?" she asks.

"Wherever you want it," I tell her.

I place my hands behind my head, giving her full access as she sets the lime in my mouth.

I'm hard as a rock, and there's no hiding that. She feels me— that's why she's rocking against me. Julie trails her finger down my chest, then drags her tongue across my stomach in the same places. My eyes roll into the back of my head, and I keep my hands to myself as she grinds back and forth.

"Fuck." I groan around the lime.

She sprinkles salt and licks it up, takes the shot, then leans down for the lime I'm holding between my teeth. Our lips brush, and suddenly, we're kissing. Deep, desperate, as she still straddles me.

"Your turn," she says against my mouth.

This time, she slides off me, pulling me to sit up.

She's still in her lingerie, skin flushed, and I have to remind myself to breathe.

"Where?" My voice is wrecked.

She tilts her head back, exposing her throat again. "Here."

I take my time, kissing along her collarbone first, feeling her pulse race under my lips. After the salt and shot, I catch the lime from her mouth, our tongues brushing.

"Nick," she gasps, pulling back, "if we don't stop now …"

"I know." I'm breathing hard, my hands on her waist. "You're right."

She doesn't move away. "The wait will destroy me."

"In the very best way." I trace my thumb along her jaw. "Tomorrow night, I'm taking you on a real date."

"Like the ones we've been on haven't been real," she teases, but she's smiling.

"You have a point," I say, standing and pulling her up with me. "I want to do this right. Show you the world."

"Oh, like Aladdin?" she asks.

"You're tipsy," I tell her.

She nods. "A little." Julie reaches for my hand. Something flickers in her eyes. "Stay tonight? Just to sleep. I want … I just want you here. Nothing else."

"Whatever you want," I say with no hesitation. "But you might want to put on clothes first. My self-control does have limits."

She grabs her dress from the floor. "Come on. Upstairs we go before we do something we'll regret."

"I wouldn't regret it," I say honestly.

"Neither would I. That's the problem." She takes my hand, leading me to her bedroom. "This was a really good idea. Sad I didn't come up with it."

"I think it's the inevitable progression of this."

"So, is this Phase Two?" she asks.

I lick my lips. "Guess I should finish my PowerPoint."

"I want *this* for however long we have," she confesses.

"Six weeks," I say.

"Six weeks," she agrees. "And what happens if neither of us wants this to end?"

I shrug. "How about this? Let's decide on Halloween night. If one of us says no, we continue forward as friends. But let's live in the moment. Our future isn't promised," I say, brushing my fingertips across her cheek.

"Okay," she says. "We'll make an ultimate decision before the clock strikes midnight on Halloween. No matter what, always friends."

"No matter what," I repeat.

She disappears into the bathroom to change while I sit on her bed, trying to calm my racing heart. When she comes out in an oversized T-shirt and shorts, she's somehow even more tempting than in lingerie.

We slide into bed from opposite sides, meeting in the middle. She snuggles close to me, like we've done this a hundred times.

"For the record," she says into the darkness, "body shots are definitely getting checked off the list. Not sure how they'll ever be topped."

I laugh, pulling her closer. "And we have so many more to complete."

"Promise?"

"Oh, Little Red. I'm going to have you adding more things …"

"I'm glad it's you," she says, yawning.

"Shit, me too," I agree, kissing her hair.

She falls asleep within minutes, but I lie awake, holding her, wondering how the hell I'm going to survive six weeks of this. Even now, I know what my answer would be. November first will either make me or break me, but that's forty-two days away. And right now, with her breathing steadily against my chest, I'm going to let myself have this.

Even if it's just temporary. Even if it ends. Even if I'm already breaking our rules by feeling things I shouldn't.

The first thing I notice is how warm I am. The second is that my phone is screaming at me from somewhere far away. The third is that I'm wrapped around Nick like a koala, and the sunlight streaming through my window is way too bright for five in the morning.

"Shit!" I bolt upright, nearly elbowing Nick in the face. "SHIT, SHIT, SHIT!"

"What's wrong?" Nick mumbles, voice rough from sleep.

I grab my phone and look at the time, seeing it's 7:43 a.m. I was supposed to open at six.

"I'm almost two hours late!" I scramble out of bed, tripping over the dress I left on the floor last night. "I never set my alarm! I *never* forget to set my alarm!"

Nick sits up, his hair sticking up in twelve directions. "Jules—"

"No time!" I grab yesterday's jeans from my chair, hopping on one foot as I pull them on. Fuck it. I grab a sweater from my closet and pull it over my head. "I have to go. The morning rush. Oh God, Blaire is going to kill me."

"Let me drive you—"

"I can walk there quicker." I lean over the bed, grabbing his face and kissing him quick and hard. "Lock up when you leave. Spare key is stuffed behind my fall wreath on the door. Can't miss it."

"Your sweat—"

"Bye!"

I sprint out of my condo, my keys jangling, my hair a disaster. The three-block run to Cozy Coffee nearly exhausts me. When I burst through the back door, I nearly crash into Sierra, who's carrying a hot tray of chocolate croissants.

"Jules!" She steadies the tray. "We thought you'd died!"

"I'm so sorry!" I tie an apron around my waist, not even bothering to check my appearance. "I forgot to set my alarm. I never forget. I—"

"Jules." Blaire appears, arms crossed, trying to look stern but fighting a smile. "Breathe."

"The morning rush—"

"Is handled. Tracy came in early. We've got it covered." She looks me up and down, and her smile breaks free. "But, um … you might want to …"

"What?"

She turns me toward the mirror by the office door.

My sweater is on backward. The tag is sticking out under my chin. My hair looks like I've been through a tornado. Yesterday's mascara is giving me raccoon eyes.

"Oh my God." I cover my face with my hands.

"So," Blaire says, pulling me into the office, "Nick stayed over?"

"That's the question you ask?" I glare at her.

"You look like you've been mauled."

"We didn't have sex. We just did body shots and slept."

Tracy pokes her head in. "Jules, honey, your sweater's on—"

"I know!"

Sierra appears behind her. "Also, you have a huge hickey. Damn."

"I do not—" I check the mirror again. Fuck. I do.

"Go home," Blaire says, full-on laughing. "Seriously. You're a disaster, and we've got this covered."

"But—"

"Jules." She puts her hands on my shoulders. "You haven't taken a real day off in months. You showed up looking like you did the walk of shame. Go home. Shower. Spend the day with your boy. Get some rest. We've got this."

"Are you sure?"

"GO!" All three of them speak at once.

"Also," Sierra adds, "shower sex saves time. Just saying."

I flip them off as I leave, their giggles following me out.

The walk back to my condo is less frantic. The morning air helps clear my head, and I'm suddenly very aware that Nick might still be there. I also remember we agreed to friends with benefits, and he's taking me on a date tonight.

When I unlock my door, I hear the shower. My stomach does a little flip.

I climb the stairs, hearing him humming something. The bathroom door is cracked open, and steam rushes out. I can see his silhouette through my shower curtain, and I admire him for a second before creeping closer.

"BOO!"

"FUCK!" Nick screams, and a shampoo bottle flies past the curtain. He slips, catching himself on the shower curtain rod. "Jules!"

I'm laughing so hard that I can barely breathe. "Did you just throw shampoo at me?"

He yanks the curtain back, soap in his hair, glaring at me. "Woman, you trying to give me a heart attack?"

"Your scream!" I wheeze. "So high-pitched!"

"You scared the shit out of me!" But he's starting to laugh too. "What are you doing back? Trying to assassinate your boyfriend?"

"Blaire sent me home. Apparently, showing up and looking like I've been mauled is frowned upon."

His eyes rake over me, taking in my backward sweater and my destroyed appearance. "Mauled, huh?"

"See for yourself." I turn my head, showing him the hickey.

"Mmm." He looks genuinely surprised. "Are you sure I did that?"

I narrow my eyes at him. "Unless there's a ghost trying to suck my neck off, pretty sure. Seems our body shots got a little too enthusiastic."

"Apologies."

I meet his eyes. "Don't. I liked it."

"You like being marked by me?" Something shifts in his expression.

"Yes," I say. "Oh, look, my sweater's on backward."

"It is," he agrees, voice lower now as I pull it off of me.

"And these jeans are yesterday's." I unbutton them, letting them fall to the floor.

"We can't have that."

"I should probably shower." I unhook my bra, watching his eyes trail over me. "You know, to save water and all."

"Environmental conservation is very important," he manages.

I step out of my panties and into the shower with him. "Hi."

"Hi." His hands immediately find my waist, pulling me under the spray. "This okay?"

"More than okay," I mutter. "Turn around. Let me help you wash your hair."

He turns, and I work the shampoo through his hair, my nails scratching his scalp. He groans, leaning back into me.

"That feels incredible."

"Just wait," I whisper, pressing myself against his back.

"Jules"—his voice is strained—"we should talk about this."

"We have," I say, and he turns to face me.

He cups my face, water streaming over both of us. "You haven't changed your mind?"

"No." I'm honest. "I want you here. I want to explore this. And I know we have forty-one days to figure it out."

"Forty days until Halloween," he adds. "When we make our real decision."

"The clock is ticking." I grab my body wash and a loofah. "Now, are you going to help me get clean or just stand there, looking pretty?"

He takes the scrubber and brushes it over my body. "Definitely helping."

Nick is everywhere, and he doesn't miss an inch. I shiver when he touches my hip bones, and then I carefully trace my ribs with his strong hands. The lavender scent of my body wash mixes with the steam, and I realize waiting to have all of him will be the longest, sweetest torture of my life. No way he'll give me everything I want right now. This is a game for both of us.

"For the record," he says against my ear, his voice mixing with the sound of water hitting tiles, "I'm creating my own list with you."

I laugh as his hands find a particularly sensitive spot. "Really?"

"Yes." He presses my back against the cool tiles.

His mouth captures mine as the water cascades over his back, and I forget everything except the feel of him against me. His other fingers thrust into my hair, tilting my head back to deepen the kiss.

"Nick," I whisper when he moves to my neck, carefully avoiding the hickey, but he licks around it.

"Tell me to stop," he says against my skin.

"I can't."

His hands explore everywhere, and he learns what makes me gasp, what makes me grip his shoulders tighter. When his fingers find exactly where I need them, he slides two inside, and my knees nearly buckle. It feels so good.

A moan escapes me as he continues to work me. My legs tremble with anticipation as he brings me to the edge.

"I've got you," he mutters, his other arm solid around my waist.

"This is not how I imagined it," I manage.

"Want me to stop?" His fingers slow their perfect rhythm.

"Don't you fucking dare."

He grins against my neck, picking up the pace until I'm shaking, nearly biting his shoulder to keep from screaming. The orgasm rushes through me, and I clench against his fingers.

"Mmm. How was it?"

"Better than I imagined," I whisper.

When I finally come back to reality, he's holding me up, looking entirely too pleased with himself.

"Another one off your list," he says.

"I want to make you feel good too," I tell him.

"It's not about me," he says, placing his fingers in his mouth. "It satisfies me to satisfy you. Plus, you're exhausted."

"Yes, but—" I whisper.

"You have a hard time accepting things. I'm a giver, Jules."

"I am too. I'm not used to people putting me first. It makes me feel uncomfortable."

"I'll help you work through it," he says as he steps out of the shower and grabs us both towels. I turn off the water, and he helps dry me off. "I plan to spoil you."

"We've already talked about this." All I can do is shake my head, but I'm smiling.

"Yes, and you said nothing expensive. My range of expensive is at a much higher tier than yours, so I agreed."

My hands run up his chest, and he wraps his arm around me. His body is still warm from the hot shower.

"What?" he asks.

"Nothing," I say, questioning how right this feels.

"Tell me."

"You want relationship advice, but so far, I have none. I get why women are so devastated when you leave them. You're easy to fall for."

"Are you falling for me?" Nick asks, bending down to kiss me.

"So far, it's just a hookup situation."

He nibbles on my bottom lip.

"You always test-drive the car before you buy it," I tell him, moving to my bedroom.

Nick follows behind me, checking his phone while I drop the towel to put on clean clothes.

"Wow," he says, his eyes sliding up and down my body. "I want to worship you."

I grin back at him, sliding on a pair of panties and a tank top. I open the window, allowing the cool autumn breeze to flow in. Every once in a while, I can smell the funnel cakes being made at the food truck on the corner.

"Oh, is this your balcony?" he says, opening the doors and moving outside. He notices the brick wall that secludes us from the waist down. "This is why it's on your list. Got to tell you though, during a parade is ballsy."

"The Halloween one is coming up," I tell him. "It starts at dark."

His eyes stay focused on me. "It's a date."

Nick's phone vibrates and he looks at it again as he moves closer to me.

"Shit," he mutters.

"Something wrong?"

"Asher texted. Apparently, photos from the festival made it onto some gossip blog." He shows me his phone.

The headline reads *Hockey Heartbreaker Nick Banks Cozies Up with Small-Town Barista.*

Below are three photos. One is of us kissing after his speech, him wiping whipped cream off my nose, and one where I'm looking at him like he hung the moon.

"The comments," Nick says. "Don't read them."

Of course, I scroll down.

She's pretty but so ordinary for him.

Gold-digger alert.

He could do so much better!

Why is he slumming it in some small town?

Did he knock her up? Is that why?

Life isn't fair.

My stomach drops. It's worse than what I thought.

"Hey." Nick takes his phone back. "Don't. They don't know our situation. They don't know us."

"It doesn't look like anyone wants us together," I say, trying to sound unaffected.

"They will never like anyone I'm with. Ever. You're gorgeous, and haters will try to tilt your crown. Don't let it get to you, okay? All that matters is you and me and what we think."

"Okay," I say. "What do you think?"

"Forever might be nice," he says.

I crack a smile and pull on yoga pants and a sweater.

Nick sits on my bed, watching me. "When's the last time you took a real day off and just rested?"

I try to think. "Um …"

"Exactly." His hands rub my hips. "Spend today catching up on sleep. I'm going to get us breakfast. Real food, not just coffee and croissants." He kisses me. "I'll send a car for you at seven."

"A car?"

"Trust me." He stands. "You need actual sleep if we're going to be up late tonight."

"Ooh, what does that mean?" I ask.

"Tonight is our secret," he says.

"Absolutely," I say.

The anticipation of what he has in store is almost too much. Because this, us, whatever we're doing—it's ours. Just ours. The rest of the world doesn't need to know the details.

The town thinks we're dating, but they don't need to know about our situation behind closed doors, about the list, about what really happens when we're alone.

Am I already breaking rules by wanting to shout from the rooftops that Nick Banks just gave me an orgasm in my shower?

"So pretty." He kisses me once more.

"Should I wear a dress? Jeans? A parka?" I ask.

"Yes," he says.

"Nick!"

"Wear whatever makes you comfy. But we'll be outside."

"Oh. Hmm." I think about it, wondering what he could've planned so fast.

His grin is wicked. "I'll be back with food in thirty minutes. You'd better be in bed."

"Yes, sir," I say, and he rolls his eyes. "Yes, *Daddy?*"

I hear his chuckle as he takes the stairs.

I close my eyes, replaying what happened in the shower, squeezing my thighs together at the thought of him touching me.

Fifteen minutes later, the sound of the door creaking open wakes me. Nick takes the stairs up to my room and appears in my bedroom doorway with a bag from the diner.

"Marge made a hangover special."

"I'm not hungover."

"No?" He sets the food on my nightstand.

"Okay, yes, I am."

He smirks. "Fuck, you're beautiful."

The way he says it makes heat pool in my stomach.

"If you don't stop looking at me like that ..."

"Eat, then sleep." He sits on the edge of my bed, watching me unpack the container.

"You're being very bossy."

"You like it." He tucks a strand of hair behind my ear. "Someone needs to take care of you. When's the last time you let anyone do that?"

The question catches me off guard. Craig never ... he expected me to take care of him. To be available when he wanted, absent when he didn't.

"Hey," Nick says softly. "Where'd you go?"

"Just thinking."

"About?"

"How different you are from what I expected."

"Better or worse?"

"Just different." I take a bite of the eggs. "A good different. You make me realize how much I settled for."

"Yeah?" Nick's face softens. "Eat. Sleep. Don't think about the past."

"Jealous?"

"Of your exes?" He laughs like they're a joke. "No. Who has you right now?" He leans in, kissing me slowly.

"You," I say, and we linger a little longer before he pulls away.

"See you at seven o'clock," he says, standing before this goes too far, too fast. "The car will text you when it's outside."

"Nick?"

"Yeah?"

"No regrets about this morning?"

"Are you kidding me? The sound you make when you come, it's on my highlight reel." His eyes darken. "Dream about what I'm going to do to you later."

I literally kick my feet when I hear him leave. How is this my life?

After he's gone, I eat the massive breakfast—scrambled eggs, bacon, hash browns, and toast. I scroll through my phone, looking at all the photos the book club has posted of Nick. Their Insta has turned into a fan club.

NICK

You're becoming the best part of my day.

JULIE

I feel the same.

I fall asleep, smiling, keeping our secret safe, knowing that, in a few hours, we'll be together again.

Forty-one days of secret touches and crossed-off lists.

Forty days until our Halloween decision.

This man may be the death of me. But, oh, what a way to go.

12

NICK

It's five p.m., and I'm pacing Riverside like a caged animal. Thankfully, this cabin is big, or I might go stir-crazy. I've changed my shirt three times, which is ridiculous because we'll be outdoors at night. But I want this to be perfect, an unforgettable experience.

My phone buzzes with texts from Patterson that I've been ignoring. I can't deal with his commentary right now, not after the internet decided it was obsessed with my and Julie's story, which seems to be writing itself. I'm trying to ignore it and not let it get to me, even though it is. I want to protect her from my world, keep her away from the bullshit I have to put up with. Unfortunately, that's not reality, and it never will be, thanks to who I am.

A knock at the door interrupts my spiral. When I open it, Zane's standing in jogging pants and a hoodie, holding two beers while wearing a knowing smirk.

"What are you doing here?"

"That's not the way to greet your bestie," Zane says, inviting himself inside. "You look like you're about to have a panic attack."

"I'm perfectly fine," I tell him.

"Sure you are." He hands me the beer. "That's why you've been pacing in front of the window for the last ten minutes."

I roll my eyes. "How would you know?"

He walks to the oversized windows and points at his four-wheeler. "I've been sitting there, watching you."

"Stalker," I say.

"Just trying to figure out what's going on with you," he says. "With you and Jules."

I exhale. "Nothing to discuss."

"Come on." Zane settles on my couch, kicking his feet up on the coffee table. "I know that look. I wore it when I first got with Autumn. I understand what you're going through."

I move into the living room.

He laughs. "You don't have to admit anything to me. You're practically my brother. It's written on your face."

I take a drink of the beer, noticing it's a pumpkin one from the local brewery. "It's really complicated."

"It always is." He studies me. "But isn't that the fun part? Figuring it out?"

We exchange smiles.

"Meeting Autumn changed my life. Coming here was one of the best things I've ever done. I learned a lot about what matters and doesn't. You'll figure it out. A Banks always gets what he wants."

This makes me chuckle. "Fuck off."

"Oh, it's true though. It's something I've always admired about you. If you want something, you commit and work until you have it." He drinks. "Even my fiancée."

"You're never going to let me live that down, are you?" I ask, shaking my head.

"Not on your fucking life," he says, cocky as hell.

"You're a bastard," I say.

"Yeah, I might be, but at least I didn't have *your* sloppy seconds. But," he continues, "thank you. I'm so glad you saved me from marrying her. If all that horrible shit hadn't gone down, I wouldn't have come here and met Autumn. It was because of you and her that I left. I mourned our friendship more than my relationship."

"I did too," I admit.

"It's like you took one for the team," he says.

"I never thought of it like that. I'm not a victim, but she took advantage of me when I was at my weakest," I tell him.

"I know. And while I give you shit, I've forgiven you. You know that, right? I'm not pissed. I like giving you a hard time because it makes you squirm like a little bitch. But I meant what I said earlier; you're like a brother to me. I'm thrilled that you're here. I've missed you."

"You have such a great way of showing it," I say.

"Piss off," he says, chugging the rest of his beer. "What are your plans tonight?"

"I want to do something special for Julie. Stargazing maybe? Any place with water?"

Zane's eyes light up. "I have the perfect location. But you'll need my side-by-side to get there. There's a trail behind my house that cuts into another trail that has this natural-fed lake from a spring. I found it and brought Autumn there once. Other people know about it, apparently, but it's secluded. You'd hear someone coming."

He pulls out his phone, showing me a map.

"Wow. That's perfect."

"Park at Hollow Manor, and I'll lend you my side-by-side. I'll park it at the trailhead with the keys in it when I get home." He stands, then pauses. "It doesn't surprise me that you have a thing for her. She's exactly like my wife. They could be the same person. Actually, Julie is sassier, which is just what you need. But be careful with her, okay? I can't clean up your mess if you make one."

"I don't plan on ruining this."

"I know, but she's Autumn's best friend, and she's a really good person. Just don't play the usual games you play. And know that Jules won't leave Cozy Creek. That coffee shop is her family's legacy. Make sure you understand what you're getting yourself into. It's a big commitment, and I don't know if you've gotten over that *dating for thirty days and drop them flat* bullshit."

It makes me chuckle. "I'm working on it. We've talked about it. The two of us are on the same page. On October thirty-first, we'll decide what happens. We'll end it there or continue seeing one another. Clean break. Clear ending. I'm spending the next few weeks discovering who I am and figuring out if she is the person I want to spend the rest of my life with. I'm tired of games. I want a reason to live my life. I've been miserable," I admit.

"Hey, I get it," he says. "Last year, when I arrived, I sat in silence for two days. I remember staring up at the sky, wondering if that was all there was to life. I felt … lost. Then Autumn found me. Being here changed me, and it looks like it's changing you too. Mom always said the mountain air could cure anything."

"I miss your mom," I say quietly.

"I do too," he tells me. "You know, I've found letters that she wrote for me, hidden all over the house."

"Wow," I say. "I wish I had letters from Eden."

"Your sister would be happy for you," he says. "Eden would love that you're here, enjoying the pumpkins."

I feel that burn in my nose, and I clench my jaw. Sometimes, when I think about her, it catches me.

"Moving away from the city worked for me. I'm happier, closer to the slopes," he admits. "You can make anything work, Nick."

"Yeah," I tell him. "Or maybe I'll retire early and pick up a painting hobby."

Zane snickers. "Yeah, because if I recall, we had a pact that we'd be friends forever and that we'd raise our kids together."

I stare at him. "Are you telling me Autumn is pregnant?"

Laughter roars out of him. "No, not yet. Hopefully soon. She's sent her book out to publishers, and she's hoping it gets picked up. Seeing how that goes first."

"Wait, you're trying?" I whisper. "I'm happy for you."

"Thanks. I'm not trying to convince you of shit, but I'd love you to be here as long as you're happy. Snowboarding season is incredible. I hit the slopes every damn day. I'm the happiest I've ever been in Cozy Creek. During the winter, it transforms into a little Christmas town."

I smile, letting out a deep breath. "You're living your dream."

"I am." Zane lifts his hand and places it on my shoulder. "Don't fuck this up. Got it?"

"It's funny that everyone keeps telling me that," I say.

"Falling in love looks good on you," he singsongs as he sees himself out. "Don't even knock when you show up at Hollow Manor. A side-by-side will be waiting with the keys, fully gassed and ready to go. I'll even set up wood in the firepit so it's ready for you to start when you arrive. Bring more supplies with you. A few blankets, towels, a lantern, and extra firewood. It has an incredible view of the Milky Way that reflects off the water. It's special."

"Sounds like it."

"I'm rooting for you."

"Thanks. Also, can you keep this to yourself? I wasn't supposed to tell you shit."

"Hmm, the only thing I remember discussing was a place to look at the stars. That's about it." I shrug.

"Thank you."

After he leaves, I spend the next hour planning a date night by a lake. After ransacking the cabin, I pack supplies into the back of the Range Rover. Blankets, tons of firewood, dinner from the diner, along with a cooler with champagne and strawberries. A few condoms, just in case. I even pack string lights that run on batteries that I found in a drawer. It's everything I could possibly need. I take the ten-minute drive to Hollow Manor, transfer the supplies into the back of the side-by-side, then patiently wait for her to arrive.

At seven fifteen on the dot, the car delivers Julie. She steps out, wearing jeans, a slinky blouse, a leather jacket, and boots. Her hair falls in waves around her shoulders. Her eyes are blindfolded.

I'm starstruck, looking at how damn gorgeous she is with those kissable lips.

I move toward her and grab her hands.

"Hi," she says, suddenly shy.

"Hi." I study her, wondering what she's thinking right now as the car drives away. "You look beautiful."

"Thank you. I wish I could see you …" She gestures at herself. "I can change if this isn't appropriate."

"What you're wearing is perfect. Classy." I pull her with me, holding her by my side. "Trust me?"

"Yes," she says, and I pull her with me, helping her move forward. "We're alone, right? Like, I'm not going to be in front of a crowd of people when I take this blindfold off, right?"

"We're completely alone," I tell her.

"Great," she whispers. "I hear the wind through the trees. Where are we?"

I chuckle. "It's a surprise. But you're going to lift your leg and sit, okay?"

She nods, and I help her onto the side-by-side, then climb in beside her.

Immediately, her hand reaches for me, and she holds me tight as I reach across her to buckle her in.

The drive to our special spot will take about ten minutes. The engine is too loud for us to chat, so we just enjoy holding each other. Her laughter mixes with shrieks when I hit bumps and her hair flies in the breeze. It's a dream—all of it. When we finally stop, I can hear the soft whoosh of water against the shore.

"Stay here," I tell her, quickly lighting the fire Zane set up. I unpack the supplies from the back, then quickly set it up.

When everything's ready, I help her out and position her just right.

"Okay," I say, untying the blindfold. "Open."

She gasps.

We're in a clearing surrounded by tall evergreens. String lights twinkle next to the blanket I have for us on the ground. A fire crackles in a makeshift fire ring, and blankets and pillows are arranged beside it. Beyond that, the lake reflects the evening sky that's fading to dark. Eventually, it will be fully dark, and the stars will appear.

"Nick," she breathes. "This is …"

"Too much?"

"A dream." She turns to me, eyes bright. "How did you find this place?"

"Zane. It's his and Autumn's secret spot."

"And they know you're bringing me here?"

I nod. "He read it on my face. Zane knows me better than anyone. He stopped by before I left and suggested this spot. He knows what we have is only temporary."

"Isn't it always?" She tilts her head at me.

"Usually," I admit.

She sighs. "I don't want to hide it from them, but I don't want the outside pressure, you know? That's our decision."

I tuck her hair behind her ear. "I know what you mean. We're in the same canoe."

This makes her smile. "Without oars."

"Nah, we have those. Just dealing with a headwind."

She licks her lips. "Better analogy."

"Why?" I ask, the fire reflecting from her face.

"Because headwinds aren't forever. It's only a temporary obstacle," she explains. "What is the solution to our problem?"

"First, we have to define the problem," I tell her. I remove the food from the picnic basket, handing her a plastic container. "Imagine this being a five-star gourmet meal. If we were in the city, I'd have brought you to this rooftop restaurant with the best view."

"This view is better." She meets my eyes, then opens her to-go container. "And beef tips with gravy *is* gourmet. Very happy about this."

She pulls a plastic fork from the bottom of the bag and hands me one too.

"But you're right. What are our obstacles? In our relationship?"

"I could make you a PowerPoint," I offer.

Laughter bursts out of her and echoes off the trees. It makes me happy, knowing my one-liners crack her up.

"I thought we were never to mention the PowerPoint again?"

"True," I say. "One problem is my inability to fully commit and give myself to someone."

"You sound like a walking red flag," she says.

"You'd better run," I tell her.

"Actually, red is my favorite color," she tells me.

I twirl a piece of her hair around my finger. "Mine too."

"Our locations are a problem. You'd have to be willing to move because it's a hard no for me," she says. "Oh, and I don't know if I can actually fall in love again."

"Are you trying?" I ask.

Her eyes meet my lips. "Yes."

"Will you let me know?"

"I'll tell you on Halloween," she says. "Right now, I'm happy and having an incredible time. I'm taking it one day at a time. And eventually, the future version of us will have to decide what happens."

"Cheers to that." The lingering stress about the future immediately melts away.

"Let's make the days count. Be unforgettable," she says with a soft smile.

"You're so fucking special," I mutter, wondering how I got so damn lucky.

Had I not gotten into an argument with Asher about attending my mother's engagement party, I wouldn't have been at the bar. I would never have met her. It was a combination of events I could've never predicted that kept bringing us together. And this is the third time.

"Third time's a charm," I say as we finish our food.

"Blaire said something to me along those lines. Oh no." Julie gasps. "She did a love spell."

Now I'm laughing until it echoes off the trees. I pour more champagne into both of our glasses. There is another bottle in the cooler.

"And? You think I'm obsessed with you because your friend lit a candle?"

She playfully rolls her eyes. "Yes! What if all this ends at the next full moon?"

I pretend to pull an invisible string, and she crawls over to me.

"You summoned me. Now what?" she asks.

"Oh, my string was connected to you?" I ask. "If I had known that, I would've tugged harder."

She smiles, offering a soft kiss. "You make life fun."

"I think it's you. I like the things you say when you want to fill the silence."

"I like how you appreciate it. Some don't."

I steal a kiss, and then Julie returns to sitting beside me.

The breeze slows down, and I add more wood to the fire as the sky darkens. Julie points out constellations, making up silly stories for each one.

"That one," she says, pointing, "is the constellation of the coffee goddess. She was cursed to live a life where no man ever found her bean."

"A terrible fate," I say, unable to hold back my laughter, pulling her closer.

"The worst." She turns in my arms. "What did you think the first time we met? Like, your first impression?"

"Oh, that's easy. I thought you smelled like flowers. Then, when I turned my head and saw you crying, I thought you were a Dallas Cowboys fan too."

She bursts into laughter. "I forgot they lost that night."

I stare up at the sky, my eyes scanning over the stars. "You were like a goddess, and I couldn't understand who would make you cry. Broke my heart."

She turns and looks at me. "You were a godsend. I'll never forget what you said to me."

"What did I say?" I ask, not remembering anything that came from my mouth.

"*Only piece-of-shit men make pretty women cry.* And then you asked me if I had an OnlyFans."

"Oh yeah, I remember that now. You were so shocked I'd asked. But I wanted you to smile."

"It worked."

It grows quiet for a few seconds, and we listen to each other breathe.

"That night, I knew there was something between us, something I couldn't name. I thought about that conversation for weeks. Was pissed that you had given me a fake last name, but now I understand why."

"Yeah, well, imagine how surprised I was to see you standing in Zane and Autumn's house. You lied and said you were a tourist."

"Sorry," she says. "I didn't want to see you again."

"Meanwhile, I was dreaming about your face, but—"

"I wasn't ready," we say at the same time.

"That's why I didn't text you back," I confess. "Because I knew if I did, I'd come back for you."

"And yet here you are," she whispers.

"We're unavoidable," I say, tucking hair behind her ear and sliding a kiss across her lips.

She releases a satisfied sigh. "That's how it feels."

I look up, noticing it's finally dark and more stars are out.

"Come on," I say, standing. "Ready to do this?"

"What?" she asks.

I peel off my shirt. "Stargazing while skinny-dipping."

"Right now?" she asks.

"Next thing on that list, babe." I kick off my shoes and unbutton my jeans.

"It's September."

"And? You didn't specify a season. Plus, the water's warm from the hot spring. No excuses. We have limited days to complete that list."

It's a reminder that the clock is ticking.

She tosses off her jacket and removes her shirt. Next, she's unzipping her jeans and shimmying out of her sexy lingerie until she's naked.

I watch, mesmerized, as she takes off running toward the water.

"You coming?" she asks.

"Abso-fucking-lutely," I say, moving our phones and my wallet away from everything, then undressing before following her in.

The water is perfect, warm, and silky. Julie dives in, then comes up with her hair slicked back. She treads water like a mermaid.

"Shit, I'm dating Ariel."

She hums "Part of Your World" and floats on her back, body glowing under the starlight.

"The Milky Way will be rising soon," I say, swimming over to her, pulling her against me. "Another thing marked off your list."

"Yes, thank you." She wraps her arms around my neck, and suddenly, the teasing stops.

We're kissing, hands everywhere, the warm water making everything feel dreamlike. She reaches down and grabs me, and I groan against her neck.

"Jules, if you keep doing that—"

"Mmm." She strokes me again. "Does it feel good?"

"Fuck. Yes," I whisper against her mouth.

I slide one hand between her legs, rubbing against her clit. She moans out, wrapping one arm around me as I hold on to her, treading water like our lives depend on it.

We're so lost in each other.

"There's that sound I love," I whisper against her skin. "Gonna come for me, pretty girl?"

"I'm so close," she says.

I feel the build, and then I hear voices.

"Shit!" Julie freezes. "Someone's coming!"

"I was hoping it would be you coming, but …" I say with a smirk.

With her orgasm disappearing, we're on full alert.

Through the trees, I see several flashlights bobbing closer. There are deeper voices, but they're not adults; it's a group of teenagers.

"Our clothes," Julie whispers as we keep everything but our heads underwater.

"Hopefully, they won't notice," I say. My cock aches for her.

I speak too soon.

"Dudes, a fire!"

"Look at this setup. Someone was getting laaaaid!" another guy says.

I chuckle, and Julie glares at me.

"Check out this lingerie! Oh, I wonder if they're worn." The kid sniffs her panties. He has to be no older than sixteen.

I try not to chuckle.

She elbows me in my ribs. "Little perverts."

"They'll leave," I say.

But they don't.

They sit down at our fire, open the other bottle of champagne, and laugh at my boxers.

"Douchebags wear underwear like this."

"Oh my God, is that a bra? Dibs!"

"I'm going to kick their asses. I swear that one kid looks familiar."

"You're going to fight them naked?" I ask.

"Yeah, I will. Tits out and all," she says, growing pissed when they pocket her panties, then throw the rest of our clothes on the fire. "Little bastards! I loved those jeans!"

They suck down the champagne, toss the bottle, throw sand on the fire, then stumble away, laughing.

Julie frantically swims to shore. "Please tell me they didn't get our phones."

I check the rocks where I stashed them. "Still here. Thank God."

"Small miracles," she mutters, then looks at our situation and starts laughing.

"What?"

"The universe has a twisted sense of humor," she says. "We have to drive back to Zane and Autumn's, naked."

Her laughter starts light, and then we both crack up until our voices echo through the trees.

"Hopefully, they're asleep," I say.

The breeze blows, and goose bumps spread over me.

"We should go before some other asshole kids stumble upon us like this," I say, holding my junk as I pick up our mess.

Once everything is stuffed in the picnic basket and cooler, I walk back to the side-by-side, shaking my head.

Julie laughs. "Didn't realize there was a full moon tonight."

"Hush," I say, grabbing the extra blanket and handing it to her so she can at least cover herself. I crank the engine and sit on the leather seat. "Ready?"

She laughs, pressing herself against my side. "You make me feel young again."

"Same, babe." I chuckle, and then we take off.

She hangs on to me as I weave in and out of the trail and back to Zane's.

"What an experience," she screams into the silence, hair blowing in the wind, and all I can do is chuckle. Julie shrieks every time we hit a bump, pressing closer against me.

When we finally reach the Range Rover, we rush inside, the blanket barely covering me.

"I can't feel my ass," I mutter.

Julie collapses on the passenger seat, laughing hysterically. "You think Zane and Autumn saw us?"

"I hope not. We might have some explaining to do." I run around to the other side of the Rover, then crank the engine.

"Kinda pissed we got cockblocked by drunk teenagers," I say.

"And robbed!" She's wiping tears from her eyes. "They took my favorite lingerie! Bastards!"

On the drive back to the cabin, I turn on the heat. She reaches over and grabs my hand. The checkered blanket is wrapped around her like a towel, and I capture this memory forever.

"What?" she asks.

"Nothing," I say, grinning. "I want to remember you just like that."

When we arrive, I punch in the code and rush inside.

I grab us robes from the bathroom. "I'm sorry."

"Are you kidding?" She moves to the couch, pulling me with her. "Tonight was perfect. I'll never forget this."

She yawns.

"I should probably take you home. You have to be up early."

"Ugh, I know. Can't be late again." She's quiet for a moment. "I really like you, Nick Banks."

"I really like you too, Julie Loveland."

I put on some clothes, and she stays in the robe. Then I drive her home. I think about how this disaster of an evening somehow turned into something even better than what I'd planned.

As I walk her to her door and kiss her good night, I think that maybe that's what this is with Julie—perfectly imperfect, but it's ours. And that's all that matters right now.

"Nick?" she says as I turn to leave.

"Yeah?"

"Blaire will interrogate me in the morning."

"Tell her what you want."

She laughs. "She's not going to believe me. I take that back. She probably will believe me because the two of us have the oddest luck. The stories I could tell you."

"I hope to hear them one day." I lean forward, sliding my lips against hers, pressing her against the door. "Good night, girlfriend."

"You drive me wild," she whispers.

I laugh against her neck, then pull away. "It's mutual. Sweet dreams."

I walk backward toward my car, watching her breasts rise and fall.

"You're going to make me work for it, aren't you?"

"You know it," I tell her, smirking. "Are we marking skinny-dipping off your list?"

"Yes, we are," she says.

As I drive away, I can't stop thinking about her. And somehow, it was one of the best nights of my life because it was real. Unscripted. Just like us. And maybe that's exactly what makes being together so damn perfect.

13

JULIE

I'm trying to focus on the morning rush, but my mind keeps drifting to last night. The way Nick's hands felt on my skin, and how he looked at me like I was something he wanted, continues to unravel me. We almost lost control in the water under the starlight. I sigh.

If it wasn't for those meddling kids!

"Earth to Jules!" Blaire snaps her fingers. "That's the third time you've overfilled a cup."

"Shit!" I grab towels to clean up the mess.

"So …" Blaire leans against the counter, watching me when there's a lull in customers. "How was your night?"

I give her one look, and that's all it takes.

Her eyes go wide. "Tell me *everything*!"

I glance around, then whisper, "There's a trail behind Zane and Autumn's place. We took a side-by-side to stargaze."

"And?" she whispers, growing giddy with each passing second.

I lower my voice, leaning closer to her so no one overhears this conversation.

"Magical. Until drunk teenagers guzzled our champagne, stole my lingerie, then burned our clothes!"

She gasps. "Bastards! Did you recognize them?"

"No! But I swear, if I *ever* see them again, I'm telling their mothers! They have my panties and bra! I had to ride to the cabin with nothing more than a blanket wrapped around me!"

Blaire shakes with laughter. "Wait. Why were your clothes off?"

I shake my head. "We were skinny-dipping."

"Oh? Oh. *Oh!*"

"Before you say anything, we're just having fun and helping each other with relationship stuff," I say.

Blaire gives me a look. "Jules—"

"I'm just enjoying my time with him for now without stipulations and expectations. It's been nice. It is what it is right now, and I'm okay with that," I admit.

"You are *so* entirely screwed."

"Nah. It's not like that with us. It's different."

"Yeah, it sounds like it," she says, looking past me. "The real deal."

The bell chimes, and when I turn to look at the door, I see Nick carrying pink roses and a white box with a ribbon. His hair is messy from being blown in the breeze, and his button-up is rolled to his elbows, showing his delicious forearms. I breathe in, actually happy to see him.

"It's like you summoned him," Blaire says loud enough for everyone to hear, even Nick, who looks pleased.

The women in the dining room turn their heads toward him as he stalks across the room toward me. It's like they've been waiting for him to arrive too. The air in the room evaporates, and my stomach does that flutter thing when our eyes meet. My entire body heats like he set me on fire.

"Wow," Blaire whispers. "I'd die if a man ever looked at me like that."

"Morning, beautiful," Nick says so naturally, leaning across the counter.

I think he's going to kiss my cheek, but instead, our lips touch. I want to melt into him, but let it be quick, considering everyone is watching us.

"Hi," I say. "I was just thinking about you."

"What a coincidence. I was thinking about you too," he admits, his voice low and sexy.

Blaire scoffs. "He's not real."

Nick hands the fancy box across the counter to me. "For you. Open it later. When you're alone," he says with a wink.

Blaire is speechless and shocked. Nick moves to the register and pulls his wallet from his pocket.

"If you hurt my best friend, I'll chop off your dick," Blaire warns under her breath.

"Good," he says. "I'd deserve it."

He leans in and orders his drink.

A minute later, I glance down and smirk when an order for a pumpkin spice latte prints.

He walks past me and waits against the wall. "I was reminded about a surprise party tonight."

My eyes go wide, and I glance over at Blaire. "Already? I swear it was—"

"You've been very occupied," she whispers, nodding toward Nick.

I turn back to him.

"Would you like to ride with me?"

"Wouldn't that be out of your way?" I ask, lifting a brow.

He licks his kissable lips. "Never for you."

Blaire scoffs, watching us. "Next autumn, if I'm single, I'm quitting Cozy Coffee and joining a convent."

I finish his coffee, putting a lid on top.

"One extra-spicy *pumpkin spice* latte," I say, handing it over to him, our fingers brushing. "See you tonight."

Butterflies take over.

"Can't wait. Pick you up at five."

He leaves the coffee shop, and when my eyes scan across the dining room, every woman is swooning.

"It's such a beautiful day," I say out loud, and they go back to their conversations.

Blaire immediately corners me. "That's La Perla in that box."

"And? What's that?" I ask, confused.

"Expensive lingerie. Thousand-dollar nightgowns." She leads me to the back. "I want to see. Open it."

"He said *alone*," I mutter.

"I don't count," she says, encouraging me. "I'm a ghost. Ooh-ooo-ooh!"

Carefully, I untie the white ribbon and slide the lid from the top. Inside is a black lace balconette bra with matching panties.

I open the note and see his handwriting.

A replacement. :)

"Damn," she says, and I hand it to her to read. "I'm going home and putting together the same love spell that I did for you and Autumn. First, Autie finds Zane, and now you find Nick. Who will I find?"

"There's someone out there for everyone. And"—I lower my voice to a whisper—"no one has said *anything* about *love*. We're just friends."

"Hate to break it to you. *This* …" She returns the note to me. "This isn't friends-with-benefits behavior, babe. I just saw the face of a man who's falling. And look at you. Oh, you are not innocent. You've been lost in your head, daydreaming. I give it a month until you're both annoyingly in love."

"This is just a replacement."

"Right. And I'm the Queen of England." She shakes her head. "Hundred bucks says you're engaged within a year."

"You're delulu, Blaire. Seriously, I think the incense has finally rotted your brain."

"I'm prophetic. Mark my words. That man is your *forever*."

I smile, thinking about that. Is it even possible?

"See, that reaction is proof," she says. *"Doomed."*

I place the sexy lingerie in the office, then return to the front.

The rest of the shift passes in a blur of customers, combined with Blaire's teasing.

"Stop looking at me like that," I tell her as we stock the fridges for the next shift.

"I can't help it. My best friend is getting properly romanced by a billionaire who looks at her like she hung the moon."

"It's not romance. It's a hookup situation, one that *you* suggested, if I recall correctly."

"Keep telling yourself that." She carries several gallons of milk from the back and moves me out of her way. "What are you wearing tonight?"

"I don't know yet," I admit.

I feel like Autumn reminded me two weeks ago about that party. It's like I blinked and now it's here.

"I heard Autumn invited fifty people," she tells me. "Mostly Zane's friends from New York."

"I'm not prepared," I admit. "I dunno what to wear."

She places her hands on my shoulders. "When we leave here, I'll come over and help you pick something out. Remember, you're lovable and you just need to be yourself."

"Thank you."

"I won't steer you wrong," she says.

"You never have."

An hour later, Blaire is in my bedroom, in my closet. She grabs three different dresses but changes her mind at the last second.

"This is the one," she says, sliding a maroon velvet-crush dress off the hanger. "Classy but sexy. Also, very easy access. And it's vintage Dior."

"What? I got that from my mom's closet."

"Mama has class. Also, wear your black boots with the zipper. A man only gives a woman expensive lingerie if he's planning to take them off. Let him enjoy unwrapping you like a gift."

"Sold," I say, grabbing it and sliding it over my body with a grin. I move in front of the full-length mirror. "Do you remember when we were twenty-one and you, Autumn and I made that dumb wish list of all the naughty things we wanted to do with our partners?"

"You told him about it?"

"I gave it to him."

She gasps, and her jaw hits the floor. "And?"

"He's helping me check things off."

"Eek!" Blaire squeals. "Which ones?"

"All of them."

She's shocked. "Does he happen to have a clone?"

"I kinda wish because …" I say, and Blaire shakes her head.

"You're naughty as hell. But also, same."

My phone buzzes, pulling my attention away.

NICK

On the way. Also, just got the guest list from Autumn. Tonight will be very interesting.

JULIE

Um … in a good way?

NICK

My brothers are at Hollow Manor now.

JULIE

Oh, so it's like a family reunion?

NICK

I told them to behave. See you in a minute!

Blaire points to the door. "I'll see you there, okay?"

"Yes. Thank you for everything!"

"Happy for you. Find out about the clone, okay?" She snickers, and a minute later, I hear the front door click closed.

I put on some makeup and curl my hair to give it some volume.

The lingerie is a secret against my skin, and the burgundy dress, paired with these boots, makes me feel confident. Blaire was right. She has a sixth sense for picking the right outfits.

When Nick picks me up, he does a double take. "Wow. Stunning. Fall queen."

"A nickname I will happily take."

I lock up, and he interlocks his fingers with mine as we walk to the Range Rover. I shouldn't like it when he claims me for the world to see, but I do. Then I remember that part is fake. Isn't it?

It's like he senses my mood shift. "What?"

"Fake?" I ask.

He glances down to our hands and shakes his head. Then he's pulling me into his arms, walking closer, taking up the entire sidewalk. "I don't want anyone thinking you're anyone's but mine."

The sidewalks are much busier than they were last week.

"And the lines keep blurring," I mutter with a smirk.

"Babe, I never had a line. That's yours that's blurring," he says, and my heart does a pitter-patter.

We navigate through the crowds of festivalgoers to his vehicle that's parked across the street. Nick steals glances at me as much as he can. Sometimes, I catch him, and other times, I pretend not to notice.

He opens my door for me, and I climb in. Before he walks away, he leans forward, sliding his lips against mine. I melt into him, running my fingers through his hair at the back of his neck.

"What are you doing to me?" he asks.

"Teaching you how to live a little," I tell him, and he immediately smiles, brushing his thumb against my cheek.

"You're my favorite part of fall," he says, kissing me again.

Moments later, he's moving to the driver's side. He cranks the engine. After he reverses, he takes my hand, and we drive away.

"Should I be nervous about meeting your brothers?" I ask.

"No, I know they'll love you. They're embarrassing as hell and sometimes say the quiet parts out loud."

"Oh." I chuckle. "This should be fun then."

As we pull up to Hollow Manor, it looks empty, until we pull to the side, where Autumn told us to park. The house is lit in the setting sun, and warm light spills from every window. The house looks alive, buzzing with energy I can feel, even from here. My stomach does a nervous flip.

"That's a lot of cars," I say.

Nick squeezes my hand. "We can leave when you want. Just say the word."

"Pumpkin spice?" I tease, but my voice trembles.

He turns to face me. "Hey. They're going to love you. And if they don't, fuck 'em."

The way he says it is so simple and sure.

"Ready?" he asks.

I take a breath, looking at this man, who's turned my life upside down in the best possible way. "Yep. Let's do this."

He kisses my knuckles, then rounds the car to open my door. As we move toward the house, I see shadows moving past the windows and hear laughter drifting out.

This is it. I'm about to meet his brothers.

14

JULIE

The house is filled with voices that echo from the open front door. My stomach does somersaults as we climb the steps to the porch of Hollow Manor. This black mansion with the tall Gothic windows was the center of every spooky story and triple dog dare when I was a teenager.

Our fingers interlock, and Nick gives me an encouraging grin as we step inside. A group of people turns toward us, and he squeezes my hand.

"Relax," he whispers.

It's like he feels me tensing. I'm sure he does. Unlike him, I'm not used to attention like this. He's relaxed, calm even, completely unaffected. I somewhat feel like a fish out of water.

As he leads me through the living room, I search for Autumn and Zane, knowing they're at the pumpkin patch in town. She did that purposely to give everyone time to arrive, hoping to surprise Zane. I think he knows she's planning this, and he's playing along to appease her.

I scan around the room and don't see Blaire either. She's probably befriending every new person she meets because that's just how she is.

Blaire doesn't stay a stranger for long with anyone, which has been both a blessing and a curse throughout the life of our friendship.

As we stroll toward the kitchen, a guy rushes over and pulls me into a tight hug. My feet lift from the ground. He smells like expensive cologne and trouble.

"Do I know you?" I ask, knowing I've never seen him in my life. That fact doesn't seem to matter.

"Put her down," Nick says sternly. "Right now."

I'm returned to the ground in seconds.

"I'm Asher. Nick's *favorite* brother," he announces. They have the same color eyes. "And you're Julie."

Nick places his arm around me, and I like the feeling of him close and claiming me in front of everyone.

Asher grins. "Wow. Sparks already. You're perfect together."

"Thanks," I offer with a chuckle, trying to match his energy. "But I don't need your flattery."

"Oh, it's not," he says. "I'm genuinely happy to meet the woman my brother will marry."

"Oh, for fuck's sake," Nick mutters. "Please don't listen to him. Asher, please don't."

"Whatever. You're a changed man. Look at you. Practically glowing."

I glance at Nick. "Is that true? Have I changed you?"

"Oh, sweetheart, change happened the moment I met you," he says.

My breath catches, and I almost melt into a puddle on the floor.

"Yeah?" I ask.

"Abso-fucking-lutely."

I remember the night so clearly. Our conversation that night changed me too. It shook me out of the haze that Craig had put me in, made me realize I deserved better. After meeting Nick and learning men like him actually existed, I promised myself I'd not settle again. And when Craig came crawling back, Nick appeared like a cockblocking angel.

"I can't believe it's almost been a year," I say, breaking myself from my thoughts.

Asher's brows furrow. "A year?"

"We've known each other since last October," I explain.

Nick glances at me. "Don't tell him our secrets."

I love that cocky smile that plays on his lips.

Asher looks like he's trying to piece timelines together. "How?"

"Don't worry about it," Nick mutters.

His mouth falls open. "The blind items that were posted about you …"

"What's a blind item?" I ask.

"Ahh, Julie, Julie, Julie. *You* were the whole reason my dear, *secretive*, loving brother chose to visit Cozy Creek. All this time, I thought it was because he wanted to be close to Zane. This makes sooo much more sense." Asher glances between us. "Sooooo much sense!"

"You're being dramatic," Nick tells him, rolling his eyes.

"Leave them alone," Billie Calloway says, looping her arm in Asher's.

Her dark bob is perfect, as always, and she's dressed to kill. I met her last year at Zane and Autumn's wedding. This woman is gorgeously intimidating with piercing blue eyes and a perfect resting bitch face.

"Nice to see you again, Julie. Beautiful dress. Is that 1994 Dior?" she asks.

"I believe so," I tell her with a laugh. "It was a random steal from my mom's closet a few years ago. Honestly, I had no idea it was anything special. I just thought the waistline was cute."

"It's a great find, and it looks *incredible* on you," she says.

"Thank you." My confidence instantly rises.

"Oh, Billie is my fiancée," Asher announces.

"Oh! Wow! Congrats! That's amazing," I tell them both. "You're a very lucky guy, Asher."

"The luckiest." He meets her eyes, then steals a quick kiss.

They do that thing where they communicate without speaking. I notice the way Asher looks at her, how his whole demeanor changes.

"So, how long have you known each other?"

"Over a decade," Billie answers, then places her hand on his cheek. "I hated him for most of it."

"A total waste of time, if you ask me," Asher says, and they kiss again.

They're cute together, totally meant for one another.

"You know, I was always supposed to get married first," Nick says playfully.

"You still have time," Asher tells him with a pat on the back. "Considering we set the date for early spring, I think that gives you seven months. Almost enough time to have a baby if you wanted."

My mouth falls open.

Billie grins. "That's very true."

Just as Nick tries to deliver his rebuttal, a guy with messy blond hair, light-blue eyes, and contagious laughter bear-hugs Nick from behind.

Nick turns and lights up with excitement when he sees who it is. "Patterson! What the hell are you doing here?"

"Autumn invited me, and I had a few days off. Thought I'd crash with you if that's cool."

"Whatever you need," Nick offers. "The house I rented is huge. You're more than welcome to stay, even though I might not be there much."

Patterson's light-blue eyes lock in on mine. "Ooh la la."

"This is my *girlfriend*, Julie," Nick says, his arm conveniently sliding around my waist. "This is Patterson. We used to play hockey together on the Angels."

"If things don't work out with you two, call me," Patterson says, barely able to get his words out.

Nick swats him away. "I'll literally kick your ass."

The front door opens and pulls our attention away. This time, it's Harper with a bulky, tattooed guy standing beside her like he's her bodyguard. I notice the ring on her finger and how they look at one another and know it's more than that. When Harper spots Billie, they rush toward one another to hug. When they pull away, she sees me and Nick and smiles.

"Wow," Harper says, glancing between us. Her eyes unfocus. "*Whoa.*"

"What?" Nick asks.

"Forever is right in front of you," she says. "Love doesn't follow rules. Love doesn't have expiration dates. The third time isn't just a charm; it's destiny correcting itself, righting its wrong. I see two paths, but they both lead to the same place—home. You've already found what you're looking for."

"And what are we looking for?" I ask.

"Endgame."

"Did you seriously just give me a love prophecy?" Nick blurts out.

"I can't help it!" She grins as she glances between us. "Right now, I feel like I should be saying congratulations."

Everyone is staring at us, and my cheeks heat.

The energy builds, and my head spins.

Blaire's whistle pierces through my thoughts. "They're here! Everyone, hide!"

"There you are!" I yell toward her, and she smiles before I lose her in the crowd.

People scramble in every direction. Some dive behind couches and duck into side rooms. Nick grabs my hand, pulling me into the coat closet and pressing us together in the narrow, dark space.

"This is cozy," he whispers against my ear, his breath warm on my neck.

"Shh." I try to sound stern.

His hands are on my waist, and we're so close that I swear I can feel his heart beating against my chest.

Before I can tell him to behave, his mouth finds mine. Suddenly, I forget we're hiding and the house is full of people. My hands tangle in his hair as he presses me against the wall, kissing me like tomorrow will never come, like we have all the time in the world.

"Surprise!" The room bursts into muffled cheers, but we're too lost in one another to break out of it.

Seconds later, the door opens, and I hear Zane laugh. Nick's lips are on my neck, and my hands are still twisted in his hair.

"Surprise," Nick says, not even slightly embarrassed. "Happy birthday, buddy."

"Thanks," Zane says.

Autumn appears behind him, laughing. She hands him their coats, and he hangs them at the opposite end before closing the door.

I collapse against Nick's chest, laughing.

"You make my heart race," I whisper.

"It's mutual, babe." He steals a few more kisses.

"Does Harper usually give love prophecies?" I ask before he tugs my bottom lip into his mouth and sucks.

"Yes, and she's never wrong."

His words force streams of electricity through me, and there's a part buried deep inside that wants her to be right. I can't deny that.

"We should join everyone," he says.

"Yeah," I tell him, knowing we can't stay in here all night.

We lost control, and I don't know how to feel about that.

He reaches for the door and opens it, and the two of us step out. I glance at myself in the golden-framed mirror on the wall. My lipstick survived, thanks to the super-stay formula, but my lips are swollen, and Nick's hair is messy from my fingers running through it. Everyone gives us knowing looks, but there's no judgment, only support.

Spooky music plays in the background, and the lights are lowered. The ambience is perfect and makes me excited for the huge costume party they're throwing on Halloween.

Zane and Autumn offer us drinks, and we take them.

"Were you at least surprised?" I ask Zane.

"Not even a little. She's been trying to return last year's favor since I threw her the best surprise party of the century," he says, smiling at her.

It's so easy to see how in love they are.

"At least act surprised," Autumn says, feeding him a nacho. "One day, I'm going to get you so hard."

"You've already got me, Pumpkin."

More of his friends walk up to chat, and Nick pulls me away. We refill our drinks at a giant cauldron that's lit up and smoking. The purple punch smells like bad decisions, but right now, I welcome it. We both gulp it down, and I take a moment to notice how many fall decorations are in the house. Autumn must've spent all morning decorating. There are at least fifty pumpkins in different shapes and sizes.

"Do you think she did that while he was sleeping last night?"

Nick chuckles. "So, when he woke up, it was like the Autumn Santa visited."

"Exactly. But he was born on the first day of fall, so that would be fitting."

Nick glances around, taking it all in. "I think there are at least a hundred pumpkins in here."

"That many? No way." I begin counting. "Okay, maybe I have pumpkin blindness. I just counted eighteen on the mantel."

Nick leans in close and points across the room to a serious-looking man by the window. "Oh, that's my older brother, Dyson."

Dyson turns just as Nick says his name. His blue eyes glance at me, like he misses nothing.

"Wow, he's intimidating."

"I know," Nick mutters.

Seconds later, Dyson's moving toward us.

"You must be Julie." His handshake is businesslike, but firm. "Nick said you own a coffee shop."

"Family business. Three generations."

"Profitable?"

"Dyson, come on," Nick warns. "Leave your finance bullshit in New York."

"It's fine," I say, grabbing Nick's hand. "It's not possible to stay in business for eighty-one years without turning a profit. What do you think?"

Something shifts in Dyson's expression. Is it respect maybe? I hope.

He smirks. "You're better than his usual type."

"Which is?" I can't help asking. "If you're going to mention it, I'd like to know what I'm being compared to."

"He's never found a woman who was on a level playing field intellectually."

I'm surprised he answered. "You believe I am?"

"Yeah. At least, I hope you are, or it won't work out," Dyson says, and I'm not sure if it's supposed to be a warning or not. "Anyway, good chat."

Dyson walks away, and Nick shakes his head.

"He can't help his honesty, even if it's brutal."

"Lots of reality checks tonight," I mutter.

We refill our drinks and escape outside to the firepit. The cool evening breeze feels amazing after being in the crowded house that's full of conversations that feel too real at times. We both let out a sigh, then chuckle.

"This is better," I say as he settles on a log bench.

The fire crackles, casting shadows across Nick's face. He pulls me onto his lap, and I lean against him.

"Much better," he says, wrapping his arms around my waist, his chin leaning on my shoulder. "Sorry about my brothers. Neither of them has a filter, but they mean well."

I reposition myself where I can see his honey-brown eyes. "Was what Dyson said true? About your usual type?"

Nick studies me in the firelight. "Yeah. I think it is true."

"Is that a warning he gives to everyone?" I ask.

"Not that one," he admits. "That was a new revelation."

We sit in the silence, watching the flames flicker upward.

"You live like you're happy," Nick says. "It inspires me."

"I am happy," I admit. "Right now is all we have, all we're guaranteed. Are you happy?"

He leans closer, and I think he's going to kiss me when an angry voice cuts through the moment.

"I don't give a shit about Kendall!" Patterson storms past us, phone pressed to his ear, pacing near the tree line. "No, she's Satan. If she's there, I won't be! I don't care if I have to play. I don't want her at any of my games. I don't want to be anywhere near her. Not after what she did to Jameson."

He sees us, waves apologetically, but keeps pacing.

"Addison, you just don't get it—" His voice fades as he moves farther away.

"Who's Kendall?" I ask, noticing Patterson is worked up.

"She's his brother's ex-fiancée," Nick explains, pulling me back against him. "His sister, Addison, just moved back to the city and has been hanging out with Kendall every weekend. They're basically inseparable."

"Sounds like drama."

"Oh, it is. Patterson and Kendall have this weird hate thing. They can't be in the same room together. It's been going on for about five years."

"So, lots of unresolved sexual tension."

Nick laughs, his chest rumbling against my back. "Don't let him hear you say that—ever. He'll lose his shit and crash out."

"You know what they say when a man doth protest too much …"

"What's that?"

"He wants insideth her panties."

Nick's still laughing when Harper appears.

"Cake time, soulmates! I've been told to grab everyone."

We ignore the nickname, but we get up.

Patterson continues to argue in the shadows as we head inside. It makes me wonder what the real story is.

"Oh, Kendall is also our coach's daughter and about seven years younger than him," he whispers in my ear.

"Oh, damn. This *is* juicy drama."

"Or is it moist?" He chuckles.

"Ew, don't ever say that again," I tell him as he opens the door for me.

Once we're back inside, we gather around the table as we sing "Happy Birthday." Zane and Autumn are wearing their Pumpkin King and Queen crowns, which I'm sure was one hundred percent *her* idea. The chocolate cakes Harper brought are arranged beautifully on the counter. They're so pretty that they almost shouldn't be eaten. Autumn whispers something in Zane's ear that makes him grin wickedly.

Nick feeds me a bite of cake, and then he leans forward, kissing icing off my lips. It's not performative. I hum against him.

When he pulls away, he stiffens in front of me.

"Mom?" He stands a little straighter. "I didn't know you were coming."

"Surprise!" she says.

My stomach drops. His *mother*. I'm meeting his mother, and her first impression is that my mouth was locked with her son's. Not to mention, I'm slightly drunk on purple punch.

"Ambrose wanted to see Zane. A little birdie named Asher told me you were in town, and I wanted to see you. I've been worried about you, Nicky, but it seems like you're doing fine."

"I am, Mom. I'm doing great. Oh, I want you to meet Julie."

Her smile is exactly like Nick's, and I can tell she doesn't miss details by the way she's studying me. She's elegant in a way that makes me very aware of my flushed cheeks and messy hair.

"She's my girlfriend," Nick says so casually that I almost believe it myself.

"We're just friends," I blurt, the purple punch making me too honest. I don't want to lie to his mother under these circumstances.

"Yeah?" Nick's voice carries something I can't identify.

The room seems to pause. Asher clears his throat dramatically, like he overheard our entire conversation.

"Attention, everyone! Quick vote!" He's grinning mischievously. "Who here thinks Julie is Nick's girlfriend?"

I watch as every single hand goes up. Autumn, Blaire, Zane, Dyson, Asher, Patterson from across the room, and even people I haven't officially met cast a vote.

"Great! Who thinks they're just friends?"

My hand rises alone in a sea of smiles.

"Thanks for participating." Asher smirks.

I open my mouth but can't find words.

"Well, whatever you are, congratulations." Nick's mom smiles, and I immediately relax. "Autumn raves about your chocolate croissants. Says they're the best in Colorado."

"She's too kind," I manage. My voice is much steadier than I feel. "The secret's in my great-great-grandma's dough recipe."

"We're staying at our cabin through the holidays. You two should come to dinner soon."

"You're not going back to New York?" Nick sounds shocked.

"Honey, I like the city as much as you do," she says with the perfect amount of sarcasm.

Zane's dad calls her over, and she gives Nick a hug. "Please don't be a stranger."

"Okay," he tells her with a smile. "I won't."

After his parents leave, the party continues, but I feel like the ground shifted while I wasn't paying attention. Everyone sees something that I keep denying. Or maybe they know what I'm too afraid to admit.

Before I can speak, Blaire appears, definitely tipsy now. "There you are! Jules, we're doing shots!"

"I think I've had enough purple punch," I tell her with a laugh, not wanting to take a trip to Wastedville tonight.

"Lightweight," she teases, then looks between us. "Oh, am I interrupting something?"

"No," I say, but Nick's hand slowly finds mine, and the slightest touch from him causes goose bumps to trail up my arm.

"Actually," he says, levelheaded, "I think we're going to head out."

"Already?" Autumn appears, carrying empty cake plates. "We've barely seen you."

"Because you're popular," Nick points out.

And I'm happy for the escape, especially with him.

Nick tells Zane, Patterson, and his brothers goodbye.

I follow Autumn to the sink, where she sets down the plates.

She turns to me and gives me a tight hug. "I'm so happy for you."

"Stop," I whisper, but I can't stop grinning.

"This looks good on you."

"What?" I ask.

"Love."

Before I can say anything, Nick comes over and slides his hand in mine. "Ready?"

"Yes, so ready," I say, happy he can read me so easily.

"Have fun, you two!" Autumn tells us.

We move through the house and walk out onto the porch.

"Better?" he asks.

I nod.

"Zane and Autumn rented limos to drive everyone back to Cozy Creek or to the resort, where several people are staying," Nick tells me, leading me toward one.

"What about your Range Rover?" I ask.

"I'll come get it tomorrow."

We climb into the back of the car, and Nick wraps his arm around me as we drive away.

"This feels like the twilight zone, doesn't it?" I ask.

"Kinda, but in a good way." He glances at me, his face illuminated by passing streetlights.

The truth sits between us as we stare at one another, and then our lips crash together.

At first, our kisses are soft, lingering, but they quickly turn to desperation.

We have a little over a month to figure this out, but time is flying by.

And all I can think right now is how I don't know how I'm going to give him up.

Nick Banks has quickly become my new addiction.

15

NICK

The limo pulls up to Julie's condo, and neither of us moves to get out. We've been kissing like teenagers for the entire ride, only breaking apart when we needed air. The driver clears his throat for the second time.

"We should go inside," Julie whispers against my mouth, but her hands are still fisted in my shirt.

"We should," I agree, kissing her again.

When we finally stumble out of the limo and into her place, the fire between us is scorching. After Harper's prophecy, after everyone voting that we're together, after my mother meeting Julie, and my brothers giving their approvals—everything feels different. More real. It's almost terrifying that I can imagine spending more time with her.

Julie kicks off her heels and turns to face me. "What are we doing?"

"I don't know," I admit, moving closer. "Do you?"

"No," she whispers.

"We can stop. We can walk away."

"That's not possible." She takes a step toward me. "Letting you run away from me is the last thing I want, unless you're having doubts."

"No doubts, sweetheart."

She searches my face, then decides. "Come upstairs with me."

Julie takes my hand, leading me to the top of the stairs and into her bedroom.

She turns to face me, green eyes sparkling. Her fingers play with the zipper of her Dior dress. Slowly, she unzips it, letting the material fall and pool at her feet.

My breath catches when I see the lingerie set I bought her. It highlights every gorgeous curve.

"You're stunning." I breathe out. I run my fingers along the lace at her hip. "You know exactly what you're doing to me."

"And?" She starts unbuttoning my shirt. "You're just as guilty."

My phone rings, and we freeze.

"Please make it stop," she says, capturing my lips.

I forget what we were even discussing, but my phone keeps vibrating.

After five missed calls, I pull it out to see Patterson's name on the screen.

I answer. "What?"

"I can't get into the cabin," he says.

"Four-seven-eight-two," I say, then end the call, turning my phone off.

Julie pushes my shirt off my shoulders, and it joins her dress on the floor.

I back her toward the bed and lay her down. That's when *her* phone starts ringing.

"Ignore it," I say, pulling her to the edge, kissing between her thighs.

But it rings again. And again. And a-fucking-gain.

Julie groans and sits up.

She grabs her phone from her dress pocket on the floor. "It's Autumn."

She answers and puts it on speaker. "This'd better be life or death."

"Put Nick on," Zane states.

"What do you want?" I ask.

"Patterson's calling everyone. He's locked out of your cabin and about to break a window. Deal with it before the cops get called. That's the last thing any of us needs."

"Can't you—"

"No. He's *your* hockey friend. I'm sending a car to get you since your Range Rover is here. Be ready in five minutes."

The line goes dead.

Julie flops back on the bed, still in that lingerie, looking like every fantasy I've ever had.

"You have to go, don't you?" she asks.

I join her on the bed. "I don't want to."

I place my hand on her hip, watching her breath catch.

She pulls me down for a kiss that makes me groan.

"Do you really have to?" she asks.

"I want to tell him to sleep outside," I admit against her lips. "He will break windows though. We don't need a headline about the billionaire who trashed the rental."

"Fine," she says, twisting her body to push me down onto my back. A moment later, Julie is crawling onto my lap and straddling me. I place my hands behind her back and watch her, grinding against my rock-hard cock. "I want you so bad."

"Jules," I say, barely able to speak.

The only things keeping us apart are my clothes and her extremely thin panties. A grunt releases from me as her breathing increases. We can't stop kissing, can't stop touching, and she keeps going. If Julie keeps this up, she might find her end.

Right before I think she might lose herself, a car honks outside with two quick beeps.

"No," she whispers, defeated. She's breathing heavy in my ear, her lips swollen.

"I'm so sorry. I don't want to leave."

"You have to." She climbs off of me, and when I stand, it's like I have a damn circus tent in my pants. "Please go, before I beg you to stay."

"Look what you do to me." I bend down to kiss her. "Rain check, I promise."

Twenty minutes later, I'm at Riverside, letting a very drunk Patterson inside.

"You're a lifesaver," he slurs. "The door *hates* me. Almost punched my fist through it."

"The door's fine. You were putting in the wrong code, which is why it locked you out for twenty minutes."

"Bullshit! Four-eight-seven-two."

"No, dumbass, it's four-seven-eight-two."

"Oh." He crashes on the couch, face down. "Whoops."

I move to the window and see if his rental car is outside, but it looks like he had a limo drop him off.

"Fuck," I whisper.

When I turn around, Patterson's already snoring.

I go upstairs to the main bedroom and sit on the edge of the mattress.

NICK

I had fun today.

JULIE

I did too.

NICK

Patterson's already passed out. I'm going to bitch him out tomorrow.

JULIE

He deserves it.

NICK

I can't stop thinking about you in that lingerie.

JULIE

I'm still wearing it.

NICK

Don't tease me.

She sends a photo of herself from a side angle. She's in bed, showing just a hint of black lace against her skin.

NICK

You're playing with fire.

JULIE

Maybe I want to burn.

NICK

Tell me what you're doing right now.

JULIE

Lying in bed. Still in the lingerie you bought me. Thinking about your hands on me. Squeezing my thighs together.

NICK

I'm so fucking hard, thinking about you.

JULIE

Show me.

As I get ready to snap her a picture, my phone rings, and it's a FaceTime call.

"Hi," she says when I answer.

The screen lights up, her face glowing like an angel, but I know better. She's no saint. Not tonight. Her lips part, and I can already see the flush creeping up her neck. She's nervous. Good. I like her timid, unsure, but willing. So damn willing.

She's propped up against her pillows, the black lace perfect against her skin. Her nipples poke through the fabric, hard and begging for my mouth. Julie moves the camera lower. Her legs are spread just enough to let me catch a glimpse of her through the sheer fabric that she's soaked.

I flip the camera around and show her exactly how much she affects me.

"God, Nick." Her breath catches. "This is torture."

"Touch yourself," I say. "Let me see."

"Only if you do too." Her voice is soft. "I've never done this before."

I smirk, leaning back on the mattress. The sight of her has me throbbing. "I know, sweetheart. That's why I'm gonna make it good for you. You trust me?"

"Yes." She nods, biting her lower lip.

"Take your panties off for me," I order, my voice rough, desperate even. "Show me what's mine."

She props her phone up on a pillow, then hooks her fingers into the waistband of her panties, pulling them down her legs and tossing them away. Then she repositions the phone, putting me back between her legs. The sight of her bare, almost breaks me.

"Good girl." I growl. "Now, I want you to do exactly what I say. No rushing. No coming until I tell you. Understand?"

"Yes." She bites her bottom lip, and I love how eager she is to do this with me.

Fuck, I can't wait to ruin her.

"I'm so turned on," she whispers, and it's music to my ears.

"Touch yourself," I say. "Slowly. Just like that."

She rubs circles on her clit, her hips rocking with her so slowly and sensually.

"Now slide your fingers over your hole, sweetheart, before returning back to that clit. Damn, you're so wet. And you look so damn beautiful, teasing your wet little cunt."

"Yes," she whimpers.

"One finger, Jules. And curl it."

She does as told. Her finger traces the outer edge of her slit before she plunges inside.

"You feel that at the end? That's your G-spot, sweetheart. Massage it."

Her breath is coming faster now. "I've never felt that before."

"Mmm. Enjoy the sensation. That's it. Palm your clit and rock up into it," I encourage her. "Tell me how it feels."

"It's … it's so much," she whispers. "I want you. I want you so bad."

"I know you do," I mutter. My cock aches with need. "But don't you dare come, Jules."

Her head falls back as she moans softly, and she takes her time working herself. "Oh God," she whimpers.

"You want more, don't you?" I ask.

"Yes," she admits.

"Good. Add another finger for me. Show me how you fuck yourself when you think about me."

Her free hand grips the edge of the bed as she adds a second finger, her moans growing louder, more desperate.

"I can't keep going," she says breathlessly. "I'm already too close."

"Not yet," I tell her. "But let's go to the very edge together."

Her body trembles with need. "Please," she begs, her fingers working her cunt furiously. "Please, let me come."

"Patience is a virtue," I say.

"And what if I don't listen?"

"Then I'll punish you," I say.

"Oh my God. Is this domination play at the same time?"

I give her a simple nod.

She squeals.

"Try me, Jules. That pussy pulses, and I will refuse to see you for a week."

She laughs. "Okay. I'll be a good girl and follow the rules."

Her motions slow, but I notice how her mouth falls open and her breathing grows more ragged.

"How does that feel?"

"So damn good, but I wish it were you."

"You're so beautiful," I say, my cock twitching at the sight. "Now, taste yourself, sweetheart. Describe it to me."

Her cheeks flush crimson, but she does it, sliding her fingers between her lips. Her eyes lock on mine. I can hear the soft suck of her mouth, the way her tongue swirls around her fingers. Her red lips glisten with saliva.

"Good girl," I mutter. "Now bring those wet fingers back to your swollen little clit. Say hello."

"I want you to do this with me," she says between pants.

My hand slips under the waistband of my boxers to grip my cock. It's hot and heavy in my palm, pre-cum already beading at the tip.

I turn the screen around to show her. "Look what you do to me, Julie."

I rub my thumb across the tip, showing her what she desperately wants to see.

"Proof that you're under my skin."

"It's mutual." She bites her lip, circling her clit with teasing strokes. "After you left, I was thinking about how badly I want your cock inside me. How, tonight, I wanted you to fuck me so hard that I wouldn't be able to walk at work tomorrow. I fantasize about you."

I stroke myself, my eyes locked on her. "Tell me what you want me to do."

"I want you to pin me down on the mattress." She moans, her fingers slipping inside herself, moving in time with my hand, just how I taught her.

She continues, "I want you to … spread my legs … and bury your face in my pussy until … I'm screaming. Then I want you to flip me over and take me from behind, spanking my ass until it's red and raw."

"You think you can handle that?" I offer, my hips thrusting into my fist.

"Yes."

She's writhing now, her fingers moving faster, her pussy so wet that I can hear the sound. "Shit, I'm so, so close …"

"Pull away," I tell her. "No coming until I say."

She does slowly, carefully, like she's afraid I'll vanish if she doesn't. "I'm throbbing for you."

"Show me," I demand, and she does.

"I need you." Her breasts rise and fall.

I'm still stroking myself, my balls tightening. "Back to your clit, babe."

She returns her hand, doing slow circles as desperate pants escape her. I can tell the orgasm is building because her entire body tenses.

"Are you close?" I ask.

"Are you?"

"Yes," I admit. "Can you come for me on the count of three?"

She bites her bottom lip.

"One." I wait at least ten seconds. "Two."

"Please," she whispers.

I smirk like the devil. "Waiting for that next number, aren't you?"

She slows her pace, nearly straining as my orgasm builds like a storm at sea.

Her back arches off the mattress. When I see she's stranded on the very edge, I wait five more seconds, then speak.

"Three," I tell her.

She groans out, and I can't hold back my release any longer. The orgasm crashes over me, and I forget that I'm not alone as I moan out. Ropes of thick, hot cum spill all over my stomach. Her body convulses as she cries out. Her fingers stay buried deep inside her pussy. Watching her come apart on-screen, hearing her moan my name, knowing she's watching me do the same—it wrecks me. We're desperate, needy, as the sexual frustration pours out through our phones.

"Julie." I groan, my vision blurring as I ride out the wave of pleasure.

Her breathing is ragged, body still trembling as she looks at me. "That was …" A satisfied smile lingers on her face. "Incredible. Thanks for busting my phone-sex cherry. I want to do it again."

"Right now?"

She laughs. "Um … no. But that's an option?"

"Yes," I say, chuckling. "I aim to satisfy even the greediest of girls."

"Oh my. You'd better stop, or I'm coming over tonight."

"It's too late for that. I'll see you tomorrow."

She gives me an adorable pouty face. "Do we have plans?"

"No, but I have a fall bucket list item I want to check off, and I thought you'd be a good person to ask to join me."

"Oh, where?"

"You're so damn pretty," I say, grinning. "The apple orchard."

"I love Coleman's. I would love to join you."

"Do you have to work?" I ask.

"Not tomorrow. It's my day off."

"Great. I'll pick you up around lunch. Let's go on a picnic."

"Aw, I'm excited," she says, then tries to hold back a yawn. "Sorry."

"You should go to sleep, sweetheart."

"I'm not ready to say goodbye yet."

"You don't have to," I say, cleaning myself. I walk to the dresser and pull out a pair of joggers. "I'll be here until you drift off."

"Okay," she tells me, turning onto her side, propping the phone up on a pillow.

I climb into bed, imagining lying next to her, holding her, and smelling how pretty she is.

Julie closes her eyes. "Tell me about your first love."

"Oh, wow, I haven't thought about her in a very long time." I laugh. "She was older than me by, like, two years. She was a senior when I was a sophomore. I played varsity football, and she was in the band. A saxophone player. She was the first person I ever felt love for, and when she broke up with me to go to college, I was devastated."

"Did she ever reach out to you again?" she asks.

"Yeah, once I signed my contract with the Angels to play. But I'd already moved on," I say. "Every relationship I've ever been in has taught me something."

"What do you think this lesson will be?" she asks.

"Not to give up." The truth tumbles out of my mouth.

"Yeah, that's perfect."

I continue chatting about my hockey days and training, and she eventually falls asleep.

I end the call, then lie in the dark, thinking about her, about us, about what we just did.

We were vulnerable, open, entirely focused on each other.

I think about Harper's prediction and know I'm falling in love with Julie Loveland.

No, I've already fallen. I don't need forty days to decide if I want more time with her, but she needs it. Being together would be a big step for both of us, but we'd figure it out. Whatever it took ... I'd do it.

Tomorrow at the apple orchard, we'll be one day closer to decision time. We have time, even if the universe is cockblocking us.

It will be just us, the autumn air, and the truth we've been dancing around since the moment we met.

16

JULIE

Sunlight streams through my bedroom window as my eyes flutter open. Last night was like a fever dream. Between the party, Harper's prophecy, meeting his family, the frustration of being interrupted twice, and then the FaceTime call. Oh God.

I feel my cheeks heat just thinking about it. I don't know this adventurous woman I am when I'm with him, but that was the point of my list.

My phone dings on the nightstand, and I see it's just past ten in the morning. I bolt out of bed, realizing I haven't slept this late in years.

NICK

Morning, beautiful. Still on for apple picking?

JULIE

Yes. What time?

NICK

When you're ready. Patterson's still passed out. Going to leave him here with a note, telling him to fuck off. And the code.

I laugh, already climbing out of bed.

JULIE

Poor Patterson.

NICK

Poor Patterson, nothing. His timing is absolute shit. Be there in 30?

JULIE

Make it 45. I need coffee and a shower.

NICK

Take your time. See you soon!

JULIE

Perfect.

I shower, my mind drifting to his hands, his voice telling me exactly what to do last night. It's only been six days since we started this fake-dating thing. Six days. That's nothing. So, why does it feel like so much more?

It's because this invisible string has kept us tethered together for a year.

When Nick arrives, his hair is a mess, like he just ran his fingers through it. My eyes slide down his white button-up and dark slacks. Somehow, he's sophisticatedly casual.

"Hi," I say, suddenly shy.

"Hi, yourself." He steps inside and gently pulls me against him. "I need to kiss you."

"Please," I whisper.

His mouth captures mine, and I lose track of reality. Our tongues slide together, and I'm tempted to pull him to the couch with me. Before I gain the courage, he pulls away. We're both breathing too hard, and we're too heated.

"Ready?" he asks.

"After that? I don't ever want to leave."

"Well, I kinda rented the orchard for us."

My eyes widen. "The entire thing?"

"Yeah," he admits. "I wanted it to be private. I don't want wandering eyes."

I can't help but smile. "I can't believe this. You just asked them how much they'd take?"

"I asked them how much they made per day, and I told them I'd triple it if they gave us the afternoon."

I'm shocked.

He shakes his head. "You're so damn cute."

The drive to Coleman's Orchard is filled with comfortable silence, his hand on my thigh the entire time.

Mrs. Coleman greets us at the entrance with a knowing smile.

"I was wondering if you were bluffing," she tells Nick. "Nice to see you, Julie."

"Hi, Mrs. Coleman. This is my boyfriend, Nick," I say, sitting forward to chat with her.

The entire Coleman family moved to Colorado from Oklahoma several decades ago and started this farm. It's been here my whole life.

"Nice to meet you," he says, and it amazes me how damn charming he is without even trying.

She notices me staring at him.

"Well, you two go ahead and drive through. Going to lock the gate behind you. The Honeycrisp apples are perfect right now. Back section, row fifteen. Very private with lots of shade." She winks.

I'm mortified, but Nick grins, taking the gathering baskets she offers us.

After we park, he grabs the picnic basket from the back before reaching for my hand.

We wander deep into the orchard, the mid-morning sun filtering through leaves that are starting to turn gold. When I look over at him, I capture the moment in my memory. I want to remember how he smiles at me and how our fingers brush together as we walk. I don't think I've ever felt this way about a man before.

The thought should scare me, but when he looks at me like this, I'm like a moth to a flame. At least the end will be beautiful.

Row fifteen is completely secluded, surrounded by tall grass and wildflowers.

He lays out the checkered blanket and places the picnic basket on top to keep it from blowing away in the cool breeze.

We take our time picking apples, filling our wicker baskets while stealing glances and touches. The tension between us builds with every accidental brush of fingers, every moment our eyes meet.

"Have you ever done this before?" I ask as he lifts me up to reach one.

"Nope," he admits. "It's a first."

I smile. "I like knowing there are still things reserved for us."

He chuckles. "Oh, I've had many firsts with you, sweetheart."

"Yeah? Like what?"

"Well, for starters, I've never ordered or drank a pumpkin spice latte until yours."

I gasp. "No way."

"Swear," he says. "I don't particularly care for bougie drinks. But if you make it, I'm drinking it."

That shouldn't mean that much to me, but it does.

"What else?"

"I've never done yoga in my life."

This makes me giggle.

Once our baskets are full, we make our way back to the blanket in the shade between two overhanging trees. Sunlight reflects through the branches.

We settle beside one another, and Nick unpacks the lunch he brought. He made fancy sandwiches, and he also has several containers of cut strawberries and grapes, several different cheeses, and a bottle of apple cider from the orchard.

I snag a grape and pop it in my mouth as he hands me a clear plastic cup of cider.

The sweetness dances on my tongue.

"You thought of everything," I say, watching him arrange the food between us.

"I wanted today to be perfect." He pours himself some cider. "No interruptions, no onlookers, no cosmic interference. Just us."

We eat, talking about everything and nothing. He tells me about morning practices on frozen rinks and about the adrenaline of playoff games, and I realize how much he misses playing. I tell him about early mornings at the coffee shop, about the comfort of routine, and my fear of being stuck in life.

"Can I tell you something?" he asks.

"Of course," I say as we pick up the food, putting it away.

"When I saw you that night at Bookers, something in me recognized you. Like my soul was saying, *Oh, there you are.* I tried to ignore it, tried to forget when I left. But then January happened, and now ..." He trails off.

My heart races.

"I'm not asking you to say anything back," he says quickly. "We have weeks to figure this out. Our deadline still exists. I just need you to know this isn't new. It seems like it's happening fast, but I think it's been a long time coming."

I move closer to him. "I get that. I felt it too."

"Yeah?"

Instead of answering, I kiss him. What starts timid turns desperate. His hands tangle in my hair as I shift to straddle his lap.

"Jules," he breathes against my mouth.

"I need you," I whisper. "Please. I can't wait anymore."

"Here?" But his hands are already under my sweater, finding bare skin.

"Here. Now." I'm practically begging, grinding against him. "No more interruptions. No more waiting."

He groans, flipping us so I'm on my back on the blanket. The sun filters through the apple trees above us as he pulls my sweater off, then his shirt.

"You're so beautiful." His mouth finds my neck. "So perfect."

We're frantic, desperate. The foreplay made us animalistic. When he reaches for his pocket, he freezes.

"I didn't plan for this," he admits.

"I don't care," I gasp, pulling him back down. "I'm on birth control. I haven't been with anyone since Craig over a year ago."

"I haven't been with anyone since I met you." He searches my face.

"Really?" I ask, almost shocked.

"Yes," he breathes, capturing my mouth again.

His hands are everywhere, desperate and as greedy as his mouth. We undress each other with shaking fingers, clothes scattered across the blanket. When he sees me fully naked in the sunlight, he pauses.

"You're mine," he whispers, and his eyes flash with need.

He lays me down on my back, and the blanket underneath me is rough against my bare ass. As he kisses up my neck, the cool autumn air nips at my flushed skin.

As he pulls away, positioning himself between my thighs, I lift myself upright onto my elbows. His thick cock is hard and leaking pre-cum, glistening in the sunlight. I can smell him, and I want to taste him. It's a heady mixture of masculine and expensive cologne.

When he looks at me like I'm everything he's ever wanted, it makes my cunt pulse with need.

I reach for him, pulling him down to me.

He kisses me deeply as he settles at my entrance, still not giving me what I want. There is nothing else in the entire world that matters right now. I breathe out, anticipating him, needing him with my legs spread wide. He grins against my lips.

"You're so wet for me." He growls.

His fingers trail over my slit, teasing me, spreading my folds. I gasp as he circles my clit, sending electric jolts through my body.

"You want this cock, don't you?"

"Yes," I moan, my voice full of need. "Give yourself to me, Nick."

He slides a finger inside me, curling it just right, hitting that sweet spot that makes me arch off the blanket. My cunt clenches around him, greedy for more.

"Not yet," he whispers, his breath hot against my neck. "I'm gonna make you beg first."

He adds another finger, thrusting them in and out of me, his pace quickening. I can feel the pressure building, my pussy getting tighter, wetter. His thumb rubs circles on my clit, and I'm panting, my hips bucking against his hand.

"I'm gonna—"

He slowly pulls his fingers out, leaving me aching.

He repositions himself between my legs, the head of his cock pressing against my entrance. Nick leans down, his lips brushing against mine.

"Nicolas Banks, fuck me," I state, my hands clawing at his back.

He thrusts into me hard, burying himself to the hilt in one smooth stroke. I cry out, the fullness overwhelming. He pauses, letting me adjust, his breath warm against my skin.

"You're tight." He groans, his voice strained.

"You're too big," I muster. "I feel like you're breaking me in two."

"We'll go slow. I'll let you get used to me carving my path. It will never be like this with anyone else," he tells me.

"I know," I say, my eyes squeezing closed as he moves slowly.

He pulls almost all the way out before pushing back in. Each thrust hits me deep. I moan, my nails digging into his shoulders, as he picks up the pace.

"Harder," I beg, my voice shaking. "Please, harder. It feels really good."

He slams into me, not picking up the pace, just thrusting deeper. He stretches me wide, hitting me just right. The orgasm coils tighter, and my control is ready to snap. His fingers find my clit again, rubbing it as he pounds into me relentlessly.

"Oh, oh, Nick. Keep doing that," I whimper, the build happening fast.

The sensation of him inside me with nothing between us is overwhelming. The sun warms our skin, and the apple-scented air surrounds us.

"You feel …" He can't finish.

"I know." I gasp, wrapping my legs tighter around him. "I can't describe it either."

What we're doing is something else entirely. Every thrust, every kiss, every whispered word breaks down another wall between us. Everything ceases to exist outside of this.

"Look at me," he says, and when I do, the expression on his face breaks something open in my chest.

"Nick," I moan, getting close to seeing actual stars. "I'm so close."

"Let go for me, sweetheart," he whispers.

"I want you to come with me," I breathlessly say.

I can feel the pressure building until it's unbearable.

He doesn't stop, his thrusts becoming erratic, his breathing ragged.

"I will," he promises, slamming into me one last time before he stills, his cock pulsing inside me as he fills me full.

My body tenses, my cunt clamping down around him, and then it happens. I scream as my orgasm hits me, waves of pleasure crashing over me as I squirt all over his cock, soaking the blanket beneath us. It's intense, like nothing I've ever experienced, and I don't recognize the sound coming out of me.

We're a tangled mess of sweat and satisfaction. We stay joined, breathing hard, foreheads pressed together. I can feel him still pulsing inside me, along with the warmth of what we just shared.

"That was …" I can't find words.

"Everything," he finishes.

I can still feel him between my thighs and know where he's been, will be evident later. But right now, the world feels different, like that one experience changed it all.

"We just …" I trail off.

"I know," he whispers.

His cock slips out of me, and I can feel him dripping down my thighs. He kisses me, his hands roaming over my body before he helps clean me with some paper towels from the picnic basket.

"You're a dream," he says as we get dressed.

I grin, my body still tingling with aftershocks of having him exactly how I wanted him. "And you're a fantasy."

The clouds cast shadows on the orchard as we gather the picnic supplies. We're both aware that we've crossed a line we can't uncross.

"Stay with me tonight?" I ask.

"I'd love to," he says. "I want to wake up with you in my arms tomorrow."

Butterflies flutter inside me. "I want that too."

As we drive back, I keep glancing at him, at our joined hands, thinking about what just happened.

It was a claim. A promise. A beginning to something that feels bigger than both of us. And we both know it.

"Something just changed," I whisper. My head is still screaming that six days is too fast; my heart is whispering that maybe time doesn't matter when you find your person.

"Everything did," he says. "But we have time. I'm not going anywhere."

As we drive on the outskirts of Cozy Creek, Nick glances at me. "We should stop at the cabin," he says. "I need to grab some things if I'm staying with you."

"Sure. You can turn up here on this road. It connects," I tell him.

Six minutes later, we pull up to Riverside, and Patterson's rental car is there.

Nick kisses my fingers. "Come in with me?"

I nod.

Inside, Patterson is sprawled on the couch, playing on his phone.

"There you are!" He sits upright when he sees Nick. "Dude, I've been texting you all day."

"I was busy. Visited the orchard," Nick says, and then I step into view.

Patterson's eyes land on me, taking in my messy hair, swollen lips, and the way Nick's hand rests possessively on my lower back.

A knowing grin spreads across his face.

"Yeah?" He waggles his eyebrows. "How 'bout them apples?"

"Patterson," Nick says, rolling his eyes. "Grow up."

My cheeks burn.

"Oh, I'm staying at Julie's tonight."

"Great! I'm having a party and inviting all the local single ladies," Patterson says with a laugh.

"No parties, please. The woman who rented to me lives two houses down, and she's watching the place, trust me."

He stands up, moves to the kitchen, and opens the fridge. "I'll invite her in to hang out with us."

"I'll be right back," Nick says, disappearing upstairs to pack a bag, leaving me alone with Patterson.

"You're good for him," Patterson says, his tone serious. The flirty, suave attitude is gone. "I've never seen him like this."

"Wait, you can just turn it off like that?"

He grins. "Don't break my friend's heart, okay? I don't think he can handle that right now."

"Him handle it? Are you kidding me? I'm more worried about him breaking mine," I admit.

Patterson shakes his head. "You don't see the way he looks at you when you're not watching. I've never seen him like this, and we've been friends for fifteen years."

Before I can respond, Nick returns with a duffel bag.

"Ready?" he asks.

"Yeah."

"Bye, Jules. Nice chat."

I meet his eyes. "Nice chat."

As we drive to my place, I think about what Patterson said.

"You're quiet," Nick observes.

"Just thinking."

"About?"

"About how we're supposed to be fake dating."

He pulls onto the street in front of my condo and turns to me. "No decisions. One day at a time."

"Nick …"

"You already know how this ends."

"How?"

He shoots me a wink. "You know."

My heart pounds as we head inside.

Nick Banks is staying with me, we just made love in an apple orchard, and nothing about this feels temporary anymore.

As he sets his bag in my bedroom, he pulls me against him.

"Still no regrets?" he asks.

"None," I whisper. "You?"

"Only that it took us this long."

"It's been six days," I whisper.

"It's been eleven months," he says.

And as he kisses me again, it's full of promise, and I realize then that we're not pretending.

Were we ever?

17

―――――

NICK

I wake to the weight of Julie pressed against my side.

For a moment, I'm disoriented, knowing this isn't my penthouse. Then I remember I'm in Julie's bed and what we did last night.

A smile touches my lips as I realize I'm waking up next to her for the first time. I'll never get to experience this again.

She's still asleep, red hair fanned across the pillow. I can feel her breath against my shoulder. I think about yesterday at the orchard and the sunlight against her skin.

"I can feel you staring," she mutters without opening her eyes, then smiles.

"How?"

"Your breathing changed." She stretches like a cat, pressing closer. "What time is it?"

I reach over and check my phone. "Just after seven."

"Shit." Her eyes fly open. "I have to be at work—"

"Sierra is covering your morning shift," I remind her. "You texted her last night, remember?"

She relaxes back against me. "Right. I'm not used to taking any time off."

"Maybe you should get used to it. I've heard having work-life balance is important."

"Yeah? Teach me how."

I wrap my arms around her, pulling her closer against me. "I'm trying."

She stares at my mouth. "Waking up to you is my new favorite thing."

"Me too, sweetheart."

We lie here for a moment, just holding each other. I run my fingers through her hair, and it's surreal, being with her like this.

I feel alive, to the point I want to stand on the balcony attached to her bedroom and scream it for the entire town to hear.

"I should shower," she says, but doesn't move.

"We could share," I suggest. "Conserve water."

She laughs. "We already marked it off my list."

"Partially," I tell her. "We didn't define what sex is."

She kisses me. "Join me?"

"Lead the way."

She slips out of bed, completely naked and gorgeous in the morning light. Julie is a goddess.

I follow her to the bathroom, already half-hard.

The shower is small, forcing us to press close under the spray. Julie tips her head back, water streaming over her.

"You're staring again," she says.

"Can't help it." I reach for her body wash and loofah, wanting to touch her all over. "Sometimes, I find it hard to believe you're real and that we're here."

She places her hands against the tiles, and I start at her shoulders, massaging as I go. She moans when I work out a knot.

"That feels amazing."

My hands slide lower, over her breasts, her stomach. When I reach between her legs, she gasps.

I kiss her neck, fingers teasing. "Let me take care of you."

I slide two fingers inside her, and she rocks back against me.

"See? Getting you all clean."

"From the inside out."

I work her until she's shaking. When I feel her getting close, I turn her around and drop to my knees. I spread her legs wider and taste her. Her hands immediately tangle in my wet hair. A broken moan escapes her as I take my time, learning what makes her gasp, what makes her pull my hair harder.

Before she comes, I stand up and turn her around. "Palms flat on the wall."

She does as I said, and then seconds later, I thrust deep inside of her. She screams out with satisfaction as I wrap my arm around her waist, holding her tight.

I don't stop, holding her steady as she arches her ass for me, creating more friction. Her cries echo off the bathroom walls as she comes. I chase my release, following behind her.

"Wow," she pants out as I lean forward, kissing her neck and ear. "Is this real?"

"Hell yes, it is."

She turns around, her back against the wall. She looks up into my eyes and smiles. Julie opens her mouth to say something, and before she can get it out, I hear pounding on her door.

"Are you expecting someone?"

"No." Julie groans.

The knock comes again—harder.

"Maybe they'll go away," I suggest.

"Julie Marie! I know you're home!" A woman's voice carries through the house.

Julie's eyes widen. "Oh no, that's my mother."

"Your—"

"Where are you at, sweetie?"

The front door opens and closes.

"Shit, shit, shit." Julie scrambles out of the shower, grabbing a towel. "She's inside. My mom has a key."

"What?"

"Get dressed. *Now.*"

"Your dad and I are here," she announces.

As she rushes to dry off, I hear the creak of the stairs being taken to the second floor, where Julie's room is.

Her eyes go wide. She throws me a towel. "Let me get rid of them."

I smirk. "Breathe. You're a thirty-five-year-old woman."

"True. But I'll always be their innocent little girl."

"Innocent? Give me a damn break." I steal a kiss.

Her eyes scan down my body.

"I want more of that later."

"My point," I tell her. "You're no angel."

"I'm coming up!" her mom says. "Hope you're decent."

"Go," I say, but not before I pull her against me, kissing her.

Footsteps traveling down the short hallway have us scrambling. They're heading straight toward us.

When we break apart, I rush to pull on my clothes.

"Julie?" Her mom's voice is closer now. "I brought breakfast from the shop and—oh!"

Julie steps out of the bathroom, shutting the door behind her.

"Mom. Dad," Julie says suspiciously. "Can we go downstairs?"

"Are you alone?" her mom asks.

"Uh, I ..."

I take this as my cue and open the door.

A woman who looks like an older version of Julie—same red hair, same green eyes—stands at the doorway. Behind her is a tall man with graying hair and suspicious eyes.

"I'm Nick." I step forward, offering my hand. "Nick Banks. Nice to meet you both."

Julie might explode from embarrassment, and I find it adorable.

Her mom's eyes light up. "Oh! You must be *the boyfriend* everyone has told us about!"

"Everyone?" Julie and I say in unison.

"The whole town's talking," she insists. "I thought it was a rumor, to be honest."

"Okay, okay, can we please take this conversation downstairs?" Julie asks, pushing them forward.

We all head downstairs, and I can feel Julie's tension radiating off her like summer heat. Her mother immediately makes herself at home in the kitchen, pulling goodies from the bags she brought. There are caramel apples, maple scones, and miniature pecan pies.

"Let me make you both breakfast," I offer, moving toward the stove.

"Oh, no, dear. We already ate," her mother says, but she's studying me with interest. "We stopped by the diner. Marge finally rolled out her pumpkin pancakes for the season."

"First day of pumpkin pancakes is basically a town holiday," her dad adds, extending his hand for a proper shake now. His grip is firm, testing. "I'm Richard. And pardon my daughter for being so rude, but this is Sharon, my wife."

"So very nice to meet you," I say genuinely.

"I used to watch you play, Banks. You were a monster on the ice."

I chuckle, but I'm flattered. "Yeah? I only act that way when I have skates on."

Her dad laughs. "You're a legend."

"Nah," I say.

"You're just being humble, which is fine. It's a good quality to have. You know you were the best."

I shrug.

"I saw you donated to the library," Sharon says. "That was so generous."

"Okay, please don't bombard him," Julie tells them, turning on her espresso machine. "Please."

"The donation was made in my sister's memory."

Something shifts in her dad's expression. "Sorry for your loss. That's respectable, honoring her that way."

"Thank you."

Sharon is practically beaming as she watches us.

"Oh, Julie, honey, look at you!" She clasps her hands together. "I haven't seen this look on you since Buddy Madison."

"Mom!" Julie's face turns bright red. "Why would you bring him up?"

"Who's Buddy Madison?" I ask, intrigued.

"Her first love," Sharon says. "They were inseparable."

"Until he cheated on me with Bethany Collins," Julie mutters.

Sharon reaches over and touches Julie's hand. "But look at you now. That same sparkle in your eyes, except ..." She looks between us. "This is different. Bigger."

"Mom, *please.*"

"What? I'm just saying what I see." She turns to me. "Yesterday, Mrs. Henderson cornered me at the grocery store, said you two were glowing at the festival."

"Mrs. Henderson needs a hobby," Julie mutters.

Her dad laughs. "She has one. It's called being in everyone's business."

"Pot, meet kettle," Julie says, gesturing at her parents. "You literally broke into my house."

"We have a key. That's not breaking in. Besides, we wanted to meet Nick properly." She turns to me. "So, you're from New York City?"

"I live there now, but I grew up in a small town a few hours outside of the city. The population is about the same as Cozy Creek."

Richard nods approvingly. "Good. City boys don't usually understand places like this."

"Dad's not a fan of tourists," Julie explains.

"Pumpkin peepers," Richard says with disdain. "They clog up the streets, can't drive worth a damn, and act like we're here for their entertainment."

"Richard," Sharon warns, but she's smiling.

"He's not wrong," I say. "That's why I rented out Coleman's Orchard yesterday. I want and need privacy."

Julie's parents exchange surprised looks.

"You rented the *entire* orchard?" Richard asks.

"For the afternoon, yes."

Sharon's eyes shine. "Oh, that's so romantic! Richard, remember when you—"

"Sharon," Richard warns, but his mouth twitches with a suppressed smile. "I didn't have hockey money."

He looks at me with something that resembles an approval, and I take it.

"You're here through October?" she asks me.

"Yep," I say. "I have to be back in the city on November first."

Julie's hand finds mine, squeezing gently.

"Well," Sharon says, brightening, "I hope not forever."

"It won't be," I say, meaning it. "My mom and stepfather are staying in Cozy Creek through the holidays. I always spend Thanksgiving and Christmas with my mom, no matter where she is in the world."

Julie's mouth falls open, and then she quickly closes it. I lift a brow at her.

"Oh, wonderful! We should have a family dinner sometime," Sharon says.

"Mom, slow down," Julie pleads. "You're already planning holiday dinners, and you just met him."

"When you know, you know," Sharon says, looking at her husband. "I knew your father was it for me after our second date."

"First date," Richard corrects. "You just didn't admit it until the second."

They share a look that speaks of decades of love, and it makes me grin.

Richard pulls Sharon with him. "We should let you two get on with your day. Sorry for barging in."

"Though not really sorry," Sharon adds with a wink. "I had to meet the man who has my daughter glowing like this."

"I'm glad you did," I say.

After they leave, Julie drops her head on the counter. "I can't believe she brought up Buddy Madison."

"Your first love?" I pull her in front of me.

"High school boyfriend. Ancient history." She looks up at me. "And they definitely knew we were having shower sex."

"Your parents are great, Jules."

"Really?"

"Yeah. They love you. They want you to be happy." I brush hair from her face. "Your mom's right though."

"About what?"

"You are sparkling."

She hides her face in my chest. "Stop."

"Never."

My phone buzzes in my pocket, and I pull it out.

PATTERSON

Coffee shop is AMAZING. Your girl's friend with the crystals is hot. Also, I may have told everyone we're brothers. Roll with it.

I show Julie the text. She laughs.

"Blaire will destroy him."

"Probably. But I have a feeling Patterson isn't quite her type," I say, studying her.

"You're right. Blaire goes for the artsy, intelligent, nerdy boys. Patterson's about as subtle as a freight train. Should we go rescue her?" she asks.

"Let him figure it out. Besides, it's your day off. When's the last time you took one?"

She thinks about it. "Yesterday."

"Exactly. Before that, you have no idea." I pull her closer. "Spend the day with me."

"You say it like I need convincing."

"Do you?"

She shakes her head, then pushes up on her toes, kissing me. "You're sweeter than you let people see."

"Don't tell anyone. I have a reputation."

"Your secret's safe with me."

"What do people do here when they're not working?" I ask.

Her eyes light up. "The farmers market is today. It's the last big one before October."

"Perfect. Let's go."

"Really?"

"Yeah. Lead the way. I want to go everywhere with you."

She blushes, and I love that I can make that happen.

"Let me grab my bags," she says, sliding a few recycled totes over her arm, then we leave.

We walk hand in hand through town toward the square where white tents are set up in rows. The morning air is cool, and I can smell fresh bread, apples, and a hint of cinnamon.

"This is one of my favorite things about fall," Julie says, swinging our joined hands. "Local vendors, fresh produce, Melanie's apple cider doughnuts ..."

"Apple cider doughnuts?"

"Life-changing." She pulls me toward a tent where an older woman is frying doughnuts. They smell incredible.

"Julie! And the famous Nick Banks!" Melanie beams at us. "I heard all about you."

"Of course you did." Julie laughs. "A dozen, please."

"A dozen?" I ask.

"Trust me. We'll want them later," she whispers and tries to pay, but I insist.

"Absolutely not," I tell her, handing my card to Melanie before tipping her big.

"Uh," she says, looking down at it, "I think you added too many zeros."

"Oh? Let me see." I look at the slip and see a thousand-dollar tip. "Nope, that's right."

As Melanie bags our doughnuts, she winks at me, adding extra ones. "Thank you so much. Now, you'd better take care of her. She's special."

"I know," I say, squeezing Julie's hand.

We wander through the market, Julie introducing me to vendors she's known her whole life. She buys honey from the beekeepers, Granny Smith apples from Coleman's stand, and fresh herbs from the community garden. I carry her bags, watching her light up as she chats with everyone.

"Nick Banks?" A man with a thick Southern drawl approaches. "Holy shit, it really is you."

"Hi," I say, taking his hand.

"Huge fan," he says, shaking.

Julie watches the interaction.

"Mind if I get a picture? No one will believe that I ran into you."

"Of course," I tell him.

Julie takes the phone, snapping a few shots.

After we're alone, she looks at me thoughtfully. "Wow, you must really be a big deal."

"Shh," I say. "I'm not, trust me."

"You're just being humble. I mean, I knew you played hockey, but these people are fangirling over you. Even my dad did."

Laughter releases from me. "Didn't realize who your boyfriend was?"

I wrap my arm around her, and she holds me tight.

"I guess not."

We move between a vegetable stand and the craft booth to check out another section.

"Nicolas?" Another voice interrupts. "Nick Banks?"

We turn to find a woman with a professional camera around her neck. Not a local. Her clothes are too polished, her smile too calculated.

"I'm Amy from *Sports Daily*. What brings you to Cozy Creek?"

My body tenses. Julie must feel it because she steps closer.

"I'm not here for interviews," I say.

Amy's eyes slide to Julie, taking in our joined hands, the market bags, the domestic scene. "I don't think we've met."

"I don't think we need to," Julie says, but doesn't offer more.

"We're actually in a hurry," I say, steering Julie away. "Have a good day."

"Just one picture?" Amy calls after us.

I don't respond, guiding Julie through the crowd toward the edge of the market.

"Who was that?" Julie asks once we're clear.

"Trouble." I scan the area, looking for other photographers. When there is one, there are usually others. "She's a sports journalist, but she focuses more on gossip than games."

"Oh." Julie's quiet for a moment. "Is she going to write about us?"

"Probably."

"About our fake relationship?" she asks, but there's something in her voice.

Julie spots another photographer near the honey stand.

"Maybe," I say, realizing we're surrounded. "Come on. We need to get out of here."

She grabs my hand, squeezing my fingers. "Want to go home and eat apple cider doughnuts in bed, naked?"

"That's the best suggestion you've had all day," I say with a laugh, loving how she so casually pulls me away from my mini spiral.

"Better than shower sex?" she asks.

"Different category, but equally appealing."

I was afraid of the outside world bursting our perfect bubble. I just wanted more time with her before reality came crashing in.

As we walk back to her place, I keep watch for photographers, knowing I need to text Asher as soon as we're out of the public eye.

Julie hums beside me, swinging her market bags, occasionally feeding me bites of a warm doughnut. She acts as if she doesn't care, but I know better.

Regardless, I soak in the morning sun, enjoy the peacefulness of the town, and try to forget people from my world are here, watching us.

"Nick?" Julie says as we reach her door.

"Yeah?"

"Whatever happens with the media stuff … I'm glad it's me."

"Me too."

She fumbles with her keys, and that's when I realize she's nervous.

"Let me help," I say, taking them, unlocking the door while shielding her.

Once inside, Julie sets down the market bags on the counter and turns to me.

"What parts are real, and what parts are fake?"

"When we're alone. All real." I move closer to her. "The way I look at you. Real. How I feel when I wake up next to you. Real. The panic I experienced when I saw those photographers getting near you. So damn real." I take her hands.

"So, you're just really bad at fake dating?"

"The worst," I agree, pulling her closer. "But it will work out."

"Even with photographers following us?"

"Especially then." I kiss her forehead.

My phone vibrates, and I pull it from my pocket.

PATTERSON

Blaire just read my palm and told me I'm going to see my soulmate in November. Then she kicked me out of the shop. I'm so confused.

I show Julie the text. She laughs, and some of the tension releases from her shoulders.

"This doesn't surprise me," she admits.

I tuck loose strands of hair behind her ears. "Now, about those doughnuts in bed …"

She smiles, the tension immediately disappearing. "Race you upstairs."

"What do I get if I win?"

"Me," she says, snatching the bag of goodies and taking off running.

I catch her halfway up, spinning her around, kissing her against the wall. The market bags drop, and an apple rolls down the stairs, but neither of us cares.

"I already won," I tell her.

"We both have," she whispers.

And for now, we have apple cider doughnuts and each other.

It's more than enough.

I wake up to find Nick already awake, propped against my headboard, scrolling through his phone in the early morning light.

"Morning," I mumble into his chest.

"Morning, beautiful." He sets his phone down, running his fingers through my hair. "Happy October."

"Mmm." I stretch against him, then freeze. "Wait. Do you hear that?"

There's noise outside, like a small crowd has gathered.

I get up and move to the window, pulling back the curtain. My stomach drops. There are at least thirty photographers on the sidewalk. Some are sitting in lawn chairs with coffee from Cozy, like they're camping out for the day.

"Oh my gosh." A few of them snap pictures of me, and I step back and let the curtain fall. "Nick."

He joins me at the window, wrapping his arms around me. "Shit. There's more than yesterday."

"Yesterday, there were five. This is …" I turn in his arms. "This is psycho level."

For the past week, we've been followed anywhere we go. At

first, it was almost amusing how far they'd go. Several tried to catch us doing something scandalous, only to get pictures of us grocery shopping, holding hands, or trolling them. But each day, more arrived. I've been followed to work so much that Nick started walking with me. They've waited outside the coffee shop, taken pictures of me while I work, and even tried to interview my customers. Yesterday, one followed my mom to her book club meeting.

As soon as the thought leaves my mind, my phone buzzes.

MOM

DO NOT go to the shop today. I've taken you off the schedule for the rest of the month. This is too much, honey.

JULIE

Mom, I can't just NOT work. It's October!

MOM

I'm not asking you. I'm telling you. Lie low until this dies down.

JULIE

This is ridiculous. It's the busiest time of year!

MOM

Which is why I don't need photographers blocking the entrance for our customers. Take a vacation, sweetie. You haven't had one in years. Enjoy the season for once.

JULIE

Mom … please.

MOM

I've spoken. Stay with Nick. Be happy. The shop will survive.

I show Nick the texts. "She's banning me."

"Your mom's smart," he says, kissing my temple. "She's protecting you."

"But October is busy. The pumpkin drinks, the tourist rush—"

"Which your mom has been handling for decades." He turns to face me.

My phone vibrates again, and I expect to see another text from my mom, but it's Craig.

CRAIG

Saw the circus outside your place. I love you, Julie. I will always love you. I would've never put you in this position. If you need an escape from him, I'm here.

Nick reads it over my shoulder. "Fucking vulture."

"He's trying to use this against you," I say.

Nick pulls me closer. "What do you want to do? We can't stay here."

"We could go to Riverside," I offer.

"Yeah?"

"It's private. They can't follow us there." I glance back at the people down below. "Truthfully, I need a break from this. And if I can't work ..."

"We could enjoy October. Like normal people." He grins. "Well, as normal as we can be with all of this."

"How long does it take for them to leave us alone?" I ask.

"It's impossible to predict, but we can play it by ear."

I sigh. "A week at Riverside doesn't sound so bad."

"No, we have the hot tub under the stars with actual privacy. I'll cook for you every night. Plus, the view."

His eyes slide up and down me, and I fall into his arms.

"Will this be what destroys us?" he asks, and I can hear the pain in his voice.

I pull away, meeting his honey-brown eyes. "It will take more than this."

"I hope so." He's already reaching for his phone on the bedside table. "I need to call Asher and tell him what's going on."

While he talks, I start packing, trying not to feel guilty about abandoning the shop during peak season. But Mom's right—the photographers are affecting business.

"Zane's on his way," Nick says, hanging up. "He's going to create a distraction so we can slip out the back, where Autumn will be waiting for us."

"This is unbelievable," I tell him.

"I know. I'm sorry they're making our lives difficult."

"Not your fault."

"Kind of is."

"Nick"—I cup his face—"stop blaming yourself for things that are out of your control. If you could snap and make them disappear, I know you would. We're handling it. Together."

"Together," he agrees. "Are you sure your parents don't hate me for this?"

"Are you kidding? She's probably thrilled I'm finally taking a vacation and dating someone. She's been trying to get me to take time off and hook me up, but I've refused."

I finish packing two weeks of clothes in an oversized duffel. Nick gets dressed and continues to stand by the window, watching everyone outside.

Ten minutes pass, and he gets a text. "Zane is here."

"Great," I tell him as he takes my bag and swings it over his shoulder.

Seconds later, there's a knock at the door.

"Should I answer it?" I ask.

"No, let him pull attention," he says as we move to the back door.

I take one last look at my invaded sanctuary.

"Hey." He stops me before we walk outside. "This week, no photographers, no drama, just us and October. Got it?"

"Sounds perfect."

"Good. Because we still have a list we need to complete."

Despite everything, I laugh. "Priorities."

"Always." He grins. "Now let's go enjoy your favorite season."

As we sneak out the back, hearing Zane arguing with photographers about "private property laws," I realize my life has become surreal.

We creep through my small backyard toward the fence, and Nick suddenly stops. "Jules, where's the gate?"

"There isn't one."

"What do you mean, there isn't one?"

"We have to jump the fence."

He stares at the six-foot wooden fence, then at me, then at the duffel bag. "You're joking."

"Nope. Come on. I used to do this all the time as a teenager."

"In those boots?"

"Just help me up," I tell him.

Nick drops the bag over first, then makes a step with his hands. "This is insane."

"This is an adventure," I correct, placing my foot in his hands.

He boosts me up, and I swing my leg over, dropping down on the other side with a thud.

"You okay?" he calls over.

"Perfect! Your turn, city boy."

I hear him muttering something about "ridiculous" before he pulls himself up and over with surprising grace.

"Not bad for a hockey player," I tease.

"Piss off," he says, but he's grinning.

"Hey! You two!" A photographer has spotted us from the side of the house. "Nick! Julie!"

"Shit, run!" he says.

We grab the bag and sprint toward Autumn's idling car. She already has the back door open, and we dive in like we're in an action movie.

"Drive!" Nick shouts.

Autumn peels away from the curb as photographers start running toward us, cameras flashing.

"Thanks for being our getaway driver," I pant, trying to catch my breath.

"What are best friends for?" Autumn grins at us in the rearview mirror. "Besides, this is the most excitement I've had in weeks. Very Bonnie and Clyde."

"Less murder, more paparazzi," Nick says, pulling me against him.

"Same level of drama though." Autumn laughs. "Riverside?"

"Please," we both say in unison.

"How bad is it?" Autumn asks, glancing at us in the mirror.

"Bad enough that my mom took me off the schedule," I explain.

Autumn gasps. "In October?"

"And Craig's trying to start shit," Nick adds.

Autumn's hands tighten on the wheel. "That asshole had better stay away."

"He's irrelevant." I squeeze Nick's hand.

"We just need some time to breathe. Oh, did we forget Zane?" I ask as we travel through town.

"He drove himself," Autumn explains. "It's easier to separate in situations like this."

Nick whispers in my ear, "I'm sorry about all this."

"Don't be," I whisper back. "I'd jump a hundred fences with you."

As Cozy Creek disappears behind us and we head toward the cabin, I realize that despite the chaos, I'm exactly where I want to be.

I'm next to Nick, heading toward a week of privacy, with my best friend making jokes about our ridiculous escape.

And in a weird way, I'm grateful for it all.

19

NICK

I wake up before Julie, which has become my new normal. The morning light filters through the massive windows of the Riverside cabin, and I can hear birds instead of photographers. The silence is perfect.

Julie's sprawled across me like a starfish, red hair everywhere, one leg thrown over mine. The tension from leaving town has almost melted away.

I think about jumping fences, diving into Autumn's car like criminals, Julie laughing despite the chaos. She didn't break. We didn't break. The photographers tried, but we're still here.

Patterson left a few days ago, claiming the "small-town witches" were trying to marry him off. He had to get back to New York—hockey season starts soon, and he's the team captain. But not before Blaire read his palm one last time and told him about his love line. He's been texting me about this nearly every day.

My phone buzzes on the nightstand.

ASHER

> Media's calming down. Give it another couple of days. But it could be a false alarm.

NICK

Thanks for handling it.

ASHER

That's what I'm here for. How's Julie?

NICK

Perfect.

ASHER

You're so doomed. Congrats!

He's not wrong. Every morning, I wake up more fucked than the day before. More attached, more certain this isn't just temporary, more terrified of the November 1 deadline.

We've been at Riverside for a week now, and I don't ever want to leave. The past few days have been just us, this ridiculous cabin, and October. We've cooked together, used the hot tub every night, taken walks around the property without anyone watching, and made love under the moonlight. We've both needed this.

My phone shows 5:47 a.m. Too early to be awake, but I can't stop staring at her. The way the predawn light catches her skin, how peaceful she looks.

Then I remember her list. *Wake up to oral.*

She's asleep this time, not pretending. This is my chance to check this one off properly.

I carefully shift down the bed, moving slowly so I don't wake her yet. She mumbles something in her sleep but doesn't stir. I gently ease her legs apart, settling between them.

She's just wearing one of my T-shirts, nothing underneath. It's something she's gotten comfortable with.

I start with soft, barely there kisses on her inner thighs. She shifts slightly but doesn't wake. I work my way between her legs, and that's when she gasps awake.

"Nick?" Her voice is thick with sleep and confusion. "Oh my God."

Her hands immediately tangle in my hair as I continue, not stopping now. She's already wet, her body responding even before her mind catches up.

"Best alarm clock ever," she moans, hips rocking against my mouth.

I work her clit with my tongue, wanting to taste every inch of her, making sure she's fully awake and aware of every sensation.

When she comes, it's with a cry that echoes through the cabin.

I move back up to kiss her deeply, both of us breathless and connected in this perfect morning moment.

"Good morning to you, sweetheart," I say.

"That was …" She's still panting. "So good. Bucket list item achieved."

"The list is sacred. What will we do when we complete them all?" I ask.

"Add more." She pulls me down for another kiss, tasting herself on my lips.

My cock waits at her entrance. She's so wet and warm.

My phone buzzes.

"Don't you dare answer that," Julie says.

"Could be important," I mutter against her mouth.

She backs away, meeting my eyes. "Do you think it's more important than this moment with me?"

"Hell no." I let it go to voicemail.

"I can't believe we've been here a week already," she says as I slowly slide into her. She gasps. "Part of me doesn't want to leave."

"Then we don't." I trace patterns on her skin. "We could stay here a few more days."

"Tempting," she says, leaning up and then somehow moving me to my back before straddling me.

I groan as she takes me in.

Julie leans down and kisses me, and I'm lost in her as she rides me. Her breathing increases, along with her pace. I thrust upward, adding more friction, going as deep as possible. Our skin slaps together, and we lose ourselves.

"You were made for me," I grunt, slamming up into her.

"I was," she confesses, her mouth falling open.

Julie's head rolls on her neck as her titties bounce. I push up on my elbows, and she meets my mouth.

"Damn, I love kissing you."

"It feels so good," she moans. "So close."

I roll her over onto her back, and her thighs spread wide as I pump into her.

"Yes, yes, yes."

Each muscle tenses, and when she groans out her release, I slam harder, filling her full.

I tuck her hair behind her ears as I kiss her. We don't say anything, just settle in the moment, communicating without whispering a word.

My phone rings again, ripping us from our reality.

"Oh, for fuck's sake." I bury my face in her neck, inhaling her hair.

"You should answer it," she says.

I grab it, seeing my brother's name across the screen.

We break apart, slide out of bed, and move to the shower.

"What, *Asher*?"

"Good morning to you too. How's the love nest?"

"It's not a—"

"Whatever. Listen, the TMZ story about your fence-jumping escape is working to your advantage. But I do have something to tell you."

I sit up, not knowing what's being said. I promised myself I wouldn't check and would just wait until Asher told me pertinent information. Ignoring the media is easy; it's something I've been doing since I stopped playing hockey and began working at the firm.

"What?"

"*Hockey's Bad Boy and Barista's Great Escape.* Very romantic. Comments are supportive. But there is a blind item that was posted."

"Asher—"

"I'm just saying, the narrative has shifted. You're not the playboy ex-hockey star who will stick his dick in anyone anymore. You're the protective billionaire, trying to live a private life, who's protecting his small-town girlfriend from media harassment. The blind item says the barista is the woman you've had a crush on for the past year."

"What?" I ask.

The phone stays silent for seconds.

"Who did you tell about Julie last year?"

I stare out the window, noticing the leaves changing on the mountain. "No one."

"Think about it, Nick. You had to have told someone that you'd met her when you visited Cozy Creek. I need to figure out who's posting these blind items."

"Zane and Autumn knew," I say, then hesitate. "And Dyson."

The silence draws on.

"If it's our older brother who's feeding this beast, I'll *never* forgive him."

"Asher," I whisper, "don't do this. Let it be."

"I'm going to find out who the fuck it is," he says between gritted teeth.

"What will it solve?" I ask.

"I'll know who continues to sell us out. Think about everything that's been posted about Easton, Weston, me, Brody, and you. It's not a coincidence. It's someone in our inner circle."

"Who cares what's posted? Maybe they're helping? Every single person you mentioned has found their person, Ash. It's nothing but harmless matchmaking."

"Harmless?" I can tell he's upset. "Love has blinded you. I'll solve this mystery if it's the last thing I do. With or without your help."

"Asher."

He groans, and I can imagine him sitting at his desk in New York, staring out his office window toward Billie's office since their buildings face each other. I smile, thinking about them.

"Oh, and LadyLux wants an exclusive."

"Not happening," I mutter.

LadyLux is an anonymous pop culture blogger who posts about many people in my circle. She writes for LuxLeaks and is always fair and balanced.

"She's a good resource, and she'll tell the truth. Think about it."

I shake my head. "I don't care. I don't want a bigger spotlight."

"It will stop many of the rumors that aren't being addressed. Take care of them before the snowball becomes an avalanche," he tells me.

"Nope."

"You know exactly what you're doing, so handle it however you see fit. Don't mess this up."

"What part exactly?" I ask.

"Julie. She's the best thing that's happened to you, and I know your thirty-day deadline is soon."

"She's different," I explain.

"Yeah, but are *you*?" He hangs up before I can respond.

I move to the bathroom and step into the shower with Jules.

"Well?" she asks.

"Everything is *great*. Asher's in a mood."

"Oh. Sorry to hear that." She smiles. "Can we really stay a little longer? I like our bubble here."

"A few more days in the grand scheme of things won't matter," I say as she takes her time washing me.

Her touch comforts and calms me as we stand under the warm water.

The stream cascades over us. She starts at my chest, then moves up to my shoulders. She touches me like she's memorizing every inch of me.

"Turn around," she says softly.

I do, bracing my hands against the tiles as she washes my back. Her fingers work out knots I didn't know I had, and I groan.

"You're so tense," she whispers. "Everything is going to work out how it should."

"I know it will." I glance at her over my shoulder, and our eyes meet. "It's us against the world right now."

"A battle I will happily fight next to you."

She moves lower, taking her time, and it's not sexual. It's intimate. When she's done, I turn to face her.

I wash her hair first, massaging her scalp until she's practically purring. The suds slide down her body, and I follow them with my hands. She watches me with those green eyes, and something unspoken streams between us.

"Nick," she whispers.

"I know."

And I do. I feel it too. I feel this thing we're both too scared to name.

The steam surrounds us, the water still perfectly hot. It's like the cabin knew we needed this.

I pull her against me, and we just stand there, holding each other. Her arms wrap around my waist, her cheek pressed to my chest. I rest my chin on top of her head, breathing in the scent of the shampoo, mixed with steam.

"I don't want this to end," she says so quietly that I almost miss it.

"Which part?"

"Any of it. *All of it.*"

I tighten my hold on her, and we stay like that for who knows how long. The luxury of endless hot water lets us exist in this moment.

When we finally step out, it's not because we have to, but because we choose to face the day together.

We dry each other off in comfortable silence, stealing glances and soft touches. Julie wraps herself in one of the plush robes while I pull on sweatpants.

"Breakfast?" I ask.

"I'll never say no."

In the kitchen, I pull ingredients from the fridge—eggs, bacon, and fresh fruit we picked up from the farmers market earlier this week. Julie perches on the counter and doesn't take her eyes from me.

"I love watching you cook," she says. "You get this concentrated look. It's cute."

"Cute? Pfft. I'm going for *sexy* chef."

"That too." She steals a strawberry from the bowl. "What's on our agenda today?"

"Whatever we want. That's the beauty of hiding from the world."

"We can't hide forever?" She playfully pouts.

"No," I tell her, cracking eggs into a bowl. "But we can today."

My phone buzzes on the counter. Julie glances at it.

"What's it say?" I ask her.

"You trust me with your phone?"

I chuckle. "I have nothing to hide from you. Go through it if you want."

"No way. I trust you too."

"Read it to me then," I say as the bacon sizzles.

"Patterson said Blaire texted him about his 'romantic future,' and he doesn't know if she's flirting or threatening him."

I laugh. "Hilarious."

"Getting under people's skin is her superpower." Julie gets quiet. "I miss her. And the shop. And my normal life."

"We can go back—"

"Not yet." She meets my eyes. "I'm not ready to share you with the world again."

"Julie—"

"I know we only have three weeks left. I know this has a

potential expiration date, and no decisions are to be made until then. But right now, it's just us. Can we just … pretend for a few more days?"

I abandon the eggs, moving to stand between her legs. "We don't have to pretend anything."

"You know what I mean. I want to pretend there isn't a shitstorm outside, waiting for us."

"Yeah, I do." I cup her face.

She kisses me, then pulls back. "I think the eggs are burning."

"Shit!" I rush to save breakfast while she laughs.

I plate everything and even make a few slices of buttered toast. We eat on the deck overlooking the mountains, wrapped in blankets to help with the October chill. The landscape is painted in red, orange, and gold. It feels magical.

"We should use the hot tub tonight," Julie says. "Under the stars."

"Clothing optional?"

"Clothing is highly discouraged," she says.

We look at the mountains, and I think about how different being here has been from my everyday life. No meetings, no pressure, no performance. Just Julie and me and this ridiculous cabin that's become our perfect bubble.

"Damn, I love spending October with you," I say out loud, and she grins.

20

JULIE

I wake up at Riverside, and the weight of the world sits heavily on my chest. Nick's already awake, staring out at the mountains through the massive windows.

"Can't sleep?" I ask, curling into his side, pressing my cheek against his heart, listening to the steady beat.

"Just thinking." He kisses the top of my head.

I sit up to look at him. "Tell me what's wrong."

"I have a bad feeling about going back."

"Nick—"

"I know; I know. It's just the feeling." He pulls me closer to him. "It's just … this week with you has been perfect."

"Does that have to change?" I ask.

"No, it doesn't. But it will." He traces patterns on my bare shoulder. "I'm afraid this will scare you away."

"Why? Talk to me." I kiss him.

"The media, the gossip sites—they have ruined every relationship I've ever been in. This—all of this—is usually the catalyst and the cause of the end."

We're quiet for a moment, just holding each other as morning light fills the room.

I exhale. "It's a lot to deal with. I've never craved attention. There are times when we're alone when I question this."

He studies me. "I have a lot of baggage. It's what stopped me from pursuing you before."

"That makes me sad." I sit up. "Ready for a relationship tip?"

He nods with a smirk.

"This?" I wave my hand around. "You're mourning the end before it's begun."

Nick licks his perfect lips, sitting upright too. "We have a deadline, Jules. Less than a month to decide if this is something you want to deal with for the rest of your life. The public scrutiny won't change. The rumors won't change. The tracking of us and our life and our relationship status, lies, rumors—all of it will not magically disappear. If you choose me, you choose everything that comes with it, and I need you to think long and hard about that."

He leans forward, his hand slides up the back of my neck, and he grasps my hair. He presses kisses down my throat, and my breathing grows ragged.

"This is just a taste of it," he warns, his teeth grazing across my sensitive skin as he leans me back, pushing up my T-shirt.

My chest rises and falls, the cool morning air brushing against my nipples, already hard and begging for his attention.

He kisses up my stomach, then captures my nipple in his mouth before sliding to the next one.

"You have to be absolutely sure I'm what you want on Halloween." His voice is low.

"I know," I whisper, my breathing increasing.

The sun filters through the curtains, casting a golden glow across the bedroom. The silk sheets are cool against my bare skin, and I try to remember every feeling. As he continues to kiss lower, my stomach tightens with anticipation. I want him, and the delicious craving of having exactly that makes my pussy clench. He sits upright on his knees between my thighs.

I tilt my head, my eyes sliding over his shirtless body. His chest is a masterpiece of muscle, and his abs are carved like a sculpture. The gray sweatpants hang low on his hips, and I can see the outline of his cock, already hard, straining against the fabric. My mouth waters from just thinking about it.

His brown eyes lock on mine, and that sexy-as-sin smirk makes my thighs tremble.

"If you have any doubts, your answer should be no," he purrs, his voice dripping with dominance.

I love it.

I swallow hard because, his voice alone is enough to make me wet. He leans forward, pushing my shirt over my head. Then he pins my wrists to the mattress. His breath is hot against my neck, and I can feel the heat radiating off his body, searing into mine.

"I've been thinking about a few things on your list." His lips brush against my ear. "Do you want to play?"

"Yes, I do," I whisper.

"Close your eyes. Stay right here. Do not move." Nick moves off the mattress. "Don't peek either."

"Okay." I stay exactly where I am, eyes closed, hands resting above my head.

I can hear him slide open the drawer, then close it. I run through everything on my naughty wish list.

There are several I can automatically cross off from happening. A moment later, fabric is sliding around my wrists, and then I'm being attached to the headboard. Gently, he places something over my eyes, tying it. The world goes dark, and my senses sharpen. I can hear his breathing, the rustle of the sheets as he moves, the faint creak of the bed beneath us.

"Ready?" he mutters, his hand sliding down my body, fingertips grazing my ribs, my stomach, stopping just above my dripping pussy.

"Yes," I say breathlessly.

"Think about every sensation and enjoy it. Right now, you're mine, Little Red."

His fingers trail down my thighs, parting them slowly, and I can feel his breath on my inner thigh, so close to where I need him most.

He growls, his lips brushing against my sensitive skin. "I can smell you, baby. You're begging for it."

He doesn't make me wait. His tongue drags up my slit, and I arch off the bed, a gasp tearing from my throat. He laps at my clit, sucking it into his mouth, and I scream, my wrists straining against the silk. My body is on fire.

"That's it." His voice is muffled against my pussy. "Scream for me. We're going until you beg me to stop."

I immediately laugh, loving that this is what we're doing. "Oh, yes. Thank you. Let's cross this off."

He plunges two fingers inside me, curling them just right, and I swear I see galaxies. His tongue is relentless, his fingers pumping in and out of me, and I'm losing it. My hips rock against his scruff, and I greedily chase that sweet release, knowing he'll give me as many as I want, until I beg him to stop.

"Come for me, my greedy girl," he commands, his voice gravelly.

And I do.

The orgasm crashes over me like a tidal wave, my body trembling, my screams echoing through the room. He pulls away, watching my pussy pulse for him.

"I wish you could see what a beautiful sight you are," he says, slowly giving me a finger.

He pulls away, and I hear him suck on his finger.

"Mmm. You're my favorite flavor."

Once I come down from my high, he moves back to my clit, adjusting to how sensitive I am. He starts slow until the build happens again.

He laughs against me; the sound filled with wicked intent, and then his tongue is on me, licking a long, lazy stripe from my entrance to my clit.

I cry out, my body buckling as pleasure crashes through me again.

This time, he doesn't stop, doesn't give me a moment to recover. His tongue swirls around my clit, flicking and teasing, and I'm already trembling, already on the edge.

"Damn, your cum tastes so good," he whispers. His voice sends shivers down my spine. "Like fucking honey."

His tongue dives into me, plunging deep, and I cry out again, my thighs shaking as he fucks me with his tongue, slamming into me like I'm made for him.

One hand grips my hip, pinning me down as his mouth works me. He's so filthy.

The other hand slides between my thighs, fingers dipping into my slick folds, and I moan, my hips jerking uncontrollably.

"Your cunt is dripping for me," he rasps against my clit. "Perfection."

Two fingers slide into me, curling, stroking that rough, spongy spot inside me. I scream, my orgasm crashing over me, ripping me from my reality. His fingers pump in and out of me, fast and hard, while his tongue latches on to my clit, sucking and flicking, driving me higher, deeper into the pleasure until I'm shaking, crying, begging.

"Please," I sob, my voice wrecked. "I'm so close. I've lost count."

"Enjoy the ride, sweetheart." He growls, his words muffled against my pussy. "I'm not done with you until you tell me to stop. I'll eat this pretty little pussy for the rest of the day. Now, relax for me."

His fingers withdraw, and I whimper at the loss. I hear the click of something—a bottle maybe.

"I'm going to try something. If it's too much, tell me to stop," he whispers.

I feel the press of one digit against my asshole, teasing, probing with lube and my juices.

At first, I tense, but he shushes me, his voice soft and reassuring.

"This is going to feel so good, baby." His tongue is circling my clit again. "Let me in."

I melt for him, and his finger slides into my ass, filling me in a way that makes me gasp. His tongue is back on my clit, licking and sucking, while two of his fingers move in tandem. Two in my pussy, one in my ass. I don't recognize the sound coming from my throat or the sensation traveling through my body. The pressure is almost unbearable, but delicious. I'm split open, stretched, filled to the brim, and I can't stop moaning, can't stop shaking as he works me over, driving me toward the edge.

"That's it, sweetheart." His voice is full of lust. "Take it. Take everything I give you. You're so fucking beautiful. Let me keep worshipping you."

I take all of him—his fingers, his tongue, his praise—until I'm coming again, my body spasming, my cunt clenching around his fingers, my ass tightening around his pinkie. He doesn't stop. He holds me through it, his mouth and fingers relentless, until I'm exploding again.

He returns to my clit, and it's too sensitive.

"Please."

"Is that you crossing it off your list?" he asks.

"Yes," I say, barely able to catch my breath. "Now, I need more. Harder. Break me, Nick."

Seconds later, he's opening my thighs wide. "You're glistening for me, babe."

"I need you so bad."

He growls—a sound so primal that it makes my clit throb—and then he's on me, his cock pressing against my soaked entrance. He slides into me in one smooth, brutal thrust, and I scream, my body arching off the bed as he fills me, stretches me, claims me.

"Is this how you wanted it?" He groans.

"Harder," I scream out, my back arching off the bed.

I'm lost in the sensation, lost in him, until there's nothing but pleasure, nothing but him and us.

His hips slam into mine, the sound of skin against skin filling the room. My legs wrap around his waist, pulling him deeper, and he growls, his hands gripping my hips, pounding into me harder, faster, until I'm screaming his name, over and over.

This orgasm is like nothing I've ever experienced. I squirt all over his dick, feeling it everywhere.

"Damn, baby." His voice is strained.

"Come deep inside me," I beg.

He pumps into me, and I can feel his hot release flooding me. He collapses on top of me, his breath ragged, his body trembling.

He removes the blindfold, kisses me, smiles. "Are you okay?"

"I'm a changed woman," I tell him.

He looks over his shoulder, and I see his phone on a tripod.

My mouth falls open. "I got blindfolded, tied up, devoured until I begged you to stop, *and* you recorded it? I'm so lucky."

"Seems like you got a three-for-one deal," he says. "Not many things left on your list now."

He unties my hands, and I wrap my arms around him.

"Do you think we'll be able to complete it?"

Nick laughs, then presses kisses to my neck and shoulders. "It's my civic duty."

When he pulls back and I meet his light-brown eyes, I've never felt more alive or wanted. I understand that he was creating one last perfect memory before our reality check, and it's so damn thoughtful.

Nick kisses me one last time, then moves to the phone and turns it off.

"What are you doing to me?" I ask, sitting up.

"The same thing you're doing to me," he says over his shoulder.

We both know, but neither of us will say it until Halloween.

"Okay," I say. Seeing his naked body against the fall colors in the backdrop has me taking pause. "Now I don't want to leave."

He laughs, but it's tinged with sadness. "Shower? Pack? Then face the world?"

"That's a logical order."

We move through our morning routine, but everything feels heavy.

"You okay?" Nick asks as I fold my clothes into my duffel.

"Just memorizing it all."

"We can come back."

I zip my bag. "This has been a fantasy, Nick. A beautiful, perfect fantasy. But none of this is real life."

He crosses to me, cupping my face. "It can be."

"I know. I just mean—"

"I know what you mean. We're safe here, but it's not reality." He kisses me. "Being alone with you is the only time we get without interruptions. Outside of our private walls, there are spotlights."

"And you really don't think it will ever stop?"

"Slow down? Yes. Stop completely? No. That's an unrealistic expectation."

My phone buzzes, pulling us away.

MOM

> I just got a text from Blaire. Craig has been by the shop every day, asking about you. I contacted his mother. She told me to mind my own business.

I show Nick the text.

"Every day?" His jaw clenches. "That's stalking."

"He's probably just—"

"Jules, no. Stop making excuses for him. He's waiting for you, and I don't like it."

"You're right," I admit.

I don't understand how I could be with someone for three years and not even know who he was.

"We should document everything when we get back. Maybe talk to the police," Nick suggests.

After we're packed, I look around the cabin one last time. "Ready?"

"No. You?"

"No. But let's go anyway."

We load the Range Rover with our bags, taking our time, like we're both reluctant to leave.

"At least we can come back whenever," Nick says, reading my mind. "I have this place until November."

We drive down the mountain road in comfortable silence, NPR on the radio. The leaves are bright and colorful, fluttering in the light breeze. Everything feels peaceful, like the world is welcoming us back, like everything is going to be okay. I slightly relax until we turn onto Main Street.

"That car's been behind us since the turnoff," Nick says, checking his rearview mirror.

I look in the side mirror and see a black SUV with tinted windows. "Maybe they're just—"

Another car pulls out from a side road ahead of us, camera lens visible through the passenger window.

"Shit," Nick mutters. "How did they know?"

A third car appears, boxing us in.

Nick checks the rearview mirror. His knuckles are white on the steering wheel.

"Maybe they're just—"

"Jules"—he glances at me—"that's a telephoto lens hanging out the window."

The black SUV speeds up, trying to get alongside us. Nick suddenly yanks the wheel right, taking a sharp turn onto Cedar Street. My hand grabs the door handle.

"Sorry," he mutters, but his quick hockey reflexes are in full effect.

"Take the next left," I say. "Then an immediate right onto that dirt road."

"What dirt—" He sees it at the last second, tires squealing as we turn.

The SUV overshoots, brakes screeching.

"Now right again, behind the old Miller farm."

Nick follows my directions without question. We weave through back roads only locals know—the shortcut to the quarry, the hidden turn by the creek, the unmarked road that connects to Mountain View.

"How many are still with us?" I ask, afraid to look back.

"Two ... no, three." He accelerates through a yellow light. "Hold on."

He takes another hard turn, and I see one photographer's car get stuck behind a delivery truck.

"Yes!" I cheer, then immediately feel ridiculous.

Nick's jaw is clenched tight, but there's something almost amused in his voice. "Where now?"

"Straight for two blocks, then left at the old church."

We lose another car at a stop sign, but the black SUV is persistent.

"Shit, he's calling others," Nick says, seeing the driver on his phone.

My stomach drops. "They're coordinating?"

"Welcome to my world." He takes another sharp turn. "Actually, no. This is worse than usual."

My phone pulls my attention away. I glance down at a text.

BLAIRE

Where are you?

JULIE

I'm heading to my condo.

BLAIRE

DON'T. Media circus downtown. I just heard someone say you're on Main Street.

JULIE

How did they know?

BLAIRE

No idea. All these photographers have been huddling outside of the shop since this morning.

JULIE

Ugh. We're being chased by photographers. I'll keep you updated.

BLAIRE

You'd BETTER!

"We can't go to my place. Blaire said downtown is packed. Let's go to Autumn's. It's the most private. I have the code to the gate."

Nick takes the next turn, but two cars follow. He speeds up, taking random turns until we lose them, then heads up the mountain to Hollow Manor.

When we make it to the private gate, he punches in the code, and it jolts open. Nick drives through, stopping to make sure the metal snaps closed before taking off. Colorful leaves line the paved road that winds up to the mansion.

As soon as we park, Autumn opens the door and walks to the edge of the porch, wrapping the cardigan tighter around her thin frame.

"What the hell is happening? We've been watching the news."

"The news?" My voice goes up an entire octave. "Why do they care?"

"You're the talk of the town."

Nick ushers me inside, his hand protective on my lower back.

Autumn practically drags us to the living room. "You both look shell-shocked. Zane, look who showed up!"

"Speak of the devils. You know you're everywhere right now? All the social media sites, TMZ. Even the local news is giving updates." He slides his laptop off the counter and moves toward us.

Hockey's Playboy Returns with Small-Town Girlfriend

Secret Love Nest Exposed: Banks and Barista's Hidden Romance

Is Julie Pregnant? Close Sources Say Yes!

Hockey Star Dates a Barista to Repair His Reputation

"We were supposed to get married." Ex Speaks Out!

I LEAN FORWARD AND CLICK THE LINK ABOUT CRAIG. HE GAVE THEM photos of when we were together—some of which were intimate, showing us lying in bed together.

Nick's jaw clenches as he reads it with me.

The article quotes Craig as saying he's concerned for my well-being, and he hopes I know he'll be there when this ends. He told the world I am a sweet girl and would never date a man like Nick. He's calling it a midlife crisis and that I'm being brainwashed.

"That manipulative bastard." I growl.

"There's more," Zane says quietly, swiping to another page. "It looks like he's been posting old photos of you. Leaving captions like you were recently together."

I see pictures from years ago but cropped and filtered to look current. We look happy and in love.

"I think I'm going to be sick," I say.

Autumn immediately goes into mama-bear mode. "Okay, everyone, stop. Zane, close the laptop. Nick, sit down. You're pacing like a caged animal. Jules, breathe."

She disappears into the kitchen and returns with tea and fat slices of pumpkin bread. It makes me smile, per usual.

"This is my fault," Nick says, not touching anything. "I should have listened to Asher. Should have done the interview, controlled the narrative—"

I move next to him on the couch. "This isn't your fault."

"Isn't it? Your life was normal before—"

"My life was *boring* as hell before." I take his hand. "And Craig was still a manipulative ass. This just gave him an excuse to show it."

Autumn sits across from us. "The question is, how did they know you were coming back today? You didn't tell anyone, right?"

"Just you guys and my parents," I say.

"And Asher," Nick adds. "But he wouldn't—"

"Someone's been watching you," Zane interrupts, pulling up security footage on his phone.

Nick's phone rings, and he shows Zane the screen.

"Put him on speaker," Zane says.

"Warning: he's going to be an utter asshole," Nick warns.

"This is an absolute shitstorm," Asher barks. "This is exactly what I warned you about!"

"Nice to hear from you too," Nick says dryly.

"Don't. Just don't. I told you almost a week ago to do the LadyLux interview, and you didn't. I also explained how rumors don't just disappear. You know all of this, Nick. So, pull your stubborn head out of your ass. You don't get to stay in your little love bubble and ignore reality, for fuck's sake."

"Asher—"

"I'm not done. Do you know what's trending right now? *Hockey Playboy's Latest Victim*. There's a whole thread on Reddit analyzing how long until you dump Julie. They're all trying to figure out the first day you two got together.

"And that's not even the best part," Asher continues. "One of your ex-girlfriends—Virginia? Vanessa? Whatever her name is— well, she just did an interview, talking about your toxic cycle. Love bomb for thirty days, make everything seem great and perfect, then ghost."

My stomach drops.

"Vanessa was stalking me. I had to get a restraining order!" Nick explodes.

"Doesn't matter. The story's out there now, and they've officially dug into all the people you've dated in the past five years and put them in chronological order. This headline: *Exes Confirm Nick Banks's Romantic Countdown to Ghosting.*" Asher pauses. "Now admit I'm right."

"You're right," he says, but his voice is neutral.

"Did you hear about the hometown hero trying to save his ex from the big bad wolf?"

Nick's jaw clenches so hard that I swear I hear his teeth grinding.

"Oh, it gets soooo much worse," Asher snaps. "Someone leaked your location at Riverside. Sold the information to the highest bidder. That's why you have a parade following you."

"How do you know all this?" Nick asks.

"Because, unlike you, I don't ignore problems, hoping they'll go away. I have people monitoring this shit. Yes, even you. This is a PR nightmare," he says. "You're worse than our bitchiest clients. Diva."

This makes Nick laugh.

"Think about the interview with LadyLux." Asher is direct.

"Look—"

"And get a restraining order against Craig. Document *everything.*" He pauses. "How's Julie handling this?"

Everyone looks at me.

"I'm fine," I say.

"No, you're not. Even I can tell when you're lying." Asher can detect bullshit through the phone. "I'm sorry you're dealing with this. My brother should have listened to me."

"Your brother was trying to live his life for once," Zane finally says to defend Nick.

"By ignoring the problem? Very effective, Alexander. Even you know that's not logical, and you don't do this shit for a living." Asher scoffs. "Nick, it's a shit show at the office. So, thank you. Thank you so much. Every day, I have to push my way through a horde of people, hoping it's you."

"I'm sorry. I didn't ask for any of this."

"This is beyond normal paparazzi stuff. You've become a sensation, which is what I was concerned about. People are obsessed with both of you, and it's dangerous." Asher's voice turns serious. "Be careful. This has escalated over the past three days, just as I feared. Do the interview."

Nick looks at me but doesn't confirm. "I'll think about it."

"Good. And, Nick? Next time I tell you to get ahead of something, listen."

"Love you too, asshole."

"Julie …" Asher says.

"Yeah?"

"Welcome to the family circus. Sorry that it's like this."

He hangs up before I can respond.

I lean back on the couch and close my eyes, trying to understand how any of this happened.

My phone vibrates and pulls me away from my mental spiral.

CRAIG

Crazy about all those photographers. If you need somewhere safe to stay, I'm here.

I show everyone the text.

"What the hell?" Zane mutters.

"I should have known he wouldn't leave you alone." Nick's pacing now. "The way he grabbed your arm at the coffee shop, him showing up randomly—"

Zane scrolls through messages. "How long has this been going on?"

"Since he returned to Cozy Creek."

Nick leans over and reads all the text messages Craig has sent.

CRAIG

Hope you're getting the rest you deserve.

CRAIG

Beautiful weather in the mountains today.

CRAIG

I went to the coffee shop today. Was hoping to see you.

CRAIG

Can we please talk about this?

CRAIG

You said you'd always love me and that we were meant to be together. We will be together, Jules, baby.

"Wow," Nick breathes out.

"This has been going on since he saw me at the coffee shop." My hands are shaking.

"I'm going to find him and make him pay." Nick moves toward the door.

I follow him. "No. Please—"

"This ends now."

Zane stands and places his hand on Nick's shoulder. "No. Your emotions are running high. This is a trap, one he has been setting up for weeks."

"He's right," Autumn offers. "This is exactly what Craig wants. You're a good person, Nick. Don't let him make you do something out of character, okay?"

I grab his hand and lead him back to the couch. "He wants you to be violent. He needs to be the victim and prove you're the bad person. Don't give him what he wants. For me. Please."

"Okay." Nick presses his fingers to the bridge of his nose. "You're right. We need to document everything and file a police report. We handle this the right way."

I squeeze his hand. "Thank you."

"Save everything," Nick tells me. "It's all evidence."

"It's harassment and emotional manipulation," Zane adds. "I can call the chief of police. He's friends with my dad."

Nick shakes his head. "We go the proper routes so it can't be twisted. But I should've handled him a week ago."

"How?" Zane asks. "Beat the shit out of him? That's exactly what he wants. *Hockey Player Attacks Local Hero, Craig Downing.*"

"Local hero?" I ask.

"That's how he's positioned himself with the media," Zane explains. "He's good at this."

Autumn nods. "Many believe he's the hometown boy who lost his girl to the rich playboy outsider. Half the town feels sorry for him."

My phone rings, and I glance down and see it's my mom. I immediately answer.

"Julie, honey, are you safe? I just talked with Blaire."

"I'm at Autumn's."

"Sierra told me Craig came back to the shop this morning, asking when you'd be back. They didn't tell him anything, but he seemed to know already." She pauses. "Sweetie, be careful. He's not himself lately."

"What do you mean?"

"He's been telling people Nick is using you, that he'll leave you broken when he goes back to New York. That he's just trying to protect you from a monster."

"Nick isn't a monster. Craig's lying. He has no idea wha—"

"I know, honey. Nick is a fine young man." She sighs. "But please keep me updated, okay? I'm worried about you."

"I will. Love you."

"Love you too."

I end the call and place my face in my hands.

Nick places his arm around. "It's going to be okay."

"You promise?" I ask, meeting his eyes.

"Yes." He gives me a small smile, and with everything I am, I want to believe him.

21

JULIE

Autumn stands, breaking the awkwardness. "Right now, we need to figure out the next step. What do you want to do, Jules?"

"Truthfully? I want to go home. I want to sleep in my own bed. I want to wear my cute sweaters that are in my closet and enjoy October. This is my favorite time of year," I explain. "I don't want to be forced to hide."

"Then we'll make sure you get home," Autumn says. "Don't let this ruin your favorite time of year. And if things get too bad, come back here. We have plenty of room and food. We'll have a slumber party."

"Yes, absolutely," Zane says. "Are you ready to go home now?"

I look at Nick, then at Zane. "Yes."

"Okay, I'll drive the two of you," Zane offers. "My truck is less recognizable."

"I'll follow separately in the car," Autumn adds. "Create confusion, but also, I need to pick up some more ingredients from the store. Everyone is getting pumpkin bread soon. I've just been in the mood."

"Thank you," I whisper, hugging Autumn.

"Hey, it's going to be okay," she tells me, squeezing me tight.

"It will. It's just a lot right now," I whisper.

She pulls away and moves my hair over my shoulders. "A year from now, no one will care about any of this. I promise."

"Come on. Let's get going," Zane says. "We're taking the truck."

Nick wraps his arm around me, and we move to the oversized garage in the back. Zane clicks a button, and the door lifts.

I gasp. "I didn't realize you had all of this."

Zane chuckles. Inside is a jacked-up truck, a couple of motorcycles, a classic Mustang convertible, and a Lamborghini.

"All of this is really subtle," Nick says.

Zane chuckles. "I hardly drive any of it. And if anyone gets in my way, it will be a monster-truck experience."

Nick laughs, and it relaxes me. "Shit, let me grab our bags."

A minute later, he's running to his Range Rover, unpacking our things, then rushing back.

We climb into the back seat, and the windows are tinted so dark that no one is taking any photos of us.

"Just like old times," Zane says, adjusting the mirror. "Remember when we used to sneak out in your mom's Suburban?"

"You *forced* me," Nick corrects.

"Oh, whatever." Zane starts the engine, and it rumbles like thunder. "It was your idea half the time."

"Revisionist history."

"Remember the Denver concert incident?" Zane grins, pulling out of the garage.

Autumn is waiting in her Lexus.

"We agreed never to speak of that again," Nick says.

"Now I need to know," I say.

"No, you don't," Nick insists, but he's fighting a smile.

"Nick tried to crowd surf and—"

"Zane, I swear to God—"

"And security thought he was rushing the stage. Spent three hours in concert jail."

"Concert jail?" I laugh.

"It was a misunderstanding," Nick mutters.

Zane navigates down the mountain, and the reality of what we're heading back to settles over us. Our fingers interlock as I stare out the tinted windows.

Zane takes a turn fast enough that we slide across the seat.

"Sorry. Thought I saw someone following."

My stomach drops. "Following?"

Nick turns to look. "Silver Honda?"

"That's the one."

"Take the next left," Nick says. "Then double back through the gas station."

Zane follows his instructions, and the Honda continues straight.

"You two have me paranoid." Zane's fingers grip the wheel tight.

"How often does this happen to you?" I ask Nick.

"More than I'd like," he admits. "Since I retired, it's not been like this."

The rest of the drive is tense. Zane takes back roads like he's a local, doubling back twice more just to be safe. Finally, he's parking on the street in front of my condo.

"The coast looks clear," Zane says, but then I see the crowd of photographers waiting.

"Shit," Nick mutters. "This is more than before."

"You sure you want to do this?" Zane asks. "You could grab more clothes and come back to our place."

I shake my head. "I'm not letting them chase me from my own home."

Zane turns and looks at us. "If you need anything, call us."

Nick places his hand on Zane's shoulder and squeezes. "Thank you."

"When I said best friends forever, I meant it," Zane says.

They meet each other's eyes for a long moment before Nick turns to me. "Ready?"

"No. But let's do it anyway."

"I think that's our official motto," he says with a smile.

"It's a good one."

This time, we're more prepared for the crowd that surrounds my condo. Or at least, that's what I tell myself over and over.

The moment we exit Zane's truck, I get lost in the flashing lights, bodies that press in from all sides, and the shouting. It's overwhelming.

The questions fly from every direction.

"Julie! Are you pregnant?"

"Nick! How much did you pay her?"

"Is this real or a publicity stunt to fix your reputation?"

"Julie, what will you do when he leaves you?"

"Did you cheat on Craig?"

"Nick! How many women have you destroyed?"

Nick's arm comes around me, his body becoming a shield. I can feel the tension radiating off him. This is his enforcer energy—the same thing that made him legendary on the ice.

"Stay close," he mutters in my ear. "Don't let go of me."

We push forward. A photographer shoves a camera in my face—so close that I can smell his coffee breath. Nick's free hand comes up, not touching but creating space.

"Back. The. Fuck. Up." His voice is deadly.

The guy stumbles backward.

Someone grabs my arm from behind, trying to stop me, to separate us.

That's when instinct kicks in.

I spin, using the momentum to break his grip, and in one fluid motion, I palm-strike him in the chest. He flies backward, his ass landing on the pavement.

"Don't touch me without permission," I warn.

The crowd of photographers goes silent for a second.

Nick stares at me, mouth open. "Are you the Karate Kid?"

"I need my keys," I say, but my hands are shaking now, adrenaline making them tremble. "I need—"

They slip from my fingers.

"I got it," Nick says, scooping them up, still looking at me with something like awe. He uses his body to create a barrier.

Finally, we're inside, and we both lean against the door, breathing hard.

"Are you okay?" Nick immediately starts checking me over. "Your hand—"

"I'm fine," I say, though my whole body is shaking now.

"You just … you laid that big dude out flat."

The adrenaline is fading, leaving me shaky. "Yeah, and I'll do it again."

"He was two hundred fifty pounds minimum. Nearly three times bigger than you. Where the hell did that come from?"

Despite everything, I laugh. "I'm a black belt in karate. Have been since I was sixteen."

"You're what?" He's confused. It's cute.

"I was a very paranoid kid. Ask Autumn and Blaire. I'm usually very hyperaware of my surroundings, and I was afraid of being kidnapped because I was a cute kid. So, I begged my mom to put me in karate so I could learn self-defense. Also, I played roller derby for about a decade." I flex my arm. "These guns aren't just for show."

Nick stares at me like he's seeing me for the first time. "Roller derby?"

"Oh yeah. They called me Red Menace."

"Of course they did." He starts laughing—a real belly laugh. "My girlfriend just knocked a photographer on his ass."

"He *grabbed* me. Anyone touches me without consent, they get dropped."

"That was"—he pulls me against him—"the hottest thing I've ever seen."

"Really?"

"You went full-on ninja. That palm-strike was perfect."

"My sensei would be proud." I'm still worked up. "God, I haven't had to do that in years."

"Why didn't you tell me you could fight?"

"It never came up. *Hi, I'm Julie. I make coffee and can break your arm in three places.*"

He's grinning wider now. "What else don't I know? Secret spy? Assassin?"

"I'm also really good at pool."

"Of course you are."

"And I can juggle."

"Now you're just showing off."

"Oh, and I won a hot-dog-eating contest once."

"Stop."

"Sixty-seven hot dogs in ten minutes."

"That's physically impossible."

"Okay, that one's a lie. It was only seven, and I almost threw up afterward." I grin at him. "But I did win. The trophy is at my parents'."

"What else? Please tell me you weren't in a biker gang."

"Just derby. We did have rivals though. The Silver Sky Slayers. *Bitches.*"

We're both laughing now, and the tension breaks. It feels good after everything we've been through today.

"I'm dating Red Menace," he repeats, shaking his head as I lead him into the kitchen.

"*Retired* Red Menace. I haven't skated in four years."

"We should go sometime."

"You want to go to the rink?"

"Oh yeah. Rollerblading is something I did a lot as a kid to practice in the offseason."

I pat his cheek. "I'd love to see it."

"You tell me when, and it's a date," he says, his face softening. "Have you ever ice-skated?"

"Yeah, a few times at the resort. It was fun. Though busting your ass on ice is just as bad as a rink."

He smiles, tucking hair behind my ear. "I'm so sorry about all of this."

"It's not your fault. I won't let you take the blame for their actions," I say.

He pulls me closer to him. "Jules, I don't know what's going to—"

Before he can finish, a knock taps on the door, causing us to both freeze.

Nick moves to the peephole and looks out. Seconds later, he opens the door, and Blaire rushes inside.

"Oh my goodness!" She drops everything to hug me. "Are you okay? I heard you dropped a photographer!"

"How did you—"

"Someone got a video, and it's trending. I think the caption said something like *Barista Goes Ninja on Handsy Photographer*." She shows me her phone. "The comments are wild. Even the other photographers backed off after that. *Don't mess with Red Menace* is trending locally."

"Wow," I say.

"No, it's good! People are on your side. Even Craig's supporters are saying the photographer deserved it."

My brows furrow. "Craig has supporters?"

"He's been playing victim all week. But this?" She gestures at her phone. "This shows you're not some damsel he needs to save."

"I've *never* been a damsel."

"I know that. Now everyone else does too. Red Menace strikes again." Blaire grins.

Nick looks between us. "Did you do derby too?"

"Only for a year, and then I quit. I learned that I'm too fragile. Look at me," Blaire says.

"What was your derby name?"

She laughs. "I was The Blair Witch Project."

"Of course you were," Nick mutters, but he's smiling. "You know, I have a friend I should hook you up with."

Blaire immediately shakes her head, her cat earrings jingling. "I don't do setups. I want the universe to put the right man in my path. Oh, before I forget … I brought supplies." She gestures at the bags. "Wine, tequila, chocolate, whipped cream." She waggles her brows, then moves to the next bag. "Sage to cleanse the negative energy and Chinese food because I know you both probably haven't eaten since breakfast."

"Thank you so much," I tell her. "You're the best. Do you want to stay and hang out?"

She shakes her head. "Nah, I'm going to go home and pet my cat, then rot in my bed."

Nick gives her a look. "What does that mean?"

"Exactly what I said. Take it how you want." Blaire bursts into laughter. "If you need anything, please let me know. Happy to deliver it to you."

After a deep breath, Blaire opens the door and steps out. She uses the sidewalk like a runway and then disappears through the crowd.

"Now what?" I ask.

Nick lifts the bottle of tequila. "We continue the party."

We do shots, then collapse on the couch with the Chinese food. While we eat, my phone continues to buzz with notifications and texts. When I've had enough, I finally check it.

MOM

Are you okay? Dad saw the video of you defending yourself. He's so proud.

JULIE

Fine. I'm home. Safe. Nick is with me. We're eating Chinese food.

I open the next text.

CRAIG

I saw what you did to that photographer. That's not the gentle Julie I know. Nick's changing you for the worse.

I show it to Nick. "He's still watching everything."

"Block him."

"I can't. We need evidence for the restraining order."

An hour later, after we've finished eating, we lounge on the couch and watch TV.

"It's quiet," Nick says with me wrapped in his arms, a tequila buzz swarming me.

He's right; there's no more shouting or camera flashes.

Nick creeps to the window, staying to the side so he can't be seen. "The street is empty."

"Completely?"

"There's one car …" He leans closer. "Black sedan on the corner."

My blood goes cold. "Craig?"

"Can't tell. Windows are tinted."

I get up and join him, and we stare at it for a moment.

"Should we call the police?" I ask.

"And say what? There's a car parked legally on a public street?"

The car's headlights suddenly turn on, illuminating my building for just a second before it drives away.

"That's not creepy at all," I mutter.

Nick pulls the curtains closed. "Tomorrow, we will file that restraining order."

"Tomorrow," I agree. "But honestly, where did all those photographers go?"

Nick's already checking his phone. "Something bigger must have happened."

"Is this the calm before the storm?" I ask.

"Potentially."

I sink deep into his arms, and he kisses my forehead.

"Whatever's coming, we'll face it together," I say.

"Together," he agrees.

We stay holding each other in the quiet, knowing this peace won't last. But right now, in my little condo with empty Chinese food containers scattered on the coffee table and tequila warming our blood, we're safe.

For tonight, we're just Nick and Julie, not the hockey star and the barista or any of the other headlines. We're just us.

22

NICK

I stand outside on the balcony with the doors open while Julie gets ready for our double date. The cream curtains flap in the breeze as I people-watch. The closer we get to Halloween, the more bloated the town becomes with tourists. Downtown has been gridlocked for days, and the sidewalks are packed with festivalgoers dressed in costumes and cozy sweaters. We're in the center of it all, the mecca of Cozy Creek.

Julie's balcony gives a front-row seat to the festivities. Honestly, I could stand here for hours. The weather is brisk, and I can feel the excitement floating through the air.

Most of the paparazzi who were following us left three days ago, but I know it's short-lived. Asher explained they're chasing a scandal involving a senator's son in Denver. He'd fabricated a story for them to salivate over, and they took the bait. I appreciate the reprieve more than he'll ever know. This is why my brother is the best in this industry. He can bury anything, and I believe my sister knew Asher was a powerhouse, an asset. At first, I didn't understand why Eden had chosen him to be CEO when I had worked beside her for years. Now, I get it.

A chill rushes over me.

Asher lives for strategy in intense situations and is obsessed with causing or putting out fires. Nothing intimidates him, and he genuinely loves New York. She knew Asher would be a lifer at Banks Advertising and Marketing. I think she knew I wouldn't.

Eden. My dear, sweet sister. She'd have *loved* Cozy Creek.

"Are you okay?" Julie asks from her closet door. She's leaning against it, dressed in her bra and panties, watching me. Red hair is twisted up on her head in small pinwheels.

I glance at her, unable to deny how damn pretty she is.

A smile touches my lips. "Of course. Why?"

"You looked sad," she says.

I suck in a deep breath, confirming she can see straight through me. It's a gift she's had since we met.

"Oh, babe. I'm *very* happy, I promise," I say. It's the truth.

"Just making sure. Want to talk about it?" she asks, returning to her closet.

Hangers slide against metal as I go back to my thoughts.

"I was just thinking about my sister and how much I miss her." I smile and turn back to the balcony. My mind drifts back to Eden.

A month ago, I could hear her voice scolding me in a way that was perfectly, uniquely her. But since I've been here, my sister's disappointment no longer haunts me. I think my happiness has settled her soul, or maybe it's settled mine. Regardless, I'm not the same person I was a month ago. My outlook on life has changed, and a part of me has too. Even I can recognize that.

Julie hasn't returned to the coffee shop yet, but she's supposed to soon. Her parents have stated several times that they don't want her returning until November, but my girl is very stubborn. She decided yesterday that she would continue to do inventory throughout the month. Her dad caved.

"I'm ready!" Julie announces.

I turn and see she's wearing a black dress with a white collar, and it's giving off a Wednesday Addams vibe. My eyes scan down her spiderweb fishnets to her clunky Doc Martens boots that make her look like a vampire hunter. I believe she could kick ass in them after watching her knock the piss out of that photographer. It's an energy I can match.

"Are you sure about going out tonight?" I ask, moving into her room.

"Yeah." She grabs her pumpkin head from the edge of her bed and puts it on. Her voice is muffled inside the pumpkin. "No one will know it's us. We'll have anonymity. Your turn."

Julie hands me my ridiculous pumpkin head.

"You'd better be glad I like you," I tell her.

"Oh, I'm *so* damn glad," she admits. I can imagine her wearing a cute little smirk.

I stand beside her, looking at us in the mirror. "You're sure we'll fit right in?"

"Do you trust me?" she asks, moving closer, causing our pumpkin heads to bump together.

"Absolutely."

"Good. Ready?" She grabs my hand. "Come on. Autumn and Zane are meeting us there."

"Are they wearing pumpkin heads too?"

"Nope. But Autumn said she was trying to convince Zane to wear a matching cozy sweater."

I crack up. "Hmm. He's never been the type."

She grins. "Yeah, well, he's a changed man."

"For the better," I admit. "I'm happy they found one another."

"Me too," she says. "Ready?"

"Yep."

We make our way downstairs.

"Want to pregame?" she asks, moving toward the kitchen.

"Pregame?" I lift my brows.

"Oh, are you too old to do that?" She places her hands on her hips.

"You're joking. I'm only a few years older than you."

"Still older." She shrugs, antagonizing me.

I slide the pumpkin from my head, and she does the same. Julie opens the cabinet and pulls out a bottle of Fireball.

"Shots for courage," she says, pouring two generous ones.

"Courage is drinking that." I nod toward it.

"We'll need it for what we plan to do in that corn maze." She winks.

"You're trouble, Little Red."

"Not the first time I've heard that."

We clink glasses and down the cinnamon whiskey.

"Ew."

She snickers. "One more for luck?"

Before I can answer, she's pouring the shot glasses full.

"For luck," I say before we down them. "That tastes like shit."

"You get used to it." She looks up at the clock on the wall. "We should get going."

Julie grabs my hand and drags me outside. The walk to the carnival grounds is hilarious. Julie keeps trying to take selfies of us, causing us to slam into tourists who have zero self-awareness.

"These pics are terrible." She laughs, showing me a blurry photo where we look like demented vegetables. There's another one where our heads aren't even in the frame.

"We're pumpkin perfection." I wrap my arm around her as we laugh down the sidewalk together.

We cross the street and enter the festival grounds. String lights are everywhere, and torches light the paths. Over half the people here are in costume. I've counted countless zombies, witches, vampires, and even pumpkin heads.

"We fit right in," I say.

"See? Told you!" Julie's voice echoes.

"Nick? Jules?"

I hear Autumn's voice behind us. The two of us turn as she and Zane approach, both in regular clothes but wearing matching sweaters.

"How did you know it was us?" Julie asks.

"For one, Nick's wearing a hundred-thousand-dollar watch," she says.

"Shit," I mutter, removing it from my wrist and placing it in my pocket.

"And I'd recognize your ass from a mile away," she says, slapping Julie on her butt.

Zane pulls his phone from his pocket. "Get together. I need to memorialize Nick being a little bitch."

Laughter falls out of my mouth.

"You're going to run your mouth, Mr. Matching Sweater?" Julie glares at him.

"Oh, sorry. Don't want to set off Red Menace." He chuckles. "Come on. Be good little pumpkins."

We pose for him, and then the four of us take a photo together.

"Apple cider time!" Autumn announces, pulling Zane with her.

We wait in a line that's twenty people deep. Our conversation floats from topic to topic. It's easygoing.

"Are you still leaving in November?" Zane asks.

"Yes," I admit. "I have a meeting on the second that I can't miss."

"Oh." Autumn glances between us. "But you're coming back afterward?"

"I don't know yet," I say. "Ask me at midnight on November first."

"Is that when you turn into a pumpkin?" Autumn asks.

"Possibly."

We each order large apple ciders that are steaming with cinnamon sticks slid inside.

"How do we drink this?" I ask, removing my pumpkin head.

"Cheater," she accuses.

"It's called being adaptable, babe," I say.

She removes hers as well. As we drink our ciders, we stroll through the patch with Autumn and Zane. Many of the pumpkins are carved into extravagant designs and are lit, glowing in the night.

"Look at this one!" Julie points to a pumpkin in the shape of a haunted house, complete with tiny windows. It's Hollow Manor.

"Isn't that incredible? You both have to see this one," Zane says, leading us to a massive pumpkin carved into a dragon, scales and all.

"I can't imagine how much work this took," Julie says, smiling as she takes photos of it.

Autumn clears her throat. "I think this is the perfect time to announce the news."

She's giddy.

I glance between Zane and Autumn, wondering what it could be.

Julie grows impatient. "Hurry and tell us!"

"My book is going to auction! The one I wrote last year." She's ecstatic.

"Autie!" Julie squeals, hugging Autumn as tightly as she can. They're both giggling and laughing. "*All I Want* will be published?"

"*Yes*! Can you believe this?" Autumn laughs. "I got a call from my agent today. Publishers are *fighting* for it!"

"Oh my goodness! My bestie is going to be a *big deal*. Finally, the world is going to meet Mr. Dreamy." She waggles her brows.

Zane chuckles. "It will be a hit. I mean, considering who the hero is based on, of course it will be."

I laugh. "Who's Mr. Dreamy?"

"A fictional character," Autumn hurries and says.

"The man Autumn dreamed about for thirteen years, who happened to weirdly be Zane," Julie explains.

My brows lift. "Wait, is that true?"

Autumn nods. "It's true. I still remember the first time we met."

"Me too," Julie says, reminiscing. "It kinda feels like yesterday."

Autumn's expression softens. "Zane ordered an asshole Ristretto."

"Not a Ristretto," I mutter. "Seriously, all the finance assholes in New York drink that. It's a red flag."

"Exactly," Autumn agrees. "Anyway, he told me my coffee tasted like shit and stormed out when it was perfect. Pissed me off."

Julie snickers. "She was convinced he had a shitty palate."

"My palate is refined," Zane offers.

I glance between them. "So, that's how you met? At Cozy Coffee?"

"Yep," Zane says. "The moment our eyes locked, I knew she was the one. I wasn't ready. I had come here to escape, to heal. Falling in love wasn't on my agenda."

Autumn smiles wide. "I've wanted this since I was a little girl. And now magic is happening."

Zane's arm wraps around her, and he kisses her hair. "I'm so proud of you."

It's obvious how much he loves her.

Autumn turns to him, standing on her tiptoes to kiss him. "You inspired me."

"You changed my life," he tells her.

It warms my heart that my best friend has what he always wanted—someone to love and see him for who he is.

"I'm happy both of your dreams have come true." I reach for Julie's fingers and take her hand as we wander through the displays.

It feels good, being with her without photographers or drama. We're hanging out with our best friends, enjoying October. It doesn't feel real.

She puts on her pumpkin head and turns to me. "What?"

"Nothing," I whisper, realizing we're doing everyday couple things. It's something I've wished for, but I never thought I'd get this.

"Remember when we tried to carve pumpkins last year?" Zane asks Autumn.

"You mean when we *attempted*?"

"Yeah." He chuckles, and Autumn chews on her bottom lip.

We finish strolling the winding path. Music drifts through the speakers, and I can't remember the last time I enjoyed myself so much.

Once we leave the patch, we stop and eat caramel apples, then continue forward.

Zane tries to win Autumn a spooky stuffed ghost at the ring toss and talks smack the entire time.

When I turn my head, I see Craig by the kettle corn stand with a blonde woman.

"Don't look," I tell Julie, but in the pumpkin head, she can barely see anyway.

"What is it?"

"Craig."

Her body tenses. "Has he seen us?"

"I don't think so."

I move toward Zane and lift my pumpkin head. "We need to split up, okay?"

"Okay," Zane tells me. That's when he spots Craig—I can see it in my best friend's expression. "Be safe. If you need anything, text me."

"I will."

I slide my fingers through Julie's and lead her away from Zane and Autumn. With them, we're too obvious; away from them, we blend in.

I try to steer Julie away, but the blonde woman who was with Craig approaches us.

"Excuse me," she says, her voice shaky but clear. "Julie?"

"Who?" Julie asks, attempting to disguise her voice.

"I saw you with that dark-haired woman earlier. Autumn, right? The way you two hugged, I knew it was you." The woman wraps her arms around herself. "I need to talk to you."

Julie's body goes rigid, and I can feel the tension radiating off her. This is the woman Craig proposed to after dumping Julie.

"We should go," I mutter, sensing Julie's discomfort, but she surprises me.

"No, it's okay." Her voice is steady despite everything. "I'm listening, Sarah."

She looks surprised that Julie knows her name. "You remember me?"

"I'll never forget you. Craig brought you to my parents' anniversary party three months after we broke up." Julie's voice is neutral. "You wore the necklace I'd given him."

Sarah touches her neck, though she's not wearing it now. "He told me his mother gave it to him."

I place my hand on Julie's back, feeling her trembling, but she continues to stand her ground.

"Is that all?" Julie asks.

"No." Sarah looks around, making sure Craig isn't close. "He's not over you. He talks about you nonstop. Julie this, Julie that. He even …" She pauses, tears welling in her eyes. "He calls me by your name sometimes."

Julie is silent for a moment. "Why are you telling me this?"

"We broke off our engagement a month ago, but we've been trying to work things out. Or at least, I thought we were." Sarah wipes at her eyes. "But all he cares about is you."

"Sarah—"

"I'm pregnant," she whispers.

We both freeze.

"What?" Julie's voice is barely audible inside the pumpkin.

"Ten weeks. He doesn't know yet. I came here to tell him, to try to make things work, but he keeps photos of you on his phone. He drives by your place at night. I followed him once." She looks desperate. "I need to know if you plan on getting back with him."

"Never," Julie says. "It's over. I've moved on."

"But he's sure you'll get back with him."

"Not this time. Not *ever* again." Julie pauses. "Look, I don't want to get in your business, but you deserve to be more than someone's second choice. You deserve someone who doesn't call you by another woman's name."

Sarah's face crumples. "I know, but with the baby …"

"A baby will never fix a broken relationship," Julie says.

"Sarah!" Craig's voice cuts through our conversation. "Who are you talking to?"

"I was just—these people were asking about directions for the corn maze."

Craig approaches, not glancing at us.

"The entrance is over there," he says, pointing behind him.

He grips Sarah's wrist and pulls her with him. "Come on. You said you wanted kettle corn."

"Craig," Sarah says, "you're hurting me."

"Not now." He's impatient, still not looking at us. "Let's go."

"Be careful with me. I'm *pregnant*," Sarah blurts out.

Craig freezes, and his head snaps toward her. "Who have you been seeing?"

"You," she cries. "Just you. I'm ten weeks," she whispers.

I grab Julie's hand, moving us away from the conversation. "We need to get out of here," I say.

"Yes," she whispers.

Their conversation can still be overheard.

"This is …" He runs his hand through his hair.

I see it the moment recognition dawns.

"Jules?" His voice is angry now. "I'd recognize those boots anywhere."

Julie doesn't bother ignoring him and turns around with her arms crossed over her chest. "What do you want?"

"You …" He looks between Sarah and Julie, his face reddening. "You were talking to her? Sarah, what the hell? What did you say?"

"She deserved to know the truth," Sarah says, finding her courage. "You calling me by her name, driving by her house every night, keeping her photos—"

"*Shut up*," Craig snaps.

"I'm concerned about you, Jules. There's a difference," he says. "Sarah is jealous. She always has been."

"Concerned people don't drive by someone's house every night," Sarah interjects.

Craig's attention shifts back to her, his jaw clenching. "You have no idea what you've done."

"Please," she says, reaching for him, but he ignores her, moving toward us.

"Take those ridiculous things off. If we're having this conversation, at least have the courage to show your faces."

Julie pulls off her pumpkin head, hair static wild, chin raised with defiance. I do the same, moving closer to her. She's pissed—I can tell.

Craig glares at me. "How long until you get bored, Banks? How long until you move on to the next small-town girl looking for excitement? Everyone knows about your reputation."

"Finished?" I ask, not affected by him.

I deal with assholes who make him look like child's play. Asher is one of them.

"You're making a huge mistake with him," Craig warns Julie. "This is a game he plays with women. You're just entertainment. His personal whore."

"Shut your mouth," Julie says, glaring at him. She's livid, and I don't know if I've seen her quite this mad. "I will never give you a chance again. Ever. I'd rather be alone."

Craig's mask slips, and I see pure rage underneath. "When he leaves, remember that you chose humiliation."

There is venom in his tone, but all I can do is laugh because he's trying too hard.

"The only one who will be humiliated is you," I tell him. "Look at you. You're pathetic."

"Yeah, but I'm not fucking your sloppy seconds, am I?" Craig takes a step toward me, fists clenched, and I'm ready to lay him out flat.

I look down into his eyes, with nostrils flared. "I'll destroy you. Throw the first punch. I dare you."

"Craig, stop!" Sarah grabs his arm. "Please. You'll go to jail."

He shakes her off, but the mention of being arrested seems to snap him back to reality.

He glances at Sarah, then at Julie, then back at Sarah.

"We're leaving," he says. "Now."

He grabs her arm and pulls her away, but not before throwing one last look at Julie. "This isn't over."

"Yes, it is," Julie says. "I'm filing a restraining order. And this time, I have witnesses."

Craig's jaw clenches, but he doesn't respond. He drags Sarah away, and we watch them disappear into the crowd.

Julie's shaking, and I pull her against me.

"You okay?"

She takes a deep breath. "At one point in my life, I envied her. Now I feel sorry for her."

"That's because you're over it," I say. "Congrats. That's huge."

Julie looks up at me. "Thank you for having my back."

"Always."

Autumn and Zane find us a few minutes later.

"We saw Craig storm off," Autumn says. "What happened?"

"His ex is pregnant," Julie says.

"What?!" Autumn's eyes go wide. "Are you serious?"

"Ten weeks. It's his."

"That bastard," Zane mutters. "He was trying to get back with you while—"

"While he was still seeing her on the side. Classic Craig. He did the same thing to me." Julie gasps.

"You okay?" Autumn asks, studying Julie's face.

"That could've been me," she whispers, inhaling with her eyes closed. "That could've been me."

I move closer to her. "I'm glad it wasn't."

"He traps women," she says. "Last year, he wanted me to get off my birth control, making me believe we were getting back together."

"You escaped him. I'm so damn proud of you, Little Red," I say.

Julie grins. "It's because I met you. That night"—her voice lowers to a near whisper—"my life changed."

The words hit me square in the chest because mine did too.

"I'm finally seeing things clearly," she says.

"I think we're witnessing something we shouldn't," Zane says to Autumn, but his voice is warm, understanding. He wraps his arm around his wife, then spins her around to face the opposite direction. "We're going to look at more pumpkins. Over there. Far away from you."

"Subtle," I call after them.

"We're giving you privacy," Autumn calls back.

"I married Captain Obvious!" Zane adds, and Autumn smacks his arm.

As their laughter drifts away, mixing with the sounds of the festival, I lean forward. Julie's still glowing with this newfound freedom, her cheeks flushed, eyes bright. I close my eyes and slide my lips across hers. She tastes sweet, like apple cider. Our tongues twist together, and I swear the entire world stops spinning on its axis.

When we break apart, we're breathing hard.

"Thank you," she whispers against my mouth, eyes still closed.

"For?"

"For being here. For having my back. For helping me be brave."

"You did that yourself."

"Maybe." She kisses me again, quick and sweet. "But you showed me what I should be looking for. What I deserve."

"Jules—"

"Twenty-two days," she says.

I know she's thinking the same thing I am. We have twenty-two days to figure out if this is real or just another beautiful disaster waiting to happen.

"I think we're on the same page," I say, studying her.

"I hope we are," she tells me.

"Now, I think we have a corn maze to discover."

A wicked smile crosses her face. "I already love where this is heading."

"Shall we?" I reach for her hand.

She takes mine. "Yes, we fucking shall."

We return the pumpkins to our heads and move toward the corn maze, excited to knock another thing off our list. Because, yes, I've adopted it too.

She grabs my hand, and this time, goose bumps trail over my arms and through my body, causing a whirlwind of emotions to flood through me.

I don't want to let Julie go in twenty-two days. I think I want forever.

23

JULIE

The corn maze entrance looms before us, lit by dim orange string lights that make the stalks glow gold. I'm high on the thought of fulfilling this fantasy. The cool October air carries the scent of kettle corn and distant bonfire smoke.

"Ready for an adventure?" I ask, my voice muffled.

"With you? *Always.*"

We enter the maze, and the sounds of the festival fade. It's just us, the rustling corn, and the occasional distant laughter from other lost souls. The paths are barely lit, creating more shadows than light.

"Left or right?" Nick asks, hooking his pinkie with mine.

"Always left at first. That's the secret."

"There's a secret?"

"Oh, there are lots of secrets in Cozy Creek."

I pull him with me, and then we immediately turn right. I get us lost within minutes, but we keep walking forward.

When we're at the edge of the maze, I pull him a little farther, then remove my pumpkin head. He removes his too. The string lights don't reach us.

"You know what I realized tonight?" I ask, moving closer to him.

"What's that?"

"For the past few years, I've been going through the motions of living."

I wrap my arms around his neck, and he slides his around my waist.

"And now?"

"Now I feel alive. You make me believe I can have the things I want."

"What are the things you want?"

"Lazy Sunday mornings in bed. Inside jokes. Someone who looks at me the way you're looking at me right now."

He cups my face in his hands. "Tell me how I'm looking at you."

"Like I'm lightning in a bottle."

"You are," he confesses, leaning forward, fingertips brushing against my cheeks.

His lips meet mine with a tenderness that makes my knees weak. It's not the desperate, heated kisses we've shared before. This is something else. His mouth moves against mine like he's memorizing the shape of my lips. I can't help but sigh when he tilts his head just right, allowing his tongue to swipe against mine.

I melt into him, my fingers tangling in his hair, and I need more of him, like I can't get enough. It's almost as if my life depends on it.

Nick tastes sweet from the cider, and he's being so damn gentle as his thumbs stroke against my cheek. We kiss like we have unlimited time, like we're not in a corn maze, where someone could stumble upon us.

One hand slides into my hair, pins falling out and scattering on the ground, causing red waves to tumble down my back.

"Jules," he breathes against my lips, not pulling away, just needing to say my name.

"I know," I whisper.

I feel the magic between us. This shift. This change. This

wonderful, terrifying thing that's been percolating between us over the past year.

He kisses me again, backing me up until I'm pressed against the corn stalks. They rustle around us, creating a curtain of sound that makes this feel even more private, more ours. His body cages me in, but I don't feel trapped. I feel protected. Cherished. Wanted.

When we break apart, we're breathless. My lips are swollen, tingling, and I feel dizzy, drunk on him. His forehead rests against mine, and we hold each other for a moment.

"That was …" I don't know how to describe it.

"Yeah," he agrees, knowing what I mean.

"I want …" I pull him down so I can whisper in his ear. "I want you to make me forget my name. I want you to make me come so hard that I see pumpkins in the stars."

He groans. "Damn, girl. Never heard the word used during foreplay."

I snicker. "First time for everything."

His hand slides under my dress, to the edge of my slit, and I gasp. "Bad *fucking* girl."

I gasp. "I'm prepared."

"And so wet and ready."

"You're a turn-on," I breathe out.

"Tell me something," he says.

His fingers tease me, but don't quite touch where I need and want them.

"When twenty-something-year-old you put this on your list, did you think you'd ever do it?"

"No," I admit, inhaling as his fingers make contact between my slick folds before he slides one digit inside. "I never thought I'd find someone who could satisfy me."

"And I do?"

He steadies me as he continues to torturously move in and out of me. When his thumb rubs against my clit, my eyes roll in the back of my head.

"Yes."

I feel his body heat as he leans in, the warmth of his breath causing a delightful tickle on my neck and sending thrilling shivers down my spine. His scent, pine needles and leather, wraps around me. It's then that I realize how much I want him, how much I've always wanted him.

He continues to tease my clit with his thumb and adds another finger. Two digits deep. I wrap my arms around him, hanging on to him as I take the ride of a lifetime on his hand.

A gasp escapes me at the intense pleasure that sweeps through me. Anticipation dances in my trembling legs as I rock against his hand. I hear voices surrounding us, and the thought of getting caught makes my pussy clench around his fingers. I've never done something so risqué or taken control like this, but I'm so turned on that I can't help it.

Nick continues to finger-fuck me and leans forward, kissing me. His mouth slides to my ear and down my neck. "Your skin tastes so good."

Everywhere his lips touch, sparks ignite. His teeth graze my skin, and he plunges deeper into me.

My breath catches in anticipation as I approach the precipice at a sprint. My heavy breaths mingle with the gentle rustling of corn stalks swaying in the breeze. I can barely handle how good his hands on me feels. A moan releases from me, and Nick laughs against my neck.

"Shh, Little Red. Don't want anyone to overhear."

He continues to touch me, and I feel safe, even as we're doing something so risky.

The intensity builds, and I hold on to him, fingers digging into his shoulders as waves of sensation wash over me.

Voices float through the maze, and my heart races. The thrill of this is almost too much. I squeeze my eyes tight.

"You're close," Nick whispers against my ear. "You're so beautiful."

His words affect me as much as his touch. This isn't just physical. Right now, it's emotional, and I'm finally claiming what I want.

The rustling corn creates a symphony around us as I get lost in the moment, in him. My breathing increases.

I bite my lip, trying to stay quiet as everything intensifies.

I place my hand over my mouth, stopping myself from screaming when the orgasm pulls me under. It's euphoric, and I have an out-of-body experience. He holds me upright so I don't collapse.

"Nick," I breathe against his chest, still trembling.

"I've got you," he murmurs, holding me close. His heart is racing as fast as mine.

"This feels different," I whisper.

"How?"

"Like we're not pretending anymore."

His arms tighten around me. "We haven't been pretending for a while now."

"Tonight, seeing Sarah …" I take a shaky breath. "That could have been me. Trapped, pregnant, as he screwed around."

"But it's not you."

"No. And I'm grateful. You showed me what I deserve."

The voices are closer now.

"Quick!" I grab our pumpkin heads, squeezing my legs together.

We barely get them on before a group of teenage boys rounds the corner.

"Dead end," one says.

"Nice pumpkins, weirdos." Another laughs as he passes us.

"Wonder what they were doing back here," the taller one says.

"Hey, you little bastard," I yell. "You stole my panties."

"Oh, shit!" the teenager screams.

He and his friends sprint away from us, laughing hysterically.

"I'm going to find out who your mom is and tell on you!" I scream.

When they're out of sight, Nick turns to me, wearing a smirk. "I'm sure they're scared."

I chuckle. "I hope they are."

Nick reaches over, pulling a piece of corn silk from my hair. "You're a beautiful mess. Was it worth it?" he asks.

"Hell yes. Happy I had that on my list," I say, grinning.

"Did you see pumpkins when you came?" he whispers.

I nod. "I think I saw the spice too."

He grabs my hand and chuckles. "Corny."

I turn to him. "Am I the type of woman men want? Do you think I'm too much?"

"Not for me. I can never get enough," he confesses. "And, yeah, I think you are the type of woman men want."

"Why am I single?" I ask.

He turns to me. "Because you're not a fucktoy, Jules. You're the type of woman men want forever with."

My heart skips a beat.

We finish wandering through the maze, stopping to kiss one another when we can. I hear music, laughter, and the occasional scream from the haunted house.

"Did you know we're almost at our thirty-day mark?" Nick asks as we take another wrong turn.

"Yes, I'm aware. One week. I've got your expiration date programmed into my phone."

"I'm not running, Jules." He places his hands on my shoulders. "I don't want to, and that's never happened before."

"What does that mean?"

"What we have is different."

"Does that scare you?" I ask.

"Not this time," he tells me, kissing me.

I grab his shirt, pulling him to me. "Love to hear it."

After we break away, he grabs my hand and leads us toward the exit of the maze.

"Thank you for making my silly list seem important," I say.

"I don't think it's silly." He kisses my forehead. "I know we're not supposed to talk about this yet, but I'm—"

"Don't jinx it." I press my finger to his lips. "Tell me on Halloween. We agreed."

"You're right," he says. "I got lost in the moment."

After forty-five minutes of purposely being lost, we find our way out.

"There you are!" Autumn calls out. She takes one look at us and smirks. "Have fun getting 'lost'?"

"Too much fun," I say, but we're not fooling anyone.

My lips are still swollen, my hair is a mess despite attempts to fix it, and we both have that telltale glow.

As we walk back through the festival, Nick's thumb brushes over mine. It's such a simple gesture, but it makes my heart race. Something has shifted. This isn't just about checking things off a list anymore. This isn't just a hookup situation. This is something more. Something that scares and excites me at the same time. Something that might be worth risking everything for.

We're in the middle of where we were and where we're going. It's almost purgatory because I have my answer, but I'm giving it space to breathe, to make sure Nicolas Banks is who I want.

I'm just worried something will change between now and then, and our answers won't match.

24

NICK

I wake up to the smell of bacon and coffee, and for a moment, I think I'm dreaming. Then I see Julie standing in the bedroom doorway, holding a tray and wearing nothing but a T-shirt and panties.

"Happy thirty-one days," she says with a sweet smile. "Ready to disappear and pretend I don't exist?"

"As if that's possible. I tried that last year, but it didn't work out for me," I tell her, sitting upright to lean against her headboard.

She sets the tray on the nightstand and climbs onto the bed, straddling my lap. Julie leans forward and kisses me, tasting like coffee and promise.

"How does it feel to make it past your infamous thirty-day mark?" she asks against my mouth, then pulls away. "Wait, does this even count? I mean, *technically* ..."

"Hell yeah, it does." I wrap my arms around her, leaning in to kiss her again. "The countdown began the moment I kissed you in the coffee shop."

"So, you're finally admitting that *you* kissed *me*?" She laughs, running her fingers through my messy hair.

"I wanted to."

I love the way she looks at me. It makes me believe I'm something special, something worth her time.

"Good, because I woke up early and made breakfast to celebrate this record-breaking occasion."

"Thank you."

The words *I need you and want you forever* sit heavy on my tongue, begging to be said, but I'm keeping emotions to myself. We agreed to wait, and it's still two and a half weeks away. It's hard.

"Thank you for not sliding out of bed last night and disappearing." She grins. "Or suddenly deciding you need to find yourself in Tibet."

"The only thing I need is more of you," I admit freely.

"You have me."

"Forever?" I tease as she crawls off of me.

I sit up straighter, and she sets the tray on my lap. There are two plates, one for each of us, and two cups of steaming coffee. She prepared crispy bacon, scrambled eggs with cheese, and hash browns.

"Wow," I say. "This is the first time a woman has ever made me breakfast in bed."

"Really?" She looks proud of herself. "I feel special to have one of your firsts."

"You are special," I admit. "No one ever cared enough."

Her smile fades. "That makes me sad."

"Aw, don't be." I chuckle. "I wasn't the best partner. Being with you has made me realize I was an entitled asshole for no reason, who had zero respect for myself or anyone else. Thank you for that."

"You're welcome." She sips her coffee, eyeing me. "So, I kept my end of our fake-dating bargain?"

"Hell yeah, you did," I say. "I'm not the same person I was when I arrived. Truthfully, I don't know how I'll transition back to my life."

"You'll figure it out," she says. "You know why?"

I shake my head.

"Because what's meant to be *always* has a way of working itself out."

"You believe that?" I ask.

"Yep," she says. "Think about the things in your life that have worked out. For me, I didn't have to force anything because it fell into place. That's how relationships should be too. Try because you want to and because you care, not because you *have* to. Pour your energy into what matters. It's impossible to force a square peg into a round hole."

I smile. "I'm so damn lucky to have met you."

"I feel the same," she confesses. "You know, the Nicolas Banks they talk about on the internet and the one eating breakfast in my bed aren't the same."

This makes me laugh. "I'm aware."

"I'm glad," she says. "Not sure I'd like that asshole very much."

"Oh, I'm still *that* asshole, but you make me soft."

"Aw," she says. "That's kind of adorable though."

We finish eating and talk about anything and everything. It feels nice to be with her. I imagine this is what she meant when she said she wanted lazy days with someone.

"Don't forget, tonight I have to do inventory at the coffee shop," she says, stacking the plates on the tray, then moving it to the bedside table.

"You don't *have* to," I tell her.

She grins. "I want to. I miss being at work. Not being able to help makes me feel guilty because it's the busiest time of the year. It's similar to being one of Santa's elves and not working during December."

I turn to her. "I understand, but your safety is more important. Speaking of, today I'd like it if you filed a temporary restraining order on Craig," I say, catching her hand and kissing her palm.

"Okay," she tells me. I can hear the disappointment in her voice. "I was hoping he would calm down."

"But he hasn't, and after speaking with Sarah, I don't think he will. Once Craig's served papers, he will know to leave you alone. No more games, Julie. I worry about you, and I can't follow you around everywhere."

"Are you sure you can't? I enjoy having you around all the time." She playfully bumps my shoulder.

I take a sip of coffee. "I love it and wish I could, but I also want you to be protected. If something happened to you …"

She grabs my hand and squeezes it. "Nothing will happen, Nick. We'll go today, even if it's just for peace of mind."

"Thank you," I whisper as she leans over and kisses me.

I meet her eyes, knowing I've never made it past thirty days with anyone. And maybe it's because with Julie, it's different. It's comfortable without the normal pressures. I'm not counting down the seconds, waiting for when it's over. I watch the clock because I never want it to end.

With anyone else, I'd be halfway to Europe, giving excuses about needing space or time to figure things out. Instead, I'm pulling her down for a kiss, wondering how I ever lived without her.

"Are you ready for the real celebration?" she asks against my lips.

"Breakfast wasn't it?"

"Oh, no." Her eyes sparkle with mischief. "This was just the appetizer."

Before I can move, she's straddling me again, pulling her T-shirt over her head.

"Thirty-one days deserves a proper celebration, don't you think?" she whispers.

"Hell yes."

THE COURTHOUSE SMELLS LIKE OLD PAPER AND DISAPPOINTMENT.

"Reason for requesting order?" she reads aloud, then pauses, pen hovering over the small box. She takes a deep breath and begins writing.

Julie fills out form after form, and I watch her hand cramp as she writes, detailing every incident—from the constant texts to the festival confrontation to Sarah admitting he drove by her condo at night.

I can see some of the words from where I sit. *Harassment, unwanted contact,* and *stalking* her are just a few things she's scribbled down. Her handwriting gets shakier with each sentence.

Once she's signed her name at the bottom, she returns to the clerk with her head held high. The woman—probably in her late fifties and with kind eyes behind thick glasses—reviews everything.

"What are the odds of this going through?" Julie asks, fingers tapping on the counter.

The clerk looks up at her. "Honey, with what you've documented here, it's enough for a temporary order. He'll be served within forty-eight hours. After that, if he does this again, it's considered a violation."

"And then what happens?" Julie's voice is just above a whisper.

"Then he can be arrested."

Julie nods, swallowing hard. "Thank you."

"You're doing the right thing," the clerk adds. "I know this is uncomfortable, but too many women wait until it's too late, and something terrible happens to them. You have to protect yourself where you can."

Julie flinches, and I step forward, placing my hand on her waist, needing to be close to her.

As we walk out, I wrap my arm around her, feeling her lean into me. The October sun is bright, and it makes her squint.

"You okay?" I ask.

"I hate that it came to this," she mutters. "I just wanted Craig to move on. To be happy with Sarah, have his baby, live his life. He moved away, and I thought he would be gone forever. None of this should've happened."

"I do understand him not wanting to let you go," I tell her, tilting her chin up to meet my eyes. "But he has to. It's become an obsession, Jules. Driving by your house, keeping your photos, calling Sarah by your name ... that is not normal behavior."

"And what happens if he doesn't respect this?" She waves the copy of the order. "Will they actually do something?"

I don't answer because I don't know. Restraining orders work if the person respects them. And Craig has already shown he doesn't care about boundaries.

"Come on," I say, leading her to the Range Rover, needing to change the subject. "Want to get lunch?"

"Hmm ..." She looks up at me with those green eyes, still glassy with unshed tears. "Can we just go home?"

The word *home* does something to me.

She continues, "I want to spend the rest of my free time with you today. Just us. No wandering eyes or whispers."

"Whatever you want, Little Red."

When we return to her condo, Julie kicks off her shoes and collapses on the couch. "Want to be a potato with me?"

"Hell yeah," I say, joining her.

I position myself behind her body, holding her as she flicks on the TV. Her phone buzzes, and she pulls it from her pocket.

AUTUMN

Just checking in. How are things?

BLAIRE

Yeah, let us know!

SHE TEXTS THE GROUP CHAT, NAMED THE SANDERSON SISTERS, WHICH includes the three of them.

JULIE

I'm surviving!

SHE RECORDS A VOICE MEMO TO CATCH THEM UP. THEIR RESPONSES come fast, and it's all supportive messages. Autumn even threatens to deal with Craig herself if he violates the order.

Then she texts her mom and updates her too.

MOM

Oh, sweetheart. Good for you.

JULIE

You're not upset?

MOM

Upset? I'm relieved! Your father and I have been worried sick about his behavior. It's unacceptable. I'm proud of you for standing up for yourself. How are you and Nick?

She turns her head toward me, smiling. "My parents adore you."

I snuggle into her neck, kissing the softness of her skin. "I adore them."

JULIE

We're great!

MOM

I like him. Seems as if you two really hit it off.

JULIE

Thanks, Mom!

MOM

I'm serious. I've never seen you so happy. Hope you're having the best time.

JULIE

I am. It's been incredible.

Julie tilts her head and looks at me, aware that I can read everything. "Guess they don't need any convincing."

"Do you?" I ask.

"No," she says, setting her phone down, then completely turning toward me until we're face-to-face. "Whatever happens on Halloween, know that I will always cherish this time with you."

"I will too. It's been the best autumn of my life." I kiss her, wanting her to know.

She smiles against my lips. "Want to watch *Dumb and Dumber*? I could use some ridiculousness."

"If you asked me to watch grass grow with you, I would."

She twists around, pressing her ass against my cock. Our bodies mold together as she reaches for the remote, then clicks on the movie. I wrap my arm around her, holding her, smelling her, appreciating how she fits in my arms, wanting this moment to last a lifetime.

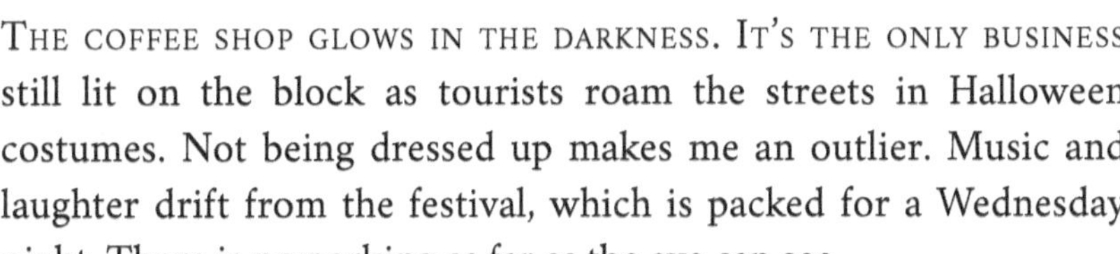

THE COFFEE SHOP GLOWS IN THE DARKNESS. IT'S THE ONLY BUSINESS still lit on the block as tourists roam the streets in Halloween costumes. Not being dressed up makes me an outlier. Music and laughter drift from the festival, which is packed for a Wednesday night. There is no parking as far as the eye can see.

Through the large walls of windows of Cozy Coffee, I see Blaire and Tracy behind the counter, finishing their closing duties.

I push through the front door, and the bell chimes, announcing my arrival.

Three hours ago, I walked Julie to Cozy Coffee so she could start counting her inventory. She told me she'd be finished around closing time. While she was doing that, I had a very long discussion with Asher. It was productive.

"Sorry, we're closed," Tracy says, and then she realizes it's me. "Hey, Nick! Julie's in the office. You can go back there, but can you lock the door for me first?"

"Hi. Sure," I say, doing what she asked.

Blaire wipes down the espresso machine and lifts her brow at me. "Hey, stranger."

"Stranger?" I say with a laugh. "Sorry I haven't been around much. I've been busy."

"'Busy.'" She uses air quotes.

Sierra laughs as her head pops up from the pastry case she's cleaning. Tracy finishes counting the register and slides the drawer out.

"We're heading out in ten," Blaire says with a knowing smirk. "Then the shop will be all yours."

"Great," I tell her. "How have things been?"

"Quiet," Blaire admits. "No signs of the ex, which is either a blessing or a curse. I haven't decided yet."

"Total blessing," Sierra says. "He's weird AF."

"He wasn't always like that," Tracy explains. "I think he started losing it after he realized Julie had moved on."

"What did he expect? For Julie to sit around and wait for him?" Blaire scoffs. "They've been over. He can kick rocks. If he doesn't watch out, I'm going to put a hex on him."

A part of me feels guilty, and I wonder if I instigated something.

I make my way to the back office, finding Julie bent over the desk, calculator in hand, surrounded by clipboards. Her hair is piled on top of her head, held up with a pencil. I watch her for a few seconds, loving how pretty she looks when she concentrates.

"How's it going?" I ask from the doorway.

She looks over at me and grins. "Oh, hi! I was just thinking about you."

"Really?" I ask. "I was thinking about you too. Almost finished?"

"I've counted all the cups, lids, syrups, and, well, everything. Now I'm trying to reconcile it with last month's numbers and calculate what we need to order."

"Want help?"

"You know how to do inventory?"

"I help run a multibillion-dollar company, remember?"

"You're right." She scoots over, making room for me at the desk. Our thighs press together as she slides the keyboard toward me. "These numbers go in this column."

"Bye, Jules!" Blaire calls out. "We're leaving! I miss you!"

"I miss you! Thanks for everything!" Julie calls back.

The front door chimes, and then there's silence.

We're alone.

I work through inputting the numbers into the computer system as she logs things in a book. Every few minutes, she shifts, her leg brushing against mine. The office feels smaller, more intimate.

"You're good at this," she says, watching me work.

"You sound surprised."

"I'm not. Maybe having you here will be my new tradition."

I laugh. "Maybe so."

She smirks and stands, moving between me and the desk. "We're alone."

"What about finishing the inventory?"

"The numbers can wait. I can't," she says.

"You're sure?" I ask, glancing at all the family photos on the wall.

"Yes," she says. "Make my fantasy come true."

The air shifts between us, and it's full of anticipation. I pull her onto my lap, feeling the warmth of her body pressed against mine as she straddles me.

Her hands fly to my belt, and it's desperate, but I catch her wrists before she gets it undone.

"Not yet," I murmur, rougher than I intended.

Her eyes flash up to mine, all fire and need, and, God, it nearly kills me to deny her, but I want her strung tight. I want her begging for me. I want to watch her lose control piece by piece because she needs this.

I slide my palms up her thighs, dragging out the touch, savoring the way her skin burns under my hands. I grip her ass, pulling her hard against me so she feels the thick length of my cock pressing into her. She rocks against me and releases a gasp. Pride overtakes me, knowing that I can affect her this way, that she trusts me to give her what she wants.

Her mouth crashes into mine, lips feverish, tongue greedy, and I taste her, never able to get enough. My fist tangles in her long hair, tilting her head just enough to steal more of her moans. I push her back against the desk, papers sliding to the floor, but I don't care. The only thing in this room that matters is her.

I unbutton her blouse one slow pop at a time, holding her gaze, as if to remind her that she belongs to me. Like she could forget. When her bra falls away and her breasts spill free, I cup them, tweak her nipples until they're tight peaks against my palms. Her head tips back, and she whispers my name like it's a prayer.

I could worship her for eternity.

I drop to my knees, shove her skirt up, and press my mouth against the damp lace of her panties. The taste of her teases me, even through the fabric, and my cock jerks painfully against my zipper. I slide the lace aside and lick her. I take my time savoring the sweetness, how she shudders when I brush against her clit. The desperate cries she can't hold back have my cock throbbing in anticipation.

When she starts to shake, I pull away, grinning.

"Mmm. Patience, Little Red," I whisper, standing again, my lips slick with her arousal.

Her eyes blaze with frustration. "You're torturing me."

"It's worth the wait," I mutter, spinning her around and bending her over the desk. "Arch that perfect pussy for me."

She braces herself, palms flat on the wood, ass high. I thrust my hand through her hair and grab a fist of it, tugging her head back, needing to hear her.

"Do you know who you belong to?"

"You," she gasps, voice breaking. "I'm yours, Nick."

Her confession burns through me.

"Now tell me what you want."

"Fuck me," she says, her voice almost strangled.

I free myself and drag the head of my cock along her slick folds, coating myself in her wetness, teasing until she's whimpering.

"Please," she begs.

That's all I need.

I slam into her in one hard thrust, burying myself to the hilt. She screams my name, her body clenching tight around me, and the sensation nearly undoes me.

"Yes, sweetheart." I groan, gripping her hips and driving into her again—harder.

The desk shakes beneath us, her moans filling the room, and I know this isn't just sex. It's something deeper.

I thrust into her over and over, my hand still tangled in her hair, pulling her back against me. I want her to remember this, to feel me everywhere tomorrow. Her cries are desperate, broken, her body rocking with every slam of my hips. I reach around, grabbing her breast.

"You were made for me," I pant, leaning over her back, pressing my mouth to her ear. "Every inch of you."

Her response is a sobbed moan, her body tightening, fluttering around me. And then she shatters, screaming my name, coming so hard that her legs quake. The sound, the feel of her pulsing around me, wrecks me.

I pound into her a few more times before I lose it, spilling deep inside her with a guttural groan. My vision blurs, my body convulses, and all I can do is hold her hair, her hips, like she's the only thing keeping me tied to this reality.

When it's over, we collapse forward. My chest to her back, sweat dripping down my temples. I press a kiss to her shoulder, still buried inside her, unwilling to break away.

"That was amazing," she whispers, still unable to catch her breath. "Exactly what I needed."

"You're amazing," I say, kissing her neck.

I realize that I have everything I've ever needed with her. I want more of this. I want her laugh, her fire, the way she challenges me. I want every piece of her. We break apart, and she turns around, sliding her skirt over her body. We're still breathing hard, trying to straighten our clothes and the paperwork that's scattered everywhere.

"We just …" Julie starts, then laughs.

"Made some memories in this office?"

"That's one way to put it."

"You started it," I tell her, tucking her hair behind her ears, then kissing her.

"And you finished it." She grins, looking up at me. "I'm so lucky."

"No, babe, I am."

After our heart rates settle, we sit back at the desk and finish doing inventory. Every few minutes, we catch each other's eye and smile like teenagers with a secret.

"Thank you," she says.

"For?"

"For today. For all of it."

"You never have to thank me for being there for you."

She reaches over, taking my hand. "I know things are going to get complicated when Craig is served. But having you here with me … I feel safe."

"You are safe. I won't let anything happen to you," I promise.

An hour later, Julie submits the reports and places the order for next week's shipment. We walk out into the cool October night, holding hands. Not because anyone is watching, but because it feels right.

"Did you think it could be like this?" she asks.

"Only in my dreams," I say.

As we stroll to her condo, I can't shake the feeling that this peace we have won't last and that something's coming. But for tonight, we're together, and that has to be enough.

25

JULIE

With Nick's hand in mine and the October wind whipping my hair around, the three-block walk from Cozy Coffee to my condo feels shorter. We're both giddy from what happened in the office, and we steal glances at each other.

My parents would be pissed if they knew, but that's the allure of it.

"I can't believe we just did that," I say, squeezing his hand.

"Inventory or—"

"You know which part." I bump his shoulder. "My grandmother is probably rolling in her grave."

"Or giving you a high five from heaven."

"Nick!"

"What? I'm sure she'd want you to be happy, even if that meant getting dicked down in her sacred office."

I feel my cheeks heat.

We pass the closed boutiques, their windows decorated with scarecrows and autumn leaves. The streets are still packed with festivalgoers in costumes, along with drunk tourists stumbling home from Bookers. My body still tingles from his touch, and I'm already thinking about what we'll do when we get home. I could go for round two.

We turn down the sidewalk toward my condo, and I'm mid-sentence about wanting kettle corn when something makes me stop.

The porch light is off, and I know when Nick walked me to the coffee shop, we left it on. I always do. It's been a habit since I moved in six years ago.

"Nick, did you turn off the porch light?" I ask.

"No," he says, and then he sees it too.

My front door isn't completely closed. It's been broken off the hinges and is cracked open. Darkness from inside bleeds onto the porch like spilled ink.

"Stay here." His entire demeanor changes.

The playful, relaxed man from seconds ago is gone, replaced by someone ready for combat. His shoulders square and jaw clenched tight, Nick positions himself between me and my condo.

"But what if—"

"Please, stay here." His voice is commanding in a way I've never heard before. He pulls out his phone. "I'm calling the police."

But I can't just stand scared on the sidewalk.

This is my home. My safe space.

I follow him up the sidewalk, my heart pounding so hard that I can feel it in my throat.

Nick pushes the door open wider with his foot, not touching the handle. Smart. Fingerprints. He reaches inside to flip the light switch, his body still blocking mine.

The living room illuminates, and my stomach drops like I'm on a roller coaster going down.

Everything is wrong.

The couch cushions are at odd angles, with indents in each one. I can imagine him sitting on each of them. Picture frames on my bookshelf have been moved—the one of me and my parents is face down; the one of me, Autumn, and Blaire is turned backward. My grandmother's quilt, which is always draped over the back of my couch, lies crumpled on the floor. Craig knows how much that means to me and he tossed it aside like trash.

"Don't go in," Nick says, already on the phone with 911, but I'm pushing past him.

"My things—"

"Don't touch anything." He grabs my arm, gently pulling me back to him. "This is a crime scene, Jules. I don't know if he's still here or not."

The words hit me like ice water. Crime scene.

I'm shaking as we move through the apartment, careful not to disturb anything. In the kitchen, every cabinet door hangs open. My spice rack has been reorganized, the labels all facing different directions. The junk drawer is pulled out, contents rifled through, but nothing obviously missing.

"Why would someone—" I start, then stop because I know why.

This isn't about theft; it's Craig showing me that he's touched everything of mine.

The bathroom is worse. My medicine cabinet is open; bottles of ibuprofen and vitamins are in the sink. The shower curtain is pulled back. Even my makeup bag has been unzipped, lipsticks and mascara scattered on the counter, but it's my bedroom that makes bile rise in my throat.

My underwear drawer isn't just open; it's been picked through. I know because I organize by color, and now it's chaos. Black mixed with nude, lace mixed with cotton. He's touched every piece.

The photos of Nick and me from the festival that Autumn took were on my dresser. They're all ripped in half. And there, in the center of my bed, where I can't miss it, is a note written in his familiar handwriting.

HE'LL LEAVE YOU, LIKE THEY ALL DO. YOU ALWAYS COME

BACK TO ME. YOU ALWAYS WILL. NO ONE WILL EVER LOVE YOU, JULIE. ONLY ME.

"Fuck you, Craig," I whisper, my voice breaking on his name.

Nick is still on the phone with dispatch, but I see his free hand clench into a fist so tight that his knuckles go white. The muscle in his jaw tics. I've never seen him this angry—not even when Craig confronted us at the festival.

"Someone broke into my girlfriend's apartment," he says, voice controlled but full of fury. "Yes, we're safe. No, we haven't touched anything. We need officers here now." He gives my address, then adds, "The intruder left a threatening note. We know who did this."

I sink onto my ottoman chair—the one my grandmother gave me when I was a little girl—unable to stop shaking. Craig was in my bedroom. He touched my panties, my photos, and my bed. The violation of it makes my skin crawl, and I want to shower for hours. I want to burn everything he might have touched.

"Hey." Nick crouches in front of me after ending the call, taking my face in his hands. His touch is gentle. "Look at me. You're safe. You're okay."

"He was in here. He touched—" My voice cracks.

"I know. I know, sweetheart. But you're safe. He's gone."

"The restraining order. Do you think he was served and this set him off?"

"Possibly," Nick says. "I don't know what he's thinking."

The police arrive ten minutes later, though it seems like hours have passed.

There are two officers—Grady, who's older with tired eyes, and a younger one who looks fresh out of the academy that I've never met before. His name badge says *Officer Sanders*. They take photos of everything, dust the doorknob and light switches for prints, and bag the note as evidence with gloved hands. They're professional, but their questions make me think I've done something wrong.

"Any security cameras?" Officer Grady asks.

"No," I say.

"Alarm system?"

I shake my head.

"Witnesses? Neighbors who might have seen something?" he continues.

"I don't know. Maybe. You can ask them."

"Okay," he says, but his tone suggests they won't find anything useful. "Any idea who might have done this?"

"Craig Downing," I say. "I literally filed a restraining order against him today. He's my obsessive ex who's been stalking me."

The officers exchange glances that make my stomach sink.

"Without proof he was here—" Officer Sanders starts.

"Who else would leave that note?" Nick's voice is dangerous. "Who else has been stalking her? Showing up at her work? Driving by here at night?"

Grady starts. "We understand your frustration—"

"Do you?" Nick steps forward. "Because from where I'm standing, you're more interested in making excuses than catching the person who did this."

Officer Sanders clears his throat. "With all due respect, sir, without evidence placing Mr. Downing here—"

"The note is evidence. The pattern of behavior is evidence," Nick says.

"We'll look into it," Officer Grady says in that placating tone that tells me nothing will happen. "We'll talk to him, see where he was tonight."

"And he'll lie," I say. "He'll have an alibi. His mother will lie for him. She always does."

The younger officer looks sympathetic but useless. "We'll add this to your restraining order file. It will help establish a pattern if anything else happens."

"If anything else happens?" I laugh, but it's hollow. "He broke into my home. What else does he need to do? Hurt me?"

They don't answer because we all know the truth. Until he gets physical, until there's proof, until something worse happens, they can't do much.

It takes them two hours to finish taking pictures, taking my statement, and finalizing everything. It's two hours of standing in my violated space, trying not to touch anything that he might have touched, trying not to think about Craig's hands sifting through my belongings. Every surface feels contaminated. Every object out of place feels wrong.

"We can't stay here," Nick says once the police leave, their cards left behind with case numbers.

"I can't let him run me out of my own home—"

"Jules, sweetheart." He places his hands on my shoulders. "Please. Just for tonight. I'll have a security system installed for you, complete with cameras, new locks, and anything else you need. But tonight, we can't stay here. He could be lingering."

I look around my sanctuary, my safe space, and see it through a different lens. Craig has poisoned it.

"I hate him," I sob, the tears coming violently.

Nick pulls me into his chest, and I break.

"I hate that he can do this. That he thinks he owns me. That he won't just leave me alone."

"He doesn't own you. He never did." Nick holds me tight, one hand in my hair, the other rubbing my back. "Pack a bag. We're leaving."

"I don't want to go to Riverside."

"Then we'll stay at Hollow Manor. With Zane and Autumn. Just … not here. Not tonight."

I nod against his chest, wiping my tears on his shirt. He doesn't seem to mind.

While I pack, trying not to think about Craig's hands sliding through my dresser drawers hours ago, Nick makes calls. First to Zane, speaking urgently, then to someone else. I only catch bits and pieces of his conversation.

"Yeah, I know it's late in New York. Someone broke into Julie's apartment and … we think it was her ex. Can you? Yeah, that would be perfect. Tomorrow? Even better. Thanks, man."

"What was that about?" I ask, zipping my overnight bag. I've packed enough for several days, not wanting to come back here anytime soon.

"Asher. He fixes things. I just want him to be aware, just in case this explodes into something else."

"I'm sorry. I feel—"

"This isn't your fault." His voice is fierce. "You didn't ask for any of this. I'm here with you, Jules. We'll figure this out together."

"Okay," I whisper. "Thank you."

"No need to thank me."

We drive to Hollow Manor in silence. One of Nick's hands holds mine, and it's pure comfort. His other hand grips the steering wheel with white knuckles.

"I want to find him and fuck him up," he says as we wind up the mountain road.

"Nick—"

"I won't. But I want to." He glances at me, and in the dashboard light, his eyes are dark with rage. "No one should ever make you feel unsafe in your own home. No one should be able to violate your space like that."

"I'm okay."

"You're not." He pulls into Hollow Manor's driveway and turns to me. He reaches toward my face, and his thumb brushes my cheek. "And that's allowed. You don't have to be strong all the time, Jules. You don't have to minimize this."

The words break something in me, and I cry again, ugly sobs that I've been holding back since we found the door open. Nick wraps his arms around me, letting me fall apart in his Range Rover.

By the time we reach the front door, I'm cried out. Autumn takes one look at us and goes into best-friend mode.

"The guest room is ready," she says, not asking questions. "There's wine if you need it. Or something stronger."

"Thanks," Nick says while I collapse on their couch, feeling boneless and exhausted.

"That bastard," Zane says, his jaw clenching.

"My thoughts," Nick mutters.

"What did the police say?" Autumn asks.

"Nothing useful," I manage. "Without proof it was him ..."

"Bullshit," Autumn spits. "Who else would it be?"

Zane makes me chamomile with honey. Autumn sits with me, not talking, just being there, her hand holding mine. It's what I need.

"He took some of my panties," I tell her while the men talk logistics.

"We'll go shopping tomorrow. All new everything. He doesn't get to make you feel this way."

Later, in the guest room with its soft blue walls and white curtains, Nick holds me in the dark. The bed is comfortable but unfamiliar. Everything smells like lavender instead of my usual vanilla.

"I should have been there, waiting for him," he says.

"You were with me. I had fun with you tonight."

"I did too, sweetheart. But I should've insisted on the security system sooner. Should've been more prepared for this. Should have—"

"Please stop." I turn to face him, barely able to make out his features in the moonlight. "This isn't your fault. It's Craig's. Only Craig's."

"I just ... I can't lose you."

"You won't."

We both know that October 31 is coming, whether we're ready or not. And now, I'm terrified of what might happen before we get there. What if Nick decides this is too much or I'm too much?

"Does this make you want to run away from me?" I ask in the smallest voice.

Nick's lips press against my forehead. "It makes me want to hold you closer."

The certainty in his voice makes me feel safe, and for the first time since we saw my condo door busted open, I relax.

"Now, let's get some sleep. You're safe," he says against my skin, holding me. "I'm with you."

26

NICK

It's been three days since the break-in. Three days of Julie startling at every creak in Hollow Manor, of checking and rechecking locks, of barely sleeping, even with me holding her. This morning, she insisted on returning to her condo. The security company is installing everything today. I special-ordered state-of-the-art equipment.

"I'm letting him win," she says as we pull up to her building.

"You're not. And it's not about winning or losing. This is about protecting you. Not just from Craig, but from anyone else who tries to snoop." I squeeze her hand. "This company is the best. They've completed several celebrity homes across the US."

"Of course they have." But she's smiling.

The installation team is already at work. Cameras are at every angle, motion sensors, and smart locks that'll alert her phone if anyone even approaches the door. The lead installer—a former military guy named Jeffrey—walks us through everything with professional efficiency.

"No one's getting in here without you knowing," he assures Julie. "This system is—"

Julie's phone rings, cutting him off, and she silences it. "Sorry, please continue."

She shows me the screen, and I see Autumn's name. She calls three more times as the guy continues walking Julie through how to use everything. He finishes his explanation, and her phone rings again.

"Answer it," I whisper to her.

"Okay," she says, putting it on speaker while she watches them install a camera. "What's up?"

"Jules, don't freak out." Autumn's voice is serious in a way I've never heard before.

Julie goes still. "What happened?"

"I don't know how to tell you this." Autumn doesn't speak for a very long time, and my heart begins to race. "There are photos of you posted online."

"What kind of photos?" I ask.

Autumn sighs. "Intimate ones. They're … they're everywhere."

The blood drains from Julie's face. She drops her phone, and it crashes to the ground. She hurries and picks it up. "Please explain."

"It's Craig. He posted things he had no business posting. Said you were a whore who deserved to be exposed."

"No." Julie's hands start shaking. "No, no, no."

I'm already calling Asher as Julie breaks down while she talks to Autumn. My anger builds with every cracked word that releases from her mouth.

"We have a situation," I tell my brother when he answers.

"What kind of situation?"

"Revenge porn. Julie's ex posted intimate photos of her online."

"Have you seen them?" he asks.

"I haven't."

"I will be in Cozy Creek as soon as I can," Asher tells me. "Tell her not to look at anything online. It's counterproductive. I'll start making calls. We're in crisis mode."

Asher ends the call, and Julie rushes over to me with devastation in her eyes. She's got the pictures pulled up on her phone, and she's sobbing.

"Everyone's seeing this, Nick. My parents, my coworkers, everyone in town."

"We'll fix it," I say, grabbing her hand.

"You can't!" She's growing hysterical. "I'm so exposed. Those photos are out there forever. People have already screenshotted them. I'm probably on porn sites already."

"Sweetheart, I don't think you understand how powerful my company is. I will fix this." I study her. "Is there anything else I need to be aware of? Are there videos? More pictures?"

"No," she whispers. "No, he posted everything he has."

The security team leaves, and within fifteen minutes, the doorbell rings.

We freeze until she checks the live video feed on her phone. I lean over her shoulder and see it's Mrs. Patrick, with several more of the Fairy Godmothers, all carrying casserole dishes and flowers.

"It's Mrs. Patrick, Mrs. Mooney, Mrs. Henderson, Mrs. Caldwell, and Mrs. Lutcher." She points to all of them, then sighs. "They won't let me ignore them."

I squeeze her shoulder. "I'll answer it."

"Okay," she says.

I open the door, and Mrs. Patrick speaks.

"We're here for Julie! That bastard Craig needs to burn in hell for what he's done!"

They sweep in like an avenging army of grandmas, surrounding Julie with a fierce, protective energy. I try to stay professional while these women plot Craig's demise.

"The whole town's talking about it," Mrs. Caldwell says. "But not how Craig wanted. This is criminal."

"Sarah's at the police station right now," Mrs. Patrick tells us. "Apparently, he did the same thing to her. Posted her photos on some disgusting website months ago."

"Sarah?" Julie looks up. "Craig's pregnant ex-girlfriend, Sarah?"

Mrs. Patrick nods. "She's been too ashamed to report it until now. But seeing what he did to you gave her courage."

Julie looks stunned, her face pale as she processes what Mrs. Patrick just said. "He did this to Sarah?"

The Fairy Godmothers nod, sharing their outrage; their voices surround us.

"You did nothing wrong, Julie," Mrs. Mooney insists, patting her shoulder. "It's shameful he went this low."

Mrs. Henderson adds, "The whole town knows it. We're furious for you. And we're not going to let this go. I've already had choice words with his mother."

Julie leads them into the kitchen, where they set their casserole dishes on the counter. "I thought … I thought this would ruin me."

I slide my arm around her. "You are not ruined. You're the strongest woman I've ever met. I'll burn the world down before I let anyone make you feel like less."

Her eyes glisten, but I see something spark behind the tears. It's pure anger.

Mrs. Patrick crosses her arms. "Sarah's already pressing charges. We'll all testify if needed—because many of us were in the coffee shop the day you told him to leave. Men like Craig don't get to keep destroying lives in this town."

The other women agree. Their voices are a chorus of determination.

Julie looks around at them, at me, then takes a shaky breath. "Then I'll press charges too. He doesn't get to take any more from me. Not my privacy, not my peace, not my future."

I'm filled with pride and fury as I kiss the top of her head. "Asher's already mobilizing PR and legal. Craig has no idea what kind of war he just started."

The Fairy Godmothers clap like it's settled.

"We'll handle the gossip," Mrs. Patrick says. "You handle the lawyers."

Mrs. Mooney smiles. "I know this is hard to handle right now, but, honey, when you're my age, you'll be proud of a body like that. If I could go back in time, I'd personally walk around naked everywhere I went. I didn't realize what I had in my youth."

Julie bursts into laughter. "Thank you. I guess that's a silver lining."

And as the women around us talk strategy and vengeance, I know one thing for sure: Craig Downing picked the wrong woman to cross. He hasn't gone after just Julie, but after every single one of us. He won't win.

Once everyone has left and we're alone, Julie leans into me. "We're in this together, right?"

"Always," I promise.

She seems to relax.

Four hours later, Asher arrives and doesn't bother with pleasantries. Behind him are two people I don't know.

"Status?" he barks at one of them as soon as he enters Julie's condo.

"Photos went up at eight a.m. across all major platforms," the woman reports. "We've got them down from Instagram and Facebook. Twitter's being slower. Working on DMCA takedowns for the rest."

"Criminal charges?" Asher asks.

"Colorado has revenge porn laws. Class 1 misdemeanor, but with the restraining order violation and pattern of behavior with multiple victims, the DA might bump it to a felony," the guy with him says.

"Sorry, who the fuck are you two?" I ask, glancing between them.

"Oh, this is Laurel and Patrick. The new interns I hired two weeks ago, who are learning how to handle crisis management," Asher explains, then turns back to them. "Make sure it's a felony. I want him buried. No one messes with my brother's girlfriend."

Hearing Asher be so protective makes me smile.

"Do you know where Craig is now?" I ask.

"No," Patrick says. "After posting the photos, it seems as if he's disappeared. We have a private investigator trying to track him. His apartment is empty."

Julie goes even paler. "He's hiding?"

"He's screwed, and he knows it," Asher says. "This is a crime with more than enough evidence to convict. Because you filed that temporary restraining order, this will not be taken lightly. This is retaliation."

Julie turns her phone back on against my advice, and the notifications are overwhelming. I read over her shoulder—some messages are supportive, but others are disgusting. Strange men explaining what they'd do to her. Some are even calling her horrible names.

"Sweetheart, turn it off," I whisper. "Seeing it won't help."

Her phone rings before she can speak, and it's her mom.

"Mom," Julie says, voice breaking.

"Oh, honey." Her mother sounds upset. "Your dad and I saw … we're sick for you. Craig is a monster."

"Mom, I'm so sorry—"

"Don't you dare apologize. He betrayed you."

Her father's voice comes through. "I'm going to find him and make him pay for this."

Julie excuses herself and goes upstairs so she can chat in private while more people arrive to support her. Autumn and Zane enter, and Blaire follows behind them with crystals and sage. Coffee shop employees stop by with messages of support.

"Julie is trending," Laurel says, shaking her head. "The story's going viral."

"Shit." I run my fingers through my hair. I can't help but notice the spotlight is burning brighter because of me. Had Julie been dating anyone else, this might have been swept under the rug sooner, but because I'm attached to her, it's getting unneeded visibility.

My phone rings from an unknown number.

"Don't answer—" Asher starts, but I don't listen.

"Is this Nicolas Banks?"

"What do you want?"

"This is TMZ. Would you like to comment on your girlfriend's revenge-porn situation? We—"

I hang up, my jaw clenched.

Julie comes downstairs and hugs Autumn and Blaire, and they stay huddled together for minutes.

"LadyLux has emailed you," Asher says to me. "Do the interview tonight."

"Okay," Julie says, turning toward me.

"What's wrong?" I ask, holding her cheeks in my hands, looking into her shining green eyes.

"I'm worried this will ruin what we have. I could hurt your reputation, and—"

"Don't worry about me," I say, taking her hands. "I'm used to this. You matter more."

She searches my eyes. "I'm a liability. Your girlfriend's nudes are *trending.*"

"My girlfriend is trending because she was brave enough to stand up to an abuser."

A moment later, Autumn moves over to us with her phone open. It's a video of Craig at the brewery, fighting.

"Is this live?" Asher asks.

"Yes," Autumn tells him.

"We need to call the authorities," Zane says, unlocking his phone, but I'm already on it.

Craig's behavior is out of control.

"He's escalating this," Asher tells us. "A security system, even though it's as locked down as Fort Knox in here, isn't enough. You need personal protection."

Julie's mouth falls open. "I can't have a bodyguard. That—"

"You go nowhere alone," Asher explains. "Not until he's caught."

As I report the commotion going on at the brewery, Julie breaks down.

"I feel so violated. First my home, now my body—my privacy. He's taken everything."

Blaire holds Julie tight as she cries, and I hate this. It's breaking my heart.

"No," Autumn says. "He's tried to take everything. But you're still here. Still fighting. Still with Nick. You're strong."

Zane and Asher stare at me.

"Okay, sir, we already have a squad car heading out there now," the dispatcher tells me.

"Thank you," I say and end the call.

I move to Julie, and the girls step away as I wrap her in my arms. I kiss her hair, tell her how pretty she is and how we're going to work through this.

Asher clears his throat, moving close to us. "The LadyLux interview will be published tomorrow if you can return her email tonight. I know this sucks, but trust me when I say, I've cleaned up bigger messes than this. I am in no way minimizing what happened. It's utter bullshit, and if I could chop off that guy's dick and shove it down his throat, I absolutely would. However, it could be a lot worse. We will remove all instances of it that are posted. Eventually, a new scandal will happen, and everyone will move on to that. It's the nature of this."

Julie nods, finding that fighting spirit. "Do you promise?"

"Yes," Asher confirms, then glances at me. "I'll do whatever I can to fix this. Not to brag, but I'm the absolute best in the business."

"I know that," I say, grinning.

"Thank you. I'm … I'm so lucky to have all of you. I don't know what I'd do without you."

Autumn and Zane head out, promising to keep an eye on the town chatter. Blaire leaves crystals on every windowsill, kisses Julie's cheek, and threatens to hex Craig into oblivion before slipping out the door.

Asher lingers the longest, running through a list of follow-ups with his interns until I all but shove him out the door.

"We've got it from here," I tell him.

"You'd better," he warns, pointing at me like *he's* the older brother. Then his expression softens when he looks at Julie. "Don't worry. I've got you. I'll check in first thing tomorrow."

When the door shuts behind them, the silence feels heavy and welcome at the same time. Julie exhales, slumping against the counter like she's been holding her body upright with willpower.

"Alone at last," I mutter, crossing the room to pull her into my arms.

She lets herself melt into me for a long while before pulling back to meet my eyes.

"Alone except for the countless casseroles, flowers, and half a dozen military-grade security cameras."

"Isn't it romantic?" I ask, kissing her forehead with a smile.

She snorts. "Okay, let's get this interview over with before I lose my very last nerve."

I grab my laptop and lead her to the couch. She curls into me, her legs tucked under her. Julie's chin rests on my shoulder as I open the email from LadyLux. A neat list of questions waits in my inbox, half thoughtful, half nosy in that classic LadyLux way.

Julie groans when she sees the first one. "Who is this person?"

I grin. "Well, that's the thing. No one knows because she's anonymous. The rumor is that she's a widowed socialite who's part of all the elite circles. She writes the truth though, and she's fair, even when many I run with don't deserve it."

"Really?" Julie asks.

"Yes. I've tried to figure out who it is, and I think I almost have it pinpointed, but I'll never tell her secret."

"Who do you think it is?" Julie looks up at me.

"One of my friend's wives."

She bursts into laughter. "Scandalous."

"There's something about the way she watches that makes me

believe it's her. However, her husband is an asshole, and I don't want to stir the pot," I say.

"Wow." She inhales. "Is this how your life is?"

"Sometimes," I admit. "Other times, it's quiet. But enough about that. We should probably get started."

I read the first question out loud. *"How are you coping with such a personal violation becoming public?"*

Julie rolls her eyes. "How does she think I'm coping?"

"Some of this will be shit, but she has a way with words, I promise. Just speak your truth," I say, fingers hovering over the keys, ready to type whatever she says.

"All I can do is survive. Having intimate and private photographs of me displayed in such a crude manner has been tough. There was a time when I thought I'd marry that man, and every day, I'm thankful I didn't. I refuse to let his jealousy try to ruin and sabotage me. I have a strong support system—my friends, family, and the entire town of Cozy Creek— and I'm focusing on that instead of what Craig did to me." She tilts her head. "How's that?"

"That's good. I'm adding on the end ... *casserole. Lots and lots of casserole.*" I laugh.

"I'm excited about eating it," she admits.

"Me too," I tell her. "After we do this, we're digging in."

"Deal!" She bumps her shoulder into me.

I read the next one. *"How has this impacted your relationship with Nicolas Banks?"*

Julie's cheeks flush. "Oh no. Here we go."

I smirk. "Should I send her our sex tape?"

She swats my chest. "Nick! It is seriously too soon to even joke about that."

"Sorry. I'm not sharing it with anyone other than you. I give you my word."

She looks at me. "Can we watch it together?"

"After we finish these questions." I study her face, knowing she needs this.

I swear I see fire in her eyes.

"Okay. Give me the laptop."

"Sure, have at it," I tell her as she places her hands on the keys.

Julie reads the questions and types away, her fingers flying over the keyboard. I watch her, but I allow her to give her words, until she gets to the end.

"These questions are for you specifically," she tells me, passing the laptop back to me.

I place it on my upper thighs and read it.

How does this make you feel, knowing that this scumbag of a man did this to your girlfriend?

I'm upset for her. I'm upset that so many people are invading her privacy and supporting this cruel behavior. It makes me sick to my stomach, and I wouldn't wish this on my worst enemy. However, I will be there for her through this.

I move to the next question.

Are any of the rumors true? Is this a fake relationship to repair your reputation? You have to admit that all of this seems to have worked in your favor, and considering you are a Banks brother, it's not below you to fabricate something like this. Thoughts?

Julie doesn't react. "What does that mean?"

I glance at her. "Some people believe I'm here to repair my bad reputation and show the public I can commit so that the man-whore rumors will end."

"Did you come here for that?" she questions, tilting her head.

"No. I don't give a fuck about my reputation, babe. If I did, I wouldn't have done half the shit in my past so publicly. Also, I'd never use you."

"Oh, Nick. I'm so sorry. I never thought you'd use me. My head wasn't thinking that way."

"It's fine. I just want you to know that I'd never do anything to hurt you. After what happened with Craig, you need to hear that. I promise you that on my sister's grave," I tell her. "And I'd never lie to my sister."

She tears up and wraps her arms around me. "Thank you. I'm so scared this is going to push you away."

"I'm not going anywhere. I'm right here."

I type the answer to the last question and set the laptop on the coffee table.

"LadyLux has her email. Can we eat casserole now?"

I grin. "Later. First, victory kiss."

She arches a brow. "Victory kiss?"

I tug her into my lap, kissing her until she's laughing against my mouth. Her hands fist my shirt, pulling me closer, and suddenly, the room feels smaller, charged in that way it always does when I'm with her.

When she pulls back, she whispers, "Can we watch it together?"

I search her face. "You were serious?"

She nods, green eyes fierce despite the nerves in them. "I want to see it. To see us."

I pull my phone from my pocket, unlock the private folder Asher built for me, and press play. The Riverside bedroom fills the screen. I see her blindfolded with wrists tied to the bed, both of us raw, reckless, alive.

Julie's breath hitches. "God, you look at me like—"

"Tell me," I mutter into her ear.

"Like I'm *everything*."

"Because you are."

As she continues to watch, her skin floods with goose bumps, nipples tighten beneath her shirt, and her thighs press together. I see it, feel it.

"Show me what you need."

She swallows hard, then slides her hand under her joggers. My chest aches as I watch her. Every soft gasp, every tremble of her body wrecks me.

"You're sexy," I whisper, forcing myself not to touch her. "You undo me, Jules."

Her eyes stay locked on the screen as her hand moves, her breath stuttering, the sound of it breaking me open.

"Come for me, sweetheart," I command, knowing she's close.

She gasps my name and lets go, body convulsing with satisfaction. Julie on-screen is shattering at the exact moment as the one beside me. This is vulnerable, and so damn beautiful.

"Nick, that was so good, but I need you," she whispers, still shaking.

I drag her into my arms, kiss her until she's breathless, then lower her back onto the couch cushions. When I finally slide into her, it isn't desperate. It's slow, deep, and all-consuming. Every kiss, every brush of her hands is a promise. She clings to me, nails scratching down my back. Her hot mouth presses against my jaw, my throat, my lips.

"You're mine," I whisper against her mouth.

"I've been yours since the beginning," she breathes back.

From then on, every thrust, every kiss, every breath is mine. She wraps her legs around me, begging for me to spill inside her.

When she whispers, "Please," I give her everything and come undone with her.

My kisses are filled with so much emotion that it makes her whimper.

Later, when we collapse together, she buries her face in my chest.

"I don't ever want this to end," she confesses in my ear.

I hold her tighter, kiss her hair. "It doesn't have to."

Craig can try to take her home, her privacy, and her past, but he'll never take this.

This is ours. And I want forever.

27

JULIE

I t's been four days since my intimate photos were leaked to the world, and I'm trying very hard to pretend everything is normal. The LadyLux article that was published yesterday helped tremendously, but it doesn't erase what happened.

The Halloween costume shop on Main Street is supposed to be my escape from reality today, but I don't feel comfortable in public yet. Random glances feel personal, like people are imagining my naked body from the photos. Craig put our private moments on display for everyone to see. What he's done is unforgiveable.

"Someone said I was trying to be the next Kim K and this scandal was to help me launch an OnlyFans career," I say, reading the comments on the bottom of the post as we walk the few blocks to our destination. My laugh comes out bitter. "Wait, why did you ask me if I had an OF when we met?"

"Because you're gorgeous," he says.

I tilt my head at him. "Would you have followed me?"

"I don't have an account, but I'd have made one." Nick squeezes my hand as we walk through the door. "Let's have fun."

The bell chimes overhead, and Patty, the woman who's run this costume shop for thirty years, looks up from the register. I used to buy all of mine from her when I was a kid. As soon as she sees me, her face softens into a smile.

"Julie, baby. Come here." She rounds the counter and pulls me into a tight hug. "That bastard should rot in hell for what he did to you."

"Thanks, Patty." I sink into her hug for a moment. "Congrats on winning the autumn arrangement contest again."

"Aw, appreciate that considering some people in town are jealous." She smells like cinnamon and mothballs, and the familiarity is comforting.

"It's very much deserved," I tell her.

The shop is busier than usual with Halloween approaching. The aisles are cramped with costume racks, and I have to squeeze past a family debating between zombie and vampire themes. Some customers glance at me with sympathy. It's mostly locals who know me or my parents. Others stare with a different kind of recognition that makes my skin crawl. They saw me naked.

One man near the superhero section does a double take, his eyes lighting up. He elbows his friend and whispers something before they pull out their phones.

"Eyes forward, asshole," Nick barks out, his voice loud in the quietness.

The guys scurry toward the exit, but not before one turns to me. "Nice to know the curtains match the drapes."

Nick walks over to me, his brows furrowed.

"You can't threaten everyone who looks at me," I whisper, though part of me secretly loves that he tries. While I hate needing protection, I also love how safe it makes me feel.

"Watch me."

Patty appears beside us again. "Anyone else gives you any more trouble, you tell me. I've got a baseball bat behind the counter, and I'm not afraid to use it."

"That won't be necessary," I say. She reminds me of my

grandma. "Seriously. They're dumb teenagers who follow pop culture news. They don't understand."

She walks away, and Nick comes closer.

"We can leave."

"I'm good," I tell him.

We split up to keep our costumes a surprise from one another. It's something we decided before we got here. We'll reveal them to one another on Halloween night.

Nick heads toward the men's section while I wander through the women's racks. I already know what I want based on something he said to me a few weeks ago.

I find the perfect costume tucked between a witch outfit and a flapper dress. The teal-blue fabric is soft with gold trim that catches the light. It's sexy but not too revealing. Important now that everyone knows what's underneath.

"Princess Jasmine is a perfect fit for you. I even have the wig and crown," Patty says, materializing beside me like she has a sixth sense for customers who need encouragement.

"You don't think it's too revealing, do you?" I meet her eyes.

"Too what? Honey, you wear whatever makes you feel good. You're gorgeous. Don't let that piece-of-shit ex of yours make you believe you need to hide anything. But let me ask you this: would you have worn it before this happened?"

"Yes," I tell her.

"That's your answer then." She shifts me toward the dressing room, and I make my way down the aisle. "You'd better try it on because you know I won't do a return."

"Right. All sales final."

As I'm heading to the dressing room in the back, I hear raised voices in the front.

"You need to leave. Now." Patty's friendly voice has turned to steel.

"It's a free country. I can shop where I want," a guy says, slurring.

Day drinking on a Tuesday is so classy. But then recognition washes over me, and my blood freezes in my veins. For a second, I think it's Craig, but when I peek around the corner, it's not.

"Get out before I call the police," Patty says.

"It was posted that she was here! I wanna see if she's as hot in real life," he says to his friend, loud enough for the store to hear. "You know, the coffee chick with the great tits."

Rage and embarrassment flood through me. Before Nick can react, before I can think better of it, I'm placing the costume on the hook behind the door, and then I march toward them.

"Leave—right now," I say. My voice doesn't even shake. The steadiness surprises me almost as much as it surprises them. For a second, I'm braver than I feel.

When he recognizes me, the man's eyes light up with excitement.

"Holy shit, you really are here! Can I get a selfie? My friends won't believe I met you," he says, like he's a fan.

"Are you serious right now?" I ask.

"Come on. You're hot! Especially for a ginger!" He smirks, his eyes doing a slow scan of my body.

Nick moves so fast past me that I almost don't see him. He grabs the younger guys by their shirts and carries them outside.

"Hey! You can't do—"

One of them drops his phone, and Nick kicks it across the floor.

"Leave." His voice is calm, but it's absolutely terrifying. "Before you regret it."

Patty has already taken out her phone and is speaking to dispatch. "Yes, we have two men harassing a customer at The Costume Shop. They were refusing to leave and are standing outside. I want them charged with trespassing."

The one who took pictures of me looks at his shattered phone screen, and he's whining about lawsuits and assault charges.

"Sue me," Nick calls after them. "Please. I'd love to tell a judge what happened, and I'm sure the owner would too."

Patty nods with her hands on her hips.

After they leave, the store feels too quiet. Some customers are pretending not to care, while others' stares cause pinpricks on my skin. I feel out of place.

"I'm so sorry, honey," Patty says, touching my arm. "If anyone else bothers you, they're banned for life. I'm not kidding."

"Oh, please don't apologize," I say, but I'm shaking. My fight-or-flight is kicking in.

Nick wraps his arms around me from behind, his chin resting on my head. "We can leave if you want."

"No." I straighten my spine, channeling every ounce of stubbornness I have left. "I'm not letting creeps chase me out of here. I'm buying a costume, and we're going to the Halloween party, and I'm going to have fun for the rest of the month, even if it kills me."

He grins at me, tucking loose strands behind my ear. "Love it when you're fierce."

We continue shopping, but I'm now hyperaware of everyone. A mom with two kids gives me a sympathetic smile. Every glance feels loaded with something more, either judgment or pity. I hate this.

I glance down at my phone, realizing those little bastards posted the picture of me somehow. The comments under it are disgusting.

"Stop reading them," Nick singsongs as he hides his costume behind his back so I can't see it. "Now, go give her your costume and let her bag it up, and then I'll come pay."

I laugh, enjoying how seriously he's taking keeping it secret.

We make our purchases, and Patty refuses to let Nick pay full price. Then she leads us through the back entrance to avoid the lurkers who have gathered out front. A teenage girl watches us with wide eyes, and a few ladies from the book club give us nods of approval.

"You come back anytime," she says as we stroll hand in hand down the alleyway. "This is your town, not theirs."

I look over at Nick. "Then why am I the one in a back alley?"

Nick wraps his arm around me. "I can't help but think this is somehow my fault."

"It's not," I explain. "Craig would've done this to me, no matter who I'd moved on with. He was waiting to pounce, to use his final *fuck you* and humiliate me. He's the type of man who doesn't take no for an answer. I think you're his karma though."

"The thought of that makes me smile," he says.

When we're back at my condo, my phone rings, and it's Blaire. The picture for her contact is a selfie of us from last fall. We were laughing at something, but I can't remember what.

"Hey, Jules. Just wanted to check in. How's costume shopping?"

"We survived. Nick lifted two dudes by their shirts and threw them outside."

"Good! I'm sure they deserved it. Listen, I did a complete protection ritual at your place earlier. Sage, crystals, and even buried some black tourmaline by your door. You got the full witchy works."

Despite everything, I smile. "Thanks, Blaire."

"Also—and don't freak out—there's something you should know."

My stomach drops to my feet. "What now?"

"Craig's mom called the coffee shop, looking for you. She says she hasn't heard from him in three days. She sounded worried."

"That's concerning."

"Yeah. She said it's not common for him to do this. Even when he's being a shit, he checks in with her. Just stay alert, okay? The cards this morning were weird. The Tower kept coming up."

I clear my throat. "I don't have the energy for tarot foreshadowing right now, Blaire. Call me when The Lovers arrives."

The Tower. It means destruction, upheaval, chaos.

I laugh it off, but unease sits in my stomach like a ten-pound weight. What if the thing falling apart is me?

"You're right," she says. "Just use your karate moves if you need to, okay, Red Menace?"

"You know I will."

After I hang up, I plop down on the couch.

Nick joins me. "We need to talk about something."

"If this is more bad news—"

"It's not. You now have a bodyguard."

I stare at him. "What?"

"Don't worry; he's subtle, but he's watching when I can't. Professional guy, former military, and only temporary until November first."

"Nick, that's—"

"Necessary. His name is Brody. He's a dick, doesn't say much, but he's also marrying Zane's little sister and volunteered. He's the best in the business, and you don't tell him no. I'm sorry. I didn't hire him. He's going to do it whether I want him to or not."

"Okay," I say, and he sits down next to me.

Nick leans forward, bracing his elbows on his knees. "Brody's already watching the perimeter. You probably won't see him, but he'll see you. That's how he works."

I blink. "Wait, he's here? Like … right now?"

Nick's mouth tips into a half-grin. "I bet he's parked down the street in some unmarked truck, eating jerky and scaring kids in costumes."

Despite myself, I laugh. "That's supposed to make me feel better?"

"Yes," he says. Then his expression softens. "Look, I know it's invasive, but Brody cares about protecting your life. He said that he owed it to my sister to make sure we were okay. I can't refuse that."

I tuck my legs under me on the couch, hugging a pillow. "I'm just not used to this. I've lived in this town my whole life, and suddenly, I need a bodyguard to watch me."

Nick slides closer, prying the pillow from my arms and replacing it with his chest. "Just for a little while longer, I promise."

For the first time all day, I somewhat relax. I want to argue, to roll my eyes, but a part of me exhales at the thought of someone else watching the shadows when I can't. With Nick's arms around me and Brody keeping watch, the panic moves to a simmer instead of a rolling boil.

"Everything will be okay," I say, closing my eyes, wanting to believe it.

Nick doesn't move right away. His chin rests on the top of my head, his hand tracing idle circles down my arm like he's trying to draw calm into me. For a while, I let myself just sit there, eyes closed, pretending the world outside this couch doesn't exist.

It hardly works.

I can still feel the stares in the costume shop and how those men looked at me like I was public property. My body shivers before I can stop it.

Nick notices. "Cold?"

"Haunted," I admit, pulling back enough to look at him. "Faces and comments are burned into my mind. I can't quite shake it."

His jaw tightens. "Then we burn new ones in there. Better ones."

I raise an eyebrow. "Examples?"

"The Fairy Godmothers caring enough to bring you casseroles galore. Or how Blaire adores you so much she's hexing Craig at this very moment. Or maybe you should think about how my face lights up every time you walk into a room."

"The last one's the best."

"Good," he says, brushing a strand of hair behind my ear. "It's just for you."

The tension in my chest eases a little more. He doesn't minimize how I feel, but he doesn't let me drown in it either.

"I don't know how you do that," I whisper.

"What?"

"Make me feel like I'm not an embarrassment."

He cups my cheek, thumb brushing along my skin. His gaze is unwavering and fierce. "You're not. You're just a little bruised, pissed, and exhausted. And that's okay. It's okay to be all of those things."

"I am. I'm being sexualized. I hate it." Something inside me cracks, and I tuck myself into him, pressing my face against his chest.

"I hate it too." His voice drops to a low roughness. It vibrates against my skin. His eyes sweep down my body, sharp and unyielding. "I don't want anyone looking at you, sweetheart. Not like that. Not ever." His jaw tightens.

With a certainty that makes my pulse skip, he adds, "You're mine."

The words should scare me, but they don't. They ground me. They burn away the shame and replace it with something hotter. Because when Nick says I'm his, it's not possession; it's protection.

My breath catches. My body melts into him.

"Say it again," I whisper.

His mouth hovers by my ear, his hand gripping my hip like he's already branded me. "Mine."

Heat pools low in my stomach. I move closer, my thighs brushing his, my body alive with want.

"Does that please you?" he asks.

"Yes, very much," I admit. The confession releases before I can stop it.

His growl rumbles through me, his fingers tightening until I'm pinned to him. "Good. Because it's the truth, Little Red. You. Are. Mine." Each word is punctuated with his hips grinding forward, the hard ridge of him pressing against me.

I gasp, clutching his shirt, my body sparking everywhere we connect. My thighs part instinctively, and he takes advantage, shifting me against him until I'm straddling his thigh. The friction of his thick cock is right where I need it most.

"Nick," I breathe, my voice breaking as he rocks me harder against him. My panties are already damp, sliding against denim, and every move makes me ache more.

He grabs my ass, dragging me over him like he can't stand the thought of space between us. "Feel that, sweetheart? That pussy's mine too. So is every sound you make. Every gasp. Every fucking shiver. All mine."

I moan into his mouth when he kisses me, my hips grinding helplessly against him. The friction is brutal, delicious, and the orgasm builds fast. My body tenses, clinging to him as if he's the only thing holding me together.

His teeth graze my lip. His breath is hot against me. "Come for me. Right here. Ruin those panties for me."

The command tears through me, my body obeying before my brain catches up. I break apart against him, muffling my cry in his shoulder as heat floods me, soaking through the thin fabric. He holds me tight, grinding me through the final pulses, rocking me until I come down from my high.

I collapse against his chest, my breath ragged. His fingers comb through my hair as his lips brush my temple, so soft that it undoes me all over again.

"That's how I want you to forget him, Jules," he mutters, voice hoarse. "Not by erasing what he did. By making new memories. This"—his hand squeezes my hip possessively—"will be one of my favorites."

A shaky laugh slips out of me, half breathless, half disbelieving, while I try to recover from the aftershocks of that mind-blowing orgasm. "I don't deserve you."

His smile curves against my skin before he kisses me. "I think that's my line."

28

NICK

The knock at the door comes just after breakfast. Julie freezes mid-sip of her coffee, and I see the flash of panic in her eyes before she masks it. I'm so sad that she's still jumpy, but I understand how much of a paranoid kid she was. Craig just plays into her worst fear of the unknown.

"I'll get it," I say, already moving toward the door.

I open it and am confused when I see a plain cardboard box sitting on the porch with no return label. Julie's name is scribbled in Sharpie across the top. As soon as I see it, every muscle in my body tenses. Julie steps closer, squeezing in beside me so she can look.

"Don't touch it," I warn.

"What is it?"

"I don't know yet," I say, crouching to tear the tape and peel the flaps back.

The disgusting smell hits me first.

Inside is a bouquet of wilted, blackened roses, stems slimy with decay. Tucked between them is a card, smeared with something like dirt.

"What th—" Julie clamps a hand over her mouth.

I slide the card out with two fingers, and there are just three words written in sloppy handwriting.

I'M ALWAYS WATCHING.

The meaning is clear.

My vision goes red. "Motherfucker."

I pull my phone from my pocket and take a picture of it, then text it to Brody.

NICK

Did you see anything?

BRODY

No. No cars stopped by. Just a bunch of kids in costumes, going door-to-door.

NICK

How's that possible?

BRODY

Not sure. Contact the security company to review the footage from sunrise to the present.

Julie sinks into the couch as I close the door, leaving the flowers where they are. Her knuckles are white around her coffee mug. "He knows I'm home."

"I'm calling the police," I tell her.

She shakes her head. "What if this never ends? What if Craig stays lurking in the shadows?"

I drop to my knees in front of her and take her face in my hands so she has no choice but to look at me. "This will not last forever. I promise. Craig's showing signs of desperation, and desperation means he'll make mistakes. It's a cycle, and we're nearing its end. I've seen this too much over the years with our clients."

Her eyes glisten, but she shudders. "His note sounds like a threat."

"Then let me promise you something," I say. I keep my voice steady even though my blood is boiling. "He'll never touch you again. Not while I'm breathing."

An hour later, the box of dead roses is gone, sealed in an evidence bag. Another statement is written, everything is photographed, and more time is wasted. Festivalgoers stare at the house as the cops stand out in front. Julie pretends to be fine, but I've watched her eyes unfocus on the same unread page of the *Cozy News* for the last twenty minutes.

When her phone rings again, she flinches hard enough that she almost spills her fresh cup of coffee. Julie turns her phone around to show me it's a blocked number.

She answers and mutes the call. I hear someone breathing.

Julie's face goes pale, but she clenches her jaw, not hanging up until they do.

Not a word is said. Creep.

After a few minutes, she ends the call, but it rings again. This time, *I* answer.

"Hey, Craig," I say in a low tone. "I bet it pisses you off that I answered instead of Jules. But see, now you get to hear me talk about how you fucked up by letting her go. Honestly, I should thank you, buddy. Thank you for being a complete and utter dumbass and not realizing what you had. Because now she's mine and—"

The call ends.

Julie chuckles—a sound I love to hear.

"Guess I figured out what triggers him. It happens again, hand me the phone," I say.

She smiles. "You'll just irritate him."

"That's the point. Maybe he'll stop calling when he has to listen to me brag about us every damn time."

For a second, the silence in the condo is a victory. Then my phone rings.

It's the security company.

"We've downloaded and forwarded the video to the police department and to you. It appears that a man asked a child to carry the box and knock on the door. We can't see anything other than a blur of a body."

"That sucks," I breathe out. "Thank you."

"Sorry, I couldn't have been more helpful," he says, and the call ends.

I open my email and forward it to Brody.

Julie's phone vibrates again, and another knock on the door follows it.

"Damn," I whisper.

Julie checks the app and moves through the living room.

"It's Mrs. Mooney and several other people," she whispers, smoothing her hair down before opening the door.

"Jules! We came to hang out with you today," Mrs. Mooney announces. She's the secretary of the book club. "We just got news that bastard's been spotted in Silver Sky. Martha's cousin saw him at a gas station, looking like hell."

Silver Sky is thirty minutes away.

"When?" I demand.

"Early this morning. The police went, but he was already gone."

The five women set up camp in Julie's living room in a protective circle that's full of maternal energy. They've brought doughnuts and gossip and glittery cans of pepper spray, just in case.

"Now," Mrs. Patrick says, settling on the couch like a general preparing for battle, "we're here to take your mind off that piece of trash. I brought my favorite card game to help pass the time."

"Which is?" Julie asks, her brow lifted.

"Cards Against Humanity." Mrs. Patrick pulls the extra-long black box from inside her oversized purse with a wicked grin. "The *Nasty* bundle."

"Mrs. P!" Julie gasps. "The sun is still up!"

"So? We're not prudes. Honey, I've been married for forty years. I know things that would make him blush." She points to me.

For the next two hours, we play the most inappropriate card game I've ever witnessed with a group of women over sixty. Julie laughs so hard that she's crying. It's the good kind of tears too. Mrs. Henderson plays a combination so dirty that even I blush.

"I can't believe you!" Julie wheezes.

"Believe it, honey. How do you think I landed my third husband?" Mrs. Mooney smirks.

"Third?" I ask.

"Oh, yeah, the first two just couldn't keep up with this," she admits.

This sends Julie into another fit of giggles. And for a moment, it's like the weight of the morning lifts off her. She's not looking over her shoulder, not checking her phone, not thinking about Craig. She's just alive and living her best life with a group of women who've collectively become a grandma army for her.

"Okay, okay," Julie says, wiping her eyes. "I need to excuse myself, or I'm going to pee my pants."

"TMI, dear," Mrs. Patrick says, then plays another horrifyingly inappropriate card that makes everyone scream with laughter.

My phone buzzes. I don't know the number, but I answer it because it might be important.

"Nick Banks?" a woman's voice says, sounding professional.

"Yes?"

"This is Becca Burndy from the *New York Times*. We're doing a piece on revenge porn and famous victims. Your girlfriend's case—"

I hang up.

"Who was that?" Julie asks, returning with bottles of water for everyone.

"Reporter with the *New York Times*."

The mood shifts, but Mrs. Henderson takes control of the situation.

"The *New York Times* can kiss my saggy ass," she states. "Now, whose turn is it?"

Julie laughs again, but it's not as easy as it was before. "Yours, I think."

We play for another hour. The women share scandalous stories about their youth, each trying to top the other. Julie holds her stomach from laughing when Mrs. Henderson launches into a story about skinny-dipping with her boyfriend in 1962.

"The sheriff caught us, and there I was, naked as a jaybird, trying to explain that we were just cooling off."

"Seriously?" Julie asks.

"Oh, yeah. I told him Bobby Henderson had the finest ass in three counties and I was doing my patriotic duty by appreciating it," she says and gives a salute.

"You did not!" Julie gasps.

"I did! The sheriff laughed so hard that he let us go with a warning, but somehow, the entire town knew before we got back into city limits."

"Wait," Julie says. "Bobby Henderson? As in Mr. Henderson? As in your third husband?"

"He was my first love. As they say, the third time's a charm." Mrs. Henderson winks. "Some asses are worth keeping forever, dear."

Julie tips sideways against me, giggling so hard that she can't breathe. I memorize the sound—the laugh I'd burn down the world to protect.

The afternoon passes with moments of genuine joy, punctuated by reminders of why they're here in the first place.

When someone knocks on the door, everyone tenses until we confirm it's another false pizza delivery, which has been happening for the past hour. But then Mrs. Mooney starts a story about the time she accidentally ordered thirty pizzas instead of three, and the tension in the room eases again.

That evening, after the women leave with promises to check in the next day, Julie and I have an early dinner, then move to the balcony. She's still smiling from the day's unexpected turn.

"I didn't know the Fairy Godmothers had it in them," she says.

"I might be a little traumatized," I tell her playfully.

"Oh, you loved it." She pokes my ribs. "I saw you trying not to laugh at Mrs. Patrick's story about the church bell incident."

"True. They're hilarious, and they have a good sense of humor."

She leans against me. "I think they enjoyed hanging out with us. I appreciate that they care."

"You're loved, sweetheart," I say. "Everyone wants the very best for you."

"You know, sometimes, I forget that no matter what's going wrong in life, it's still possible to have fun."

"You're damn right about that."

The sunset paints the mountains orange and gold as the carnival rides light up and glow. In the distance, I can see Hollow Manor tucked up on the hill overlooking Cozy Creek. Even though a lot in my life is unsettled and it's not perfect, that doesn't take away from how peaceful it is with Julie by my side.

"Oh, by the way, Autumn is going to force us to carve a billion pumpkins the day before Halloween," she says. "I'm going to out-carve you."

"Oh, really?"

"*Really*. I've been watching YouTube videos for the past ten years. I'm basically a professional now."

"I'll have you know that I was pumpkin carving champion three years running in my hometown," I explain.

Her mouth falls open, and she turns her body toward me. I notice how her face glows at golden hour.

"You're kidding."

"Nope. And it was extremely competitive because there was a lot of money involved."

She laughs—a real laugh. "You're making it up."

"Scout's honor. I have a trophy somewhere." I pull out my phone, scrolling through old photos until I find the one I'm looking for. "Boom. Carving champion. Need me to zoom in so you can see it?"

"Pfft." She glances at the photo of teenage me holding a genuinely impressive pumpkin carving trophy. "Oh my goodness, you weren't kidding."

"I wasn't."

"Aw, look at that baby face. You were so adorable. I'd have had a crush on you as a kid."

"I was fifteen and *very* serious about my pumpkin art. So, I'm going to kick your ass at carving pumpkins."

She's laughing again, and I save this moment in my memory. "I forgot you were competitive."

"Babe, you have no idea. Not to mention, I always win, and I always get what I want."

"Noted."

Julie's wearing one of my hoodies; her hair is messy from the wind, and she's giggling about pumpkins while the world tries to break her.

"You're so pretty," I whisper.

She grins, and her phone buzzes with a security alert. We check it together, and it's the back-door sensor. There's nothing on the camera. I lean over the railing to glance at the back door.

"Nothing there," I tell her.

"Must've been the wind," she agrees.

"Or a ghost," I say.

"I can handle a ghost all day, every day," she tells me with a snicker. "I'd prefer it over Craig."

Once the sun sets, we return inside and shut the balcony doors.

As we're getting ready for bed, Julie puts on some '90s pop and starts dancing around her bedroom.

"Dance with me," she says.

"To the Backstreet Boys?"

"Yes. I want it *this* way."

So, I give her what she wants.

She spins under my arm, and I dip her dramatically. We're ridiculous, and it's perfect.

After several songs, we collapse onto the bed, both smiling.

"I needed that," she whispers, kissing me.

"I know you did," I tell her.

Craig can send dead flowers. He can lurk in the shadows. He can even try to break her. But he's already failed because Julie Loveland doesn't break.

She keeps living.

"We can go back," Nick says for the third time as we walk toward Cozy Coffee.

He senses my unease, but I continue to push forward. Being in public right now is my version of exposure therapy. I want to desensitize myself to the stares, and I'm done hiding.

While it's only ten in the morning, Main Street is bustling with Sunday funday energy. It's the last weekend before Halloween, and spooky excitement floats through the air.

Families head to the diner on the corner, and the line is wrapped around the block. Many tourists window-shop. Locals gather their groceries for the week because starting tomorrow, the sidewalks will be nearly impassable with people. Trust me, I once learned the hard way. So far, everything looks normal for this time of year.

Behind me, Brody is watching, wearing a *go to hell* look that makes Nick's seem soft.

I keep my eyes forward, ignoring those who glance in my direction.

"It's not too late to turn around," he offers in my ear with his arm wrapped around me.

"I want a lavender latte," I explain. "Time to rip off the bandage."

"Stubborn girl," he says with a chuckle. "But I'm proud of you. The quicker you stop giving a fuck what other people think about you and us, the better. They're going to talk anyway."

Brody chuckles behind us, and Nick mean-mugs him over his shoulder.

"Shut the hell up."

"Asher was right. You're whipped."

Nick's glare could cut glass, but I bite back a smile. If this is whipped, maybe I like him this way.

"Just like you are with Harper," Nick tells him.

"Oh, I'm not denying that at all. I worship the ground Harp stands on," Brody tells him as Nick opens the door for me.

The bell rings, and as soon as I enter, everyone says, "Jules."

I feel special, like Norm on *Cheers*. Instead of beer, I'm here for lavender lattes and to show the town I'm not backing down or hiding. I immediately grin.

As we move toward the register, Nick's grip is tighter than usual. I can feel the tension radiating from him. He's been on edge since we left the condo, and he eyes every person we pass like he's ready to kick their ass.

"Breathe," I whisper. "We're just getting coffee."

The two of us find our way to the back of the line, and Brody stands behind us. I glance around, noticing how the decorations have doubled since last week. I automatically know it's Blaire's doing. No way she'd let the fall decor sit in boxes through the season.

We step up to the register, and Blaire glances between us, grinning. "Wow, you two. My Goddess. You're in love, *love*."

I chuckle nervously. "What?"

"The look on your faces. I haven't seen you in days, and it's just … lightning in a bottle."

Nick smirks. "Mmm. I think I'd like a *pumpkin spice* latte."

I chuckle and chew on the corner of my lip. "And I'd like a lavender latte, extra sweet."

He glances at me while pulling his wallet out. I lift my brows and grin. Love talk made him uncomfortable.

"Oh, and I'd like a large black coffee and a chocolate croissant," Brody says behind us. "He's paying for it."

Blaire tilts her body so she can look past me. "Oh, hey, Brody. I didn't realize you were here. Is Harper with you?"

"You two know each other?" I ask.

"Yeah, we met at Autumn's wedding. Oh, and then I chatted with him and Harper at Zane's party last month. Did you know he's engaged to Harper? Zane's little sister."

"Yes," I tell her.

Brody chuckles. "I'm great. Thanks. Have you been well?"

"Fantastic! Still single. Living my best life." Blaire leans forward, glancing between me and Nick. "Is everything okay? He's a literal killer."

Nick chuckles. "He's also very stubborn, and he does whatever he wants. I didn't request his services."

"You know, I can hear you," Brody says.

Blaire clicks a few buttons, and when Nick tries to pay, she shakes her head. "You're comped."

"Oh, come on," Nick says. "Please let me pay."

"No," Blaire says.

"Okay then. I'd like to pay for every single person in here to treat themselves," Nick says, raising his voice.

Thirty people clap, and many line up behind us.

"Give them whatever they want," Nick tells her, handing over a thousand dollars. "Keep the change."

She scoffs. "You're not serious."

"I wanted to support my woman's business," he says with a wink. "This is even better."

When our drinks are finished being made, Sierra hands them over to us. "I've missed you so much. You're the best schedule maker in the world. Just know that I will never complain again once you come back."

I laugh, because of course that's what I'm known for—not the scandal, not the photos, but the girl who makes sure nobody misses their life events. The reminder that my old life still exists is somewhat of a relief. I can't let what Craig did define me.

I give her a smile. "Just glad you're not going to take me for granted when I return."

She's one of our youngest employees, and I try to give her every request she makes because I know what it was like to work away my youth. Shit, I'm still doing it.

"I definitely won't," she says as the printer goes off with orders. Marianna, another one of our employees, works the other machine. "Anyway, I gotta get to it. Please come back soon. Tracy is a hard-ass!"

"Don't talk about your aunt that way," I tell her. "I'll be back soon."

Mrs. Patrick waves from her corner table, where she's chatting with a few book club members. Tom Valley is in his usual chair, mustache waxed to perfection. Everything seems normal—maybe too normal.

Once Brody grabs his coffee and croissant, I get ready to lead the way across the room toward an open table by the window. But as I open my mouth to chat with Nick, the door chimes.

Craig.

My mouth falls open.

He's unshaven and wearing wrinkled clothes. He's lost weight since I last saw him, and there's something uneasy in his expression that makes my blood run as cold as the river in the winter. His eyes are bloodshot. When they lock on mine, it's dangerous, like a rattler uncoiling.

The hum of the espresso machines, chatter, and clinking cups all die at once. The silence is louder than the noise ever was.

Before I say a word, Craig has spotted us. His face transforms with anger when he sees Nick turn and glance at him.

"Julie." He says my name like it's a prayer and a curse.

"You need to leave," Blaire says from behind the counter. "Now."

"I just want to talk to her." Craig takes a step toward us. "Five minutes. That's all."

"You're violating a restraining order," Nick says, his phone already dialing the police station.

"I don't care!" Craig's voice cracks. "I've lost everything because of her. My job, my home, my reputation."

The room tilts. Somehow, in his mind, I'm both the villain and the only thing that can save him.

Anger overrides my fear. This is enough. "You've been stalking me since you got back in town. You broke into my house, stole my panties, and destroyed my pictures! Then you posted our private moments on the internet. What you've done is unforgivable."

"Because I love you!" He's screaming. "Don't you get it? We're meant to be together. I wanted to marry you, have kids, and build a life—"

"You broke up with me! You left me! You aren't going to twist this. I would've married you, Craig. You ruined it." I'm surprised at how steady my voice is. "You led me on a year ago. I was your pathetic side piece, Craig. That's who I used to be. But not anymore."

People gasp.

"Then you proposed to someone else while you were still sleeping with me! Now I have self-respect, and you don't know what to do about that. Your ego can't handle it. It's *over*. O-V-E-R! You have Sarah. She's carrying your baby."

"No, she's not! This is utter bullshit," he shouts. I hear a coffee mug drop and shatter on the floor. "I never wanted her forever. She was just a distraction."

Gasps ripple through the shop. Sarah isn't even here, and somehow, he's humiliating her too.

"For fuck's sake," Brody says from behind me.

Craig's eyes snap back to me. "You're leaving with me. Right now."

His words make my stomach turn. My pulse spikes so hard that I feel it in my throat.

"No, I'm not."

He lunges toward me, and everything happens too fast.

The scrape of his shoes on the hardwood.

The twisted snarl of his face.

His hand stretched for me.

Before I can move away, Nick is there. His arm slams into Craig's chest, shoving him so hard that he stumbles back into a table. Craig topples to the ground with it, and I can tell he's scared shitless.

"Don't you dare touch her." Nick's voice is both dangerous and calm, in a way that shakes my bones.

Craig hops to his feet, and Brody moves beside Nick. The two of them are a wall of muscle, stopping any path Craig has to me.

Blaire watches in horror as I back toward the coffee bar. If I need to, I will run to the emergency exit at the back and not stop until I reach the police station. The look in Craig's eyes is what nightmares are made of.

But before I have to do that, customers rise to their feet. Tom Valley, who usually polishes his mustache and keeps to himself, stands from his chair, with his fists balled like he's ready to fight. Mrs. Patrick plants herself beside him, wearing a glare sharper than any knife. Behind her are the other Fairy Godmothers, each with their pepper spray activated. One by one, customers fill the space, acting as human shields.

"I'll take you away from here, Julie! You'll never see any of them again!" Craig threatens, jerking free.

He's determined to get to me, but before he can, Brody grabs him by the collar. In one terrifyingly easy motion, he lifts Craig clean off his feet and hurls him across the room. Gasps ripple through the shop as Craig crashes into a chair, scrambling on the floor like a cornered rat. For the first time, I see fear in his eyes.

After a few seconds, he gets up and tries lunging toward me again, but some customers catch him by the arms and wrestle him to the ground. The sound is chaos, and sirens follow it. They wail down Main Street and grow closer until it's blaring.

The bell above the door clangs as two uniformed officers rush in. Relief floods me so fast that my knees nearly buckle. They detain Craig, my customers practically handing him over. He starts to fight, but they have him cuffed too quickly.

"You'll never be enough, Julie! He'll never love you!" he screams as they pull him through the shop. "Never!"

His words fall flat. For once, I'm not the one breaking. He is.

The officers drag him through the shop, past Blaire's narrowed eyes, past the book club women, who talk shit under their breath like they're casting spells. Every eye in the shop is on Craig, and not one of them is sympathetic.

The door slams shut behind them. Craig resists as they drag him across the parking lot.

For a heartbeat, everything is silent except the hiss of the espresso machine and the pounding of my pulse in my ears.

Nick turns to me, his hands cupping my face. His eyes search mine like he's cataloging every inch of me. "Are you okay?"

I let out a shaky breath. I can't believe Craig tried to pull that in my family's business. "I am now."

Applause starts from the back, hesitant at first, then louder. Blaire bangs a spoon against a mug like a victory bell. Someone cheers, and another person whistles. The sound crashes over me, drowning out Craig's threats in my head. They're celebrating.

Nick pulls me into his chest. "It's over," he says.

"Thank you. Thank you all so much," I say to the room of customers staring at me.

"We should get out of here," Brody tells Nick.

"You're right," Nick mutters, escorting me through the room, leading me outside.

The cool October breeze and sunshine feel nice on my cheeks. Police cars are parked in the middle of Main Street, causing a traffic jam, and the sidewalks are full of people watching what's going on. I'm utterly embarrassed as Craig screams from inside the car.

I see flashes of cameras and notice cell phones are being held up, but I ignore them. We rush down the sidewalk and disappear into the sea of tourists. The cheers still echo in my ears as we walk toward my condo. My legs wobble, and Nick immediately steadies me.

"You okay?" he asks quietly in my ear.

I nod, dazed. "I will be."

"You stood up to him," Nick says.

"I thought I'd feel relief," I whisper. "But I feel hollow. Like I've been holding my breath for months, and my lungs still don't know how to let go."

Nick threads his fingers through mine. "That's normal. It's a trauma response after being violated. Know your feelings are valid, even if you don't feel anything right now." He lifts my hand, brushing his lips over my knuckles. "But it's over, Jules. I'm hiring the best attorney in the country for you. He can't and won't hurt you anymore. I'll make sure of it."

I let his words sink in as he watches me. When I meet his eyes, his expression is raw, like he's holding me together with his gaze alone.

"Let's take this conversation inside," I say, unlocking the door.

I glance behind us and notice Brody is nowhere around. He's like a ghost.

Nick grins. "Shall we celebrate?"

"What do you have in mind?" I ask, twisting the doorknob.

Nick grins, eyes swirling with something that makes my stomach flip. "You'll see."

30

NICK

Four days. That's how long it's been since Julie stood up to Craig and the cops dragged him out of Cozy Coffee in handcuffs. It's been ninety-six hours since the town applauded her like she'd slain a dragon. In a way, she did.

Since Craig was arrested, she's actually slept and relaxed. It's a relief.

This morning, I wake up and can't remember the last time I felt this. There's no adrenaline in my veins. No stress of waiting for the next shoe to drop. It's just peace.

Julie stirs when I press my lips to her forehead.

"Morning," she says, her voice rough with sleep.

"Morning, beautiful," I whisper back, not wanting to break the early morning spell.

Her hand slides across my stomach. "Don't forget, we're carving a lot of pumpkins at Hollow Manor later for the party tomorrow."

She sounds excited.

I chuckle. "That's what you wake up thinking about?"

"Of course," she says, propping herself up on an elbow, like there's no other answer. "It's my *favorite* time of year."

I pull her down for a kiss. "Are you sure you're ready for me to out-carve you?"

She kisses my shoulder. "Oh, you can try."

I kiss her, slowly. She smiles against my mouth. We don't rush the moment; that's the luxury of having peace.

An hour later, we're at Hollow Manor, moving toward the back porch of the gothic mansion. Autumn has turned Hollow Manor's backyard into a pumpkin battleground. Fifty pumpkins—no exaggeration—sit in rows like an orange army, surrounded by bins of tools and bowls for seeds. Battery-operated candles wait in boxes.

Autumn adjusts her high ponytail on her head, and then she smooths down her black-cat-print apron like a seasonal general.

"We're carving all of these?" Julie asks.

It seems like a lot.

"Oh, yeah," Autumn says. "I want the sidewalk to glow and greet every guest. Oh, please keep the seeds. I want to roast them before the party."

Julie drags her palm over a lineup of gourds like she's choosing a racehorse. "This one's mine." Then she beelines for a deeply unfortunate, wart-covered pumpkin. "And I want that one too."

"Absolutely not," I say. "I get the troll pumpkin."

"Possession is nine-tenths of the law," she says, already hauling it to her side of the picnic table.

Zane appears, carrying a tray that has apple cider, cinnamon doughnuts, and a bowl of candy corn, which he pretends he's not eating by the fistful.

"Saw Blaire this morning. She said Mercury is no longer in retrograde," he announces.

Julie snorts. "Very good to know. Perfect timing actually. Is she coming?"

"She said she was going antiquing with her mom."

"Oh, good!" Julie says.

I lift a carving knife like a saber. "Ready?"

Julie grabs one as well. "Oh, yes. Prepare to be humbled."

We work across from one another. The first slice of the lid releases that sweet, earthy smell of pumpkin. Julie lets out a contented sigh that I file under top ten sounds I'd like to hear for the rest of my life. She draws her design with a marker and chews on the inside of her cheek with concentration.

I steal glances more than I carve.

"Eyes on your own gourd, Banks," she says without looking up.

"Oh my *gourd*. I can't help it. You're gorgeous."

She slings a handful of pumpkin guts at me.

I throw some back with a laugh.

She gasps like I've violated the Geneva Conventions and retaliates with a scoop that lands across my sweatshirt. I move to her side of the table, closing the distance.

"Dirty play," I say.

"Fair play," she counters. "You started it."

I pull her closer until the scoop drops to the table and her palms slide to my shoulders. The kiss starts playful and goes somewhere else. Her fingers curl in my shirt, and the world shrinks to nothing. I taste the cider on her mouth and hear the sound of her soft, happy sigh.

Someone coughs.

Zane.

"Don't let Autumn see you getting distracted," he says. "Especially not mid-triangle-eye."

Julie buries her face in my chest, laughing.

"He's right," I tell her, tucking hair behind her ear. "Autumn, apparently, takes this very seriously."

"I heard that!" Autumn says, carrying ghost decorations to hang in the trees. In the corner of the large, manicured field next to the house, a stage is being constructed, along with a haunted house.

"How many people are attending this party?" I ask.

"Two hundred, but not everyone RSVP'd."

"Wow," I whisper. "So, you're all obsessed?"

"Yes," the three of them say.

I settle back in across from Julie, who's been carving something creative.

"What are you making over there?" I ask.

"You'll see soon enough," she tells me.

Julie's focused on her pumpkin when I hear tires roll over the pavement. It's a Jaguar.

I glance up and groan. "Who's that?"

Zane doesn't even look away from his knife. "Patterson."

"Patterson? Why?" I ask, just as he steps out of a sleek black sedan like he's about to negotiate a billion-dollar hockey contract instead of walking across a patio full of pumpkin guts.

"I invited him to the party tomorrow," Autumn says.

Patterson surveys the porch and the pumpkins, then looks at Julie.

"Oh, shit, you two are carving pumpkins. You know he's the champ, right?"

Julie looks up at him, grinning. "I'm aware. I'm going to kick his ass. Anyway, it's good to see you again. How's the season going so far?"

"Everything is good. Leaving the morning after Halloween, so won't be here very long."

"Coincidence," Julie tells him. "So is Nick."

Patterson slides his sunglasses on top of his head. "Wow. It's worse than I thought." He tips his head at me.

"What is?" Julie takes a break from her carving.

Patterson barks out a laugh, then turns to Nick. "When do you plan to stop playing games and admit you're never going back to the city?"

Julie glances at me, but I don't take my eyes off Patterson.

"I'm returning on November first," I confirm. "I have a quarterly investors' ball on the second that I can't miss."

Patterson smirks. "And how long will you stay in the city?"

Julie arches a brow, and I wish I could read her mind.

"Damn. How many questions do you plan on asking me?" I snap out.

Autumn waltzes by us. "Patterson, you're here. Perfect timing! I need your height. Don't interrupt their carving. They have fifty pumpkins to finish, and I need help hanging string lights in the gazebo, please."

He gives her a look. "I'm *not* getting on a ladder. Last thing I need to do is get injured."

"It's a step stool. Quit being a baby," she says, shoving the stool into his hands. "You're helping. Come on."

Julie presses her lips together to keep from laughing.

"You're so bossy," Patterson tells her, but he's following Autumn.

"You have no idea," Zane says with a laugh.

We carve until the table is a battlefield of lids and pulp.

Zane gathers up the seeds while Autumn puts on a playlist of 2000s throwbacks that makes Julie shimmy her shoulders while she carves. I pretend she doesn't undo me but fail. By the time the sun starts to slide behind the mountain, we finish the last of our pumpkins.

"Okay, well, I carved faces," Zane says, glancing between our pumpkins. "You two assholes decided to be artists."

"Ready for the reveal?" I ask Julie.

"Yes. We should line them up on each side."

Autumn comes to us. "I'll turn the fake candles on, and then I'll give you a thumbs-up when they're all lit, got it?"

We nod, standing at the end of the sidewalk as she does what she said. Zane and Patterson light the ones on the porch.

"You're good to go," Autumn yells as she, Zane, and Patterson move inside, leaving me and Julie to ourselves.

"This is the reveal I've been waiting for," I admit.

I take her hand, and the two of us stroll down the sidewalk.

The soft glow throws light across us, and for a second, I forget we're here for the pumpkins.

We start at the end, and I realize she's carved a sea of stars across all twenty pumpkins. There are hundreds of stars, cut delicately, like a constellation map. At the very end, she's carved a couple kissing in a window.

"Holy shit," I mutter. "Is that us?"

"Yes," she admits.

"This is incredible, Jules." I place my hand on my heart. "I've been humbled. I'm not worthy."

Julie nudges me with her shoulder, her eyes still glittering like the constellations in the pumpkins. "All right, champ. Let's see if the legend lives up to the hype. Show me yours."

The first few pumpkins are apple trees. Their branches carved so thin that they lace together like veins of light, tiny apples dangling like lanterns. Julie's lips part, and she leans closer.

"The orchard," she mutters, seeing a couple lying on a blanket.

"It was so damn special, being there with you," I say.

I move us along, and the light from the next set spills across her face. It's the building of Cozy Coffee, downtown, followed by a coffee bar. I nearly lost my mind, getting it right. The final one is a steaming coffee cup. The steam patterns are so delicate that they almost look like lace.

Her laugh breaks the silence. "Wow."

"Did I win?" I tease, though my throat feels tight.

Julie's face softens. "Nick … these are …"

She doesn't finish, but I see it in her eyes.

The next ones are how I view us. Two hands threaded together, every line deliberate so the shadows make them look alive. A couple silhouetted beneath a shower of falling leaves, the shapes of their bodies leaning close.

Her breath catches as she stares at the last few.

The first is a blazing sun, every ray carved with razor precision. Next to it, a starry night sky with bold shapes and imperfect stars. They shine like they're burning straight out of the pumpkin.

Then the final is a couple in a heart silhouette, kissing. The one that almost undid me to carve because it felt like I was putting my heart on display. It's us.

Julie takes in the pumpkins.

She lifts her hand to her mouth. Her voice is a whisper, but it knocks the air from me anyway. "You carved our love story."

I rub the back of my neck. "I wanted you to see what I see when I look at you."

Her hand falls, and before I can take another breath, she's on me —fingers twisting into my shirt, tugging me down. Her lips meet mine with a force that's soft but also desperate.

It's a kiss that two people exchange when words aren't enough. It's as if I'm her air, and she's been waiting for this moment just as long.

I slide my hands to her waist, pulling her closer until the glow of the pumpkins washes over us. Her mouth parts against mine, and I taste cider and sweetness and Julie. Her hair brushes against my cheek, and she exhales into me. It's a sound I carved into those pumpkins without even realizing it.

For a moment, there's no chill in the mountain air, and nothing else exists. It's just her, us, and the way she kisses me, like every wall we've held up has crumbled.

When we break apart, her forehead rests against mine, and her breath is uneven. In the glow of flickering pumpkins, I know I'd carve a thousand more if it meant keeping this look on her face.

AFTER WE'VE HELPED AUTUMN COMPLETE EVERY ITEM ON HER checklist, we return to the condo. Julie showers and pulls on an oversized sweater while I make tea. We move around each other comfortably.

"I thought we would write our letters tonight," she says, setting down a stack of paper and a handful of gel pens that look like they belong in a middle-school pencil pouch.

I sit across from her at the kitchen table. "Great idea."

She chooses a glittery orange pen, turning it between her fingers. I pick up a plain black one. It feels right. She's color and stardust and constellations. I'm solid lines. This is why she makes me a better man.

The page in front of me sits blank. For someone who's spent his whole life knowing exactly what to say in press conferences, contracts, negotiations, this is the first time my hand doesn't quickly move.

I want to write *I love you.* Three simple but obvious words. It's too much and not enough, so I start smaller. I write about her laugh and how she looks in the morning light. Write about how I appreciate her fearlessness, even if her voice shakes.

I glance up. Julie's hunched over her page, hair falling around her face, pen hovering, but not moving. She chews the inside of her cheek—the same way she does when she's lost in thought.

"Stuck?" I ask.

Her eyes flick to mine, then back to the page. "No. Just trying to find the right words for everything I need to say."

"Same," I admit.

I want to tell her everything. How the moment she walked into my life again, the noise in my head quieted. How I thought I was too far gone to deserve this and she proved me wrong without even trying. How she makes me want things I've spent years convincing myself I couldn't have. But every thought feels too heavy.

Fuck it, I think.

I let the pen move and don't stop until the page feels full, and then I turn it over. My chest feels lighter and heavier when I spill my heart. Once I've reread it three times, I fold it.

Julie slides an orange envelope across the table to me, and I stuff my letter inside, then write her name on it. She does the same.

We stare at the two festive envelopes, which seem almost innocent. They might as well be sticks of dynamite, waiting for a spark.

I don't know her answer, but in my heart, I believe there's a future for us.

There is a chance that, after everything that's happened with Craig, she might decide that we're better off as friends. I have not counted that possibility out.

If that happens, at least she'll know my truth because I put my heart on the line.

She exhales. "No matter what, I've loved every moment with you. You know that, right?"

Her words should reassure me, but the way she said "no matter what" hooks something in my chest. I hate how it sounds like an ending.

"Yes, sweetheart. Friends, no matter what." I remind her of our original rules.

The silence that follows hums with anticipation.

I think about reaching for her envelope, tearing it open, not waiting another second. But I don't. I will be impatiently patient.

Julie moves to the seat next to me and wraps her arms around me.

She tips her head back. "You okay?"

I kiss her hair, breathing her in. "Yeah. Just thinking about tomorrow."

My fantasy future with a redhead in a sweater already feels like home. Being with her is a thought I could get lost in.

"You know, I couldn't imagine spending my autumn with anyone else," I confess.

She kisses my jaw. "Don't get sappy."

"Oh, just you wait."

After another few minutes, we get up and make our way to her bedroom. We climb into bed, and the two of us stare at the ceiling, holding one another.

We finally drift off around two a.m., wrapped together like we're afraid to let each other go.

Tomorrow, we'll open the envelopes that contain our confessions.

Tomorrow, no matter what, everything will change.

31

JULIE

The first thing I notice when I wake is the empty space beside me. I rub my hand across the mattress and feel cold sheets.

Nick is gone.

My heart lurches forward, and panic claws up my throat.

Today is our deadline.

Halloween.

The deadline to our fake-dating and hookup situation.

I hope this isn't the end.

I sit up too fast, scanning the room, like maybe he's just in the bathroom, but his shoes and his jacket are gone; even his cologne that always lingers in the air is faint.

It's easy for me to convince myself I've been ghosted, like how Asher warned over a month ago. He said Nick would be gone without warning.

Just as I'm getting ready to spiral, I see a folded note propped against the bedside lamp with my name written across it in his elegant handwriting.

I unfold it with anxious fingers.

Julie,

I had to take care of some business things today. I'll see you tonight at the party. In the meantime, Cozy Spa in town is expecting you. Massage, facial, the works. My treat. Don't argue.

Enjoy your day, sweetheart.

Nick

RELIEF CRASHES OVER ME SO HARD THAT MY EYES STING.

He didn't leave for good. But still, the ache of him doing that doesn't disappear. This deadline has made me anxious and paranoid. And I'm aware that when we open those envelopes, everything will change between us for better or worse. We will leap together, or we'll walk away. It's that simple.

I'll respect his decision, but I've been trying to prepare myself for all options.

The thought of us going our separate ways after we've shared so much has me reeling. Crossing this line with him was a risk, but it was one that I was willing to take. I just hope this doesn't hurt me.

If it does, I'm swearing off men for an eternity.

After I take a shower and eat a bowl of Cinnamon Toast Crunch, I grab my keys and head to the spa. Inside smells like lavender and eucalyptus. The soft music and trickling water feature in the corner are calming. As soon as I arrive, I'm escorted into a room where I lie face down on the table. A warm blanket is draped across my lower back, and I try to remember the last time I felt this relaxed.

Nick did this because he knew I was tense and needed it.

The masseuse presses her palms along my shoulders, working out knots I've carried since Craig returned. I close my eyes, and instead of the calm ocean sounds, I imagine Nick's laugh, his real one. I think about how he walked into Cozy Coffee the first day he was here and confidently invited me to dinner. It's impossible for me to forget the cute grin he gave me when he pretended to be my boyfriend.

The firm pressure moves down my arms. My mind drifts to the nights we spent together at Hollow Manor. How he kissed me on the blanket in the apple orchard as the sunlight flickered through the tree branches. Him holding me close after the break-in, jaw set like he'd burn the whole world before letting anyone touch me.

The masseuse circles her thumbs along my lower back, and my body sinks deeper into the table. I think about Nick's hands on me. The way he held me in the Range Rover when I straddled him, teasing him in the beginning. Or how he pulled me against him after the Fairy Godmothers left my condo and whispered sweet words to me.

A lump rises in my throat. I can't imagine being with anyone else. Nick has been my everything, even among the chaos, and I'm not ready for it to end yet. Our time together overshadows the drama with Craig, the naked picture scandal, or any of the town gossip. I think about the sexy moans he releases right before he comes. And how he calls me sweetheart, like the word was invented for me.

The massage shifts to my legs, kneading out the tension, and I let myself replay the moment we kissed last night after we revealed our carved pumpkins. Candlelit gourds that he'd carved our love story into surrounded us, as if they were proof that what we shared wasn't fake.

Fake. That's what this was supposed to be.

My eyes sting, and I bite the inside of my lip. Tonight, what we've written and tucked inside those envelopes will decide our future. This will either be a beautiful, fleeting October or the opportunity to keep him long after the leaves have fallen.

The masseuse presses gently into my temples, and I force myself to breathe. I need to relax and let go, but my heart keeps lurching toward thoughts of him. I'm … in love with him. The realization unravels me. And if he doesn't feel the same, I'll be ruined.

By the time the massage ends, I feel wrung out, like every knot in my body has melted away.

After my facial, I'm given aftercare instructions. My body is spaghetti as I enjoy the crisp October air. All I can think about is Nick. His hands on me and his voice.

By the time I get home, the need for him is too much.

I peel off my clothes and step into the shower. The hot water cascades down my back, steam rising, but it isn't enough. My skin feels too tight, my body restless with all the things I can't say yet. I close my eyes and see him—the upward lift of his mouth when he calls me stubborn, along with the heat in his gaze when I push back.

My hand trails lower, my breath catching as my fingers brush over my clit. I let myself imagine it's him instead. His hands. His mouth. The way he takes his time until I'm trembling, screaming his name.

I brace a palm against the slick tiles as the tension builds, my thoughts nothing but Nick.

Him holding me. Him buried inside me. Him whispering, promising me that he's not going anywhere.

My body breaks apart, a rush of heat and release that leaves me gasping his name into the steam. I lean against the wall, breathless, my knees nearly giving out as the orgasm takes over. The water washes everything away except the truth that terrifies me.

I don't just want him. I *need* him.

When I finally step out, I wrap myself in a towel and catch my reflection in the mirror. My cheeks are flushed, and my eyes are bright. I look alive, in love, and ready to conquer the night. I tell myself that no matter what happens at midnight, I will survive.

I dry off and slip into the costume. My hand slides across the teal fabric with gold trim, making me feel bolder than I am. I chose

Jasmine because Nick has shown me a whole new world. There was no other choice.

By the time I finish adjusting the dark wig with a crown, Blaire's horn honks outside. She never comes to the door. Just three quick honks, one after another, like always.

My jeweled sandals click against the porch steps. As I slide into her passenger seat, I'm hit with the smell of sage and cinnamon and her ever-present incense.

"Have you been casting spells?" I ask.

"Maybe," she admits, backing out of the driveway as I buckle. "Tell me why you're wearing a mischievous look on your face."

"No reason," I reply, though my stomach twists.

As we drive, the town flashes by in orange lights and hay bales, kids in costumes darting across the open fields. Blaire drums her fingers against the steering wheel, her rings clanking as her spooky playlist streams on her radio. She's side-eyeing me.

"So," she says casually, "I pulled your daily card before you got into the Jeep."

I glance over at her. "You did? And?"

She smirks. "Want to know what it was?"

"Actually, yes." My voice comes out shakier than I want.

Her grin widens. "The Lovers."

My pulse races as the words echo in my head.

The Lovers. *Finally.*

Blaire turns down Skyline Drive toward Hollow Manor, humming along to the radio.

"All right, spill it. What's going on in that head of yours? Because you look like you're about to be sick."

I let out a laugh. "Tonight is the night."

She arches a brow. "For?"

I exhale. "To decide if Nick and I will end tonight or if we'll keep going as a couple. No more games. It was the deadline we gave our hookup situation."

"Oh. I see."

I nod. "At midnight, everything changes."

Blaire whistles low. "That's spicy. Very poetic."

"Why?" I look at her, realizing she's a fortune teller costume.

"There's an old wives' tale about lovers' confessions on the first midnight after Halloween, when the veil between worlds is thin. Any couple brave enough to speak their true feelings under the moonlight will be bound together. *Forever.* Comparable to a fate sealed in candle wax."

I roll my eyes. "Bound together? Sounds made it up."

Blaire grins like the devil. "Maybe. But I guess we'll see."

She has me giggling. It's something she's always been able to do.

"You have nothing to worry about, Jules," she says more gently. "That man is gone for you. Everyone sees it. He looks at you like you're his past, present, and future."

"Then why do I still think he might leave?" My throat tightens, and I glance out the window at the blur of porches decked out with hay bales and fake cobwebs.

"Because you're in love." She states. "When falling in love is intense, moving to the next step in the relationship is like jumping without a net. I don't think you realize Nick's already at the bottom with arms open, waiting to catch you."

I turn to her. "You believe that?"

"Yes." Blaire smirks. "When it's right, it's easy. And if, by some chance, he screws this up, we'll slash his tires before we leave. I'll even ask Autumn to help me make some glitter glue."

A startled laugh bursts out of me. "Glitter glue?"

"Yep. Nothing ruins a man's ego more than driving around with a glittery *YOU SUCK* written across his hood. When it's washed off, it just so happens to peel paint."

"Damn," I mutter. "But thanks for having my back."

She grins. "Honestly, he's yours, Jules. I have zero doubt about that, especially after talking to his brother."

"You talked to Asher?" I ask.

"Yeah, at Zane's birthday party, I did recon. I asked a lot of questions about Nick and learned a ton."

My eyes widen. "Really?"

"Yep. No way I was going to approve of this relationship without learning as much as I could. Basically, he's a green flag who has it bad for you," she confirms.

"Thank you," I say, taking her words to heart.

"Don't be nervous. If it's meant to be, it will be."

When we arrive at Hollow Manor, there are handfuls of cars parked on the manicured lawn.

As soon as I see Nick's Range Rover, my heart races. He's been on my mind since this morning. It's the first time I haven't woken up next to him since he started staying with me. We haven't even texted one another today. It's been radio silence.

"Calm down," Blaire mutters.

"I'm trying," I admit.

"Your leg is shaking," she tells me as she unbuckles. "You have *nothing* to worry about. Now, let's go find your man."

"Okay," I say, trying to stop this spiral.

We get out of the Jeep, and Blaire grabs my hand, leading me up the sidewalk that's full of our pumpkins. Groups of people are huddled outside on the grass where the haunted houses are fully constructed. There's also an outdoor bar and a DJ. Later, a band will take the stage. The house is pumped full of low-lying fog and glowing lights.

"Do you see him?" I ask Blaire over the music.

"Not yet," she says, weaving around people.

My heart races as I wonder where he is.

As I scan the crowd, my heart hammers in my chest. Costumes blur together—pirates, witches, a giant inflatable dinosaur.

When I slide into the downstairs library, I search for him.

In the corner, standing near the bar, is Nick.

My breath catches when I see him.

For a moment, I stare at how gorgeous he is in a deep purple vest that's open. His ab muscles are on full display, and the light-brown pants sit low on his hips. A gold sash is wrapped around his waist, catching the light every time he moves.

Aladdin. My Aladdin.

Every bit of doubt I carried here, every nightmare about him walking away, burns to ash the second I see him smirking at me.

When his eyes find mine, the entire party falls away. His mouth curves into that cocky, slow smile that always undoes me, and the unease in my chest disappears. He didn't leave Cozy Creek. He's here. He's mine. And he's looking at me like I'm the only person in this haunted mansion.

The only thing that breaks our connection is Blaire nudging me. "See? Whole new world."

I can't stop the joy that bursts out of me. "We didn't tell each other what our costumes were."

"Totally meant to be," she says.

Nick casually strolls toward me. When he reaches me, he bows, extending his hand. "Princess Jasmine," he says loud enough for a few people by the fireplace to grin.

I roll my eyes, but my hand finds his anyway. "Aladdin? Really?"

"Coincidence," he says, kissing the back of my hand. "Or fate. You pick."

My cheeks burn, but I smile so hard that it hurts. "You look handsome."

"You're a dream," he says without missing a beat. His eyes sweep over me slowly, deliberately, and the heat in his gaze makes my knees weak.

Blaire coughs dramatically beside us. "Okay, I'll leave you two before I get cavities. Don't do anything I wouldn't do."

"Uh, you have no boundaries," I say.

"Exactly." She chuckles, disappearing into the crowd.

I lean in closer as the bass of the music shakes the floor. Ghost lights are strung from the ceiling, casting a warm glow over the entire space. Even so, Nick is the brightest light in the room.

"Damn, I've missed you." His mouth brushes mine.

The kiss is full of certainty.

"I missed you too."

The fear of losing him immediately vanishes. As our tongues slide together, I know tonight isn't about endings. It's about new beginnings.

32

NICK

Julie tastes like sugar. When I finally pull away from kissing her, she's breathless. Her cheeks are flushed, and her green eyes sparkle beneath the jeweled crown. I'm ruined. Absolutely fucking ruined.

The bass shakes the floors of Hollow Manor, but she pulls me toward the dance floor anyway. Her hand is in mine, and her laughter spills out of her. We dance through two songs, then three. She teases me for not knowing the words, and I tease her for knowing them. The crowd fades away until it's just us.

We eventually trade the dance floor for the outdoor bar, weaving through the crowd of costumes until I lead her toward a tall table near the edge of the terrace. A skull candle glows in the middle, casting light on our faces. Julie leans into me without thinking, like her body already knows where it belongs.

I grab us two of the signature drinks, Love Potions. When we're alone, we finally breathe. She smells like vanilla, and it's mixing with the spice of cinnamon from the drinks we're sipping. Her wig is slightly crooked from dancing. She's beautiful, her teal costume shimmering under the strings of lights overhead.

I slide an arm around her waist. "Did you have a good day?"

"It was incredible. Thank you," she says. "But it still felt too long without you."

"You're welcome. I couldn't get you off my mind."

"Same," she confesses, and it makes my heart flutter.

The music thumps in the distance, and laughter drifts across the lawn. Her warmth seeps through the silk costume. Every time my thumb slides over her hip, she exhales like she can't help herself.

She's the calm in my fucking sails.

We finish our drinks and grab new ones, and then she leads me toward the firepit. The flames lick upward, sparks flying into the night sky. A few people glance our way, smiles tugging at their mouths like they're in on the secret, but I don't care who sees us together.

I sink into one of the Adirondack chairs and open my arms. Julie takes my lap like she belongs there. My arm wraps around her waist, and her smile catches in the firelight.

When I kiss her, it's less about want and more about need. It leaves me wrecked, wanting more of her.

The fire pops and crackles, sparks shooting up into the October night. I could sit here until midnight, letting the townsfolk swirl around us, pretending the world outside of us doesn't exist.

"All right, lovebirds!" Zane shouts, cutting through the spell as we stare at the flames.

Julie startles, blinking at me as a very large crowd gathers near the stage. Autumn grins and enjoys every second.

"What's happening?" Julie whispers.

"Costume contest," I say, already groaning at Zane, who's tugging me up by the arm.

"On stage. Both of you." He doesn't give us a choice.

Julie's laugh bubbles against my chest as she takes my hand. "Come on, Aladdin. Let's dazzle the crowd."

We're moved onto the small stage, and the Fairy Godmothers sit in the front row, fanning themselves dramatically. I'm convinced they fell straight out of a *Bridgerton* episode with those petticoats and wigs.

"And for our final entry of the night!"

Julie's cheeks turn pink, but she plays along, lifting the hem of her costume to curtsy while I bow.

The crowd cheers with approval.

"Vote time! This is based on loudness, so scream for who you want to win!" Autumn calls into the microphone. "For the pirates! The skeletons! The vampires and ..." She gestures to us. "Princess Jasmine and Aladdin!"

The cheer is deafening. People chant our names, the Fairy Godmothers leading with, "Jules and Nick! Jules and Nick!" until I chuckle.

Julie turns to me and grins. I never want to forget this look on her face.

"Unanimous," Autumn declares. "The winners are Nick and Jules!"

Zane steps forward, holding up an envelope like it's a goddamn Oscar.

"Grand prize," he says, milking it for all it's worth. "Weekend trip to Napa Valley during Valentine's Day. Compliments of Autumn and me."

Julie gasps. "Are you serious?"

"Dead serious," Zane says. "Flights, hotel, vineyard tours. The works. You're welcome."

She hugs him so hard that he actually stumbles. "Thank you."

I cross my arms. "You couldn't have just given away a bottle of wine?"

Zane smirks and leans in. "That's too easy."

Julie beams at me, her green eyes shining like she's already picturing the trip. I can't wait to get away with her.

When we finally take the steps off the stage, her grin is so bright that it could light the entire town.

"We're going. No matter what our decision is tonight," she insists.

"I'll agree to that," I say, knowing that if she doesn't choose me tonight, I'm still promised one last week with her. It's a selfish agreement.

As the band returns to the stage, I steer her toward the haunted house at the edge of the lawn. "We have one last scare."

The structure looms at the front of Hollow Manor, with fog spilling down the steps and strobe lights flashing in the windows. Screams echo from inside, followed by laughter. Julie squeezes my hand tighter, her jeweled bracelets glinting in the moonlight.

"I don't think I want to get jump scared," she mutters.

"I'll protect you," I tease, tugging her closer.

She shoots me a look. "I don't need protection."

"Tell that to your death grip on my hand."

Her cheeks flush, but she doesn't let go. If anything, she clings tighter.

Inside, the air smells like smoke and dry ice. Black curtains brush our faces as we make our way through the narrow hallway. A zombie lunges from the shadows, groaning loud enough to make Julie shriek. She immediately buries her head in my chest.

I laugh, pressing a kiss to the top of her head. "Definitely don't need protection."

"I'm actually a wussy," she says, her voice muffled against me.

We move deeper, weaving through rooms full of skeletons and clowns. Every time something jumps out, Julie startles, then laughs. She's glowing in the flashing lights, her cheeks pink, her eyes bright, and I can't stop watching her.

By the time we reach the final stretch, the fog is thicker. A figure in a mask slams a fake chain saw against the wall, sparks flying. Julie yelps and practically climbs into my arms.

"Okay, okay," I whisper, holding her tight.

The chain-saw guy moves on to his next victims, but Julie doesn't let go. She's breathless.

Before we exit, she grabs my hand and yanks me through a half-open black curtain, into a side room that's pitch-black, except for a single flickering lantern in the corner. It comes on and off randomly to make it scarier.

"Jules—"

Her mouth is on mine before I can finish. I'm hard and desperate for her. I press her back against the wall as she pulls me down to her, fisting the front of my vest like she's starving for me. I groan against her lips, bracing my hand above her head. The other one grips her hip, and I pull her flush against me.

"Fuck, you're so hard," she whispers, kissing me.

Her body presses into me and I want her closer. The need to have her is overwhelming, and we're nearly insatiable.

Julie breaks away just long enough to whisper, "I need you, Nick."

She drags my mouth back down to her hungry lips.

"Careful," I rasp, my forehead pressed to hers. "I might not let you leave this room."

Her nails scrape lightly against the back of my neck, sending shivers down my spine. "Maybe I don't want to," she confesses.

Her words undo me.

I kiss her harder, deeper, until we're both gasping. Her crown clatters to the floor, along with her wig. My hand slides beneath the edge of her top, feeling the heat of her skin and the arch of her back as she melts into me.

Somewhere outside, another scream echoes, but here in the dark, it's just us. Just the sound of our breathing and the taste of her mouth.

"I don't want to either, but ..." My lips trail along her jaw, and I press my mouth to her ear. "I need you to meet me at the gazebo in five minutes."

Her breath catches. "Why?"

"Because," I mutter, kissing her softly, "it's time to exchange our letters."

Her eyes search mine, still dazed, still burning, but she nods.

I leave her with one last kiss, then force myself to walk out before I change my mind and devour her right there in the dark. My chest is heaving, my lips swollen, my body aching for her, but this moment deserves more than shadows and fake cobwebs.

I step outside alone, and the night air hits me. My heart pounds harder than it ever did on the ice. I walk across the lawn, past the chatter and Halloween music, until I reach the gazebo at the edge of the property.

Autumn and Patterson hung the lights in it yesterday, and it glows like something out of a dream. Strings of fairy lights twist around the white beams, casting everything in soft gold. Pumpkins line the steps, and their happily carved faces flicker, guiding me inside.

I take my place on the bench and pull the orange envelope from my pocket. Her name is written across it in my handwriting. It holds my truths and how I feel about her. It's light compared to the weight of what it means.

For once in my life, I'm not nervous about a crowd or an opponent or the press. I'm nervous about one woman, the *only* woman who matters. The one I've fallen head over heels in love with without even trying.

The sound of soft footsteps pulls my attention away.

Julie.

She's still in her Jasmine costume, though the wig and crown dangle from her hand, like she gave up pretending a few haunted rooms ago. Her real red hair tumbles around her shoulders, wild and perfect. She's clutching her envelope in her other hand like it's both armor and a confession.

When she steps into the glow of the lights, my lungs seize.

She's everything.

I stand, meeting her halfway. For a moment, we just stare at each other. The party is a distant hum behind us; the night holding its breath.

"This is it," I whisper.

"It is."

I glance down at my phone and watch the time click to midnight. We exchange envelopes, then sink onto the bench beside one another. Our knees brush, and the fairy lights above us twinkle like stars.

"No matter what, still friends," I say.

"No matter what, we still have time at Napa Valley," she reminds me. "Where we'll have *tons* of sex?"

"Absolutely," I promise. "Ready?"

Julie nods, biting her lip. "More than ever."

My fingers tremble as I unfold hers, the orange paper catching the lights. Her handwriting curves across the page, and every word already threatens to undo me.

That's how I feel before I start reading.

NICK,

THE NIGHT WE MET AT BOOKER'S, I DIDN'T WANT TO ADMIT WHAT I FELT. I TOLD MYSELF THAT MEETING YOU WAS BAD TIMING. BUT THEN YOU SMILED AT ME. THAT RIDICULOUS, COCKY SMILE, AND I KNEW RIGHT THEN THAT I WASN'T FOOLING MYSELF. I WASN'T ANNOYED WITH YOU. I WAS TERRIFIED THE MOMENT OUR EYES LOCKED. IN THAT SHORT AMOUNT OF TIME THAT WE SPENT TOGETHER, I KNEW YOU WERE THE MAN WHO COULD BREAK DOWN EVERY WALL I'D BUILT.

I'VE THOUGHT ABOUT THAT NIGHT SO MANY TIMES. THE WAY YOU LEANED ACROSS THE BAR TO CHAT WITH ME AND HOW YOU TEASED ME FELT RIGHT. THEN YOU LOOKED AT ME LIKE YOU COULD SEE OUR FUTURE, AND THAT TOOK MY BREATH AWAY. EVEN NOW, IT'S ALMOST HARD FOR ME TO ADMIT. BUT THAT NIGHT, AFTER MEETING YOU, SOMETHING PERMANENTLY SHIFTED INSIDE ME.

THIS WAS SUPPOSED TO BE FAKE, BUT IT WAS IMPOSSIBLE TO PRETEND. I CAN'T STOP THINKING ABOUT THE COFFEE SHOP KISSES THAT LEFT MY HEAD SPINNING; OR THE ORCHARD, WHERE I LET MYSELF BELIEVE IN SOMETHING GOOD AGAIN; OR THE NIGHT YOU STOOD IN MY CONDO AND TOLD ME YOU WEREN'T GOING ANYWHERE. I HOPE YOU MEANT THAT.

I'VE TRIED TO BRACE MYSELF FOR THE POSSIBILITY THAT, TONIGHT, YOU'LL DECIDE THAT WE WERE TEMPORARY AND THAT WE'RE MEANT TO BE FRIENDS ONLY. I DON'T WANT THAT, BUT I WILL RESPECT YOUR DECISION, EVEN IF I DISAGREE. IF THE TIME I HAD WITH YOU IS ALL I'LL EVER HAVE, THEN KNOW THAT I'LL CHERISH IT FOR THE REST OF MY LIFE. I WILL ALWAYS KEEP YOUR SECRETS AND HOLD THE MEMORIES WE SHARED CLOSE TO MY HEART.

BUT THE TRUTH IS, I DON'T WANT TO LOSE YOU. I DON'T WANT TO GO BACK TO BEING JUST FRIENDS. I DON'T WANT TO LET GO OF THE ONLY PERSON WHO HAS EVER MADE ME FEEL THIS SEEN, THIS SAFE, THIS WANTED.

SO, HERE IT IS, NICK. THE TRUTH I CAN'T HOLD BACK ANYMORE ... I'M IN LOVE WITH YOU, AND I HOPE YOU FEEL THE SAME.

YOU'RE NOT JUST MY OCTOBER, NICK. I WANT A CHANCE AT FOREVER. YOU'RE THE CALM IN MY CHAOS, THE WARMTH IN MY WINTERS, THE REASON SPRING FEELS POSSIBLE, AND THE FIRE I'LL NEVER STOP CHASING IN THE SUMMER. YOU'RE IT. YOU'RE EVERYTHING I'VE EVER WANTED IN A PARTNER.

I DON'T WANT IT TO END IN NOVEMBER; I WANT IT TO BE THE START OF OUR BEGINNING.

YOU'LL ALWAYS HAVE A PIECE OF MY HEART.
JULIE

. . .

MY CHEST ACHES AS I FINISH THE LAST LINE. *YOU'LL ALWAYS HAVE A piece of my heart.*

I can't breathe or think. Every word on this page is everything I've wanted to hear but never believed I'd deserve. Booker's. The orchard. Her condo. The pumpkins. Forever. She's fallen in love with me.

I glance up, and she's staring at me with those wide eyes.

"How did we write the same thing?" she asks.

I shake my head. "I don't know."

"How is this possible?" we ask simultaneously.

Her laugh breaks on a sob. She launches herself into my arms, straddling my lap on the bench like she can't get close enough. I crush her against me, kissing her like I've been starving for this moment my whole life.

This kiss is everything. Every confession. Every broken wall. Every fear turned into certainty. She tastes like salt and sweetness and Julie, and I know in my bones that I don't ever want to stop kissing her.

When we finally break apart, foreheads pressed together, both of us breathing hard, I whisper, "I love you, Jules."

I frame her face in my hands, forcing her to see me, every raw piece of me.

"I love you too. In every way." She smiles through her tears, a sound between a laugh and a sob spilling out of her. "Please say it again."

"I love you." I kiss her mouth. "I love you." I kiss her cheek. "I love you." I kiss the corners of her eyes, her nose, her chin. "Every season. Every day. Every second."

Her hands fist in my vest, kissing me softer as the lights hum above us and the carved pumpkins flicker at our feet.

And I know with absolute certainty that this is the beginning of everything.

"Will you fly with me to New York today?" I ask, ready to beg.

Her eyes search mine, and she whispers the only answer I need. "Yes. I will."

33

JULIE

The jet is more like a floating penthouse than a plane. Plush cream seats, a polished wood bar, and even a small bedroom is tucked in the back. I sink into buttery leather, buckling my belt as we taxi down the runway. I meet Nick's eyes as he sits directly across from me.

He's lounging like he owns the sky, one arm draped lazily over the armrest.

"What?" I narrow my eyes.

He leans forward, keeping his voice low. "I was just thinking about the things that are still unchecked on your list."

My pulse skips. "Yeah?"

He licks his lips, gaze burning into mine as the plane lifts. "Are you in?"

"You know I am." Heat creeps up my neck.

Nick smirks, knowing he's pure trouble.

The second the seat belt light clicks off, he's already out of his chair, kneeling in front of me. My breath catches as his hands slide up my thighs.

"You're so damn pretty."

I laugh, enjoying his hands on me. "Nick, what if the attendant—"

"She's been warned to give us privacy once we're at cruising altitude. Private jet perks. Come with me."

He stands and pulls me up with him. Nick's mouth brushes mine, and it's soft at first, and then he teases me. After a few seconds, the kiss deepens, his tongue sliding against mine. His hands grip my hips, guiding me against his hardness in his slacks. The low groan he lets out vibrates straight into me.

Eventually, the hum of the engines fades, and the mountains disappear beneath us. The whole world narrows to this moment.

He lifts me, strong arms sliding under my thighs, carrying me down the narrow aisle. My fingers fist his shirt, my lips clinging to his as he opens the bedroom door. I gasp as he lays me out across silk sheets, my back arching, my body already desperate.

"Nick," I whisper.

He braces over me, eyes dark with hunger, but there's something softer there too. Something that makes my throat ache. "This isn't just about the list, Jules. It's about celebrating you and making memories. You're mine, sweetheart. Thank you for choosing me."

The words leave me breathless.

"You chose me," I say.

None of this feels real.

His mouth crashes down on mine, and it's full of possession and devotion. Heat pulses through me as his hands roam, pulling at my clothes until my dress is gone. His mouth trails down my throat, biting, sucking, kissing, until I'm writhing beneath him. When he peels my panties down my thighs, they're soaked. He pauses, looking at me like he's starving.

"Mine." He growls, and it's feral.

Nick strips out of his suit pants and boxers, and the sight of him makes me whimper. He's thick, heavy, and ready, and my entire body clenches with anticipation. He drags himself through my slick folds, teasing me, circling my clit, dipping inside me just enough to make me cry out.

"Don't tease me," I beg, nails digging into his shoulders. "I need you."

He thrusts his fist into my hair. Nick's jaw is locked tight, and the pupils of his golden-brown eyes are blown.

"You'll always get what you need from me," he promises, slamming into me in one deep, claiming thrust.

I scream, my body arching, clutching him as he fills me to the hilt. For a moment, it's too much. Too good. My body grips him like every part of me was made for him.

"I love you," he whispers.

My eyes sting, but my voice doesn't shake. "I love you."

That's all it takes.

He pulls back and drives into me again—harder. The sound that leaves me is pure surrender.

His mouth closes over my nipple, teeth tugging until I gasp. He soothes it with his tongue while his fingers pinch the other peak. Pleasure spreads through me.

"More," I say, clinging to him.

He hooks my ankles over his shoulder and thrusts deeper, grinding against the spot inside me that makes me see actual stars. My fingers fist the sheets so hard that I think they'll tear.

"You were made for me." He groans in my ear.

My body clenches, spasming around him, and my climax tears through me. It's violent and consuming as I scream his name, soaking him.

The sight of me unraveling destroys him. His thrusts turn frantic, and with a guttural groan, he empties into me. Nick almost collapses, but he holds himself upright.

I cling to him, kissing his jaw, his lips, his shoulder.

"Jules," he whispers against my lips, "I don't deserve you."

I cup his face, stroking his cheek. "But you've got me."

We stay tangled together, my legs around him, his breath ragged in my ear. And for the first time in my life, I understand what it's like to love and be loved.

Finally, he pulls the blanket over us, his arm banding around me, his lips brushing my hair.

"So, how does it feel to be an official member of the Mile-High Club?" he whispers.

"Great. Do I get a member's jacket?" I smile, exhausted and glowing.

He chuckles, kissing my mouth again. "I might be able to arrange that. Just hope the next time you fly, you think about this. About us."

"It's something I'll never forget," I admit.

We don't untangle for a long time. I stay curled against Nick, the blanket wrapped around us, his heart steady under my ear while the engines hum beneath us. At some point, I drift off, only to wake to his fingers stroking my hair.

The pilot's voice filters through the intercom. "Mr. Banks, Ms. Loveland, we'll be landing in twenty minutes."

I'm sore, blissfully wrecked, and maybe the happiest I've ever been in my adult life.

Nick helps me sit up, tucking my hair behind my ear. His grin is adorable, but there's happiness in his eyes too. "Seems like we only have a few more things on the list."

"Just the elevator and balcony during a parade." My cheeks heat as I think about every experience I've shared with him. "But I wouldn't mind doing this again sometime."

"Just say when." He kisses me once more before I slide my dress over my head.

Butterflies flutter.

The jet descends, New York coming into view beneath us, the buildings glittering at night. It looks like a thousand constellations flipped upside down.

This is the first glimpse I've had into his world.

The plane taxis to the private hangar. Nick takes my hand,

steadying me as I step out into the crisp night air. His driver waits beside a sleek black car. We climb inside.

"I should warn you," he says, fingers interlocking with mine as we head toward the city. "There will be paps at my penthouse."

"I figured as much," I admit. I've been preparing myself for this moment.

Eventually, the car slows to a stop, and the driver opens the doors for us.

Just as he promised, the night explodes with camera flashes. Voices collide with questions, most of them personal and about our relationship.

"Nick, is she the one?"

"Julie, how does it feel to be the newest Banks girlfriend?"

"Engaged already? Is it true?"

"Are you pregnant?"

Pictures happen so fast that the flashes blind me. I don't shrink or try to hide. It's something I won't do anymore. For anyone.

He holds my hand tighter as we step onto the sidewalk and guides me forward. My heart races—not from fear, but from certainty. They can take their pictures and write their headlines. It will never define our relationship. Only we can do that.

When a photographer gets too close, Nick places his hand on my lower back. Questions continue to be shouted at us, and he protectively shields my body with his.

"Can't have you jacking up photographers in the city," he mutters in my ear.

Laughter escapes me.

Security waves us into the building, and the sudden quiet after the nonstop yelling is almost dizzying.

Nick glances down at me as we stride across the marble lobby.

"Good job keeping it together, Red Menace," he says, brushing his thumb across my cheek.

I grin. "I left my karate moves back in Cozy Creek."

He studies me for a long beat, and the look in his eyes makes me fall all over again.

"Glad you remembered who the hell you are," he says.

I lean into him as we step into the private elevator, resting my head against his shoulder. Right now, I'm not just visiting Nick's world. I'm proving to everyone that I belong in it.

When we enter the penthouse, my jaw practically hits the polished marble floor.

Floor-to-ceiling glass stretches across the entire far wall. Central Park is spread out below like a dark velvet blanket framed in the city's lights. Skyscrapers blink in every direction, neon and glass colliding in a skyline I've only ever seen in movies.

Nick's hand is warm at the small of my back.

"Welcome to Park Towers," he says casually, like he didn't just bring me into a space most people would sell their souls to have.

I drift closer to the windows, nearly stunned. "This is …"

He gives one of his trademark shrugs, downplaying it. "It's not bad."

I whip around. "Not bad? It's like you have the entire world laid out at your feet."

I try to drink in his space. Minimalist furniture is arranged in perfect symmetry. I can't imagine how expensive the art is hanging on the wall. This place is beautiful, but it's more like a museum than a home—untouched and curated.

Then my eyes scan the kitchen, and I squeal when I see the stainless steel espresso machine on the counter.

"Oh my God." I rush across the sleek floor and stop dead in front of a gleaming machine that resembles a NASA control panel than a household appliance. "Holy shit."

Nick follows me and leans against the counter, arms folded. "I wondered if you'd notice."

"This is a La Marzocco with custom mod panels and a straight-in portafilter. You can literally lock in a shot with one hand, not to mention the steam flush. And you have an automatic drip prediction feature!"

Nick's brows lift. "Really? That's a thing?"

I'm half offended, half giddy. "It's *the* thing. This is basically the Ferrari of espresso machines. The absolute best of the best."

He watches me like I made his night. "Want me to prepare something for you?"

I arch a brow. "You? Pulling a shot on this machine?"

"When you buy one of these, they train you on how to use it," he explains. "I'm a professional at this point."

I bite back a grin. "Oh, please show me."

He clicks it on, and after a few minutes, he hands me a tiny porcelain cup. The crema is golden and perfect. I take a sip, close my eyes, and moan out loud.

His sharp intake of breath has me focusing on him.

"Jeez, Jules," he mutters. "You can't make sounds like that in my kitchen."

I grin. "This is great. Too bad you already have a job. I'd hire you at the shop."

He takes a sip from my cup, his eyes never leaving mine, like it's not just coffee we're sharing, but a secret vow. "It's perfect. Like you."

Later, I curl up, barefoot, in the wide window nook and stare down at Central Park at night below me. The city feels alive, pulsing, but somehow quiet from up here. Experiencing New York like this makes it less intimidating.

Nick leans against the frame, watching me instead of the skyline. His expression is unreadable, but soft around the edges in a way I don't see often.

"What?" I ask, reaching for him.

That rare smile tugs at his lips. "This is the first time this place has ever felt like home."

I blink up at him. "Right now? Like in this very moment?"

He nods, eyes steady on me. "It's you, Jules. You make every space I'm in feel like sunshine."

His words crash into me. This man could live anywhere, own anything, and be with anyone. He's been chased and adored and torn apart by the media, and right now, he's looking at me like I'm the only thing he's ever needed.

Me.

Not the skyline.

Not the penthouse.

Me.

I swallow hard, not believing this is my life.

For so long, I wondered if I'd ever be enough for someone. Now he's telling me I'm more than enough. I'm *home.*

He sits next to me in the window seat, pulling me into his arms. I lean against his chest as he brushes his lips over my hair.

"Do you think this feeling will ever fade?" I ask.

"I'd bet it lasts a lifetime," he whispers, his arms tightening around me.

The words squeeze around my heart.

For so long, I thought love meant compromise, sacrifice, and losing pieces of myself to make someone else happy. But with Nick, it doesn't feel like losing anything, but finding everything.

I tip my chin, brushing my lips across his jaw. "Let's not waste it. Not a single second."

His chest rumbles against me with quiet laughter, but when he kisses my hair, it's more of a vow. "Sweetheart, I don't plan to."

The city glimmers beyond the glass, but it's nothing compared to the unshakable truth humming in my chest.

I stop wondering if forever is a possibility with us.

I already know it's ours.

34

NICK

The elevator ride down from the VIP lounge is supposed to be forty seconds. We make it two before Julie is pressed against the mirrored wall, my mouth on hers, her hands fisting my tie. I stop the elevator from moving and capture her mouth. Her dress is silk, and her laugh is muffled against my lips when I drag her leg around my hip, grinding into her.

We don't go all the way, not with a ballroom full of investors waiting, but I give her what she needs. When she's breathless and satisfied, I press the button to restart the elevator. While she smooths her gown into place, I adjust my suit. Her cheeks are flushed, her red lips kiss-swollen.

The elevator slides open, and I'm utterly wrecked. We continue our way to the skywalk that connects to the convention center. Those pretty green eyes dare me to finish what I started, and I can't wait until we're alone again.

Thankfully, the walk to the ballroom is fast.

The expansive room is lit like the inside of a diamond. Crystal chandeliers glitter above hundreds of investors, partners, and executives in tuxedos and gowns. Voices hum, deals are whispered, and champagne glasses clink.

It's the kind of room I've walked into a thousand times, but tonight, it feels different. I'm not just here as Nick Banks, the man who built this empire from the ground up with his sister. Tonight, I'm here with Julie. It's the first time I've brought a woman with me to a business event.

Julie walks beside me, her hand threaded through mine, her red hair shining under the chandeliers. Diamonds hang around her throat. The navy silk gown fits her like a second skin. When the crowd parts to stare, she doesn't even flinch. Her head turns toward me, and she grins.

"I could go for a *pumpkin spice* latte," she says, brow lifting.

I squeeze her hand, giving her as much courage as I can.

But Julie is confident, glowing, and mine. I've never been prouder to have her by my side.

I lean down, whispering in her ear, "You're beautiful. You might have half of New York's elite trying to steal you from me."

Her lips curve, teasing. "Rich assholes usually aren't my thing. You're an exception."

"Thanks."

God, I *love* her.

She's not impressed or intimidated by the glitz, the money, the politics. I've never been more certain that she's the one for me.

Julie's eyes flick down over me before she leans close enough for only me to hear. "By the way … I really love this suit on you. Especially the orange tie."

I glance down at the burnt color against black and white. "Want to know a secret?"

"Of course," she says.

"I picked it for you."

Her grin is kind. "It reminds me of us."

And just like that, the whole ballroom fades away.

I mutter into her ear, "I can't wait to get out of here."

"Same," she tells me.

The orchestra crescendos, and silence falls across the crowd.

Asher signals me from across the room, and I know it's almost time for the quarterly wrap-up. I've led this presentation a dozen times before, and it focuses on numbers, projections, and the kind of hollow wins that keep shareholders happy.

I press a kiss to Julie's temple, lingering there for a second, and then straighten my shoulders. "Wish me luck."

Her hand squeezes mine. "You won't need it."

With her sexy gaze burning through me, I stride toward the front of the room.

I step up onto the stage, the polished wood gleaming under the lights, the microphone waiting. Tonight, my chest pounds with anticipation.

Faces turn toward me. Many familiar, some powerful enough to shift entire industries with a single phone call. Usually, I'd care about that, but right now, I don't.

"Good evening," I begin, my voice carrying across the space. There are at least a thousand people in attendance, and the event is also being streamed online. "Every quarter, I stand here and walk you through the numbers. Our growth, our projections, our new contracts. And tonight, I will do the same. Rest assured, the numbers are fantastic. Banks's Advertising and Marketing Firm continues to thrive because of this team and because of the trust you've placed in us."

A polite ripple of applause sweeps over the room, and I pause, allowing it to fade.

"But tonight," I continue, "I want to talk about something else first."

All eyes are locked on me.

"For years, I thought success looked like this." I sweep a hand toward the glittering chandeliers, the polished glass, the endless skyline behind me. "Money. Power. Headlines. But somewhere along the way, *I* lost track of who I was. Of what *home* meant. And what was actually important."

My gaze finds Julie's. Her lips part, her chest rising.

"I've recently learned that success isn't always about where you stand, but who stands beside you."

Whispers spread through the ballroom. Investors lean forward, and some people look confused.

"That's why, tonight, I'm proud to announce the firm is expanding with a new satellite office." I pause, letting the words sink in. "In Cozy Creek, Colorado. The new office will be fully operational by the beginning of the first quarter next year. I'll personally be based there, working remotely with the corporate team, alongside my department. This also means that we'll be able to expand our clientele, which is always a win."

The room erupts in applause. Some people are surprised. I find Asher, and he's grinning. We discussed this a few weeks ago, and he gave me the final proposal.

I let the clapping subside before I finish. My voice is steady, my decision absolute. "The firm will continue to grow exponentially, and this is just one of the ways we'll make it happen. Now, since that announcement is out of the way, let's continue with what you're here for—numbers."

After I've run through the quarterly report and future predictions, I open the floor to questions. Several hands shoot up into the air.

I nod toward a man in the second row, and he's handed a microphone.

Before he speaks, he clears his throat. "Mr. Banks, when exactly do you plan to make this move?"

I don't hesitate. "Tomorrow."

Shock and surprise wash over people's faces. When I glance back at Julie, she's staring at me like I just set the entire ballroom on fire.

A woman with diamond bangles lifts her hand. "Nick, how will this affect your, uh … public persona? People see you as New York's most eligible bachelor. Is that changing?"

I lean into the mic. "I'm not sure if you've been on the internet lately, but that's already changed."

More whispers happen. A dozen more hands lift; their questions are variations of the ones already asked. I field them as best as I can.

"Will this decision impact your investors' confidence?" another man asks.

"Absolutely not."

And then the question I was waiting for comes.

"Do you plan on getting married soon?"

It hangs in the air. Some lean forward, waiting for me to spin or dodge it.

Before I can answer, Asher strides forward, his voice firm. "Let's keep the focus on business and not my brother's private relationship. Banks Advertising and Marketing Firm is stronger than ever, and tonight's announcement makes that clear. Questions about Mr. Banks's personal life are irrelevant here. Now, anything else?"

Asher meets my eye, his expression proud. His jaw flexes, his throat works, and for once, the man who never lets emotion show looks happy for me in the best possible way. He gives me a slow nod, then moves away from the microphone. He claps a heavy hand on my shoulder, squeezing hard, his eyes locking with mine. A silent *you did it*. A silent *I'm proud of you*.

It's the first time I've seen him look at me like I'm not just his broken big brother. Right now, he's looking at me like I finally got it right.

Even though Asher shifted the conversation, I don't let the question fade away. My silence stretches until the room hushes again, every eye on me. Then, I answer anyway.

"Marrying Julie is absolutely happening," I say.

The ballroom explodes with whispers, gasps, and lifted phones. But I don't care. I step down from the stage, walking past the tables, through the chatter and the stares, straight toward Julie.

Before I reach her, she's on her feet with tears threatening to spill down her cheeks.

I stop in front of her, cupping her face in both hands, and kiss her sweetly.

"Do you mean that?" she whispers.

"Of course I do."

When we kiss, it's without hesitation. Her hands clutch my suit jacket, her body molding against mine, and for a moment, the ballroom ceases to exist. Her eyes are shining.

I lean my forehead against hers, my voice a near whisper. "You're my endgame, Jules."

"And you're mine."

We leave before the ballroom swallows us whole. Security ushers us through a side exit, cameras still flashing, voices chasing us into the night. A limo door opens, and we slide inside, letting the chaos fade into muffled silence behind us.

Julie exhales, leaning into me, her hand still gripping my lapel, like she's afraid to let go. "You just set a bomb off in the ballroom."

I grin, pulling her into my lap, kissing her until she gasps. "I'd do it again. A thousand times."

Her laugh is soft but real.

Her fingers trace my tie. "Where are you going to stay? In Cozy Creek, I mean. With me?"

I rest my forehead against hers. "Yes. But not permanently."

Her brows lift. "Explain."

"Let's build our dream home. Zane's giving us a piece of land near Hollow Manor. I want it to be ours. Big enough for us to carve one hundred pumpkins and have space for as many kids as we want. A place that we can grow old in," I confess.

"Yes." She's kissing me again, tears wetting my cheek. "I'd love that."

I cup her jaw, tilting her face so she sees every raw piece of me. "Let's do it."

The city streaks past in flashes of light, but I don't care about any of it. Her mouth is hot under mine, hungry now, her body twisting until she's straddling me in the back seat. Her gown hikes up around her thighs, silk pooling, and the sight makes me groan.

"Jules," I rasp, gripping her hips as she presses down on me. The feel of her heat, even through the barrier of my pants, makes my head spin.

Her fingers tug at my tie, loosening it, dragging me closer. She has me cursing under my breath.

"I need you," she whispers against my collarbone.

Our mouths crash together as her hips rock against me in a rhythm that's pure torture.

It takes every ounce of restraint not to push her beneath me and bury myself inside her right here.

"You're killing me." I groan into her mouth.

Her smirk is wicked as she licks my bottom lip. "Good."

Her red hair tumbles forward, brushing my cheek, and she pulls back just enough to look me in the eye. Her voice is a whisper. "Being with you feels right."

"Because it is," I say.

Her lips curve into a slow smile before she presses her mouth back to mine. The driver turns another corner. Her warmth, her laugh against my lips, and the taste of certainty consume me.

The city blurs outside the tinted glass. She tugs at my tie until it's loose, her teeth scraping my throat as she laughs against my skin. "I love watching you lose control."

I grab her ass, grinding up into her so hard that she gasps. "You think this is me losing control? Sweetheart, I'm holding back."

My body begs to finish what she started, but I don't.

I don't want to rush; I want to remember her.

Her forehead rests against mine, her lips hovering a whisper away. "I can't get enough of you."

"You never will," I promise, brushing her mouth with mine as the limo slows to a stop in front of Park Towers.

She groans, climbing off of me. "Why did he drive so fast?"

"He didn't," I say, helping her smooth her gown into place.

My cock aches, but I rein it in.

The door opens, and the cool November air cuts the heat. Cameras flash as Julie slips her hand into mine. She's glowing as she glances over at me, and I shoot her a wink.

When we finally step into my penthouse, my mouth is on hers.

Now, I'll finish what *she* started.

35

JULIE

Nick's mouth is immediately on mine.

The penthouse is quiet; the faint hum of the city almost a hundred stories below barely seeps through. All I hear is his breath, my heartbeat, and the sound of my body sliding against the silk sheets that are cool against my hot skin.

He kisses me like he always has, like we have forever. Maybe because he knew we would.

Nothing about it is frantic or rushed. It's just hungry and consuming, as if he wants to carve himself into my heart. My body trembles with anticipation before he's even touched me.

When his weight presses me into the mattress, I greedily arch into him. My fingers tear at his clothes until they're gone. My nails graze down his chest, over hard muscles. The shiver that runs through him is confirmation that he enjoys his time with me.

"You undo me," he confesses against my skin as his mouth trails lower. He bites, sucks, kisses everywhere, leaving heat in his wake.

I gasp when his hand slides beneath my dress, fingertips teasing higher.

My panties cling to me, and when he presses the heel of his

palm against me, the moan that tears out of me echoes against the high ceiling.

"Always so wet for me." He groans, kissing me harder as his fingers stroke over the damp lace. He peels them down my thighs, slow, and savors the view, like undressing me is part of his pleasure.

Nick places hot kisses up the inside of my thighs until I'm shaking. And when his tongue slides through me, I cry out, clutching the sheets. He devours me like a starved man. My thighs shake around his head as he flicks my clit with his tongue, sucking hard. His low growl vibrates against me until I'm falling apart, nearly sobbing his name.

By the time he pulls back, my body is sweaty, my chest heaving. When he leans over me again, I feel his heavy cock brushing against my stomach.

He drags himself through my folds, circles my clit, then slams inside me until I scream with satisfaction.

He fists a hand in my hair, tugging gently until I'm staring straight into his golden-brown eyes. His jaw is tight, his chest rising and falling, like he's barely holding back. He pulls out and then takes me in one deep, claiming thrust.

My back arches off the bed, every nerve ending sparking as he fills me. He stays buried to the hilt, his forehead pressed to mine, our breaths ragged and uneven.

"You feel like home," he whispers.

"You do too."

Each thrust is slow, and he continues until I'm gasping, clutching at him. Pleasure floods through me.

"Don't stop," I beg, my voice raw.

His growl rumbles through me as he flips me onto all fours. He drives deeper, pounding against that spot inside me that makes my vision explode. The stretch is perfect, the angle brutal, and I sob his name, clinging to the sheets like I'll fly apart without him.

"You feel so good." He groans, fingers digging into my hips.

I break apart, my body spasming around him as my orgasm

violently consumes me. He curses, thrusting harder. His groans turn frantic as he buries himself deep one final time and releases inside me.

We collapse, his arms locked around me like he'll never let me go. My chest heaves, but I don't want to move. Not yet. Maybe never.

He strokes my ass, kisses the curve of my back.

"I'm so glad you're mine," I whisper, smiling against the sheets.

"Me too," he says, kissing my shoulder. "Me fucking too."

He eases out of me and pulls me into his chest, rolling us onto our sides. His hand trails down my spine like he's memorizing every inch of me. The silence stretches on, and it's comfortable.

"Why didn't you tell me that you were staying in Cozy Creek?" I ask, my fingers tracing the hard line of his chiseled jaw.

He exhales, his thumb brushing my hip. "I wanted it to be a surprise. And Asher got approval from the board moments before I went onstage."

My throat tightens with relief. "I'm so happy."

He tucks a strand of hair behind my ear. "Me too, sweetheart."

Butterflies swarm me as his mouth presses against my hair.

I close my eyes, listening to his steady heartbeat.

When he looks at me like this, I don't wonder if our love will last.

I know it will.

AFTER A WHIRLWIND THREE DAYS IN NEW YORK—JETS, PAPARAZZI, crystal ballrooms—I'm back where it all started.

The bell above Cozy Coffee jingles as I step inside. The scent of cinnamon and espresso floats through the air. Behind the counter, Sierra fumbles with the milk steamer while Tracy shoos her aside like she's been waiting for this learning moment.

"Julie!" Blaire gasps, throwing her arms wide like she hasn't seen me in a decade instead of a long weekend. "Our small-town queen returns from conquering the big city. Did you bring me anything? Chanel? Prada? A hot investor who's emotionally intelligent?"

I laugh. "Sorry. I brought you me. Nick is coming. He's outside, talking with Zane on the phone."

Blaire smirks. "You won the lottery with him."

"I did," I admit.

I glance toward the window, where Nick leans against his Range Rover. Even in jeans and a jacket, he looks like he commands the room—or in this case, the whole town.

As he chats, his eyes keep sliding back to me through the glass, like he'd rather be in here than anywhere else. The bell jingles again, and Nick finally steps inside, shaking the chill from his messy hair. The temperatures have dropped, and we're expected to get our first snowfall this weekend.

Every customer in the shop seems to freeze, but then they go about their business. I think word has spread around town that Nick isn't just visiting anymore; he's staying. Just like Zane did.

"Hey, sweetheart," he says, pressing a kiss to my temple. "Did you order?"

"Nope. I'm not sure what I'm in the mood for."

Blaire looks between us, unimpressed. "Sorry to ruin your day, but we're out of pumpkin spice lattes."

Nick glances at me and winks. "I don't think I'll ever mention wanting one again."

Our safe word makes me grin, and I realize I finally have what I always wanted—inside jokes with someone who's both a lover and a best friend.

I glance around the room, knowing this place has always been my second home. But now, with Nick here, it feels like the beginning of something everlasting.

We order peppermint mochas and wait at the end of the counter. Three minutes later, Blaire slides them across to me with a wink.

"When are you coming back to work?" she asks. "I miss you."

"Aw. Next week. There are still a few things I need to finish first."

"Can't wait," Blaire tells me. "Have fun today. Remember, I want a cottage in the woods!"

"Won't forget," I promise as Nick's hand finds mine again.

Together, we step out into the cold and head toward the Range Rover.

"Ready to check out the land?" he asks once we're buckled in.

"Yeah, I'm actually excited."

He turns onto Main and follows it until it hits Skyline Drive. "Zane told me that if, for any reason, we split, neither of us keeps the property. The resort confiscates it."

The words hang between us.

I exhale. "I really don't think we have anything to worry about."

"That's exactly what I told him." Nick reaches for my hand, his thumb stroking slow circles against my skin. "I believe in us."

The Range Rover's engine hums as the town fades behind us. When I roll down the window to feel the brisk late autumn breeze, I inhale the clean air.

In the distance, the mountains rise higher. Their ridges are painted gold and brown, while some are completely bare. The sky is endless blue. It's something I can only find in Colorado.

I sip my peppermint mocha, watching our reflections blur in the windshield. He's driving one-handed, his other hand over mine on the console, as if he can't stand not touching me, even for a minute.

When we climb the hill near Hollow Manor, I grow excited, knowing we'll live this close to Autumn and Zane. It makes me giddy. The thought of tying our lives together here, permanently, does something to me.

Nick turns onto a gravel road that cuts into the mountain. Tires crunch over stone until the trees open up, and we're met with a large stretch of meadow. Surrounding it are towering aspens. Beyond them, the mountains climb, layered in smoky blue. To the right, the slope drops into a viewpoint that overlooks Cozy Creek. I can see tiny houses, the church steeple, and even the coffee shop.

From here, the town looks like a snow globe.

"Ready?" he asks.

"Hell yes," I tell him, and we step out of the SUV.

The cold air bites my cheeks as I breathe in pine and possibility.

Nick slips an arm around my waist as we take it in. "Zane said he wanted this land to go to someone he trusted after Harper stated she didn't want it."

"It's beautiful," I whisper. "Can we really accept this?"

"Yes. And we will with a smile and a thank-you," he says. "It's selfish on Zane's part. Trust me."

Wind rushes through the aspens, causing the branches to tremble.

Nick glances over at me, wearing a soft smile. "Picture it, Jules. A house with a porch swing. A kitchen big enough for several espresso machines. And a pumpkin patch in the backyard."

I laugh, blinking away tears I didn't even realize had formed. "I can imagine it."

"I've never wanted anything more," he admits.

Nick tilts my chin, his golden-brown eyes locking on mine. His mouth claims me, and the kiss sears through me.

When we finally break apart, the cold rushes in, and I shiver, but I don't stop staring over the land. I can imagine a farmhouse with pumpkins on the porch; kids with sticky fingers, chasing each other through the grass; and laughter carrying through the trees.

I see myself in that kitchen, pulling espresso shots on a machine that hisses like a dragon, Nick sneaking up behind me to wrap his arms around my waist. I imagine us stringing lights on the porch every October. I can almost hear our kids begging for one more story before they go to bed. I picture Christmas mornings and birthdays, stupid arguments, and sexy make-ups. Whole seasons stitch together into a life I want to live with him. It's not a fantasy, but a possibility.

I see us growing old together, with gray hair and wrinkles, and still kissing because we can't get enough.

When our eyes meet again, I know he saw it all too.

The dream doesn't feel impossible.

I smile. "Did you ever think it was only going to be a hookup situation?"

Nick chuckles, pulling me closer. "No fucking way. You're the only one who ever believed that."

36

NICK

The town outside is just starting to stir on Thanksgiving morning, but in here, it's peaceful.

After my sister passed away, this holiday has been hollow for me. It used to be nothing more than a press release about how much Banks Advertising and Marketing Firm donated. There were a few posed photos at charity galas. The night was filled with endless champagne and cameras, most of which were staged and empty.

During the holidays, I went through the motions of crossing things off a list instead of celebrating.

Not anymore.

Today, I'm looking forward to spending my time with family and friends. I have so damn much to be grateful for, especially the woman who's asleep in my arms. I smile, thinking about Julie, who carved herself into me without even trying.

I tighten my hold on her.

Eden would've adored her. She would've seen what I see—how Julie doesn't give a damn about my last name, my bank account, or the skyline I used to worship. She would've loved her for giving me back the one thing I thought I'd lost forever … a sense of home.

Julie stirs, mumbling something incoherent, then tips her head back with a sleepy smile. "Happy Thanksgiving."

"You too." I kiss her temple.

A half hour later, we're wrapped in blankets on her condo balcony, peppermint cocoa warming our hands while the Cozy Creek Thanksgiving parade begins on Main Street below.

It's ridiculous and charming—exactly like this town.

A giant inflatable pumpkin bobs between two pickup trucks. Kids in construction-paper pilgrim hats wave from the back of a hay wagon. The high-school marching band stumbles through a holiday medley, horns blaring just off-key enough to make Julie snort.

I glance at her flushed cheeks and see the sparkle in her eyes. "You know, we only have one last thing to check off the naughty list."

Her head whips toward me. "You want to do that *now?*"

"When else will we have another opportunity?"

"Christmas," she tells me.

"Do you want to wait until then?" I ask her.

"Nope."

"That's what I thought."

I smirk, dropping to my knees and sliding between the balcony wall and her so she can still watch the parade. I slide her pajama shorts and panties down. She adjusts the blanket on her shoulders, then glances down at me.

"You're sure?"

"Hell yeah. Enjoy it, sweetheart."

She gasps when my tongue slides over her. Her hips jerk forward, and her knuckles go white against the railing. I can hear the parade noise of people cheering, horns in the distance, and the rumble of engines. The only thing that matters is how sweet she tastes on my tongue.

"Tell me what you see," I mutter. My breath is hot against her, and my fingers open her thighs wider.

Her voice breaks. "Th-the—oh—"

Her head tips back, her throat working as she forces herself to keep watching the parade. "The Cozy Creek Elementary cheer squad is wearing matching sweaters …"

I suck her clit between my lips, humming approval. Her body jolts, her knees already trembling.

"What else?"

Julie's laugh cracks into a moan. "N-Nick—the Boy Scout troop is in a float that's built like a giant turkey."

I thrust my tongue inside her, and she bites her lip.

"Keep going," I whisper.

Her voice is hoarse now, half breathless, half daring. "The … oh … don't stop … the middle school marching band. They're playing 'Jingle Bells,' but … oh my … they're completely off-key."

I drag two fingers along her soaked slit, circling before pushing inside, curling just right. Her words stumble, dissolving into gasps.

"T-there's … the Cozy Coffee float. It's a giant … cup of coff—"

I grin against her, continuing my war on her pussy as she tries and fails to finish the thought. Her hips rock, chasing me, her voice pitching higher as the crowd below cheers.

"You wanted this fantasy." I growl, pleasuring her with my fingers, sucking hard on her swollen clit. "So, give it to me, sweetheart. Let go."

Her cry rips out of her, muffled when she buries her face against her arm, body convulsing as the orgasm tears through her. Her body shudders, and I don't stop until she's nearly collapsing, the blanket slipping off her shoulders.

I press a kiss to her thigh, lingering there, tasting her skin. Then I look up at her, grinning. "List is officially complete."

Her laugh is breathless. "You're incredible."

I slide away from her and stand, picking the blanket up and placing it over her shoulder.

"How was it?"

"Amazing," she says, squeezing her thighs together as we watch Santa finish the parade.

Julie leads me back inside, and we climb into bed and watch the Macy's parade on TV. She teases me about which float I'd sponsor.

She grins as the parade marches on.

"Sweetheart, the list may be finished, but I think we should start a new one."

Her smile widens. "A couples one?"

"Hell yeah. And we'll check off every damn box together," I say.

Hours later, we're walking up the stone steps of my father's mansion. The air is crisp and full of woodsmoke. Julie's hand is tucked into mine, her navy coat cinched at the waist, her red hair gleaming in the fading light.

The house glitters like a cathedral behind us, windows glowing with candles and chandeliers, voices leaking out from within. Family. Friends. Everyone of importance who means anything to us is here.

Julie pauses on the porch, taking a moment to look at me. "You seem nervous."

"I'm not. Not even a little," I admit, my pulse steady. "I've never been more certain of anything in my life."

She smiles, but before she can say anything, I drop to one knee.

Her gasp catches in the cold November air; her white-gloved hand flies to her mouth.

"Julie Loveland," I say, pulling the ring from my pocket. It's the one that's been burning a hole in my pocket since I picked it up from Easton Calloway in New York. "You turned my October upside down. You made me believe in forever again. You are my home, my peace, my true love, and I don't want to waste another second without you. Will you please make me the happiest man on the planet and spend the rest of your life with me? Will you please marry me, sweetheart?"

Tears slide down her cheeks as she laughs. "Yes. A thousand times, yes."

The door behind us opens wide, and suddenly, the house erupts with cheers. My mother, stepdad, Asher, Billie, Harper, Brody, Dyson, Miranda, Zane, Autumn, Blaire, Julie's parents, and even the Fairy Godmothers are here. Every face we love is gathered inside, clapping, and some are already crying.

Julie turns to me, and I slide the orange diamond onto her finger.

She covers her mouth. "Nick … this is too much."

I chuckle, brushing a kiss to her knuckles. "Never. No limits for you, sweetheart."

Our mouths crash together on the porch of my stepfather's mansion, which is close to the ski resort. Everyone we love steps outside to congratulate us. It's messy, loud, and perfect. The people who matter most to us are sharing in this moment.

Blaire shrieks so loud that downtown Cozy Creek probably hears it. The Fairy Godmothers fan themselves dramatically, declaring it was better than television. Asher claps me hard on the back with a rare, unguarded smile, and even Zane tears up as Autumn squeezes his arm. Billie smiles as Harper and Brody lift their champagne glasses toward us. Everyone who matters is here.

When we finally break apart, Julie presses her forehead to mine, her voice full of joy. "I love you so much, Nick Banks."

"Love you too, Little Red."

Our friends' and families' excitement echoes through the yard, and suddenly, we're being pulled inside. We're hugged and congratulated, and champagne flutes are placed in our hands. Everyone wants a piece of this moment, and I don't mind sharing it with them.

Just a few months ago, Julie and I made a fake-dating pact that quickly turned into a hookup situation.

Now, this gorgeous, stubborn, pumpkin-obsessed woman is going to be my wife.

Guess the old saying is true, and the third time really is the charm.

EPILOGUE
PATTERSON

Billie Calloway doesn't throw parties; she creates memorable experiences.

Tonight is no exception. Her Manhattan penthouse, which is one of many, looks like the inside of a champagne bottle exploded. It's gold glitter with diamond chandeliers and sequined dresses that cost more than what some people make in a lifetime. The skyline outside blazes with spotlights. The Empire State Building is lit like it's competing with this party. Music throbs through the room, laughter echoes off the marbled walls, and cameras randomly flash. It's a safe space though.

Billie doesn't just decorate; she designs arenas. This isn't just another Calloway spectacle or a New Year's Eve celebration, which the entire family is known for. Tonight, we're here to celebrate Nick Banks's engagement to Julie Loveland.

Nicolas fucking Banks is getting married.

He's one of my best friends and a brother in everything but blood. He once swore off commitment harder than I swore off carbs during preseason. Now? He's across the room in a clean-cut tuxedo, wearing an orange tie, smiling at the beautiful redhead on his arm like they just shared an inside joke. She's his fiancée. His forever. The love of his life.

He doesn't care that half of New York's elite is watching him kiss her. It almost makes me believe in something fictional like love.

But if Nick can change … Nick, who used to treat women like they came with expiration dates … then maybe there's hope for the rest of us.

I'm the exception.

Love isn't in my playbook and never has been. I'm Patterson Cross—center for the New York Angels, fan favorite, notorious tabloid headline maker. I'm the guy who breaks hearts and builds rivalries. I'm known for ruining happy endings, not living them.

Still, watching Nick hold Julie tight makes something hollow in my chest ache in ways I don't admit to anyone.

"Patterson Cross," someone slurs, clapping me on the back. It's Wyatt King, our rookie winger, already drunk on Billie's bottomless champagne fountain.

"Smile, man. It's New Year's Eve. Tomorrow is a brand-new year," he says to me.

Yeah, no pressure.

I force a grin, tip back my drink, and scan the elite crowd. Anything to distract myself from the bullshit. It's a mistake, though, because that's when I see her.

Kendall Hart.

Her name is bitter on my tongue.

She's my coach's daughter, my little sister's best friend, and my brother's ex-fiancée. Kendall is the ghost that shows up in my memories, and she's always haunting me.

I hate her. *I fucking hate her.*

She shouldn't be here. Not in this room. Not in this city.

But still, she persists, and this time, she's not alone.

Her hand is tucked possessively around the arm of Damien Blackwell.

Yeah. *That* Damien. Captain of the Brooklyn Cobras, my biggest rival on the ice. He knocked my Angels out of the playoffs last season and hasn't stopped smirking about it since. He's dangerous on skates, insufferable off them, and now he's strutting into Billie Calloway's penthouse with Kendall on his arm like she's the Stanley Cup. I won't even mention the influence his entire family has in New York.

The crowd parts like their movements are scripted. The event photographer's camera flashes, and champagne bubbles. Damien whispers something in Kendall's ear, and her laughter floats across the room toward me. Her dress is silver and cut low enough to start wars. Sequins catch the light like she wore it to personally blind me.

And the worst part is, she easily finds me in this crowded room.

Our eyes lock together, and I can't break the hold she has on me.

Not even as the countdown to the new year begins.

Ten, nine, eight ...

Everyone moves closer to the windows to watch the ball drop. Nick and Julie are front and center, commanding the spotlight with their perfect, glowing love story. All eyes are on them or the ball.

But not mine. Mine are locked on Kendall. Her mouth curves in that cocky smile I've never been able to scrub from my damn head.

Damien's arm clamps tighter around her waist, staking a claim that makes my blood boil. Kendall wraps her arms around his neck but holds my gaze. She knows exactly what she's doing. This is her opening move in a game that I told her I wouldn't play.

Three. Two. One.

"Happy New Year!" everyone screams.

Confetti rains inside and outside. Champagne corks pop, and cheers fill the night. Nick and Julie kiss under the glittering gold, sealing their future.

But all I can think about is Kendall's eyes still burning into me.

If she keeps this up, I will give her hell.

The only thing that pulls me away from my thoughts is Regina, the model I brought as my date. She's tugging at my arm, shouting something about a toast, her champagne nearly spilling onto my suit.

When I glance back, Kendall slips out of Damien's grip like smoke. She weaves through the crowd in that silver dress that clings to every curve. The sequins catch the light like a thousand tiny knives. My pulse races with every step she takes closer, closer, until she's standing directly in front of me.

For a heartbeat, the world narrows to just us.

My jaw clenches as her perfume hits me. It's sweet and familiar. It's memory and poison, all wrapped into one. Her gaze rakes over me before she meets my eyes. Her smirk is merciless, and her eyes are cold. Calculated even.

Kendall doesn't say a single word, but neither do I.

The noise of the party rages around us, but it also blurs.

It's just her and me, toe to toe, trading silent daggers. Her eyes dare me to break first, to break the promise that I made years ago. *I will never fucking speak to you again,* I swore to her. Though I have a million things I want to say, I won't give her the satisfaction.

The silence stretches on for too long. It feels too heavy, too loaded. Her not speaking is a blade sharper than anything she's ever said to me.

Damien barks her name, and it causes my jaw to clench tight. She doesn't flinch or even acknowledge him. Instead, she spins around, her dress swooshing with every movement as she walks away.

She shouldn't sparkle like a damn diamond, but somehow, she does.

Regina scoffs. "That was weird."

"Yeah," I mutter, sipping my drink as she chats about champagne towers.

I barely register that I have a date to entertain because Kendall's presence has wrecked me. I've avoided her for years and made it crystal clear to my little sister, Addison, that I do not want to see Kendall. Ever.

I let out a frustrated sigh as the party continues on.

Nick kisses Julie like she's his forever. And me?

I stand there, gutted, because Kendall gave me nothing.

No words I can fight. Zero insults or rude comments. I have a comeback for everything and she usually has a lot to say. Not tonight, though.

Her silence will take up space in my head. Somehow, she's suffocating me without even trying.

Fuck, have I mentioned I hate everything about her?

Well, I do. And that's a problem because hate also feels a hell of a lot like wanting her.

That can *never* happen.

**Continue Patterson's love story in
THE HOCKEY SITUATION
https://books2read.com/thehockeysituation**

**Need more of Nick & Jules?
Download an exclusive bonus scene featuring them here:
https://bit.ly/thehookupsituation-bonus**

WANT MORE OF LYRA?

The Billionaire Situation Series

The Wife Situation

The Friend Situation

The Boss Situation

The Bodyguard Situation

The Hookup Situation

The Hockey Situation

The Royal Situation

Fall I Want (connects with this world)

Valentine Texas Series

Bless Your Heart

Spill the Sweet Tea

Butter My Biscuit

Smooth as Whiskey

Fixing to be Mine

Very Merry Series

A Very Merry Mistake

A Very Merry Nanny

A Very Merry Enemy

Every book can be read as a standalone, but for the full Lyra Parish experience, start with book 1 of the series, as they do interconnect.

KEEP IN TOUCH

Want to stay up to date with all things Lyra Parish? Join her newsletter! You'll get special access to cover reveals, teasers, and giveaways.

lyraparish.com/newsletter

Let's be friends on social media:
TikTok 🤍 Instagram 🤍 Facebook
@lyraparish everywhere

Searching for the Lyra Parish hangout?
Join Lyra Parish's Reader Lounge on Facebook:
https://bit.ly/lyrareadergroup

ACKNOWLEDGMENTS

I will never be able to tell my readers thank you enough. I will never be able to express my gratitude. Thank you so much! Let's go, baby!!!!! I have so much more in store!

Huge thanks to Erica Rogers and Kate Kelly for being amazing! Big thanks to Bookinit! Designs (Talina & Anthony) for creating this cover and all the covers for this series. Thank you to my editor, Jovana Shirley, for always helping me meet my deadlines. Thank you to Nikki Hendren for your incredible proofreads, and to Marla Esposito for the final sweep.

Appreciate all my writer friends and strangers on 4thewords who kept me on track while writing this book. Having people to write with when I'm under deadlines like this is invaluable.

And as always, gigantic thank you to my hubby, Will (@deepskydude). What a year this has been...wow. Not sure what I'd do without you being my number one cheerleader. Writing about love is easy when I have a partner like you. I'm *your* number one fan.

ABOUT LYRA PARISH

Lyra Parish is a hopeless romantic obsessed with writing spicy Hallmark-like romances. When she isn't immersed in fictional worlds, you can find her pretending to be a Vanlifer with her hubby and taking selfies with pumpkins. Lyra loves iced coffee, memes, authentic people, and living her best life. She is represented by Lesley Sabga at The Seymour Agency.